POLES APART

By Anna and Jacqui Burns

Poles Apart
Escape to Pumpkin Cottage

a&b

POLES APART

ANNA AND JACQUI BURNS

Allison & Busby Limited
11 Wardour Mews
London W1F 8AN
allisonandbusby.com

First published in Great Britain by Allison & Busby in 2024.
This paperback edition published by Allison & Busby in 2024.

A CIP catalogue record for this book is available from
the British Library.

10 9 8 7 6 5 4 3 2 1

ISBN 978-0-7490-3190-9

Typeset in 11/16 pt Adobe Garamond Pro by
Allison & Busby Ltd.

By choosing this product, you help take care of the world's forests.
Learn more: www.fsc.org.

Printed and bound by
CPI Group (UK) Ltd, Croydon, CR0 4YY

To Harry Edward Conway,
who encapsulates all our hopes for the future.

Pole Dancing Fitness Classes!

With Feather Starr

Find your inner goddess

A chance to lose the pounds, firm up those problem areas
and spice up your sex life!

Only fierce, fearless and feisty women allowed

Morlan Village Hall
Thursdays 7.30–8.30 p.m.
Starting 10th April

Leave your inhibitions at the door . . .

Chapter One

Gwen

Gwen puts her foot down, taking her chances on the treacherous bends in the steep cliff road. Her white Audi A5 convertible is totally impractical on these bloody village roads. She's lost count of the times she's clipped her wing mirrors on some overgrown hedgerow. When Gareth told her to choose a new car for her fiftieth birthday, vanity got the better of her. She saw herself driving to St Davids, the roof down, and the salty sea air ruffling her hair. The gasps of envy she would draw from the residents of Morlan Village. Truth is, Pembrokeshire weather is erratic at the best of times and in the last six months, she's only had the top down once and her hair ended up like a particularly unkempt Bearded Collie.

Up ahead, Gwen can see a tractor trundling up the hill, Gwion Morgan at the wheel with his ruddy cheeks and flat cap. He is turning into the lower field and, if she's lucky, she'll miss the back of his tractor by a whisker. The post office is closing in ten minutes and Lydia has a pile of her trashy clothes to send back. With the Easter Bank holiday weekend looming, Gwen is determined to get these sent off. As if she doesn't have enough to do. She feels like Lydia's personal assistant sometimes rather than her mother. Never mind, this time next year Lydia will be in uni. God willing! She barely did any work for her GCSE or AS levels, pleading how tough it was on her generation with Covid. Tough? Gwen thought back to Lydia lying in bed until midday and then joining her surfer friends mid-afternoon, her exams the very last thing on her mind.

Gwion draws into the field, blissfully unaware of how close he's avoided a collision. Gwen glances at the sea to her left, grey and sullen today. When she and Gareth first found the plot of land above the village of Morlan, they'd been enchanted, gasping every time they caught a glimpse of the coastline, marvelling at their good fortune. Now, she barely noticed. She supposes if you slept with George Clooney every night, you'd soon get used to him, those melty brown eyes having little effect on you after a while.

Gwen reverses into the small space next to Morlan's post office, reaches for the packages on the back seat. Feeling a twinge in her back, Gwen curses the fact the car is a two-door. The bell rings behind her as she enters the musty little shop.

'You've missed the last post, I'm afraid,' Hannah Thomas says with glee. 'They won't go until Tuesday now.'

'Oh, well,' Gwen smiles, 'at least they're out of the house.'

She's far too houseproud, of course. The price for owning the biggest and most ostentatious in Morlan. All the others, two hundred or so, are tiny little fishermen's cottages, clinging like lichen to the cliff. Some have been modernised, with appendages clad in that ubiquitous grey. Grey is everywhere these days, every wall in every new build, every show home in

10

that estate in Haverfordwest she and Gareth had visited when they were looking to buy somewhere bigger in Pembrokeshire.

Gwen's house is not grey. It's a riot of colour, rich jewel-red walls, modern navy units in the kitchen, emerald green sofas and scatter cushions in shades of turmeric, terracotta and clashing pinks. It's Gwen's way of injecting a bit of colour into her life. She loves to survey her territory every morning and it is *her* territory. This architect-designed house with windows reaching from the bottom to the very top, maximising the spectacular view. She'd had to have her Norwegian spruce Christmas tree specially delivered from John Lewis in Cardiff at an eye-watering price. She'd hidden the credit card bill from Gareth – he'd have had a coronary. Totally worth it when she sees people stopping whilst driving up over Morlan's hill to reach the main road to Fishguard. They often point to their house and Gwen feels a glow of pride just imagining their conversation. 'Wow! What an incredible house! Must have cost a fortune.'

Gwen's nose tingles. Burnt coffee. Hannah Thomas has tried to expand the post office and has a few rickety tables in a corner covered with wipeable floral tablecloths and stainless-steel IKEA pots in the middle. Fancies herself as a barista. She has slabs of Bara Brith, rich fruit cake, on the counter and some dry and floury Welsh cakes. Neither look particularly appetising. An elderly couple sip their coffees. Visitors for the day, by the looks of it, doing the Pembrokeshire Coastal Path. Their oversized rucksacks, stuffed, no doubt, with Swiss army knives, guy ropes and Marmite sandwiches, are propped against the post office counter. Morlan is Welsh for lagoon, and this is what draws the visitors, the shallow pool protected by a wall of rocks at the headland. Lydia and her friends are always swimming there. Lots of the teenage boys from the village enjoy a spot of 'tombstoning' further up. Gwen was horrified when she learnt what it meant. It puts her worries about Lydia vaping with her mates into perspective. The lagoon seems to have become the property of the teenagers of Morlan. Gwen had only swum there once about fourteen years ago when they'd first moved into the new house. It was freezing cold and Gwen remembered screaming when she stood on a piece of seaweed. Gareth laughed his head off. Now, he barely raises a smile at anything Gwen does.

'So, more packages to go back?' Hannah says superfluously as she opens the side window when Gwen hands them over to her. Can she inject any more venom into that question? Gwen knows she thinks her children are spoilt.

'Kids, you know what they're like,' Gwen sighs. She gazes absentmindedly at the posters on the wall as Hannah keys in some numbers very officiously. That old one about protecting your passwords. Another about travel insurance. She and Gareth had booked to go on that Caribbean cruise in the spring of 2020. Thank God they'd had their money back. That holiday cottage in Kendal last year was not the same. Jasmine, their eldest, had refused to come, wanting to spend time with her boyfriend and they'd taken Lydia and that awful friend of hers from school, Sophie, who laughs like an apoplectic donkey. It rained all week and she and Gareth had exhausted all conversation after the first day. They had so little in common these days. He could never switch off from the business.

'Seen this?' Hannah asks, pointing a finger at the poster nearest the counter.

'Pole Dancing Fitness Classes,' Gwen reads. 'In Morlan? Feather Starr. That can't be her real name. Come to a sleepy Welsh village to inject some life into it, is it? Trying to modernise us Neanderthals?'

'It's sparked quite a lot of interest. I said I'd keep a list of names for Miss Starr. She's quite a character. There's about half a dozen who've already signed up.' Hannah tilts her head to one side. 'Fancy it, then, Gwen?'

Gwen snorts, 'As if!' She conjures up a picture of Feather Starr, with her pink hair and nose piercings and an arse you could balance a tea tray on. 'What about you, Hannah? Fancy thrusting your stuff around a pole?'

Hannah shakes her head. 'I only had the hip replacement six months ago. Besides, it's not my cup of tea. It's more for your age group – fifties – those who need to shift a few pounds.'

Bitch! Gwen snatches the receipt from Hannah and heads outside, the door rattling behind her. She won't let that woman and her catty remarks ruin her day. She inhales deeply and stops to gaze at the sea. She shouldn't take it for granted. If her schoolfriends could see her, wouldn't they just envy all she's achieved? Make no mistake, Gareth wouldn't have got half so far in the business without her. The third biggest car showroom in South Wales. She's an ideas person; Gareth is more practical, lacking in imagination. He used to do up cars in their garage on the side of the house on the estate they lived in in Haverfordwest. The neighbours complained bitterly. The place looked like a scrapyard. But Gareth was good at fixing

13

cars and doing them up. He made a tidy profit but it was small-time. It was Gwen who saw the potential in that warehouse outside town. It was she who persuaded the bank manager to loan them the money. She also did all the advertising and saw to the books. It was Gwen, too, who convinced Gareth to buy some electric vehicles, long before anyone else realised they were a 'thing'. Now Gareth thinks he's Elon Musk.

As Gwen heads up the hill, stopping every few yards as she passes another car coming down, she thinks about the pole dancing. Is it seedy? It is certainly a novel way to tone up. It will also piss off Lydia and Jasmine and that has to be worth something! Youngsters these days think they have the monopoly on sex, believing their parents dead from the waist down. To be honest, she and Gareth might as well be. It's ages since they've had sex. God, it was at their neighbours Joe and Sasha's wedding. She'd had a few too many Proseccos and it got her in the mood. It was partly watching the happy couple on the dance floor and realising how they couldn't keep their hands off each other.

She and Gareth used to be like that. She does a quick mental calculation as she pulls in to let a motorhome pass. For God's sake, on these roads! Joe and Sasha's wedding was in September. That was seven months ago. Was it really that long?

Gwen slides the car onto the drive and rushes upstairs. Perhaps this pole dancing class is exactly what she and Gareth need. She wonders what the appropriate attire for a class like that is. Tracksuit bottoms and a T-shirt?

Her dressing room always gives her a thrill; it's her favourite room in the house. It has recently been redecorated, with navy

14

and gold roses inspired by the Palace of Versailles. Eighty quid a roll at Laura Ashley. She searches through a drawer and finds a red leotard. She hasn't worn it for a few years. It was when Zumba was all the rage. Pausing, she wonders if it still fits. She can always wear leggings underneath. Peeling off her jumper and white jeans, she slips, or rather rolls and yanks, the leotard over her thighs. Jeez, she looks a mess. More sausage than sexy. Squidgy mounds of flesh have escaped at the top of her thighs, and she looks at least five months' pregnant. The dreaded menopausal middle! There's nothing for it. It has to be thrown and she'll order something new, more flattering.

'Oh. My. God!' Suddenly Gwen hears hoots of laughter from behind, followed by the unmistakable sound of a convulsive donkey. Lydia and that daft friend of hers. 'What the hell are you playing at, Mum? Have you completely lost your mind?'

Gwen flushes 'What are you doing in here? What do you want?'

'Sophie and I are going into Haverfordwest. Can I have some money? I need to get something for Saturday night.'

'What am I, your cash machine?'

'God, Mum, you always say that. It's soo old.' Lydia rolls her eyes.

'What's happening Saturday night, anyway?'

'Don't say you've forgotten? The party?' More eye rolling. 'You promised to drive us there.'

Gwen really can't remember. She doesn't know whether it's her menopausal brain or Lydia playing some gaslighting trick on her. Gwen reaches for her dressing gown and then her bag, handing over three twenty-pound notes. Lydia keeps her hand open.

'You've *got* to be kidding me!' Gwen sighs and Lydia trots out. 'What time are you back?' Lydia doesn't answer.

Gwen hears the pair of them laughing as they descend the stairs, and she vows that she will not be humiliated again. She will go to that pole dancing fitness class and say hello to a new, svelte and sexy body shape. In the meantime, she'd better get the shepherd's pie on. Gareth will be home in a couple of hours.

Chapter Two

Meg

'I'd like a glass of Merlot,' Meg says to the waitress, 'please.'

'Small or large?'

She wants a large. She needs a large tonight. 'Small, please, I'm driving.'

Meg turns back to the man sitting opposite her who winces.

'Red wine with fish.' He grimaces as if she'd just let rip at the dinner table.

'I've been fancying a red all day,' she says, trying to remain placid with every fibre of energy left in her. This guy is really testing her patience.

'A Sancerre is more appropriate,' he offers. 'The Loire wines really benefit from the continental climate.'

'I'll make it a Sancerre, then,' she orders begrudgingly.

Meg sips from the glass, keeping her head low so he can't see her roll her eyes. Her date for the night thinks he's some kind of wine aficionado just because his mate from uni grew up on a vineyard.

'Mmm,' she pretends. It tastes like wine to her. A nice crisp white. Is there really any more to it than that?

'The citrus notes really complement a fish like bass . . .'

She should have known this was a mistake. His Tinder profile picture was of him in sunglasses on a vineyard, posing with a glass of red, fingers carefully curled around the stem, not the bowl of the glass. Gregory Jones. Twenty-six, Pontypridd. Software engineer.

It's never going to work. Greg and Meg? For a start, they sound like characters from a children's TV show. Secondly, if he mentions his summer backpacking across the Champagne region one more time, she's going to throw this wine in his face. Then she'll see how much he really likes the citrus notes.

Tinder dating really is a frightful landscape, especially for someone from a village like Morlan. Men in Pembrokeshire between the ages of twenty-five and thirty-five seem to be a niche market. The ones that aren't already married or taken are usually single for a reason: too weird or too much of a jackass to find someone to settle down with. And to be fair, Meg knows most of them from her schooldays and it's hard to find someone sexy when you remember them wetting themselves in front of the year six badminton class because they were scared of the shuttlecock.

Meg's dating life looks like a supercut from a bad romcom of awful-date clichés, complete with comedy music. And so she's decided to expand her Tinder search, to a fifty-mile radius. Is that too far to travel for the man of her dreams?

It seems she isn't going to find him with Greg, anyway. She watches him prodding his steak with his knife, inspecting it as though he's Jamie fucking Oliver.

'Barely any marbling in this rib-eye,' he says with disdain.

Pompous prick. They are in a Marston's inn off the A48, what does he expect? The menu has come laminated and covered in stains. It's hardly going to be a Michelin-worthy experience. The pub was chosen because it was precisely halfway between the two of them. Meg wishes she hadn't bothered now.

They pass the date with small talk about jobs but neither of them can kid themselves this is going anywhere.

'What do you usually look for in a date, then?' Meg asks as they wait for the bill, the conversation completely dry by now.

'Blonde, petite, nice eyes, good tits.' He cackles as if he's said something hysterical. 'I'm a boobs man. Love a curvy figure.' He holds his hands up, faux innocently.

Even though Meg has zero interest in him, she can't help her heart sink just a little bit. That definitely isn't her.

The question doesn't come back at her, as Greg continues to drone about his own life. Meg knows exactly how she'd have answered, though.

Someone that's interested in other people.

It seems to Meg that everyone is so wrapped up in their own lives these days, glued to tiny screens where they compete with others to post the best picture or funniest video, and compare themselves without really thinking about other people. She's been through the most monumental changes in the last few years, and yet those same people she'd been to school with just continue on their mission, sharing pictures of them *living their best lives* or at least pretending to. No one cares what other people are going through, as long as they are doing better than them and can share their *#goals*.

She knows she sounds bitter, and Meg really tries to put

the melancholy aside most days. That is all behind her now. It's just wasting nights with men like Greg that makes her feel disheartened.

'I'll pay twenty quid on my card,' Greg says, handing it over to the waitress. Meg checks the bill. Thirty-five pounds in total. How generous of him!

'The rest on here,' she pays the remainder and slips her card back in her purse. 'Thanks for tonight,' she turns to Greg.

'Glad you enjoyed,' he says. Meg's repulsion is growing with each second. How can she extract herself as quickly and painlessly as possible?

'I've got an early start tomorrow, so I'd better hit the road.'

He stands up and kisses her on the cheek. 'Me too. I'll go to the loo first,' he says. Meg walks out to the car park alone, noting that neither of them had even pretended there was a chance they'd see each other again. Should that make her sad? Is she such a lousy date that she isn't worth a second one?

It's ridiculous. She doesn't even want a second one with Greg.

The drive back to Morlan is long and boring. Meg listens to Dua Lipa on the one radio station her car can pick up, singing along badly. Her car must be the only one left in existence that still has a tape player and roll-up windows. It will be in a museum one day. It was her grandfather's, then her mother's, and now hers.

She crests the hill to Morlan, past the big Beverly Hills houses on the left, and down towards the sleepy village. She loves this time of night when the beach is quiet, all tourists packed up in their tents on Morlan's campsite. She parks up outside the post office and lets herself through the door with her key.

'Is that you, love?' Hannah's voice calls down the stairs.

'Yeah, Gran.' She moves to the back of the shop and steps through the little door that leads to the back office and the rest of the house behind.

'Do you fancy a cuppa? I was just about to put the kettle on.' Hannah pauses by the sink, already in her nightie and pink dressing gown, or 'Hollywood robe' as she calls it.

'No thanks, I was thinking of going for a run now,' she says, kissing Hannah on the cheek.

'Dare I ask how it went?'

Meg sighs.

'That bad? I knew it wasn't good if you were home before 8 p.m. You didn't fancy going home with him?' She raises her eyebrows in an expression that makes Meg laugh.

'God, no. He was a bit too fancy for me.' She rushes to carry her gran's tea to the table for her.

'No one's too fancy for my girl,' Hannah admonishes.

'You know I wouldn't do that anyway,' Meg sits opposite her at the little kitchen table. She prises the biscuit tin open and retrieves a Malted Milk.

'Sleep with someone on the first date? Don't knock it. It worked for me and your grandad.'

'That's an anecdote I could do without,' Meg laughs. 'I'm not ready yet . . . to sleep with someone . . . it doesn't feel right after the operation.'

'You'll have to put yourself out there one day,' Hannah says. 'You never used to be this shy.'

'Yes, well, a lot of things have changed, haven't they?' Meg

21

suddenly wants to change the topic of conversation.

'I know. I'm sorry.' Hannah reaches across and strokes Meg's hands. She smiles, unable to stay irritated at her grandmother for too long. 'I just wanted to say you know I think you're beautiful, don't you? Any guy would be lucky to have you, with or without clothes on.'

Meg groans, this time good-naturedly.

'Ooh, that reminds me . . . speaking of taking your clothes off . . . look at these posters we had through yesterday. Someone called Feather Starr dropped them off.'

'Feather what? That can't be a real name.' Meg takes the flyer from Hannah and reads aloud. 'Pole dancing fitness classes . . . In Morlan village hall? I can't imagine she'll get many attendees. Most of the women round here count the school run as exercise.'

'You could go to get the numbers up,' Hannah suggests. 'Or at least to give me some entertainment in my old age.'

'If I can go in my gym gear, then maybe . . . Although I don't know if I fancy seeing the women of Morlan gyrating around poles in the village hall.' Meg can't think of herself gyrating anywhere, but she does like the idea of a new fitness class. She was the first to try hot yoga when a studio moved into Haverfordwest a few months back. Keeping her body in motion helps to keep her mind off things, and keeps her healthy, or as healthy as she can be.

'You'd better get your run in before it gets too dark out there,' Hannah prompts.

'Thanks, Gran,' Meg says, going upstairs to get changed. She gives the armpits of her dating dress a quick sniff, deciding she won't have to wash it before wearing it again. That would be a waste of valuable time after her crappy date with disappointing Greg.

She chooses tight black leggings and a loose T-shirt with an open fleece jacket. She's an expert at picking clothes now, emphasising her bottom and drawing attention away from her stomach. That's the key. The more layers she has on, the less likely people are to notice the one underneath to hold her stoma bag in place.

On second thoughts, maybe pole dancing classes aren't a good idea. What if she has to take layers off, or worse, move upside down? Then her top might fall up and reveal her entire stomach contents collecting in her bag. No one wants to see that. Come hell or high water, Meg will make sure no one catches even a glimpse of what's under her top.

Still, her life could do with a shake-up. She could always feign injury or an emergency that means she has to leave the class if she's asked to do anything that would reveal too much. She'd had to do that at hot yoga, in fact.

Meg relishes the cold air on her face as she ventures outside. Gran always keeps the house at twelve million degrees. She picks up her pace and jogs the path to the beach. She can't run on the sand, but the little path follows the beach closely, and leads straight up the hill to the lagoon. Meg loves it, as long as she can dodge the canoodling teenage couples on the benches.

Meg has lived with her grandmother at the post office for six months now. She moved in just before her gran's hip replacement. Things were getting a little bit of a squeeze at her mother's house, especially since Graham had moved in with them. She loved Graham, but a twenty-six-year-old needed her own space. Only instead of getting the cool city apartment she'd dreamt of as a child, Meg moved in to help her grandmother, both at home and in the post office. That city pad seems a long way off sometimes, especially on her post office salary.

One day, she'll do something better with her life, something more exciting. One day she'll get out of Morlan and find the man of her dreams. One day she'll give uni another go, get that journalism degree she really wants. And she won't have to drop out this time due to sickness. One day Meg will make it in the world.

But for now, she can try pole dancing.

Chapter Three

Ivy

Ivy sits back on her haunches and surveys the living room floor. Yesterday, she'd ripped up that grubby, mottled-green carpet and it's now rolled up against the shed, ready for the tip. Hiring a sanding machine, she'd stripped the old varnish off, working late into the night and coughing on the dusty fumes. Her arm muscles ached and her back felt sore, but she'd carried on.

Today, she's applied the new varnish, marvelling at the natural wood floors. It has turned out better than she expected. Ivy had spotted a beige Scandi-style rug that would look perfect in the living room. She loves neutral colours, that pared-back style. She'd have some macramé plant holders, a geometric bookcase. It's exciting. For the first time in her life, she is making her own decisions, doesn't have to defer to anyone.

Jim would have hated it . . . but he isn't here any more. Everywhere she looks, there are traces of him: in the heavy dark cabinet holding his trophies – he was cricket obsessed and played for Haverfordwest back in the day – in the half-finished shelving in the dining room, even in the imprint of his heavy bottom on their ancient brown sofa, almost as if he's just popped out to the shop for a newspaper. They've lived in this house for over forty-five years, just a year after they'd married, brought up Matthew here.

'Co-eee! It's only me.' Wendy, her next-door neighbour stands in the hallway. 'What the heck is going on here?'

'I took the carpet up and thought I'd varnish the floorboards. Do you like it?'

'Well, it's certainly different. Won't it be a bit cold in winter?'

'I'm going to put a rug down. It freshens the place up, don't you think?' Ivy says, deflated.

'You should have mentioned you were doing this. Martin would happily have done it for you.'

'I wanted to see if I could do it myself.' Ivy smiles broadly. 'And it turns out I could.'

'Gosh, Ivy, you should be resting at your age, not tearing up floorboards. I wonder what Jim would have made of it.'

'Did you want something, Wendy?'

'I just wanted to know if you need a lift down to the village hall tonight.'

Ivy looks puzzled.

'Don't tell me you've forgotten. The WI's first meeting back after lockdown and you've forgotten.'

'I'm shattered after sorting this floor . . .'

'They've got someone from Milford tonight to give that talk on quilting. It'll be nice to see everyone again.'

Ivy gives an inward shudder. She might have just turned seventy-two but a Friday night sitting with Morlan's branch of the WI is the last thing she feels like doing. There's that new Norwegian thriller on Channel 4 and Ivy's looking forward to a glass of red. Wendy is a decade younger than her, but she fits like a glove with some of the fusty old ladies catching up on the latest episode of *Midsomer Murders* or chatting about the joys of tessellating tile patterns. Ivy's an ardent supporter of her fellow females, but she wants more excitement in her life. The WI had gone online through Covid and it gave Ivy the perfect excuse to miss meetings, pleading that she couldn't get on with computers. It couldn't be further from the truth, but since Jim's death, she can't really concentrate on anything for long.

'So, come on, then, run a comb through your hair and get a jacket on. Martin will be taking us in ten minutes. You've got some varnish on your nose.'

There really is no arguing with Wendy, Ivy thinks, as Martin drives them down the hill to the village hall. They could easily have walked, but her overbearing neighbour wouldn't hear of it. No wonder Martin's so introverted; he can't get a word in edgeways.

'I was telling Ivy, Martin, that you would have done the flooring for her. Not that it needed doing, mind you. That carpet was perfectly good.'

'It was down for twenty years, Wendy. Besides, I felt like a change.'

'All I'm saying is that you don't need to feel alone now Jim's gone, rattling around in that cottage of yours. You're welcome to come to us. A woman on her own is a target for all sorts. Predators, scammers, murderers, rapists. Don't open the door to just anyone, Ivy. You never know who to trust. You hear of old ladies being mugged every day.'

'I'll keep an eye out for axe-wielding murderers, shall I?

27

I'm not old, anyway.' Ivy catches Martin's eye in the rear-view mirror, but his face is inscrutable. How on earth does he put up with her? But people might have thought that about her and Jim.

Outside the light is fading, and Ivy gazes at the walkers on the beach, a group of teenagers heading for the lagoon. The sea is miles out of reach, a thin line of darkness on the horizon. Every moment the view from Morlan changes, no two seconds the same.

Matthew had tried to get her to move to Bristol to be near him, but she loves her independence. Matthew has too much of his father in him. Physically, they are built the same and cut from the same cloth. Women are there to serve them. She does feel guilty thinking like this now Jim has gone, but it's true.

'Ooh, the car park's full tonight,' Wendy comments, as they pull up outside the village hall. 'Everyone is glad to be out by the looks of things. It should be over by nine, Martin.' She kisses him peremptorily on the lips and Ivy imagines Martin's peaceful house for the next two hours, not without some envy.

It really is quite jolly when they enter the hall. Colourful bunting is strung above the stage and a long table is filled with cupcakes, whilst two of the regulars are pouring cups of tea. The cavernous room booms with the noisy chatter of women pleased to be out socialising after a couple of years of intermittent lockdown, in out, shake it all about.

'Welcome back, Ivy, Wendy.' Cynthia, the Treasurer, smiles warmly. There is an awkward moment where they decide whether hugs are allowed and, although things are back to near normal, there is still uncertainty in these early days.

'How have you been keeping, Ivy? I was so sorry to hear about Jim.' She shakes her head in sympathy. 'It must be nearly two years now. I was telling Mike earlier that he passed right at the beginning, didn't he?'

'Yes, two years next week. I'm OK, though.'

'Covid. A terrible thing.'

'Well, Jim didn't look after himself, as you know,' Ivy says. She remembers his nightly visits to The Mariners, eating fat like it was going out of fashion, smoking. He swore he'd given up, but his yellowing fingernails and the lingering smell of tobacco told a different story. Ivy is grateful when Sally comes over and pours her a cup of tea.

'Help yourself to a cupcake, Ivy. Butterscotch or strawberries and cream?' Firmly, she takes Ivy's elbow and steers her away.

'Thank you,' mouths Ivy.

Soon, the quilter, Delyth Parry, takes her position in the middle of the circle of chairs, a ruddy-faced, practical woman who is so enthusiastic Ivy actually enjoys listening to her extolling the virtues of quilting.

'Quilting can be traced back to medieval times . . .' she begins, her neck reddening with all eyes on her.

It's nice to be out of the house, Ivy thinks, and absence has made her view her fellow members kindlier. As the women gasp with 'Oohs' and 'Ahhs' as Delyth holds up her intricately patterned patchwork pieces, Ivy's phone buzzes in her pocket. It's Matthew. He calls at seven-thirty every night like clockwork. Sometimes Ivy thinks being electronically tagged would give her more freedom. She punches in a quick message, 'At a WI meeting. Will call later xx.'

Suddenly, there are peals of polite laughter as the quilter holds up a Greek-themed quilt, with homoerotic images of athletic male nudes with penises longer than their swords. Sally sniggers next to her, but Wendy sits stony-faced on her other side.

Later, as the women drift out, Ivy waits in the foyer as Wendy pops to the loo.

'There's a position for Secretary becoming available, Ivy,' says Cynthia creeping up behind her. 'It might give you something to do.'

Sometimes, Ivy wishes people would stop interfering in her life and trying to find her 'something to do'. As if without a husband, her life has no purpose.

'I'll think about it.'

'Well, we'll be voting at the next meeting so don't think too long. I hope you can come along.'

'Oh, I will,' Ivy says. There's someone doing a talk on upcycling old furniture and Ivy thinks it is definitely something she would enjoy.

Ivy picks up one of the flyers spreadeagled on the table in the entrance. Pole dancing exercise classes. Well, that's novel. Feather Starr is obviously a pseudonym.

'Disgusting!' Wendy says, reading the flyer from over her shoulder. 'It's the talk of the village. Who in their right mind would join something like that? This is not the place. Haverfordwest, Carmarthen, maybe, but Morlan?'

'How did it go, love?' Martin asks, as Wendy opens the car door.

'I think I'll walk,' says Ivy.

'No, you will not,' Wendy grabs her firmly. 'It's pitch-black. Have some common sense.'

The glow from her lamp greets Ivy as she enters the cottage and she smiles at her new floor with satisfaction. Pouring herself a glass of wine, she gazes out at the sea, the tide now in, the water shimmering in the light of the half-moon. Ireland is the other side, the county of Cork. She's always wanted to go. Nothing's stopping her now. Just like nothing is stopping her joining the pole dancing exercise class. She watched a YouTube video once about it and admired the athleticism of the women winding and twirling their bodies into impossible shapes around the pole. It was beautiful. And it must be so good for your flexibility, your joints. Ivy has always thought yoga seemed a bit tame. She glugs her drink and grins, imagining Wendy's face when she finds out.

Chapter Four

Summer

'Mam! Mam, mam, mam, mam, maaaaaam!'

The little shout comes from the room next door. Summer's heart rate immediately speeds up, rousing her from the half-asleep fog that is feeding time. With one arm, she sweeps up her new baby currently latched on to her left nipple and pushes the magazine off her lap. It's optimistic, anyway. Magazines, like books, and anything intended for adults, are a distant memory for Summer Griffiths.

She runs towards the screaming child in the next room, terrified of what she'll find. She shouldn't have left Nia in the dining room alone.

'Wee,' is the word that greets her.

'Do you need a wee, darling? That's OK, let's get your potty . . .' She starts as she approaches the child. 'Oh, you've had a wee. Already. On the carpet. Well, that's all right, don't worry . . .' She casts her eyes around uselessly for something that will soak it up.

Bloody Aled. He's introduced this whole concept of nappy-less time in the afternoons. Apparently, it hastens potty training.

He's read it on some daddy-forum online. *It forces the infant to learn to use the potty . . .*

So far, it has forced nothing. Nia continues to treat their house as an enormous toilet. Why couldn't she have done it on the laminate floor? A few pieces of kitchen roll and an antibacterial wipe are nothing Summer can't handle. But no, the dark puddle is now soaking into the new rug.

'Let's get a pull-up on you and we can watch Peppa Pig. Does that sound good?'

'Peppa Pig!' Nia shrieks and toddles to the living room. That is another of Aled's new-wave theories gone out the window. No TV before dinner time. Fuck it, he isn't the one dealing with two totally dependent life forms all day.

Summer retrieves a pull-up nappy from the stash in the hallway and joins her daughter on the sofa. Jordan is still latched onto her breast, thankfully. She tries to put the memory of bleeding nipples and a screaming new baby with tongue-tie from her mind. Jordan seems to have reached a glorious plateau at the moment. He is feeding nicely, sleeping for a good five hours with only one feed in the night, and is infinitely quieter than Nia had been at that age. Summer doesn't know if she could handle two divas in the house.

Two under two. That's what they called it. An exclusive club of women who were stupid enough, or mad enough, to agree to have a second child within a year of the first.

Summer can still remember the moment. Exhausted, sore, but on a high from Nia standing up for the first time, Aled had caught her, started kissing her neck in the way she always liked. And she'd given in – one of a handful of times since Nia was born – and had sex with him.

And nine months later, her son was born. And rather than adding to the sleep-deprivation and stress levels in the cumulative way she'd expected, the stresses seemed to multiply inexplicably.

Jordan clings to her breast with his little hands. A flood of oxytocin fills her veins as her heart swells with love for him. Until one of his tiny razor-sharp nails digs in.

Summer sighs, too tired to move him. A mother is able to endure pain. Endure wees on the carpet. Endure loops of Peppa-bloody-Pig. But the sleepless nights, those are the worst.

It's fine for Aled. She'd swap places with him in a heartbeat. She often feels like calling up the oil rig in North Wales, begging them to take her on for the three-week rotation, instead of Aled next time. Three blissful weeks of sleep would be worth it.

Instead, Aled gets to swan in on his ten days off like a hero, equipped with information he's read online, pumped full of restored energy ready to play with Nia. Those ten days are the highlight of Summer's calendar. She knows she should be happy to see her husband again, but in her heart the moment she hears Aled's key in the door, she is not filled with the elation of her love reunited, but the elation of knowing she'll have another pair of hands for nearly two weeks. Someone else to bathe and change and feed and burp and soothe the kids. Summer could have showers, long glorious showers, and even a shit in peace on a good day.

When Aled leaves again, it's like grief sweeping over Summer. He's based off the coast of Conwy – only a four-hour drive away but he might as well be in Siberia. Still, only one week left until he's home again.

Nia laughs at something the pink blob has done on television. Summer feels instantly guilty. She should enjoy this time with the children. In reality, she knows that if she really had the chance to leave the children for a week, she wouldn't cope with it. It would be like tearing out her organs. Gut-wrenching. But would a weekend be too much to ask for? A day? Even an hour?

Jordan finishes his feed and Summer lifts him up on her shoulder to burp him. She loves the newborn smell and the weight of him against her heart, and she holds him to her and pats his back. Now she can put him down and tackle wee-gate on the dining room rug. She grabs the carpet spray made for pet messes, and the antibacterial wipes.

While Summer is scrubbing on her hands and knees, glancing up every now and again to make sure Jordan is OK in his baby bouncer, her heart leaps at the sound of the doorbell. Their doorbell never rings. Summer practically knows everyone in Morlan by first name from her schooldays, but they never call round. A zombified mother with two screaming children is usually at the bottom of people's visiting priorities.

Her instant fear is that she's forgotten some play date arranged last week and disappeared into the fog of her brain. She scans her mental diary as she walks to the door but no, it's empty. Like it always is. No lifeline or loving family she can take the kids round to. Just her mother-in-law in the next village along who insists she 'isn't up to it' every time babysitting becomes a distinct possibility.

Summer swings the front door open to an apparition.

She would be less surprised had the ghost of Michael Jackson been moonwalking on her front doorstep.

'Mum?' she asks, as though she needs confirmation it's her.

'Surprise!' Her mother sweeps her hands up and down, displaying herself like a prize on a Nineties' game show.

'What are you doing here?' Summer demands. She knows she should be more welcoming but the shock has overcome any last reserves of politeness.

'I've come to see you. To help you,' she says, leaning in to give her daughter a hug. 'Steve is staying in Haverfordwest for a work event, so I thought I'd call in.'

That makes more sense.

'How long are you here for?' Summer asks. She doesn't know whether to scream or cry. Of course, her mother would call when she has urine drying into the dining room carpet and two-day-old baby sick in her three-day-old unwashed hair. Of course, she wouldn't call first to warn Summer. That is her mother's style, flit in and out of Summer's life like a heatwave in Britain – once in a blue moon and never with a warning.

'We're going back to Cardiff tonight, I've only got a few hours.' She grips Summer's arms. 'Oh darling, you look awful. Is Aled away?'

'Thanks. Yes, he is. Back a week tomorrow. Come on in, I'll put the kettle on.'

'You don't have any wine, do you?' she asks as she squeezes past Summer in the tiny doorway. Wine is a luxury Summer doesn't allow herself while Aled is away. She's tired enough as it is, and Summer worries that if she adds alcohol to the mix she might never wake up.

'Look who's here, it's Nanny!' she shouts at Nia, who immediately gets up and stumbles towards the new arrival.

'Nanny, Nanny!'

Summer moves past, picks up the wipes from the dining room floor after deciding it's clean enough, and flicks the kettle on. She can hear her mother cooing over the two kids in the next room. It's nice for them to see their grandmother. She wishes it were more often.

'Oh, it's a mess in here.' Her mother joins her, Jordan bundled in her arms and gurgling happily.

'It's always like this. I don't exactly get time to clean while Aled's gone,' Summer says, unable to shake the self-pitying tone from her voice.

'It's hard for you, isn't it?' her mother asks in a rare moment of insight. 'I remember when I had you, I was on my own, too. It's impossible on a woman.'

'I'm not on my own,' Summer says, although she isn't far off. 'It is exhausting, though. I'd love to have some time to myself.'

'When was the last time you went out on your own?'

'Probably . . . when I went into hospital to have Jordan.' Hardly a luxury break, but Summer had to travel to Withybush Hospital alone in a taxi while Aled dropped Nia off with his brother in Aberystwyth.

'Bless you,' she says, insincerely.

'I'd love it if someone could have the kids, even for an hour, just so I could have some time to reset. Wash my hair even!' Summer is aware she is pushing it, but this is a one-time opportunity.

'Absolutely. You only have to ask. I'll stay here with these two and you go out and have a bit of time to yourself.'

Summer is taken aback. Shocked. An offer of help from her mother.

'Thank you . . . I didn't mean to hint then, and you don't have to if you don't have time.'

'Darling, take offers when you can. You go out and have a break.'

Summer chews on a thumbnail, unsure of what to do. She is being offered a kid-free hour here, only she doesn't want to take it. After all, where will she go? She is hardly in a fit state to be seen in public. It would be better if her mother took the kids out and she could stay home, have a bath, tidy up a bit, maybe even snooze on the sofa with something on TV that isn't a cartoon.

'Go on, I'll put the kids to bed in a little bit,' she says.

It *is* nearing bedtime. Summer can't ask for them to go out of the house. She is the one who has to leave.

Yes, she can do this. 'Okay, Mum. Only if you're sure.'

Her mother smiles at her before turning to Nia who is now tugging on her cardigan. 'Say bye to your mummy!'

Summer thinks she could cry for a moment. She kisses the kids, then grabs her parka and heads out the door.

The sky is darkening outside, and the street is quiet. Summer can't remember the last time she has been out of the house after 5 p.m. It's surreal. Is she really on her own, out in public? She reaches the corner of the little row of terraces, is about to cross the street, then realises she has absolutely no idea where she's going.

The fresh air is helping her levels of alertness, but she hardly feels up to a long walk. Any coffee shop will be closed by now. She can't go to the pub; people might see her and worry she's having some kind of breakdown.

Summer crosses the street anyway, feeling horrendously self-conscious as a car passes, its headlights seeming to illuminate her stained outfit of trainers, black leggings, and loose-fitting sweatshirt covering a maternity bra and pants. Sports clothes that clearly aren't made for any kind of physical activity beyond feeding a newborn.

Where the hell is she going to go? There are no shops in Morlan, and her little shitreon car is in the garage. She finds herself wandering through the village centre, wondering if it's too sad to sit on the beach and maybe doze off a little bit?

'Summer!'

Oh God. She spins round towards the cheery voice.

'Meg. How are you?'

'I'm good, thanks. I thought it was you. Yes, all good.' Meg crosses the street towards her and Summer hopes she won't look too closely at her get-up. 'I haven't seen you for ages. Do you still live in Morlan?'

'Yes, I do. I've just been a hermit for the last year . . . having two kids means my life isn't exactly the most social.' She fiddles with her hair nervously, aware it is both greasy and crusty in different places. 'Are you still at the post office? How's your nan?'

'Yes, I'm there helping her out. She's good.' Meg speaks as Summer tries to rack her brain. She knows Hannah Thomas had been through some kind of health issue but she can't remember what it is. How is she meant to track villagers' health issues when she can't even keep track of her own bowel movements?

It's too hard, so she just smiles and hopes for this conversation to be over as soon as possible.

Summer went to school with Meg. Meg was in the year below her. Or was it two years below? Summer feels it's a miracle she remembers her name. They weren't close friends but had ridden the school bus together back and forth from Morlan to St Davids for a few years.

'So, are you doing anything tonight?' Meg asks, her eyes sparkling.

'Nothing in particular, just got an hour off from the kids.' Before she can think of an excuse, she sees Meg's face light up. Oh no, is she about to be propositioned?

'Well, if you're free, you can come with me to the hall. There's a new fitness class tonight. Starting in about . . . well, right now.'

'I don't know,' Summer says. A fitness class sounds dreadful.

'Come on, we can catch up. Plus, I don't think it's going to be too strenuous. I'd love to have someone to go with.'

Shit. Summer scolds herself for revealing she's free.

'I don't think I'll have much energy,' she says. Her voice sounds meek, and she can tell she has already given in, even before Meg links her arm through hers.

'You'll be fine.'

She's being dragged towards the village hall and sees a woman with short hair up ahead going into the hall. Isn't she in her seventies? Her mum has spoken to her before, what's her name, Eva or Ivy or something like that?

'Don't say this is a ballroom dance class?' she says to Meg. 'I don't have the co-ordination for that.'

40

'It's not,' Meg says, pulling her into the bright room.

An overweight woman bounces up and down on the little stage in the hall.

'Thank you for coming everyone. I'm Feather Starr and welcome to pole dancing!'

Chapter Five

Gwen

Gwen sits in the car outside Morlan's Village Hall, an ugly, generic, white prefab building. Her stomach is churning with nerves and she can see movement inside. Is it all a bit seedy, she wonders? Should a woman her age really be considering pole dancing classes?

She hasn't told Gareth yet. He's away, anyway, at some conference in London. But it's partly embarrassment, she admits to herself. As much as she convinces herself that pole dancing is great for upper-body strength, the sexual undertones of the class and its association with stripping makes it seem a bit illicit. Truth be told, Hannah at the post office and her comment about Gwen needing to shift a few pounds stung. She wasn't wrong, Gwen knows that. She has let herself go a bit. The menopause has done her no favours. She's textbook: sweaty, flabby in the middle, tearful and emotional.

Gareth looks every bit of his fifty-two years but no one ever seems to judge men. If there was ever a hint of criticism about his weight gain, he always stroked his paunch like a pregnant woman possessively protecting a growing infant.

'I love my food,' he'd say as if that was all the explanation necessary. And his hair loss? 'Makes me look distinguished,' he'd grin. Women, on the other hand, are bitchy and competitive, too quick to notice a few extra pounds or some rogue chin hairs. Oh yes, the rules are different for men.

The sea is angry this evening, the water slapping the shore. In disapproval? Gwen grips the door handle. Come on, you're being ridiculous, she scolds.

'Coo-ee!' Hannah Thomas raps sharply on the side window. 'You decided to join the class, then!'

Fuck! Gwen has no choice now but to go to the bloody class. She climbs out of the car, determined to hide her reluctance. Brazen it out. 'As you said, Hannah, I could do with shifting a few pounds. It's as good a way to do it as any other.'

'I was just walking the dog and thought I'd check out who was actually going to attend these classes. I would have put money down that you would, Gwen,' she grins.

The self-righteous cow! 'If only I had your time to monitor everyone's business!' Gwen says, giving the car door a good shove and striding ahead. She pulls the leggings from her buttocks as they seem resolutely compelled to burrow between her cheeks. They're new, of course. Sweaty Betty and expensive as hell. She's teamed them with a very loose, forgiving, sky-blue T-shirt.

In the foyer, Gwen takes a few deep breaths. She feels ridiculously nervous. Perhaps it's because she has a niggling feeling that women in the village don't really like her. She has always excused it as jealousy, but Gwen has never really encouraged friends or made herself part of the community.

Does she feel a bit superior to them? Now is not the time to pick at that scab.

As she pushes the door open, there are about eight women already there. At the centre is the already infamous Feather Starr, setting up in a chaos of chrome poles, locks and circular bases. She has her back to Gwen but turns around as she hears the door.

'Welcome,' she says, distracted. 'It'll only take a few minutes to set up. I have four poles with me, and they should be enough.'

Gwen takes her all in. Feather Starr is exactly as Gwen imagined she would be. She's wearing a tight yellow T-shirt stretched over her ample bosom. She's so top heavy, Gwen wonders how she stays upright and an image of *Sesame Street*'s Big Bird flashes through Gwen's mind. Her bottom half is covered by stretchy grey leggings that have seen multiple washes, but she has strong thighs, testament to her ability to twist around a pole with ease. Her hair is indeed purple and knotted in a loose bun. Studs and hoops puncture her ears, and her arms are covered in tattoos, technicolour images of hearts and roses on one arm, a weird-looking octopus and a temple on the other. Gwen realises she's staring and flushes.

'Come on in, my lovely. I don't bite. I'll take names later and you can pay at the end.'

Gwen looks around at the others. They're all ages and all shapes and sizes. Even Ivy Bevan is there, and she must be in her seventies. Gwen has only ever exchanged a few words with her, about the weather if she's bumped into her. She sent her a sympathy card when her husband died but she never called. It's always difficult to know what to say in those circumstances.

44

Besides, she doesn't know Ivy that well. Ivy gives her a welcoming smile, which Gwen returns nervously. And there's Hannah Thomas's granddaughter, Meg. A lovely girl, not a bit like her sour-faced, busy-bodying grandparent. She's a few years older than Jasmine. Gwen remembers her being away a while and then returning to Morlan. She'd heard somewhere that Meg has been ill. For once, Hannah was unusually reticent about the matter.

'Can you hold this?' a skinny woman in a red leotard asks, gesturing to a circular base.

Once the four poles are set up, Feather takes charge. 'Right, my lovelies, I want you all to sit around in a circle on the floor while I go through a few health and safety issues and dispel a few myths.'

Dutifully, Gwen struggles to fold her legs as she sits between Red Leotard and Ivy Bevan. She does a quick mental count and sees there are ten women there, including herself.

'Welcome, my lovely ladies. You should be proud of yourselves.' Feather smiles widely, revealing a gold tooth. 'It's quite brave to join any new class and especially one that could be a bit ambiguous, like pole dancing.' She winks. 'Firstly, I want to tell you that this is primarily a fitness class. It's quite an intense workout and an excellent cardiorespiratory exercise.'

Gwen tries to work out her accent. There's a slight Welsh lilt perhaps, but it's more *Eastenders* than Pembrokeshire.

'If you have any medical issues, it's really important that you chat to your GP first to get the green light.' Gwen tries not to snort. You have more chance of speaking to the Dalai Lama. 'More importantly, pole dancing is a fantastic exercise to tone you up and is especially good for older ladies who lose muscle strength as they age.' She looks pointedly at Gwen. 'Pole dancing engages all the body's muscles and develops your core, as well as your upper-and lower-body strength.' Gwen wonders how many times she's given this patter.

'You will notice a difference soon in your body confidence and that will have a knock-on effect in the bedroom.' Embarrassed, some of the women cough. Undeterred, Feather says, 'We'll always start the session by strengthening our pelvic floor muscles and finish with a few minutes of meditation.' Gwen likes the sound of this.

'Right, ladies, let's start. Firstly, I want you to relax and contract your pelvic floor muscles in ten quick bursts. Imagine you're stopping your wee mid-flow. As time goes on, we'll hold the contractions.'

Gwen always means to do these, especially as she leaks at the slightest provocation – a laugh or a cough. Well, this seems easy enough.

'Now, ladies, get into groups of three and one of you can join me. I am going to demonstrate our first move called The Fireman.' Everyone sniggers self-consciously at this. 'Stand about a metre away from the pole and hold it with your dominant arm. On tiptoes, I want you to take four steps around the pole.'

Gwen is in a group with Ivy and Meg, feeling relieved she's not with Feather Starr. Ivy goes first and Gwen notices how muscular she is. Her body is sturdy and strong, especially for a woman of her age. She manages the first move with ease.

'Oh well, that was straightforward,' she smiles.

Meg is next and Gwen wonders why she seems so shy. She has a neat figure but her T-shirt drowns her. As Gwen expects, she tiptoes elegantly around the pole. Gwen feels nervous when it's her turn, but berates herself. If she baulks at this, she'll never be able to do the full class. Gripping the pole in her right hand and raising herself on tiptoes, she moves hesitatingly around the pole. She feels as sexy as a pair of khaki-coloured Crocs amongst Jimmy Choos. Her calves burn a little with the effort of remaining on tiptoes. She breathes a sigh of relief when she manages the steps.

'My calves are burning,' Meg admits.

'Mine, too,' Gwen says conspiratorially.

'Now, when you finish that step, I want you to ensure you are still a metre away from the pole, but this time you are going to use your momentum to spin your body around the pole.' Feather Starr demonstrates the move, making it seem effortless, as if her body were as light as, well, a feather.

Gwen notices that everyone struggles slightly with this move. Ivy moves jerkily around the pole, but manages to lift herself from the spin without dropping to the floor. Gwen rubs her sweaty palms along her leggings, unsure whether she'll manage it. Meg does her spin and bounces lightly on her toes. 'That was fun!'

There's no avoiding it. Gwen grips the pole and takes the first four steps and then her hand slides down the pole as she tries to spin, but inevitably lands in a crumpled heap on the floor. Suddenly, laughter ripples from her throat. 'Well, that was clever. Trust me.' She rolls her eyes to hide her embarrassment. Ivy and Meg help her to her feet.

'It's harder than it looks,' Ivy says. 'Come on, don't give up.'

The women practise the move for twenty minutes or so. Feather helps Gwen when she sees she's struggling. 'You need to grip the pole higher up,' she advises.

In the break, the women sip tea and chatter noisily. Gwen notices that there are no satellite groups set up as she expected, the young ones separate from the older women.

'My husband choked on his breakfast this morning when I told him I was joining the class,' says Red Leotard, whose name is Carol. Everyone giggles. 'I don't know what he's expecting, but he obviously thinks it'll spice up our sex life. Which won't take much seeing as it flatlined years ago.'

'I'm doing this for me,' says a younger woman with red hair. 'I got fed up with Zumba. All that frantic activity. It's not enjoyable. This is more considered, more concentrated. It's harder, too.'

She's right, Gwen thinks, enjoying the chatter with the others. Feather Starr collects the money and jots down their names in a lilac notebook covered with glittery butterflies.

'Gwen Vimpany,' she tells Feather. The surname is unusual, and she can see that Feather recognises it from Vimpany Motors.

'It's eight pounds for the hour.'

'Do you take cards?' Gwen asks.

''Fraid not,' Feather smiles. 'You can pay me next week.' Gwen does a quick calculation – eight quid for an hour and about ten of them. Not bad. I suppose she has to hire the hall, though. She can't help doing this, she realises. Money is always at the forefront of her mind.

Ivy hands over sixteen pounds to Feather. 'This is for me

and Gwen.' She bats away Gwen's protestations. 'Don't worry, I know where you live,' she jokes. Gwen is quite touched and feels a bit ashamed that this is the first time she has chatted with Ivy or any of the other women of the village, for that matter.

In the second half of the class, Feather teaches them the Pinwheel move, an extension of the Fireman but balancing on one leg. Gwen can't manage it at all and neither can many of the others. Meg is good. She's cheerful and game for anything, but there's a shyness to her. Gwen was like that at her age. Now she looks at photos of herself when she was first with Gareth and wonders why she was so self-critical. There's one of them on North Beach, Tenby. She and Gareth must have been around twenty. Gwen's hair is long and luxurious, fanning over her shoulders, and she has a wide smile. Her figure looked great in a tiny red bikini that would have given Pamela Anderson a run for her money. At the time, though, all she could think of was her flabby thighs, imagining how the cellulite could be seen from space. The truth is her skin was firm and tanned and she exuded youthful beauty. Yes, Gareth was punching, as they say these days. Oh, how she wishes she could go back and tell her younger self to be more confident, to make Gareth work a bit harder to get her, to not try to please everyone. It's a fool's errand and now she can see how pleasing everyone other than yourself means you're taken for granted. It chips away at your confidence until you don't know who you are any more.

The last part of the class is the best. All the women lie on the floor. The windows are open and Gwen can hear the sea lapping the shore, not in angry slaps as she thought outside, but in a gentle, rhythmic and soothing way. Feather's voice is strangely hypnotic.

'Take a deep breath in through your nose. Feel your stomach contracting and hold for four seconds. Now, breathe out through your mouth for eight seconds. Clear your mind and think only of your breathing.' It's so calming listening to the breaths around her in unison, Gwen's own breathing filling her ears and stilling her mind. At one point, she thinks about Gareth arriving home to find her not there. She'd left a quick note about his dinner just needing heating. She pauses, though, and wills herself to concentrate on the moment.

'Right, my lovelies, that's the end of the class. I hope you enjoyed and I would love to see you here next week.'

Gwen sits up reluctantly. That's the fastest hour she's spent. She's crap at pole dancing but it didn't stop her enjoying herself. She helps to dismantle the poles and they're packed away in a black holdall. Some of the women help Feather carry them to her car, a red Fiat 500, 2014 number plate. Feather Starr is obviously down on her luck. Gwen catches herself, aware she's passing judgement again. She collects her bag and hovers by the door. She's really enjoyed the class, much to her surprise. Some of the women talk about a quick drink in The Mariners.

'Gwen, are you coming?'

Chapter Six

Meg

The group of women traipse in near silence to The Mariners, with Meg bringing up the rear. The last hour of surprisingly difficult exercise and suggestive dance moves around the pole have pushed Meg so far out of her comfort zone, she can't think of anything vaguely normal to say to the others.

'Cold tonight,' Ivy says, trying to buoy up the crowd. She rubs her arms in emphasis.

'Freezing,' Meg responds feebly.

'Not me, I'm still sweating,' the woman called Carol says. They lapse into silence once more as if the spell of the night, the camaraderie they enjoyed earlier, dissipated once they left the hall.

They make a ragtag bunch, Meg thinks. All different ages and sizes. Meg has met all of them before, of course. No one lives in Morlan without shuffling through the doors of the post office and her grandmother passing comment. But she wouldn't say they are the kind of women she would usually socialise with. After all, besides her and Summer, most of them are old enough to be her mother, if not her grandmother. And she's positive

Ivy could be in great-grandmother territory. Still, she seems the most cheerful of the group, and she'd been so complimentary when Meg tried to strut her stuff around the pole earlier.

'You move your hips like Beyoncé,' she'd said, with Meg giving a sympathetic smile in response. 'Or Cardi B.' Now that reference had surprised Meg. Her own grandmother would probably think she was referring to one of the knitted cardigans they sold in the post office. Meg smiles to herself thinking of it now.

'Is Gwen not joining us?' one of the women at the front of the group shouts.

'She's meeting us there,' Ivy says with enthusiasm.

At that, the white Audi speeds past the women on the pavement, the headlights snarling in the darkness like a panther.

'She couldn't have offered a lift to us?' Summer comments. 'I'm bloody shattered after that class.'

'It's only a two-minute walk, we don't need one,' Meg says, then realises she sounds bitter. It's Hannah's business to make snide remarks about Gwen Vimpany, not hers. She's never understood her grandmother's vendetta against that woman, but when she whizzes past them, Meg can't help but feel a tinge of envy. She follows Gwen's daughter Jasmine on Instagram. Always posting exotic photos from Dubai, Bali, Morocco with comments like *My second home*. You'd swear she was born on a New York catwalk, not the council house in Haverfordwest that her parents used to own before the showroom opened.

'Let's hope she saves us a good table,' someone else says.

As the group become silent again, Meg feels a rumbling from her abdomen. She clamps a hand over the opening of her stoma bag, hoping her layers will muffle any noises further. That was something no one had warned Meg about when she first had the operation to remove her bowel: that not having a sphincter would mean she couldn't control any gas that happened to build up. It would always come at the worst possible time, in work or on a date, the quietest, most inconvenient moment. It had been a learning curve and now Meg knew all the tricks – avoid fizzy drinks, stay active, Gaviscon before a date – but sometimes it couldn't be helped, like now. She feels the gas release and knows it sounds worse in her own mind than to the outside world, but Meg can't help but dart a self-conscious glance at her companions. Is she imagining it or do Summer's eyes meet hers? Does she know?

As they get to The Mariners car park, the dark is illuminated by the multicoloured lights strung around the entrance, a relic from two Christmases ago that the owners either haven't remembered or haven't bothered to take down. It looks warm inside, though, and inviting.

Gwen is getting out of her car, shaking her hair as she rejoins the group. She looks as though she's spent the journey getting powdered and blow-dried by an in-car stylist.

'You look amazing,' Summer says to her, making conversation. 'Not like me, the only workout I've done is carrying two rascals up the stairs for the last year and a half.'

'How are Nia and Jordan?' Ivy asks, and Meg feels relieved to have overheard. She's been racking her brains for the names of Summer's children since the class started. Nia and Jordan, that's it.

'Jordan's a dream, but Nia's getting to that terrible-twos stage.'

'They're beautiful children, though,' Meg adds, remembering when Summer brought them into the post office a few weeks ago. She was mesmerised by how Summer seemed to have it all together. A husband. Two children. A house that they owned. The antithesis of Meg's trajectory.

It was as if inflammatory bowel disease had pressed pause on her plans. While everyone else was working towards the classic twenties' goals of career, relationships, a family, Meg was just concentrating on how not to fart into the permanent whoopee-cushion she carried around. When was her time coming?

Meg has always wanted to be a journalist, travel journalism perhaps, or lifestyle. She used to write mock articles when she was a child and staple the misshapen pages together to form a magazine. But that dream, like every other area of her life, had been put on hold. Now, it is as if she's been overtaken by everyone else. Going back to university seems out of reach.

'What's everyone having?' Ivy asks as they enter the pub. Chatter bursts from the bar area, 'Sweet Caroline' playing from the tinny jukebox in the corner. Of all the times Meg has been in The Mariners, she doesn't think they've played anything other than 'Sweet Caroline' and 'Sex Bomb'.

'Surprised they're not repping the Tom Jones,' Summer says to her now, making Meg laugh. Summer unzips her jacket, then quickly zips back up. Meg gives her a confused look, before taking off her own jacket.

'My boobs,' Summer says, quietly. 'Don't tell the others, but they're prone to leaking when there's no tiny human being hanging off them.'

'Oh no,' Meg tries to sympathise. 'You probably need a

better sports bra.' Summer smiles then turns away, and Meg wonders if she's been insensitive.

'I'll get this round,' Ivy offers from the bar, to many protests and refusals.

'Put your purse away, mun,' one of the women says. Meg notices that Gwen has already bought her own drink. Maybe Hannah's right about her. What did she say about the rich having the tightest purse strings?

'All right?' Rhys, the bartender, greets Meg. They were in class together at school, sat together in top-set English and history, and were a constant source of teasing for their classmates. *Megan and Rhys, sitting in a tree . . .*

'Haven't seen you for ages,' she says. 'Dry white, please.' There was never any truth to the jokes. Meg and Rhys are friends and always have been. She just can't see him that way, plus she is pretty convinced Rhys has a long-term crush on her friend Natalie from schooldays.

'I know. Probably Covid,' he shrugs. 'Still hanging around Morlan, then?'

Where else would I be? Meg thinks. 'Well, Hollywood hasn't come knocking yet.'

'Only a matter of time,' Rhys smiles, putting her drink down on the bar.

'And for you? Natalie hasn't filed for divorce from the golfer yet?'

'Don't mention that name to me,' he laughs, good-naturedly. 'How many times do I have to say I'm not interested in Natalie Jones?'

'I'll believe it when it's true,' Meg jokes.

'Who are you here with?' Rhys nods to the rest of the group that have now assembled around a table next to the fire. Meg realises they must look an odd bunch.

'It's a long story.' She decides to keep quiet.

'I'm ready to hear it whenever you are. On the house,' he says as Meg gets her purse out.

'No way,' she says but Rhys won't hear of it. She's reminded of Mr Generous, otherwise known as Greg from last week, with his twenty pounds offering. He could learn a thing or two from guys like Rhys.

Meg quickly readjusts the bag under her top, making sure it doesn't pinch against her waistband, whilst no one's looking, then turns and takes the last seat with the group.

'To the best pole dancers in Pembrokeshire.' Summer holds up her glass, and Meg notices it's half empty already. Summer probably hasn't been in a pub child-free for a while.

'Did you see me? I was awful,' a short, blonde woman with green streaks in her hair says. 'I looked like a dog cocking my leg up to relieve myself against that pole.'

'Terri, I can't get that image out of my head now,' someone else says. Meg has to laugh. It seems they are all self-conscious in their own ways. It doesn't make her any less worried, though. They all own their bodies in a way she doesn't think she ever will. What if she's forced to wear some kind of costume that doesn't hide her stoma bag? Feather Starr seems to have no inhibitions, in a way that scares Meg. Surely, she can't expect the others to be like that?

'Are we all coming back next week, though?' Terri asks.

'If I can find a babysitter,' Summer says reluctantly.

'You will. In for a penny.' Someone else raises their glass and they 'cheers' again, all chorusing 'in for a pound'. A few of the women go back up to the bar to get another round. Meg finds herself next to Ivy.

'Are you OK, Ivy?' she asks. 'You seem quieter now?'

'I'm fine,' she says, although it doesn't stop Meg noticing the sheen in her eyes. She leaves it a beat, knowing Ivy will fill the silence if she wants to. 'I was just thinking I haven't been back to this place since Jim passed.'

'It was his favourite?'

'Every night in here like clockwork. Two pints on a weekday, three on the weekend. I used to join him on a Saturday. God, you don't realise what you'll miss about someone until it's too late.' She smiles but Meg can tell there's a lot of pain behind it.

'The routines of daily life, I suppose. They're a comfort.' Meg thinks about her own grandmother, how they have a pot of tea at the end of every day when the 'open' sign turns to 'closed' on the post office door.

'Don't get me wrong, we used to argue about it. "You spend your life in that pub," I used to tell him,' Ivy goes on. 'What I wouldn't give to share another drink, though.' She sighs, and Meg doesn't quite know what to say. Maybe she doesn't need to say anything.

When the moment's passed, she jokes, 'Well, the men of this village do seem to be glued to the pub. It's like they're under police curfew every night.'

'Maybe it's time for us girls to reclaim it,' Ivy says. Meg doesn't know what's funnier, whether it's Ivy referring to the group as 'girls', or the thought of their pole dancing team taking on the men of Morlan, but she laughs.

'That's very true.'

'What is?' Gwen overhears.

As Ivy explains, Meg's eyes drift to the door, which is opened, depositing a man and woman in coats and scarves. They de-robe and the man puts his arm around her protectively, while she places a hard kiss on his cheek. Meg doesn't look at them properly, not wanting to stare, but can tell they have the sort of excited intimacy of a relationship that's got past the awkward stages but is still new and intoxicating.

Meg watches as they move to the bar in tandem, before the man orders champagne, saying, 'We're celebrating.'

'We've just got engaged!' The woman thrusts her sparkly ring out, and Meg is nearly blinded from her side of the pub. A few people at the bar overhear and cheer loudly for them.

'How nice,' Summer sighs, next to her, listening in.

As the couple turn and take a seat at the table across from them, Meg realises she's met the man before.

She can't believe it.

Bile rises in her throat.

It's him. It's Greg from her date the other night.

It doesn't make any sense but it's definitely him.

'Are you all right?' Summer asks.

'I feel a bit sick,' Meg says. 'Think I'm gonna call it a night.' Call it a night before her faith in the male population is lost forever.

Chapter Seven

Ivy

'Unlike recycling, which takes a material backwards in the chain to its original properties, upcycling is very different. It adds value to an item of furniture through clever design. It makes it more desirable, financially, aesthetically and emotionally,' a woman with ruddy cheeks and blonde hair says animatedly from the front.

The village hall is quite full tonight, everyone still enjoying their post-Covid freedom. Outside the sky is pearlescent as the sun makes its evening descent into a shimmering sea. Someone has opened the windows wide and sounds drift in, the lapping waves, laughter and the revving of a car engine.

Tonight, they have two speakers and Ivy is hanging on the couple's every word. Kim and Chris Sullivan own Nooks and Crannies, an antiques and upcycling shop in Narberth. She's been in several times when in Narberth and loves some of the upcycled furniture in the store.

'Why not add a splash of colour to the inside of a chest of drawers,' Kim says enthusiastically, her blonde fringe falling into her eyes. 'Keep the colour neutral on the outside and use a more vibrant colour on the inside. It'll make you smile every time you open a drawer and see that pop of colour.'

Ivy can't help but make the analogy with her own situation. She is like an old chest of drawers in need of upcycling. She might be seventy-two and a bit creaky, but all she needs is a bit of energy and imagination to breathe new life into her. She could be as good as new.

'There are cheaper chalk paints on the market these days,' Chris interjects. 'Or you could use wallpaper on the drawers. Be bold. Don't follow the crowd.' Ivy feels they could be talking to her.

Wendy yawns loudly beside her. 'I prefer new myself. None of this shabby chic look, as they call it. Did I tell you my dining table from Leekes is due to arrive next week?'

Ivy flushes, aware that Kim and Chris might have caught Wendy's insensitive comment. She ignores her, hoping she'll take the hint that some are actually enjoying the talk.

Nudging Ivy, Wendy persists in disturbing her enjoyment. 'I heard quite a few turned up to that pole dancing class last night. Some people have no shame.' Wendy's lip curls in disgust.

Marion, on the other side of Wendy adds, 'Hannah Thomas said about a dozen turned up. Can you believe it? Apparently, Gwen Vimpany was one of them.'

'Well, that's hardly surprising,' Wendy says, warming to the theme. 'Money can't buy you class.'

Ivy feels angry now. She's never felt the need to criticise

others to make her feel better about her own life. It gives her a sense of satisfaction, though, to think that only last night she was twirling around a pole just about where Wendy is sitting now. And she had been contracting her pelvic floor muscles just where Marion is twitching in her seat.

'Idris Hopkins says he's going to lobby the council to get the class shut down,' Marion says with satisfaction.

Ivy shudders. Their esteemed councillor, Idris Hopkins. He's been having affairs for years, yet he feels it necessary to shut down an innocuous exercise class.

Everyone claps politely as Kim and Chris finish their talk. Ivy rushes to the front. 'I loved that. It was so interesting. I will definitely be in next week to buy some paint. I love what you've done with that chest of drawers.'

'Thank you so much,' says Chris.

'Ahem,' Cynthia, the Treasurer, stands at the front. 'On behalf of Morlan's branch of the WI, I'd like to thank you for that most interesting talk on furniture upcycling. It's given us all food for thought and shown us what is achievable with a bit of imagination,' she says dismissively and with all the sincerity of an estate agent. She coughs again, 'Now, to matters of business. Only one person put themselves forward for the role of Secretary, Marion Edwards. I am delighted, therefore, to say that Marion is appointed as our new Secretary. She has been with the WI for fifteen years and I know she will dedicate herself to continue making Morlan's WI a vibrant and inclusive community.'

'Hear, hear!' Wendy shouts.

As the women mill about the foyer later, Cynthia

approaches Ivy. 'I must say, Ivy, I was rather disappointed that you didn't put yourself forward for the role, especially after our last chat.'

Ivy is expecting this. 'Well, I don't feel quite ready to commit to anything at the moment.' She experiences a pang of guilt using her grief to get out of something she doesn't want to do. No, that is putting it mildly. She'd rather take an ice-cold shower in the dead of winter. She can't stand the bitchiness, the one-upmanship of the local WI. To be fair, not all the women are like that.

'Don't you think that it would have been something for you to do, Ivy? Get you out of the house, take your mind off your troubles. You don't want to become self-indulgent in your grief. Jim would have wanted you to carry on, love your life.'

Ivy has to bite her tongue. Under the guise of compassion and consideration, she can't believe that Cynthia has the cheek to tell her off for not being desperate to become Secretary of the WI. She's beginning to feel claustrophobic in the hall and it's nothing to do with the temperature.

'If you'll excuse me, Cynthia, I'm feeling a little light-headed,' Ivy says with a feeble smile.

'I'll look after you,' Sally says, and Ivy flashes her a grateful smile.

They sit on a bench outside, taking in the sea breathing softly as daylight fades.

'It's all a bit much sometimes, isn't it?' Sally says.

'I'm not sure I fit in at all with these women,' Ivy sighs.

'Some are quite good sorts,' Sally says with her usual

positivity. 'Others not so much. Don't let them get to you. Take things at your own pace.'

Ivy says, 'I joined that pole dancing class last night.' Sally is silent and Ivy continues, 'And it was the best hour I've spent in ages.'

Sally grins, 'Well, you're a dark horse! Good for you. I fancied it myself but just didn't have the guts!'

'Don't be like me, Sal. I listened to Jim for far too much of my life. We did everything he wanted. We never went for meals out because he swore we had better food at home. We never went on holidays as it was too expensive, and *You can't trust foreigners*. He didn't want me to work because there was no need and he'd always look after me.' She looks down at her hands, pinches the loose skin. 'Look at me now, I'm seventy-two and I have no idea who I am or what I want.'

Sally reaches for her hand and says nothing.

'For the first time in my life, I don't have to answer to anyone.' Ivy bites her lip, aware that it sounds bad coming from someone who has lost her husband. 'Jim wasn't a bad man and I do miss the daft bugger.'

Sally says, 'Ivy, you don't have to explain. You're a good woman – loyal, kind and I hope I can be half the woman you are at your age.' After a pause, she grins, 'A pole dancing class? I can't wait to see the reaction of the others when they hear about it. It won't come from me, of course.'

'And they will,' Ivy laughs. 'Nothing is sacred in Morlan.'

'Martin's here, Ivy. He's waiting in the car,' Wendy says, joining the two women.

'That's ok. I'm taking Ivy home,' Sally says. 'She's showing me a chest of drawers she's thinking of upcycling.'

Wendy sniffs, obviously quite put out. 'More DIY? You've got a perfectly good house there, Ivy.'

As Sally draws up outside the cottage, Ivy says, 'That's the second time you've saved me tonight. Come in for a cuppa, if you've got time.'

Sally glances at her watch, 'Of course I've got time. Simon is more than capable of getting his own dinner.'

Ivy leads them in through the front door, the lamp in the hallway casting a welcoming glow.

'Ooh, you are clever,' Sally says, admiring the sanded floor of the living room. 'I really like what you've done with the room. It's so fresh and welcoming. Modern, too. I'm hopeless at DIY and Simon is worse than me. We paid someone to decorate the hallway a few months ago.'

Ivy feels proud. 'It was only following a few videos on TikTok. Honestly, if I can do it, anyone can.' She catches herself, aware that her first reaction for anything is to put herself down. A curiously female trait, she decides.

'TikTok? You are a dark horse,' Sally says for the second time that night.

Ivy lights some candles and chooses to ignore the many missed calls from Matthew. She told him she was at her WI meeting but he never really listens to her. Sally and she sit in companionable silence for a few minutes, sipping a small glass of red wine and watching the sea below, inky-black and unmoving.

'I do admire you,' Sally says sincerely.

'Really?' Ivy is surprised.

64

'My mother is sixty-eight and she won't do anything without my father. They're like conjoined twins. Yet, here you are, alone after being widowed and you're just getting on with things.'

'I'm like the proverbial swan or is it a duck? Calm on the surface, but paddling furiously below.'

'Well, it doesn't show,' Sally says. Then after a beat, 'So, tell me all about last night. Who was there? What was it like? Did you recognise Feather Starr?'

Ivy laughs, 'I didn't recognise her, no. It was good fun, to be honest. There were ten of us. Terri Turf – the green-haired woman from the estate. Summer, the one who has just had a baby. Hannah Thomas's granddaughter. Carol, and, oh yes, Gwen Vimpany.'

Sally's eyes widen at this. 'I didn't expect her to go. She seems such a snob.'

Ivy shrugs, 'I don't think she is, actually. She seemed to be on the periphery last night. I don't think she has many friends. After all, it can't be easy being married to Gareth Vimpany, the Donald Trump of Pembrokeshire. Anyone can see that she's the brains behind the business, but he swans around like he's king pin. And only last week, I saw him in Wolfscastle with—' She breaks off suddenly.

'With who?' Sally asks.

'No one. I wasn't sure. It might have been someone else. Anyway, Feather Starr was really rather good.' Ivy deftly changes the subject. 'She's a bit out there, but Morlan needs shaking up and she has a knack of making us all feel comfortable with each other.'

'Well, she's certainly stirred up a storm here.'

'Yes, a real shitstorm,' Ivy agrees and both women laugh.

When Sally leaves, Ivy rings Matthew. He picks up on the second ring.

'Mam, at last. Where the hell have you been until this time?'

God, he sounds like Jim more and more. 'I told you I was at the WI meeting tonight. Sally came back with me, and we had a glass of wine. I rather enjoyed it.'

'I wish you'd tell me before you go off gallivanting,' he sighs.

'Do I need permission from you, Matthew? A seventy-two-year-old woman?'

'You know it's not that, Mam. I worry about you, that's all. For all I know, you could be lying in a pool of blood in the garden.'

'Thanks, Matthew,' she says stiffly.

'After what happened with Dad, I know I worry too much.'

Ivy feels a stab of guilt now. 'Look, I'm fine, Matthew. I do understand you worry but I have got neighbours who keep an eye on me. Wendy next door could work for MI5. Morlan is a safe place. Nothing ever goes on here, you know that.' Ivy crosses her fingers at this.

'Ok, point taken,' he concedes. 'When are you going to visit again, Mam? Rach was asking yesterday. It's been ages. Tabitha is missing her mamgu and she's grown so tall.'

As Ivy flicks through the channels later, she wonders if she is being selfish staying in Morlan. She has a son and grandchild in Bristol. They could do with her help. She pauses at *Naked Attraction* on Channel 4 as a young woman is describing the penis of the man in the booth in front of her to Anna Richardson. 'I like his tattoo,' she enthuses. 'The elephant is inspired,' she adds to much giggling from the presenter.

Ivy feels depressed and switches off. Maybe she will go to Bristol. First, though, she will have some fun and live a bit.

Chapter Eight

Summer

Summer reaches for the pile of clothes stacked up on the top shelf of the wardrobe, and hopes she's got the right ones. Jordan's already too big for his 0–3 months clothes, and she wants to see if she has anything neutral left over from Nia, to save a trip to the shops.

As she tugs, she feels a familiar leather box behind. She's forgotten all about her photo albums. She decides she has two minutes to flick through some pictures and reaches for the box. Summer has always enjoyed photography, nothing professional of course, but she likes documenting memories on film, holding actual pictures in her hands rather than scrolling on a phone screen. She hasn't exactly had a lot of time recently, but she decides she should add pictures of Nia and Jordan to the albums.

She flicks through some pictures of her childhood, when she was as bright-eyed and curly-haired as Nia. Summer cringes as the pictures merge to become her teenage years when braces and acne were her signature style. She can't believe sometimes that Aled fell for her at that time, but then he didn't look so hot himself with the puppy fat and curtain-hairdo. She laughs as she sees pictures from their first holiday together, Majorca, aged eighteen. They'd saved enough from their teenage weekend jobs to stay in a two-star hotel that looked like some seventies' throwback. The cheap drinks were lethal, and they'd giggled all week, enjoying their first taste of freedom from home.

Summer's life was all ahead of her then. She'd known that university wasn't for her, even if Aled went off to Swansea for engineering. She had a job as a teaching assistant at Morlan Primary School, and she loved every second of it. She loved the children, and the creativity – she remembers dressing as one of Roald Dahl's witches on World Book Day, complete with elaborate fake warts and prosthetic nose. The time off wasn't bad either, and she had the energy to go out then. There are numerous photos documenting her nights out with the other teachers, even some where they are on the beach at sunrise, with Summer in a tight dress, still boozy and eager to stretch the night that much longer.

A night out sounds like hell now, she thinks. What she wouldn't give for a night in instead, some blissful uninterrupted sleep.

And there she is on her wedding day, in a puffy white number she'd picked from a charity shop. She didn't know it then, but she was just weeks away from falling pregnant with Nia. She's tanned, lean and about to get extremely drunk.

It's like a different person stares up at her from the photographs, a different person with different worries and priorities. She looks carefree, happy, and just a tiny bit wild.

Is that Summer still inside her, or is she just destined to be someone's mum forever more?

This is why she doesn't let herself look at the pictures too often. A reminder of how life has changed.

Summer lets out an exasperated huff as she shoves the box back and removes a T-shirt from the wardrobe, sending several other items tumbling to the floor. It's hard not to be defeatist, but sometimes she feels the house is against her, conspiring to make the kids' nap time as difficult as possible. *Sleep when the baby's sleeping* sounds like solid advice, but when that two-hour window is the only time you have to shower, eat, cook, clean and maintain at least a semblance of normal life, it's completely impractical. And when the house throws up endless issues like a broken tumble-dryer, exploding porridge in the microwave, or something as mundane as fallen hangers, it makes Summer want to cry.

She would describe her attitude to cleaning as 'relaxed' at the best of times, but the day Aled comes home, she does try to make an effort. Yes, the house is filled with the chaos of crying children, but she wants it to be at least a better environment than the oil rig he works on, clinging to a rock in the Irish Sea. She does wonder, though, if that's possible.

The little moments when he comes home make it all worth it. The way his eyes shine when he scoops Nia and Jordan into a bear hug again. The shrieks Nia gives when he swirls her around the living room by the arms. The sigh he lets out when his body crumples and folds onto the sofa.

'You're at home now, babe,' she usually says, snuggling up next to him. She wonders if he gives the same sigh when he shuts the door on them at the end of the ten days. She knows she would.

'Ouch!' she grunts as she bends to pick up the tops from the floor of the wardrobe. Her hips still ache and throb like she gave birth last week. It's as if her body has been punished, she thinks sometimes, by carrying two watermelons inside her for nine months and then attending to their every need, scooping to clean up little baby bums, and collecting discarded toys. There's constant activity; she doesn't get a minute to rest. Ironically, she should be in the best shape of her life in her twenties, but Summer could still pass for third trimester even now. The chocolate bars snaffled during feeds are probably to blame, but Summer sometimes thinks they are the only thing holding her mental health together. Penguin bars and Toffee Crisps.

She dresses in her ubiquitous mum-leggings and voluminous T-shirt, then tiptoes past the nursery where Jordan is sleeping, snuffling away like a newborn piglet. The floor length mirror reveals a sight that she isn't totally enamoured by but is the best she'll get. The neckline of the T-shirt is low so you can see the straps from her maternity bra digging trenches in her shoulders, but apart from that she looks vaguely sporty.

It'll do for tonight's class, she decides. The only other young person in the pole dancing group is Meg, and although Summer knows she does a lot of sport, she hardly dresses like it. Her top looked like a repurposed sack last week. The only person in the class who Summer suspects is focused on appearances is Gwen Vimpany, and she's sure that Gwen is too enthralled by her own clothing to worry about what Summer wears. The rest are ancient.

Despite the age differences, Summer can't believe how much she'd enjoyed the class last week. It was probably just a side effect from her first solo outing in a long time, but she'd laughed like a drain with those strangers in the pub, particularly when discussing Feather Starr and her moves around the pole. Summer had felt like an androgynous lump doing most of the exercises, but she'd loved it. She might never get the hip action right, or the impressive ab muscles needed to hold yourself up on the pole, but she could give it a go. It was the only hour in the last eighteen months that she'd completely forgotten who she was, forgotten that she was a mother of two squirming dependents, and a devoted wife at the age of twenty-seven.

For an hour, she'd been Summer Griffiths, amateur pole dancer. Nearly the same Summer as the one in the pictures, she thinks.

Ridiculous, she knows, but she wants to be that person again.

At that moment, the key clangs in the front door, making Summer jump.

'Surprise!' Aled's voice calls up from downstairs.

Crap, Summer curses. The place is still a shit-tip. She hasn't even had time to run around with the Hoover downstairs. Nia had spent the morning throwing handfuls of soggy Weetabix around the kitchen while Summer cleaned up the porridge explosion. The detritus is still lying in sodden brown clumps.

'You're home early,' she says, wondering if there is a way to sound more guilty.

'No tractors on the A487 for once,' he shouts. 'I wanted to surprise my favourite people.'

Summer's next worry is that he'll wake the kids. She darts downstairs, shushing and hoping he'll get the message. 'It's nap time,' she pleads. Aled widens his eyes, getting the message.

'I thought nap time was later on?'

'It was, but Jordan was dozing off and Nia's always more tired after Thursday playgroup,' she explains. 'I thought I'd get them off and give me time to tidy the . . .' She gestures to the mess.

'So, you're saying we have two sleeping children and the house to ourselves?' Aled raises his eyebrows at Summer from the end of the hallway. He begins to manoeuvre towards her, dropping his luggage and sidling past the sideboard in their narrow hallway.

'Not for long,' she says, thinking he's probably joking. Aled's usually so knackered after getting back, they both curl up on the sofa and fall asleep in a fog of takeaway farts and police documentaries.

She relishes him putting his arms around her. They've been married for three years but she thinks the number of married nights they've spent together could probably fit inside a few months.

'It must keep the relationship young,' Summer's mother always said, not understanding her desperation to have some adult company at home. Summer envies couples that co-parent every night. How it must feel to have your teammate actually by your side, rather than over the phone. She'd kill to have more time with hers.

'God, I miss this,' Aled seems to read her thoughts.

'Me too,' she moans into him. 'I sometimes imagine the day

when we hug like this and know you're home for good.' As soon as she says it, she regrets it. She feels Aled's stomach stiffen against her.

'I know it's hard, but I have to do this. I couldn't make as much money around here, you know that,' he says gently. 'There's nothing in Morlan, or Pembrokeshire for that instance, that pays even a fraction . . .'

She knows it's true, but she can't help hope. 'Couldn't we just put up with it? Figure something out?' Summer waits for him to protest, the argument as familiar as the clothes she is wearing.

'I wish,' Aled says instead, surprising her. 'It's so hard to be away from you.'

'And the kids?'

'I'm not thinking of them so much now.' He grinds his hips into hers as he says it. Summer knows it shouldn't, but it does make her laugh, reminding her of an action Feather Starr was doing last week with the pole. She recovers quickly, lest he thinks she's laughing at him. She's already moaned at him and he's only been home for two minutes.

'Are you sure?' she says. Before the kids came along, they used to have sex relentlessly when Aled was home. As though they made up for the time he was away in frequency and quality, trying to cram in as many positions and Ann Summers' products as possible. It's less exotic now, and planned to a fine art. Ten minutes maximum whilst the kids are in bed and they have a whiff of energy remaining, every other day for the ten he's back. Like they're making up for the rest of the time.

'Let me just get the baby monitor,' Summer says as his lips

74

trail off from her neck. She remembers when they were younger and had a noise complaint from a hotel in Rhodes on one particularly rowdy trip. The complaint had only spurred them on, forced them to do it out on the balcony after too many chemical-tasting mojitos, drunkenly enjoying the excitement that they might be seen from the road. They'd whipped each other's clothes off with vigour, their Primark underwear mingling on the balcony tiles.

If they could see themselves now, Summer thinks, with the curtains drawn and every movement punctuated with a 'shhhh'. They both took their clothes off respectively, sometimes keeping the top halves on. Summer drew the line at Aled wearing socks in the bedroom, but she had once caught him folding his jeans to a neat square while she stripped off.

It isn't that sex with Aled is a chore, or even boring. She just feels sometimes like she is doing it to tick a box. To prove that they are still young and in love. That Aled does have a good life to come home to. She so wants that to be enough for him.

Summer kneels on the sofa for the final stretch, ignoring the plastic doll hand that's digging into her knee. Aled moans with pleasure, and she is even enjoying herself. They still have it pretty good, she decides.

'Mmm, I love you,' he whispers into her hair when he's finished.

'I love you too,' she says. 'Welcome home.'

'Is it nice to have me back?'

'You have your uses, I suppose,' Summer jokes, now turning to sit beside him. Their eyes flick to the monitor as a small whimper sounds. Summer holds her breath, but all seems to go quiet after a few seconds. Aled gazes at her again. Yes, now is the time she decides. 'And I've got another use for you tonight. What would you say if I told you I was going pole dancing?'

A look of confusion crosses his face, but he smiles again. 'I'd say, why didn't you tell me that earlier? I could have used that mental image.'

'You had no problems without it,' Summer says. 'I'm not joking, by the way. Someone called Feather Starr has started pole dancing classes in Morlan, and last week my mother babysat the kids while I went.'

'I . . . I'm not sure what the most unbelievable part of that sentence is,' he says. 'No, I am . . . your mother was here?'

'Some excuse about Steve having an event in Haverfordwest.'

'And she offered to help while you went pole dancing?' Aled looks as incredulous as she feels about it.

'Well, my plan wasn't to go pole dancing. I sort of got dragged into it by Meg Thomas.'

'And what was the name you mentioned? Starry Night or something?'

'Feather Starr. Insane, I know. That can't be her real name.' Summer fields off more questions. She can't blame Aled for his confusion. She would have been less surprised if he'd told her he'd been offered a million pounds to star in a 'Sexy Oil Rig Engineers' calendar.

'When can I come and watch this sexy pole dancing, then?' Aled asks now. She thinks his eyebrows have risen as high up his forehead as they can possibly go.

'It's about the furthest thing from sexy you could imagine. Basically, a room of grandmothers stretching and gyrating.'

'Gyrating, eh?' Aled says, and Summer feels suddenly affronted by his teasing tone.

'Well, I really enjoyed it and I really want to go.' Then in a small voice, 'Do you mind watching the kids?'

'Tonight? It's my first night home,' Aled says.

Yes, but I've had them 24/7 for the last three bloody weeks while you've slept and wanked and bantered with your workmates and worked just eight hours a day. She wants to explode but she doesn't. Call it the negotiating skills of a mother.

'It's only an hour. And I really want to go,' she says. 'I know it's not ideal. I promise I'll show you my moves afterwards. And I'll be home straight after it at eight-thirty. We'll put Nia to bed beforehand, so you'll just have Jordan to feed.' Why is she pleading so much? Surely Aled can do an hour of what she has to, day in, day out.

A look crosses Aled's face that tells her he knows Jordan is the worst one at that time of night. So, he remembers that much at least. The witching hour, or so it was called. If only it lasted an hour.

'It'll be great for Jordan to have some time with his dad,' she pleads.

'Go on, then,' Aled says. 'Have you got enough milk pumped?'

'I'm due a pump now,' Summer says. 'Don't worry.'

'Well, I feel like I've just been pumped.' Summer can tell he's proud of that joke, and even if it is disgusting, she laughs along.

'I'll make a cuppa now before the kids wake,' she says. As she waits for the kettle to boil and scoops a few Weetabix clumps into kitchen roll, Summer softens towards Aled. She doesn't think he's ever spent an hour alone with Jordan since he's been born. He took him to the GP once when he had a rash, and that was a disaster. Jordan had screamed the waiting room down, so much so the receptionist offered to nurse Jordan while Aled went to get a cup of tea, and he forgot to mention to the doctor that the rash wasn't just on his face but carried on down his little torso and arms. Summer had to take him back the next day.

It isn't that Aled's a bad father, just out of practice, she thinks. This will be good for him. And for her.

But deep down, as Summer squeezes two teabags against the rims of the cups, she wonders who's the most worried about the class tonight, her or Aled?

Chapter Nine

Gwen

The sun is streaming through the window and Gwen can see the sea glistening in the distance, the tide full in. The bath obscures the view a bit but that was Gareth's idea. *You can take the man out of Haverfordwest but you can't take Haverfordwest . . .* Who in their right mind would have a bath in full view of the road winding towards Fishguard? Gwen had only used it once and she wouldn't let Gareth put the lights on. Him and his ideas!

Gwen is in that lovely transition between sleep and being awake. The house is silent. Gareth went in early this morning, crashing around noisily in the bedroom but Gwen had managed to go back to sleep. Lydia is staying over at Sophie's. She sighs, her hand travelling slowly down her thighs. It's been ages. The pole dancing class has made her more aware of her body. Its needs. She even tried to get Gareth in the mood last night, but he looked at her horrified as if she'd told him she intended to shave her head. Gareth needs GPS to find her clitoris these days. She feels like his aged aunt rather than his wife. Gwen lies back on the pillow with its silk pillowcase. It's supposed to reduce wrinkles and was a ridiculous price.

She must concentrate. Oh God, not Gareth, though. She remembers that advert she saw for Light Blue aftershave last night. David Gandy was wearing his impossibly tight swimming trunks, his abs rippling in the sunlight. It wasn't that model in the boat with him but Gwen. Before she had children, of course. Pre-menopause, when her body responded to sexual tension and didn't refuse to play ball, her vagina as dry as the bloody Sahara and likely to feel like a cheese grater on any man's penis. Gwen imagines her fulsome breasts barely contained in the tight bikini top and her tan as she stretches her bronze legs out seductively, sending David Gandy wild with sexual excitement. He's grunting now like some wild animal. She can feel the sun on her skin and her long hair spills over her shoulders. There's something visceral as their bodies touch, a jolt of electricity surging through them. Hmm . . .

'Mrs Vimpany, is it ok to start on the bathroom first?' A call punctures her lovely dream.

Shit! The cleaner. Gwen forgets it's Thursday. 'Come on up, Paula.'

A second later, Paula enters the bedroom and Gwen flushes as if Paula knows what she's been up to.

'Oh, sorry, Mrs Vimpany. Did I wake you?'

'Not at all, Paula. I have lots to do today.' A lie. 'I can't laze here all day.' Another lie. If you don't count the fact that she has to pick Lydia up from Sophie's to take her to have her nails done later. The only thing she will do for herself today is go to the pole dancing class. And she's determined to go. She'll make Gareth his favourite – fish pie. He's back so late these days, she'll probably get back before him, even if she does stop for a drink in The Mariners.

She pulls a dressing gown on and steps into the en suite as Paula makes the bed. If you had told her when she was younger that she would have a cleaner and this beautiful house, she would have been delirious with excitement. In disbelief. You never enjoy it as much as you'd expect, though. Gwen lets the shower's water cascade over her body. The water is a bit colder than she would like but she read in a magazine last week that cold water is good for you. Everyone's into wild swimming these days. Especially middle-aged women. Well, this is the closest Gwen is going to get to it – a blast of tepid water in the morning.

Perhaps she'll book St Bride's for lunch and even have a massage. Yes, that would cheer her up. She'll call Lynne when she's out of the shower. As she gets dressed, she remembers that Lynne is in Gran Canaria. Some relatives have got a timeshare out there. Blast! How inconvenient!

As Gwen pours her orange juice, she admits that there is no one else she can call. That's the price she's paid for working on the business. She's missed out on the camaraderie of other females. It makes her jealous when she sees a gaggle of women howling with laughter with empty bottles of Prosecco littering the table in some pub. It's not like she enjoys time with Jasmine and Lydia to make up for it. Gwen was chuffed to have two daughters, but the reality is that they see her as a human cash machine and shun her as if she has monkeypox. She wouldn't even dare suggest going to the cinema or lunch. Not for the first time, Gwen wonders where she went wrong.

After dropping Lydia off at the nail bar in Haverfordwest, Gwen has lunch in a garden centre on her own. She's got hours to fill before the class. She could do some of the books but really isn't in the mood. She scrolls through her phone absentmindedly.

'Gwen. It is Gwen, isn't it? Gwen Lewis?'

Gwen looks up. No one has called her by her maiden name for donkey's years. She recognises the face of the woman in front of her, holding a baby with a toddler in a pushchair. Her hair has been left a natural grey and she wears a frumpy blue blouse and jeans that have seen better days.

'It's me. Florrie Beynon. Well, Florrie Jenkins now. How are you keeping, Gwen?'

'Fine. I can see you're busy,' Gwen smiles.

'My grandchildren. Yep, they certainly keep me busy. This is Oliver, eight months, and there's Maddie in the pushchair. Three now and she's a right diva!' Florrie laughs. 'What about you? Any grandchildren?'

Gwen shakes her head, 'Not yet. Lydia is only in first-year sixth and Jasmine has only just started a new post after travelling.'

'Oh well, there's plenty of time,' she says, in that patronising way that really gets under Gwen's skin.

'To be honest, Flo, Gareth and I are chockers with the business. It's hard to keep up with demand and we're considering expanding Cardiff way.' She's in full flow now. 'Yes, we're looking at buying a villa abroad, Croatia perhaps or Portugal. We're in no hurry to have grandchildren yet.'

'Well, it's lovely to see you,' Florrie says, cutting the

conversation dead. 'I'm taking these two to the rock pools in Whitesands. Take care.'

Why does she do this? Why does she feel the need to show off? It's like she has verbal diarrhoea. She regularly sees on Facebook the monthly meet ups some of her schoolfriends have. She's never invited and it niggles at her.

There are eleven women in the class tonight and Gwen joins with Ivy and Meg again. Outside, it's drizzling, but it doesn't dampen anyone's spirit. After the usual warm-up and pelvic floor exercises, Feather Starr blasts 'Despacito' on the speaker system and gives them all a demonstration of an entire routine. The moves are impressive, especially for someone who has to be in her sixties. Occasionally, she barks out a name for the move she's demonstrating.

'This is called the Baby Valentine,' she says, upside down, with one leg curled around the pole, whilst the other is outstretched. She's wearing fishnet stockings and her legs are lean and muscular. Everyone gasps in admiration.

'The Broken Doll,' she says, warming to the applause, and her body is twisted around the pole even more dramatically, spinning higher up.

'Ooh, I think the blood would rush to my head,' Ivy says, 'but it looks fun.'

Meg and some of the others have turned green. As Feather does what she calls a Cartwheel Dismount, basically splits in the air, the women give her a round of applause in admiration of her skills, which are genuinely impressive. Suddenly, they hear snorting and jeering from outside and a group of teenage boys have formed an audience at the window.

'Show us your tits!' one cheekily shouts.

Feather Starr is not bothered and gives them an indulgent wave, 'Testosterone! Ignore them,' she trills. 'So, what do you lovely ladies think of that?' Everyone responds effusively. *Amazing! Incredible! I wish I could do that. You're so skilled. Wow! How long did it take you to learn that?*

Feather shrugs. 'Well, I'm glad you enjoyed the routine, as that is the one I intend to get us all to demonstrate in Morlan's fête at the beginning of August.'

Gwen feels sick. Her first thought is that Lydia will disown her. And Gareth. The shocked faces of the women in the group mirror her own.

'Listen, you are bound to feel a bit nervous about it, but we have nearly three months and that's plenty of time to learn a routine, especially if you're determined.' Gwen notices that Feather doesn't even look sweaty or tired. Does she honestly believe they will all be up to that standard?

Suddenly, music erupts, 'Oopsie Daisy! Baby Zuzu Gets a Boo Boo!' It's so incongruous in a pole dancing class that everyone giggles, and it breaks the stunned silence. 'Peppa Pig,' Carol mouths knowledgeably.

The young girl called Summer rushes to her handbag situated at the back of the room. Her face is crimson.

'Right, I'm going to show you how to hold the pole the proper way and it will make it so much easier when you perform some of the moves. It will help if you buy some of those weights you see on Amazon,' Feather informs them.

'It's in the top cupboard,' Summer is saying in a loud

whisper. 'The one where I keep the cleaning products.' She sighs, 'Because the kids will be into them otherwise. You were supposed to put locks on the kitchen cupboards. Remember?' She rolls her eyes.

'Men are useless,' Ivy sympathises, and the other women laugh.

'When you boil the kettle,' Feather continues, 'you can do ten repetitions. It'll really build up your strength.'

What is her story, Gwen wonders? Why come to a sleepy, let's face it, dead place like Morlan? Is she running away from something?

'The class has only just started,' Summer is saying. The other women feel sorry for her. 'I won't go for a drink afterwards but come straight home.'

By the time Summer is off the phone, the women are all practising the correct way to hold the pole.

'Stand a metre from it and hold it at shoulder height,' Feather instructs.

By the end of the class, Gwen's arms are burning in pain. She has a heftier weight to lift than some of the other women, she reasons. Meg is a mere slip of a thing and Ivy is all angular and edges, like a stick of celery. She's strong as an ox. Gwen collapses to the floor for the final minutes of meditation. The teenage boys didn't hang around long, soon losing interest when the women were just holding the pole. What did they expect? Nudity? The male species is rather simple. Gwen tries to concentrate. She looks across and sees Summer, her eyes closed but her brow is furrowed. Her right leg is twitching as if she is impatient to be off.

'Well done, lovely ladies,' Feather says, as they make their way out of the hall. 'There has been real progress tonight.'

'Mariners?' Carol says, and there are mumbles of agreement all round.

Gwen watches as Summer races across the car park.

'Summer!' Gwen calls and she turns around. 'Hop in. I can take you home.'

'Are you sure?' Summer asks, sighing in relief. 'I'll be home quicker.'

'Of course.' It gives Gwen a thrill to think she can help someone and that someone is genuinely grateful. She's taken so much for granted by her own brood.

'My husband Aled is home and looking after the kids tonight. He doesn't know his arse from his elbow, though,' Summer says as she plugs in her seat belt. 'Ooh, it's close to the ground, isn't it?' she says referring to the car.

'Totally impractical,' Gwen agrees. 'You live and learn, though. You're right about men. Completely incapable!' They both grin.

As the car negotiates the bends up the hill, a call comes through on the car phone. Without thinking, Gwen accepts the call and it's on loudspeaker.

'Mrs Vimpany, it's the concierge at Wolfscastle Hotel.'

'It's probably my husband you want.'

'Actually, it's you. When you stayed with us last weekend, you left a pair of diamond earrings on the bedside table. We found your number as you're on our mailing list.'

'But I didn't stay last—' Gwen begins, cutting the call. 'Oh,' realisation sets in.

Gwen keeps her eyes fixed on the road, ignoring Summer's nervous glances towards her. She races towards Summer's house and can't even say goodbye when she hops out before Gwen barely has a chance to stop the car.

'The bastard!' she shouts at the dashboard. 'The absolute bastard!'

Chapter Ten

Meg

'How's the love life?'

Meg wonders if she wears her singledom like a face-tattoo, it seems to be up for debate in every conversation she has.

'Still non-existent,' she sighs, resting against the hard plastic NHS chair. 'Or actually, worse than non-existent. It exists but it's terrible. In the last month I've gone out with an ex-convict, an embalmer, and a man who was cheating on his fiancée.'

'Bless you,' Tanya, the stoma nurse, shakes her head. 'It's a hard scene out there at the moment. My friend is convinced she matched with the Tinder Swindler last week! Can you imagine?'

'No chance of him coming to Morlan is there? I'd at least have a posher date with him than a Harvester off the M4,' Meg jokes. It feels good to laugh. Shaking off the bad news of her appointment with the consultant, twenty minutes ago.

'So, it sounds like you're stuck with the stoma longer than we'd hoped?' Tanya says, getting down to business.

'Mmm hmm.' It's all Meg can say, unimpressed. 'No sign of my bowel recovering yet.'

'I know there's no right thing to say in this scenario, but

surely life's better than before you had the surgery?'

Meg thinks about this. The constant running to the toilet. The bleeding and pain. Not being able to eat anything more exotic than plain pasta and chicken without soiled knickers. The months of schooling she missed, her classmates leaving her behind as they launched into adulthood and she spent her youth on a hospital ward. Crohn's disease *was* a bastard. An unfair, life-controlling bastard.

But life isn't exactly a bed of roses with a stoma bag.

'In a lot of ways,' she compromises. Meg knows she should be grateful for the surgery, which has allowed her so much freedom, but sometimes she wishes she could just tear the disgusting, smelly bag right from her body and never see it again. Tanya did her best to warn her about this. But even on her best day, Meg can't stand the sight of the thing.

'I know you were hoping we'd have a surgery date booked in today,' Tanya touches her hand now, earnestly, across the desk, 'but your body will be ready in its own time.'

If ever.

Meg knows that's what these people really want to say. She was warned that her remaining colon may never recover enough to allow her small intestine to be stitched back in place. *A fifty per cent chance.* But Meg's been doing everything right. Eating fibre, drinking water, resting, exercising, taking her medications. She empties the stoma bag six times a day, lest the remainder of her bowel get any funny ideas. If anyone's going to recover, it's her.

Not today, though. Today her MRI shows the ulcers are still very much there, her weak and unused colon still fighting to heal from this random attack. She is still very much at the mercy of her bag.

'How have you been getting on with it, anyway? Any issues?' Tanya opens the pages of paper notes in front of her.

'Not too bad,' Meg answers, worried that if she says more the emotions of the day might not hold back.

'Any blood or unusual looking stools?'

'Not really,' Meg shrugs. Every stool looks unusual to her.

'Any itching, stinging, or unusual discharge around the stoma?'

'No.'

'Right, shall we get you up on the bed?' Tanya moves over to the hard table and unrolls a sheath of white tissue for Meg to lie on. Meg leans back against the headboard and lifts her jumper. She watches Tanya's face while she unclicks the bag, revealing the opening underneath. Meg marvels at how Tanya doesn't even flinch when the room fills with the smell of Meg's bowel contents, which Tanya swiftly moves to the clinical waste bin. Meg's own stoma makes her feel sick; she can't imagine handling anyone else's.

Tanya then proceeds to examine the opening with a look of curiosity. 'Are you sure it's not itching? It looks a little red on the left, there.'

'Maybe yesterday a bit, now I think of it,' Meg metaphorically kicks herself. 'Nothing major though. I've been doing all the care for it.' Twice a day, like clockwork, with a pan of warm water and cotton swabs.

'It seems OK. Nothing to worry about. And the bags are fitting well, comfortably?'

Meg nods.

'Great,' Tanya smiles. 'Hopefully it's nothing, then. The wound's come on leaps and bounds since last time.' Yes, her body is adjusting to this thing that Meg can't stand. Great news!

She softens then, seeing Tanya's look of concern as she dabs at the stoma. There is no use *reaching a pattern of negative thinking*, as the stoma leaflets advise. A state of acceptance is what Meg should be aiming towards. A comfortable *temporary* state of acceptance.

'Okay, let's get a stock of bags for you and get you out of here,' Tanya says, taking her gloves off.

'I've got plenty at home, mind.'

'A few extras can't harm.' Tanya passes a new bag for Meg to click on, which she does with practised efficiency, and a letter detailing her next appointment with the consultant. She's pleased when she can pull the high waistband on her jeans up again, tucking the stoma firmly out of sight of anyone other than her until the next appointment.

'Thanks, Tanya,' she waves, relieved the ordeal is over.

'Good luck with the dating!' she shouts after her.

Hannah is in the waiting room, flicking through a magazine. She shouldn't have come with Meg. She's twenty-six, it's not like she needs accompanying to the hospital in Carmarthen, but Hannah had insisted, stating she needed a break from the post office. 'Morlan can cope without me for a few hours.'

Meg appreciated it, but she would have to relay the bad news to her now. Hannah seems to read it on her face as they walk in silence to the car park.

'Shall we get a KFC for lunch?' Hannah asks, as they move

through the busy hospital reception.

'Don't be silly. We've got that couscous salad in the fridge.'

'Well, I fancy a KFC, so you'll have to stop for me anyway.'

'I understand your tactics, you know,' Meg warns.

'Come on. If there's one day to let go of your health, it's after your appointment. It's like those women in Morlan Slimming World who go for a big curry after class on a Monday night.'

'This is hardly the same.'

'And I know Gwion, the farmer, buys a Viccie sponge from Florrie's Treats after his diabetic nurse check-in, for his monthly treat.'

'Stop it,' Meg says. 'Is there a KFC in Carmarthen?'

Hannah smiles in victory.

'Why don't you sit here, and I'll go and bring the car round?'

'I can manage the walk,' Hannah protests.

'You need your energy for the KFC,' Meg laughs, leaving her grandmother at reception, next to a child wearing a too-big neck brace that makes him look like a sad dog in a cone.

Meg checks her appointment letter as she heads to the car. All looks well until she notices the wrong name at the top of it – Megan Richardson – with a different date of birth. Another poor sod who has to see the stoma consultant. 'Shit,' she says, turning around.

Meg could just call them to report the mistake, but she's been on the phone to the hospital before and it's an ordeal getting through to anyone with sense. It's easier if she sorts it now. The stoma clinic was just closing for lunch, so maybe Meg can go to general reception.

She scours the busy hospital entrance, looking for someone

vaguely helpful. Eventually she sees a man with an 'Ask Me Anything – I'm Here to Help' badge. He perks up on seeing Meg, probably bored out of his brains, she thinks.

'You want the general enquiries office,' he says, after she has explained the issue. 'Second floor, left wing.'

It sounds simple, but Meg realises the second floor is like a chaotic Narnia, and she has no idea where to go. There's no helpful badge-wearer up here. After some helpless wandering, Meg spots the right office, although 'office' seems a weighty name for this cramped space. The bored receptionist inside doesn't even look up at Meg as she approaches.

'General enquiries?'

The woman mutely points at the room next door.

Meg squeezes into the little room, which simply consists of a desk and two chairs. A woman is sitting at the desk, talking to an even more bored-looking man behind it, who is explaining something about the 'car park policy'. How does someone end up working in general enquiries at a hospital? Is that a lifelong dream of people out there? Is it well paid?

There is a man leaning against the wall, tapping his foot and looking frankly pissed-off. He notices Meg watching. 'I'd get comfortable,' he says.

She gives a smile of solidarity and mirrors his leaning movement against the wall.

'I completely disagree with that,' the woman at the desk is now saying, her voice raising an octave. 'In fact, I'd like to speak to your manager.'

It seems the pissed-off man is right. 'Been here a while, then?' Meg asks politely.

'Oh yeah,' he says. 'My night shift finished roughly . . .' he checks his watch, 'three days ago. But I just thought it would be fun to come and stand in here.'

Meg laughs politely. It is only now she notices he is wearing a shirt and a hospital lanyard underneath his green parka jacket.

'If only I'd noticed my letter was wrong at the time,' she smiles, waving the offending slip of paper. 'I could have saved myself a whole three days.'

'There's not even any light jazz to keep us going,' he says now, angling his body towards Meg's.

'Damn it, I love muzak.'

'These places play some great muzak usually,' he says.

'You know, I've always wondered who makes muzak?' Meg asks.

'Yes! Is that a lifelong dream of people out there? Is it well paid?' he says. Meg is so surprised, she laughs way louder than the situation needs, but he smiles in response.

'Has anyone ever had a number one album on the muzak charts?'

'Are there muzak awards?' He leans back again. 'We have enough time to google it.'

'You know, I think I'll keep the mystery going. Especially if I have got three days to wait,' Meg nods now. She can't believe that she's flirting with a man in the hospital office. But he's nice, in a kind of bookish way. He has round glasses and black facial hair, and he's attractive, without being so good-looking he could be arrogant about it.

He smiles at her. 'You should go ahead of me in the queue. If all you want to do is check your appointment,' he says now.

'No,' she begins to protest. 'I can't do that.'

'Honestly. I've got bigger beef with these guys,' he rolls his eyes. 'Someone's blocked me in in the car park and hasn't left a note. I have no idea who.'

'I hope it's not me,' she half-jokes.

'No, it's been there since I finished my shift three hours ago. I would love nothing more than to leave this hospital after a night in A&E, but no, it's clinging on.'

'Oh God, no,' Meg says. 'You're not allowed to leave. You could be saving more lives while you're blocked in.' She jokes and she likes how his eyes crinkle when he laughs.

'I'm hardly saving lives,' he says, when he recovers. 'Last night, I helped a drunk teenager call his parents to come and pick him up because he couldn't find their names in his phone.'

'What were their names?'

'Mum and Dad!' he explains. 'Honestly! I wasn't taught that in medical school, but it *seemed* the most obvious place to start.'

'Well, you said you're not saving lives but you probably saved him from a bollocking at home . . .'

They both laugh then settle into silence. Meg finds herself racking her brains for something else to say, wanting to keep the conversation going.

'At least you'll learn your lesson for next time,' she says, wishing she had more sparkling conversation.

'Actually, it's my last shift here,' he says. 'As of today, I'm an officially qualified GP. Next stop St Davids surgery in Pembrokeshire.'

Now Meg is in genuine disbelief.

'I live about fifteen minutes from St Davids.'

'No way!'

They've both talked so loudly, they've drawn looks from the woman at the desk.

'Will you be living down there?' Meg asks, not wanting to sound too keen, but also dying of excitement.

'Moving van's booked for next week. I've got a crappy little apartment to rent, but it's all I can afford on my own,' he says. She wonders if she's reading too much into it or if that *on my own* was for her benefit. 'I don't really know the area, though.'

'I can show you round,' she offers. She doesn't know where this confidence has come from, maybe the years of missing out on dating when she was in hospital, or the recent plethora of dating disasters. But Meg's proud of herself, whatever his answer is.

'That would be brilliant! I can't wait to live by the sea, eat fish and chips every day, learn to surf. I'm sorry, I should have warned you I'm a massive cliché.'

She laughs but the surfing already pings her anxiety to life. Meg can't be seen dead in a wetsuit, let alone a bikini. 'I can definitely help with the fish and chips . . . surfing not so much.'

'Shame,' he jokes. 'Here, let me take your number.' Meg types it into his phone, enjoying his screen saver of a seaside landscape. No girlfriend and no creepy pin-up. 'I'll just call you now.'

'It's ringing.' She feels her phone vibrating in her bag, and notices the missed calls from Hannah on-screen. Hannah! Of course! What was she thinking? She must be worried where she is. 'Do you know what, I'm picking someone up and I didn't tell her about the issue. I'll just call the hospital,' she says, not wanting to admit that she's with her grandmother.

'So, you endured this wait for nothing?' the man asks.

'Call me a masochist,' she says, hoping she's picked the right term over sadist. Meg thinks that the visit hasn't been for nothing. In fact, Meg has the distinct impression that fate took her into that office. If she believed in fate, which she definitely doesn't.

'Fine, leave me here to suffer alone,' he jokes now. 'I'm Josh, by the way.'

'Meg,' she feels suddenly awkward. Should she shake his hand? Hug? No, much less. She opts to wave instead.

'I'll call you, Meg,' he says. And with those words, Meg turns round and grins at the ceiling for the best hospital visit she's ever had.

Chapter Eleven

Ivy

Ivy stands outside the window of Ink Envy in Haverfordwest. She glances around in case anyone is watching her. Why does she feel so guilty? She caught the bus into town earlier and plans to have lunch in her favourite coffee shop by the river. Ink Envy is a tattoo parlour she passes endless times on the bus. Standing outside, she can see that the decor is tasteful, the walls painted a sage green, the floor a polished, rustic oak. There's a faux stag's head high above reception and the walls are adorned with prints of intricate tattoo designs. She's fascinated.

A man lies on one of the leather couches, having what looks like a parrot on his arm, shaded in bright primary colours. The tattoo artist has his back to the window, but Ivy can see his stooped figure and concentration as he tattoos the young man. His salt and pepper hair is tied in a low ponytail. The only other person is a young girl. She wears a tartan mini skirt and a black leather waistcoat, her arms covered in colourful, elaborate tattoos. The shin of her right leg is etched with a sword that has an eye on the hilt, but her other leg is bare and the white flesh seems unfinished compared with the rest of her. Her hair is short and spiky, and her dark eyes are rimmed with black kohl. She catches Ivy's eye, smiles and waves.

Swallowing her nerves, Ivy pushes open the door. The doorbell tinkles.

'Hi. Good morning. I'm Emma. Can I help you?' She flashes Ivy a warm smile.

'I'm . . . I'm . . .' Ivy starts, her voice caught in her throat.

'You're thinking of having a tattoo,' Emma says, finishing her sentence. 'It's your first time?'

Ivy laughs, 'How did you guess? Is it that obvious?'

The tattoo artist with the ponytail turns around, curious to see her.

'Something small, perhaps,' Ivy says.

'Sure,' Emma says. 'I'm free at the moment. I'll show you some designs.'

'I bet I'm your oldest client,' Ivy says, shifting her weight from foot to foot.

'Are you kidding me? You're never too old to have a tattoo. Judi Dench had her first tattoo for her eighty-first birthday.'

Ivy knows this. *Carpe diem* etched on the inside of her wrist. It's what convinced her that she could have a small one, too.

'Have you any idea of what you'd like?' Emma prompts.

'Perhaps a small bird of some sort inside my wrist.' Emma hands her a ring binder with images of designs and their meanings.

'Birds usually symbolise freedom. Then there are specific ones. Eagles, for example, represent power and strength. Swans, elegance and loyalty . . .'

'A bluebird,' Ivy says, determinedly.

'Happiness and luck,' Emma nods. 'Good choice.'

'Just a very small one.' Ivy feels butterflies in her stomach. What is she thinking, having a tattoo at seventy-two? Somehow, though, it feels right. She's always conformed to what people have wanted of her. Expected of her. Now she doesn't have to answer to anyone. Look at Feather Starr. She doesn't give two hoots what people think of her. The tattoo would mark a new stage in her life. A time for her to please herself. Take risks.

On the bus home, Ivy keeps looking at her wrist. It's covered by a bandage and it feels quite sore, but she's proud that she's had the guts to do it. Matthew will have a fit. A smile spreads across her face when she thinks of his reaction. He'll see it as a sign of the onset of dementia. She isn't prepared to fade into the background quite yet.

As the bus descends into lower Morlan, Ivy gazes at the sea. She's never bored of that view. It has a character of its own. Today it's serene, beguiling. The swell of the tide against the barrage of rocks is slow and sensuous. Ivy decides to get off at the bottom of the hill, a couple of stops from her cottage, to walk along the beach, inhale the salty air into her lungs. She's only bought a couple of things in town, nothing she can't manage up the hill.

Stepping off the bus, Ivy sees a woman in the park with two little ones. She's pushing a toddler on the swing and in a pushchair a baby is yelling extravagantly. Ivy walks over when she sees it's Summer.

'I'll push Nia. You see to the baby,' Ivy tells Summer firmly.

There are tears of relief in her eyes. 'Thank you, Ivy.'

The baby calms down as soon as Summer lifts him from the pushchair. She sits on the bench, unbuttoning her blouse, and the baby latches on hungrily.

'There, there, Jordan. Better now,' Summer soothes.

'It's like magic, isn't it?' Ivy says sitting down next to Summer as Nia joins another girl on the slide. 'I remember Matthew at that age. A hungry little devil. There's nothing like that closeness, though, when they feed.'

Summer smiles, gazing into her infant's face, 'It makes it all worthwhile. All those sleepless nights, the dirty nappies, the teething . . .'

'Isn't Aled home?' Ivy asks, remembering Summer rushing off at the end of their pole dancing class last night.

'He's still in bed. He only came home last night after long, busy shifts. He does three weeks on, then ten days off. He was worn out.'

So are you, Ivy thinks, but says nothing.

'Was your husband good with your son when he was growing up?' Summer asks.

Ivy snorts. 'He didn't know one end of a baby from the other. Neither did I, but women cope, don't they? To be honest, it was a different generation then.'

'Did you ever work, Ivy?'

She shakes her head. 'No, I didn't. I was passionate about history when I was in school. I loved studying the Tudors and Stuarts. All that intrigue! I loved all of it, though, from medieval to twentieth century. I was going to go to Cardiff to study history, but then I met Jim.' She sighs. 'The rest is history, if you pardon the pun.' The smile doesn't quite reach her eyes.

'Do you miss him?' Summer asks.

'A bit. Not as much as I should. Is that awful?' She steals a sideways glance at Summer. She doesn't know this young girl very well.

'Normal, I should think. How long were you married?'

'I got married at twenty-two. Didn't have Matthew until I was thirty. Jim died just at the start of the pandemic. Fifty years in all.'

'Gosh, that's a long time. Sometimes I think that I'll be lucky to reach ten years with Aled. It scares me sometimes that we'll just get used to each other being apart.' She closes her eyes. Above them, seagulls caw noisily in the sky. 'When he's away, I try to have a routine with the kids. Bed by seven-thirty, clothes laid out for the morning. I make their feeds, then fall asleep knackered in front of the telly. It's hard. Bloody hard. But when Aled comes home, he disrupts it all. He's the fun parent. Lets them stay up as long as they want, eat sweets.'

'Well, if you want to pay any heed to the advice of an old lady,' Ivy says, 'don't always put Aled first. Do things for yourself from the outset so he gets used to it.'

The two women sit in companionable silence.

'Look at him. He's fast asleep now,' Summer smiles indulgently at Jordan in her arms. 'It's lucky he's so cute, otherwise I'd honestly go out of my mind.'

'I tell you what, Summer. You go back home now, and I'll bring the kids back in an hour or so.'

'Aw, no, you don't need to do that,' Summer protests.

'Go on, before I change my mind. I do have a granddaughter so I am more than capable of looking after these two for a while.'

As Ivy watches Summer's back retreating from the park, she begins to formulate a plan. Summer needs these pole dancing classes more than anyone. They have to come up with a plan for babysitters for Summer's kids, otherwise this tiny taste of freedom she enjoys just once a week will be snatched from her. There must be something Ivy can do. She can't let it happen to her.

Ivy finishes her simple dinner of mozzarella, tomatoes and basil with a glass of red wine when her phone rings.

'Mum, you're home,' Matthew says in exasperation. 'You're never in these days.'

Ivy rolls her eyes. 'Well, I'm only ever around Morlan, Matthew. Nothing for you to worry about. How are you?'

'Fine,' he says. 'Well, there's talk of redundancies at the company, but my position should be safe. My skill set means I would be very hard to replace. Some of the others are more concerned, I think.'

God, Ivy marvels at his self-assurance, his lack of self-doubt. She hopes it's warranted. 'Well, that's a relief.'

'Anyway, I'm ringing to remind you that it's Tabitha's fourth birthday in two weeks' time and—'

'Really, she's my only grandchild. I hadn't forgotten.' Ivy feels irritated. He doesn't mean to offend her. Sometimes she wonders if she's so defensive with him as she sees him as a substitute for his father. It's not fair of her.

'I know. Well, look, Rachel and I have arranged a party for her in the garden and we have a magician and everything. She's so excited. So, I've booked your train ticket for a week on Thursday.

That way you can have the whole day to help Rachel set up for the party.'

And her anger returns. 'Matthew, I told you I was coming up on the Friday. I have a prior arrangement on Thursdays and—'

'Surely you can miss your exercise class for once,' he says.

Ivy flushes with irritation. She hasn't told him it's a pole dancing class as she knows he'll disapprove, but he has no right to rearrange her life like this.

'You'll have to unbook the ticket, I'm afraid. I do have commitments other than you, you know. You can't just bulldoze over any plans I've made. It's not right.'

'Sorry, Mother, I thought you'd be looking forward to coming here to celebrate your granddaughter's birthday.'

When he calls her *Mother*, he really is annoyed. And now he is trying to make her feel guilty.

'I am looking forward to it and I will be there in good time. I'm sorry, Matthew, but I did tell you last week that I couldn't be there until Friday.'

The conversation is strained after this, and Ivy is relieved when Matthew finally hangs up. She sips her red wine and watches the light fade. The tide is out and the sand looks black from this distance. The greenhouse in the far-right corner of the garden catches her eye. It's a muddle of overgrown weeds now. The onions, spinach and carrots Jim grew are all dead, neglected for the last two years. She is not green-fingered, despite everyone her age seeming to love the garden.

Ivy strokes the bandage over her tattoo. Was it just a stupid act of rebellion? Should she be acting her age? Perhaps it is too late for her to do the things she had been dreaming about for years, like getting a camper van and seeing more of Europe. She isn't that confident a driver.

Overwhelmed by feelings of flatness and pessimism, which are alien to her, Ivy closes the curtains. She'll have an early night and perhaps tomorrow she'll find her mojo again. Tonight, it seems to have hidden itself beyond her reach.

Chapter Twelve

Summer

'Daddy up!' Nia shrieks, staggering into the room. Summer follows behind. She's almost as surprised as the two-year-old to see Aled is awake and functioning. Nia has enveloped him in a hug so big it stretches around one of his thighs.

'You're getting so tall, my girl.' He's wearing boxers, and Summer gets a whiff of the stale air of the bedroom.

'What time did you come in last night?' Summer knows it was between the 11 p.m. and 1 a.m. feeds, and Aled has slept soundly since then.

'About midnight. I was out like a light. It takes me about a week to recover after shifts finish, so it didn't feel that late to me,' he shrugs, rifling through his bedside table for a clean T-shirt. Summer chucks him one from the chest of drawers. 'Thanks. Sorry I wasn't in to put the kids to bed.'

'Good night?'

'Nice to catch up with the lads. Did you know Jonesie and Bethan are getting a divorce?' He mouths the last word at Summer, lest Nia pick up on it. She's none the wiser, blissfully rolling around in their crumpled bedsheets, like a kitten. Good thing Nia's oblivious to the whiff of beer and curry too.

'No.' She shakes her head. This particular piece of village gossip has got past Summer, probably on account of ninety-five percent of her life taking place inside the house tending to toddlers. 'It's hardly a surprise though, Jonesie's an idiot.'

'The man's in pain, Summer,' Aled says. 'And what do we do with a pain? We tickle it, that's what!' He shouts the last part, chasing Nia down a fold of the duvet like she's a furrowing mole. Much laughter and yelling ensues, and Summer uses the opportunity to search for the cup of coffee she put down earlier. There it is, in the bathroom. It's cold now, but Summer drinks it anyway, not wasting the caffeine.

'I heard some other gossip as well!' Aled shouts now, and Summer comes back to the bedroom. She sits on the bed where Nia is panting, exhausted, and strokes her hair back from her sticky face. 'Lloyd did a job for Gareth Vimpany last week, and apparently you could cut the tension in that house with a knife. They're sleeping in separate bedrooms. Of course, that could be their normal state, that place is like a bloody castle. Probably enough bedrooms to house each of their cars too.'

Summer thinks back to that awkward-as-hell car journey with Gwen last week. That phone call. Summer hadn't looked at Gwen's face at the time, but the atmosphere in that car had darkened, like pouring tar into whipped egg whites. Gwen couldn't get Summer out of there fast enough after she hung up from the hotel, barely even stopped the car.

'Probably just a tiff,' she says. She's unsure why but she doesn't want to share what she knows with Aled. She doesn't want it going round the pub next time he meets up with the guys from school, doesn't want it getting back to Gwen. Morlan is incestuous enough when it comes to people knowing your business.

'She's in that class with you, isn't she, Gwen Vimpany? You should try and snoop around.' Aled's back to tickling Nia again under the covers.

'She actually isn't that bad,' Summer says, instinctively protecting Gwen. She had taken pity on her after Aled called during the class, and offered to give her a lift home. There is good in Gwen, beneath the veneers and blonde balayage, Summer can see that.

She doesn't like Aled being involved in the village gossip. Summer doesn't want to think of what people say about her, what comments are made in The Mariners after dark. Summer loves Aled, but she thinks his choice in friends really brings him down. Aled has been friends with Lloyd and Jonesie since nursery, but isn't it time to grow up from the juvenile nicknames and sticking their fingers in each other's drinks crap? There's a reason why Summer pretended to be asleep when he got back from his catch-up in the pub last night. Summer doesn't like who he morphs into after a night with them. Bold and brash, making crude jokes under the guise of banter and sizing up people in the village, waiting for their downfall. People think it's women who are the bitchy ones, but in Summer's experience, men love the drama just as much.

'What was that you say, Nia? You think we should tickle Mummy too? You do, do you?' Aled says conspiratorially in a stage whisper to the two-year-old.

'Tickle Mummy!' Nia cries.

'You'll wake Jordan,' Summer says, but she's smiling, waiting for the moment when Aled and Nia pile on top of her, tickling and scrabbling at the duvet. It feels good to laugh, and their bedroom is filled with the sound, from Nia's high-pitched tinkling to Aled's throaty chortle.

The Aled she knows is back to normal now, he's come back to them.

'You look nice, by the way,' Aled says. She's surprised he's noticed the fresh hair. Summer hasn't had a haircut since Jordan was born, and the last one she had with Nia was chaotic. She thinks the hairdresser hurried the cut just to get the screaming child and her mother out of the salon.

'I had my hair done yesterday.' Summer runs her hand through it, as if to illustrate the lack of baby-sick and split-ends in it. 'It's silky as you like!'

'It looks amazing,' Aled says, getting up from the bed. Of course, he wouldn't ask whether the kids behaved in the salon. It wouldn't occur to him that taking them would be a logistical nightmare for a mother.

'Ivy looked after them for me,' Summer explains.

'Ivy who?'

'You know Ivy? Married to Jim.'

'Of course,' Aled nods, buttoning his jeans with a look of total concentration. 'How come you're friends with her now?'

'She's in my pole dancing class. She's a lovely old woman,' Summer says, knowing she's completely underselling Ivy. There's a lot more to her than meets the eye. Summer thinks she should check in on Ivy more. It might be nice to have a friendly face in

Morlan, especially someone who might be willing to look after the kids now and again. In case of emergency.

Plus, Summer noticed Ivy's bandaged wrist yesterday. She hopes she's managing OK on her own now. She remembers her own grandmother covered in bruises from her various bumps and scrapes at home.

'Look at you, it's like adopt-a-granny,' Aled says, way more proud of his joke than he should be.

'Well, I don't know many grannies that go pole dancing,' Summer shuts him up. 'Come on, we'd better get you dressed Miss Nia, ready for . . .'

'Folly Farm! Folly Farm!'

The kids are both asleep as they turn on to their street in the car, with Aled driving and Summer stealing glances back at them. They look so perfect asleep like this, two utterly edible angels.

'I think that outing was a success,' she whispers to Aled.

'I remember going to Folly Farm as a child. It's surreal taking our two now,' Aled smiles. 'I feel just as worn out, though.'

Summer agrees, exhausted from a day of stooping to pick up little children to greet various animals. Nia's new cuddly elephant is tucked under one arm, the thumb of the other arm firmly in her mouth. And Jordan's dolphin toy absolutely dwarfs him in his car seat, but he looks adorable. Nia's eyes had widened so much when she'd seen a zebra, the sheer amazement of being a child. She had cried, though, when a camel sneezed over the two of them, and Summer's blow-dry was ruined, but it had been one of those golden family days, just the four of them.

Summer marvels at how quickly the time passes when Aled is home. Having another pair of hands is an absolute godsend. She's grateful, too, that he's around to look after the kids for her Thursday class. She knows that Aled would prefer her to stay in, but daren't admit it. There's no way she's going to miss this precious hour to herself.

'I don't know how you've got the energy to go pole dancing now,' Aled says, after they've returned from a walk on the beach.

'I don't really. But it's an easy win for you, with the kids as worn out as they are, they should sleep right through.' Summer knows that if Aled can't handle it this week, then he never will. And he'd be gone on the weekend, back to the rig. Who knows who'll take care of the kids for the next class?

'Here, let me carry them in. You go and get changed,' Aled says. Summer's grateful, and giggles when she sees Aled with Jordan's baby carrier, prancing towards the house like a bomb disposal expert. She heads upstairs and uses a face wipe to remove any remaining traces of camel from her skin and face. She'd like to put a bit of make-up on before the class, but the whole of Morlan has seen her red-faced and exasperated, what is one more pole dancing class? Plus, Summer would be late enough as it is.

'Are you sure you'll be all right this week? I've defrosted some breast milk if you need it, but Jordan should sleep through,' Summer says as she passes Aled in the hallway.

'Do you hear that? Radio silence. We'll be fine here,' Aled kisses her cheek.

When Summer's out in the evening air, she does wonder what on earth she's doing going to an exercise class after a busy day with the kids. Surely, she should be resting, not bouncing around a pole. Summer realises she's looking forward to getting back to class, though, and marvelling at Feather Starr's moves. She wants to see Ivy's smiling face, and she's intrigued to see if Gwen Vimpany is there.

And good on her, she is. Summer notices her as she opens the heavy oak door to the village hall. The class has already started, but Summer doesn't mind that she's missed out on the pelvic floor exercises. She knows she's meant to do them religiously after the birth, and they probably would help with the leaking and the looseness she feels down below, but hell, who actually remembers to do them? And who can do them properly? Summer always feels like she's tensing her entire lower body in the vain hope that she also targets the right muscle.

'Sorry,' she mouths at Feather Starr who just nods at her as she marches on the spot. Summer joins in just as she's windmilling her arms around to 'loosen up', and seeing that she's next to Gwen, she risks a look across at her. Gwen's gaze stays steadfastly ahead. Okay. So, they are going to pretend nothing has happened. Summer can understand that. She follows the warm-up exercises, already enjoying the tension fading from her body.

Summer has never understood the endorphin-high that is meant to come from exercise. Surely that is a myth made up by people who have never orgasmed or eaten a churro. But there is something about being in this room, moving in tandem with this group of women, that makes Summer feel young again. Like she is a child, all she has to focus on for the next fifty minutes is moving her body.

'It looks like we have a few new arrivals tonight, welcome everyone. We might need to get into groups of four to fit everyone,' Feather instructs.

Summer looks to her usual trio, a mother she recognises from toddler group and another woman who lives on her street, but it seems they've paired up quickly with a couple of new women Summer hasn't seen before.

She turns around, suddenly feeling like she's about thirteen and waiting to be picked for the netball team again, when she hears, 'Summer, do you want to join us?'

She turns and sees Gwen with Ivy and Meg. A peace offering perhaps, or a plea for her silence. Nevertheless, Gwen's smiling and beckoning her. It's all the encouragement she needs.

'I'd love to.' She skips over.

'The hair still looks fantastic,' Ivy whispers to her.

'Aw thank you so much. I'd never have had it cut if it wasn't for you.'

'Don't be silly, I loved my time with Jordan and Nia. Two little saints, they were,' Ivy smiles as Summer touches her arm in gratitude.

'I'm not so sure about that.'

'They were. Jordan's a dream.' Summer notices Ivy's bandage is gone and sees a flash of blue in its place.

'Is that a . . . Have you got a tattoo?'

'Ladies!' Feather's looking straight at them from the stage. There's a dramatic silence. 'As I was saying . . .'

Summer and Ivy mouth *oooh* at each other, and Meg smirks at them, enjoying. So, this is Feather Starr's fierce side. The poster had promised fierce. And it seems Ivy is a dark horse too.

'Now we've had a few introductory lessons, it's time we start building a few moves into a routine. Nothing fancy, but something we can hopefully build on to create our showcase for Morlan Fête.' A few grimaces pass around the room. Summer hasn't learnt a routine since she was in primary school, unless you could count Nia's silly handshakes with her and Aled.

'We'll begin off the poles, then work them in to the routine,' Feather demonstrates a few basic steps, walking forwards for four counts, then pivoting in a circle, and heading back for four counts.

'Let's try it without the music!' she shouts. 'Five, six, seven, eight . . .'

The movement that ensues is hilarious. The whole class masters the walking forward part, although many continue going for more than four counts. People start on different feet, meaning they head into the pivot in different directions. The whole thing is a jumble. And Summer even hears two women apologise for stepping on toes.

'Okay, that was . . . good.' Feather Starr manages to stay enthusiastic. 'Let's start on the left this time, and remember, we do the moves in blocks of four counts. Not five.'

'I'm pretty sure that was aimed at me,' Meg says to Summer, making her giggle.

'From the top,' Feather counts them in, and the result is vaguely more uniform this time. 'Better, better. Let's add in a little Beyoncé this time. Sashay those hips, ladies, especially in the pivot. We can even add in arms.' Summer marvels at the animation Feather puts into each move. Not stiff and robotic like her, but fluid, fiery. She can try her best, but God knows if it will look like that.

They practise a few times, until the room is at least going in the same direction.

'Now we're going to add in a pivot at the back, this time faster, and I've got a few new moves. Watch this . . .'

There is a cold draught from the back of the room as Feather continues. No one's heard the door open, but the next sound is unmistakeable. The shrill high-pitched piercing cry of an infant, and Summer knows immediately that it is *her* infant. *Jordan.*

She turns to see a flushed-looking Aled, pushing the double buggy, with Jordan bouncing on his hip. He looks just as distraught as the baby, but the crying continues. That's Jordan's hungry cry, and Summer can't do anything to stop the flow of milk that begins to let out from her right breast.

'Dammit,' she swears, hoping her sports bra can hold. 'Sorry, everyone,' she mutters as she sprints to the back of the room. 'Sorry!'

She just wants to usher Aled out of there, to get her baby out of the room of staring women as quickly as possible. She feels the heat of everyone's eyes on her, judging, tutting.

'Come on,' she instructs Aled, hoping her voice conveys her frustration. He opens his mouth to explain, but she snaps back, 'Now's not the time.' She wanted an hour. Just one hour in the class.

The double buggy is manoeuvred out of the village hall, and Summer can only breathe when they're outside again, away from the judging eyes, and she has Jordan attached firmly to her breast. He suckles keenly, placid now he's back with his mother. She doesn't want to look at Aled, but she has no choice.

'What happened?'

'I'm sorry, Summer. I just didn't know what to do.'

Chapter Thirteen

Gwen

The Mariners is busy when they shoulder their way in after the class. 'Born to be Wild' is blasting from the jukebox and the bar is thronged with locals. Gwen isn't really in the mood but she's had such a shitty week that she can't bear the idea of returning to that empty house again. Lydia wouldn't be home until much later. The class took her mind off her woes, albeit for a short time. She had laughed so hard at one point that she leaked a bit, being grateful that she had dark leggings on. They had all been pretty useless at the new routine, apart from Meg who had mastered it quickly. When they were counting steps around the pole, Gwen kept treading on Ivy's heels and Summer was definitely out of sync.

'I did feel sorry for Summer when Aled came in with her little ones,' Ivy says, as they grab some remaining seats by the window. 'I hope she manages to work out something more permanent for babysitting, especially when Aled goes back.'

'What a bloody useless man!' Gwen says, with more venom than she intends and not really aimed at Aled in particular. 'Poor Summer manages all on her own when he's away.'

'What are you both having?' Meg asks. The other women are standing at the bar, gravitating to whom they'd been grouped with in the class.

Gwen tries to suppress the images flashing through her mind from last week. It's a bit like the recap on a TV drama. She remembers her blinding white rage as she drove up the hill, turning clumsily in the driveway and yanking up the handbrake as she fled into the house. She sees herself stuffing black bags with Gareth's clothes, his navy Hugo Boss suits, the Armani cashmere jacket he wore on holiday in Italy, his Ralph Lauren shirts, the blue Paul Smith suit, which was far too tight on him and made him look like a Smurf. She tipped out his Rolex watches hoping they would snag on some of his John Smedley jumpers. Driven with anger and adrenaline, Gwen watched each black bag catapult down the stairs.

'Bastard!' she yelled to the empty house.

She hadn't heard Gareth entering. It was only when he grasped her wrists, his face contorted in anger, that she became aware that he was there.

'What the hell do you think you're doing, woman?' he shouted in her face.

'You couldn't help yourself, could you? You conniving, cheating bastard!'

'What're you on about? Are you out of your mind?'

'You promised me after the last time. You swore on my life. On our girls' lives. You said it would never happen again.'

'What on earth are you on about?' he yelled. Even in the vortex of her anger, she could marvel at his denial. The cheek of it!

'I tell you what I'm on about. The manager of Wolfscastle phoned me tonight.' He blanched then, the colour draining from his face. 'Apparently, I'd left my diamond earrings on the bedside cabinet. You bastard!' Gwen picked up a shoe and started hitting him across the arm. 'Who is it this time? Come on, tell me. You piece of shit.'

'I can explain,' he said, jerking from the blows. 'Will you stop that and sit down so we can talk about it rationally.'

Gwen continued for another minute or so, and then collapsed onto the bed, shattered with the effort and emotional turmoil. 'I told you last time, Gareth, that if it happened again, it would be over.'

He sat down about a metre from her, ready to pounce if she started hitting him with a shoe again.

'I've been stressed at work, as you know. The pressure on me is horrendous. Sales have dropped since Covid and then there's still the complications with moving to electric cars. It's not easy, you know . . .'

Gwen barely listened. It was as if she was watching a movie and they were acting their part. His mouth was moving but she couldn't really take in all he was saying. It was all self-pitying lies, anyway. Excuses. *What a pathetic man* was her overriding thought. She felt sad, too, for the years she had wasted on Gareth who was simply not worth it.

'So, who was it this time?' she asked in a brief hiatus. 'Elaine on reception? Someone in the bank? One of the reps?'

He looked nervous then, the corner of his mouth twitched. 'Does it matter?'

'Of course it fucking matters.'

119

'You've got to understand that we didn't set out for it to happen. Our feelings got the better of us and Lynne has been through a hard time in the last couple of years with her mother's illness and . . .' He could see straight away this was a mistake.

'Tell me you don't mean Lynne, my best friend Lynne. The one who is supposed to be in the Canaries right now.'

'The feelings were too strong. We . . .' he stuttered.

This put the tin hat on it, but she felt strangely calm. 'It is well and truly over, Gareth. I should have left you six years ago but I stayed for Jas and Lydia. I don't need to any more. I'm just angry with myself for leaving it so long.' She stood up. 'I've started packing for you. You can finish the rest. My solicitor will be in touch.' She could just imagine said solicitor, a cross between the flamboyance of Laurence Llewelyn-Bowen and the ruthlessness of Simon Cowell, rubbing his hands as he thought of his fees.

She turned to him, 'Oh yes, I'm going to hit you where it hurts – right in the wallet!'

Since that night, she'd barely left the house, her emotions swinging from rage to self-pity.

'I'll have a small glass of wine,' Gwen says, the laughter in the pub puncturing her thoughts. 'I'll get the next.'

'She's nice,' Ivy says of Meg as they watch her queue at the bar. 'She needs to leave Morlan, though. There's not much here for young people.'

'And living with her grandmother can't be much fun, especially when it's Hannah Thomas,' Gwen says.

Ivy smiles at this. Gwen has never heard her saying

120

anything bad about anyone and she wishes she could be more like her. It's hard to shake off her mood, though, after the week she's had.

'Here you are, my lovely ladies,' Meg laughs, mimicking Feather Starr.

'He seems a nice chap,' Ivy says to her, nodding towards Rhys at the bar.

'Hmm.' Meg is non-committal. 'I was at school with him. He fancied my friend Natalie, chased her for years.'

'It's always the way,' Gwen says sharply, and the two women look at her.

'Is there room for a little one?' Summer says, materialising in front of them and plonking herself down on a stool opposite them. They all laugh.

'How did you manage to escape?' Meg asks.

'I made him feel so guilty about bringing the babies to the class that he was practically insisting I join you in the pub. They're both fast asleep now, so I can spare an hour. He does try, bless him. Anyway, can I get anyone a top-up?'

'We're fine. I would have got you something if I'd known,' says Meg.

They must make an odd-looking bunch, Gwen decides, so disparate in age and circumstance, but they're nice women. She's missed out on this. Female friendship.

'I've been thinking,' Ivy says, when Summer sits with her half lager in front of her. 'Are you lot free on Sunday afternoon? I'm never going to get my head around this routine if I don't practise it. You can bring Jordan and Nia with you, Summer. I've got a stack of toys in the spare room that Tabitha plays with when she comes to stay.'

Summer flashes her a grateful smile. 'Yes, I can do that.'

'Well, my diary is quite full,' jokes Meg. 'Nah, I'll be there.'

'Me, too,' Gwen says.

'To be honest, I've got a date Saturday,' Meg confesses. 'I met someone in the hospital reception. I'll let you know Sunday how it goes.' After a pause, she says, 'So, Miss Ivy, are you going to tell us about this tattoo. We thought you'd injured yourself at first.'

Ivy laughs. 'It was on a whim. No, that's a lie. I've been thinking about it for a long time.' She lifts her sleeve to reveal a small bluebird. 'It stands for freedom and happiness. The last two years have been so hard, and I wanted to do something that represents a new start.' She shrugs. 'Daft, I know. I'd never have a sleeve like Feather Starr, of course. Do you think I'm too old?' They all protest.

'You're a dark horse,' Summer says.

'I admire you,' Gwen tells her. 'I'd love to be that fearless and not care what people say about me. I've cared too much about it.'

There's an uncomfortable silence but Ivy flashes her a look and Gwen feels that sometimes she can see right through her.

'You're nothing like I thought you'd be,' Meg says with honesty. 'I thought you were a right snob. Up your own arse!'

'Oh, you just kept to yourself,' says Ivy, ever the diplomat.

'Meg's right. I've always been too money orientated. Perhaps even thought I was better than everyone else. I'm ashamed to admit that.' She flushes. 'Well, I've certainly learnt that money doesn't buy you happiness, if that doesn't sound like a clichéd positivity quote on some happiness app.'

Summer coughs, not meeting her eye. Do the others know about Gareth's affair? She wouldn't be surprised. Nothing is kept secret for long in Morlan.

Gwen sips her wine. 'I've thrown Gareth out. He's been seeing my best friend. I found out last week.' It comes out in a rush.

'Bastard,' Meg says.

'How awful!' Ivy commiserates.

Summer shakes her head. 'What a thing to do!'

Their sympathy feels like a warm hug and Gwen feels the tears well in her eyes. Her usual recourse is to hide, pretend everything is OK, don't let anything shatter the illusion of her perfect life, as coiffed and manicured as her landscaped lawns. She hasn't even told Lydia yet, who is always busy seeing friends or at college. So far, she has got away with saying Gareth has a huge project at work and is away. She needs to tackle both of them tonight before the grapevine does it for her.

Later, as Gwen walks up the hill, she feels a bit nervous about Lydia and how she will react. She's left her car at The Mariners as she's had three glasses of wine. Dutch courage. Confessing to the women had been cathartic, but her daughter will be different. Gwen feels Lydia has always been a daddy's girl. This will not be easy.

Lydia is asleep on the couch, her hair a blonde waterfall over her shoulders. She has her fluffy grey throw draped over her and Boris, their ginger cat, curled up like a seashell next to her. It reminds her of when Lydia was a little girl, innocent and trusting. Gwen kisses the top of her head.

'Mum,' Lydia says, shaking off the fog of sleep. 'Where've you been?'

'Did you eat the pizza I made?' Gwen says, avoiding the question.

'Yeh, it was nice.'

Gwen sits next to Lydia on the sofa. 'I've got something to tell you, Lyds.'

'Is it about Dad?'

She nods. 'Why do you ask?'

'Well, he's never here these days. I can tell something is going on.' Lydia pauses. 'Are you getting a divorce?'

She braces herself. 'Probably.'

Lydia's face crumples and her body is suddenly racked with sobs. Boris sleeps through it all as Gwen pulls Lydia to her for a hug and strokes her hair.

'Can't you sort it out?' she asks.

'Not this time, darling. He's in love with someone else.' Gwen did think about just saying that they'd grown apart, but she decides there's no point. Lydia will find out. She breaks out in fresh sobs.

'Will he move out or will we have to?'

'I'm hoping to stay,' Gwen says. 'This is the home where you grew up. Eventually, I might have to sell up and buy something smaller. It'll be a while yet, though. Perhaps when you go to university.'

'He's a bastard, Mum. How can he do that to you?'

She doesn't rebuke Lydia for this. She's bound to feel angry, hurt. After all, Gwen was seething when she found out, but she's had a week to get used to it. 'It happens sometimes, my

124

love. I don't suppose he intended to hurt me.'

'I never want to see him again,' Lydia says firmly, and Gwen shushes her, stroking her hair again. Eventually, Lydia falls asleep and Gwen goes to the kitchen to make them hot chocolate. She'll phone Jasmine in the morning. She feels too emotionally drained to speak to her tonight. *What a mess*, she thinks, as she watches the mug of milk do a slow spin in the microwave.

Chapter Fourteen

Meg

Meg checks her reflection in the full-length mirror. She's worried the lipstick is too bright. It seems to mock her otherwise dressed-down appearance, but time's getting away with her, and she won't be able to remove it without causing destruction to the rest of her make-up.

'It'll do,' she mutters to herself. She's curled her hair and painted her nails, more effort than she would usually go to for a date, but this one feels different. Special, somehow.

But then it's not really a date, is it? Josh only asked her to show him round St Davids. It's just a casual thing. A friendly thing.

'It's a date,' Summer had insisted in the pub, when she'd told her how they met and the loose plans she'd made with Josh for Saturday.

'But he doesn't know anyone in St Davids. He just wants a friendly face to show him what's what, where's good to go.'

'That's the biggest load of bullshit I've ever heard,' Summer had said, buoyed up by the lager that she told them all she never got to drink at home.

'Okay, maybe it *is* a date.'

'You'll charm him, I'm sure,' Ivy had smiled kindly.

Meg's stomach stirs anxiously at the thought. Can she really be expected to charm him? It's been over a week since she met him in the hospital, and she's forgotten now what he looks like. She tried to stalk him on Facebook, but she doesn't know his surname, and there were too many Joshes in South Wales for her to narrow it down. How ridiculous, going on a date with a man whose full name she doesn't even know! What if she doesn't recognise him? What if the charm has worn off now that they're meeting for real?

She's putting too much pressure on herself. Meg will just enjoy the afternoon, and if she doesn't like him, then she doesn't have to see him again. Just like with the other dates.

So why is she so nervous?

Meg checks her side profile, making sure her stoma bag is tucked in tight to her long skirt, the movement smooth and practised. She must do this at least fifty times a day.

She's all good to go.

'Are you off out now?' her grandmother shouts from behind the post office counter as Meg tries to slip away unnoticed.

'Yeah. I won't be back late.'

'Enjoy yourself!' Hannah shouts, completely ignoring the customer who is waiting package-in-hand, with an exasperated look on his face. 'If you want to bring him back here, I can go out for the night.'

'No need,' Meg replies, dying of embarrassment. She needs to move out, she tells herself, whipping out of the door before Hannah can say another word.

It's only a short drive to St Davids, and Meg tries to listen to Radio 1, but finds her mind drifts back to Josh too often to concentrate on the news headlines. What if their conversation has dried up now? They clicked when they were waiting at the hospital, and they'd been texting all week, witty messages and weekend plans, but what if that was it? No further chemistry?

She has to calm down. They've arranged to meet at a pub at 3 p.m. Meg is twenty minutes early, but decides to go inside anyway, lest he walk past and see her waiting in the car like a loser. She does a final check of her hair and profile, and heads in.

The Bishop is a tiny white-washed pub from the outside, but Meg knows it has a good beer garden, and Josh said that it was close to his flat. Like a meerkat, her head whips from side to side when she enters, trying to spot him. There's no sign of him so she goes straight for the bar. It's noisy there, with some rugby game on the TV.

'Single gin and tonic,' she orders.

'Good choice,' a voice says behind her. Meg knows instantly it's him.

'I always turn up early when I'm nervous,' Josh smiles at her, kissing her on the cheek. 'I was planning to pretend I'd just arrived when you got in.'

'It seems we share that character trait, then. I thought about sitting in the car for half an hour,' she says. Josh laughs. Meg likes a guy that's man enough to admit when he's nervous. And the fact he's nervous for her makes her own anxiety dissipate. Josh is just as attractive as she remembered, especially now he's swapped work clothes for jeans and a T-shirt. She didn't notice how blue his eyes were before, but the stubble and glasses, and the slight lopsided smile she definitely remembers.

'So, do you travel everywhere with a giant Monstera?' Josh asks as they sit down.

'Another character trait of mine,' Meg laughs. 'No, this is for you. A moving-in present. I didn't know what to get but everyone seems obsessed with houseplants these days. At least that's what people put on social media . . .' she's babbling, but Josh is grinning.

'I love it! I was thinking of getting one. My flat is looking a bit sad at the moment. It's the first place I've rented on my own, and judging by my lack of furniture, it seems I was always the lazy housemate that didn't buy anything and relied on everyone else.'

'Please say you at least have a sofa?'

'Erm . . .' He shakes his head. 'It's coming next week. But now I have this Monstera, I have everything I need!'

'I'm impressed you know the name of it,' Meg says. 'All I know is Monstera is the one that's basically impossible to kill. Whether you water it once a month or twice an hour, it should be fine.'

'You have pretty low expectations of me, then?'

'Not just you. Maybe men in general.' Meg laughs to show she's joking, but she wonders if she's gone too far, made it too serious.

'You've had some bad dates, then?' Josh laughs too, putting Meg at ease.

'I wouldn't say bad . . . maybe awful? I met a man on Tinder a few weeks ago, but I saw him in the pub celebrating his engagement about a week after our date.'

'Ouch. Well, if it helps, my dating life isn't exactly on fire.'

'Are you telling me medicine isn't like *Grey's Anatomy* at all?'

'Shagging in store cupboards, that sort of thing? I wish! Sorry, that was crude.' Josh frowns, and now it's Meg's turn to put him at ease.

'Dammit, don't burst the bubble for me.'

'Well, the NHS isn't quite like that. It is pretty incestuous, though. I don't think I've spent time with anyone non-medical in far too long. It's refreshing to be with someone normal.'

'I wouldn't say I'm normal,' Meg laughs.

'No?'

She shakes her head. It's time to bite the bullet. 'I live in a post office. With my grandmother. And I've never lived outside my tiny village.' She expects Josh to recoil but he smiles.

'That sounds so good. I've had to move so many times for work and hospital placements. I'd love to just stay in one place, make it feel like home.' This makes her feel better. 'How come you live with your grandmother? You must get on pretty well?'

'We do, but we have our moments. She had a hip replacement a while ago and I offered to look after her, plus it got me out from under my mother's nose and I was helping in the post office anyway. It was meant to be temporary but it seems to be lasting a bit longer than expected.'

'Life never quite happens as we expect it to.'

Meg nods a little too emphatically. She wonders if Josh has his own story. It's hard, this dating stuff. It's like a dance, wanting to reveal enough of yourself but without stepping on your partner's toes, turning them off. It is too early to tell him about the stoma bag. Meg never mentions it on a first date as a

130

hard rule. Plus, Josh is a doctor, she doesn't want him to have to think medically on a date. He might think she's angling for free advice. Or it might remind him of a patient he's treated. No. There is no way to make it sexy.

'Well, if you ever want a break from your grandmother, you know where I am,' he says, then seems to cringe. 'That wasn't meant to be a proposition.'

'I was going to say that's the oddest proposition I've ever had.' Meg laughs heartily. She's really enjoying herself, she admits inwardly.

'What's the village called?' Josh asks then, changing the subject.

'Morlan. It's named after our lagoon, or so I remember from school. About fifteen minutes from here.'

'Wait, Morlan, isn't that the place with the pole dancing lessons?' Josh says, taking a sip of his beer. 'I've been here two days, but I've heard it mentioned twice now. Some women were talking about it in Tesco.'

'I can tell you from personal experience that they're excellent classes.' She waits for realisation to dawn on his face.

'You're a pole dancer?'

'I told you I wasn't normal,' she giggles self-consciously. 'Actually, I'm not a pole dancer, but I've gone to three of the classes so far.'

'And is it all writhing around in underwear?' Josh says, his face reddening. Meg feels hers too.

'About the total opposite of that,' she shrugs. 'More like grandmothers and village WAGs sweating to Girls Aloud tracks. It's good fun, though. I thought it would be naff but they're a really nice bunch. Plus, it's harder than it looks.'

Josh raises his eyebrows and Meg realises her double entendre.

'Oh dear,' she laughs.

'Well, I would love to see it,' Josh says, more serious now.

'I bet you would.' She's flirting, unbelievably. And before she's thought it through the words are tumbling out, 'We're performing at the village fête in the summer.'

'I *have* to see that,' Josh says. 'I didn't think village fêtes were meant to be sexy.'

Meg laughs a great belly laugh. 'You'll see how un-sexy it is.' She has a feeling she'll regret telling him this later. She doesn't even know if she will perform yet, but the gin is going straight to her head and she's having such a nice time. And Josh is definitely flirting with her. And she is definitely enjoying it.

The best date she's been on in a long time.

They leave the pub when it starts to get busy and the rugby crowd are getting rowdy after Wales's win. Meg walks Josh to see the cathedral. Even though she's been to St Davids countless times, the scale and majesty of the cathedral never cease to amaze her. Josh seems captivated too. She isn't planning on taking him in, but he grabs her arm and pulls her down the hill towards the cathedral entrance. The unexpected physical touching makes Meg feel dizzy with excitement. They blur past families and groups of teenagers, laughing like they're the young ones.

Meg has to check her skirt, make sure everything is tucked in as it should be. Josh doesn't notice, too busy laughing.

'I shouldn't be out of breath from running downhill,' he says, pretending to keel over. 'Too many night shift Dominos and hospital café stodge.'

'A few weeks of living in St Davids and you'll be doing Ironmans,' Meg laughs. 'There's nothing else to do around here.'

'I'm going to need to,' he says, 'especially if I'm dating a pole dancer.'

'I'm not a pole dancer,' Meg says, but she doesn't deny the other implication he's made. She hopes he doesn't notice her grinning.

'Come on,' she says, and takes him by the hand. It's meant to be gentle, loose, but Josh's grip tightens in hers. They must look so normal, strolling past these visitors and tourists, but Meg feels anything but. Inside she could burst with excitement. She hasn't felt like this in years. Not since before the operation.

They hover at the cathedral entrance, before an official-looking woman notices them.

'I'm sorry, we're closed due to a private event.'

'Oh no,' Meg says in unison with Josh. 'It was all going so well.'

'I'm going to need a minute before going back up that hill.' He pulls her over to perch on a bench nearby. Meg sits next to him, although she's not sure who's made the decision to sit so close their legs are touching. It's one of those dreary Welsh days, the sky overhead is opaque, but it's not raining, and spring is in the air. It's just on the border of being pleasant enough to sit outside. Meg couldn't care less if she was being pelted with rain, though.

'Shall we find another pub? I can probably have one more

133

'before driving back,' she says, not wanting the afternoon to end.

'What about dinner? I need to find the best pub meal around.'

She likes how keen he is. No game playing. No holding back.

'I think that sounds great. As part of my tour guide duties, of course.'

'Well, you've failed with the cathedral tour, but everything else has been . . .' He trails off, and Meg looks at him curiously. Before she can say anything else, Josh leans forward and kisses her.

Chapter Fifteen

Ivy

Ivy rings Wendy's doorbell, trying to suppress her annoyance. She's had to drag herself away from the chest of drawers she wants to start upcycling tonight. It's not everyone's idea of a fun Saturday night, but Ivy can't wait to start sanding it down. Later, she was going to have a light supper, some halloumi and roasted vegetables perhaps, and then settle in front of the telly with a glass of wine. Wendy had been so insistent when she invited Ivy for a meal at hers that she had no choice. It's hard to say no to Wendy when she lives next door and watches everything Ivy does. She hates that she's such a pushover sometimes. She's vowed that she is going to change. Reinvent herself and be more assertive.

As she stands on the doorstep, she can hear Wendy's windchimes jangling in the breeze. She glances at the view from Wendy's cottage, not very different from hers, but it catches her breath every time she sees the Irish Sea, iridescent now in the setting sun.

'Come in,' Wendy smiles.

'You look nice,' Ivy says, wondering why Wendy has put

on a dress for her casual invitation to a 'small bite to eat' on Saturday night. Ivy smooths down her bright pink T-shirt over her cropped trousers, feeling underdressed. 'I hope you like Pinot Grigio Blush,' she says. 'It's lovely on a spring evening.'

'Come in, come in. I'll have a small glass, but wine gives Martin indigestion. Anyway, go to the conservatory. They're in there. I'll be serving up soon.'

They? Ivy shoots Wendy a puzzled look but receives an enigmatic smile in return.

Martin is sitting in one of the wicker chairs in the conservatory, chatting to a man Ivy has never seen before. She has an uncomfortable feeling, like listening to a joke you don't quite understand and laughing anyway.

'Ivy, come in. Have a seat,' Martin says. He has slipped into the role of the jovial host, a side she rarely sees of him. 'Let me introduce you to Bob. He's an old friend of mine. Lives over in Narberth.'

Both men stand up and Bob shakes her hand. Ivy notices the damp sheen above his lip, the dark stains under the arms of his blue shirt.

'Nice to meet you, Ivy.'

'Bob is widowed,' Martin says.

The smile freezes on Ivy's lips, realising she has been set up. That's why Wendy was so eager she came over tonight. 'I'm sorry to hear that,' Ivy says.

'It's been seven years now,' he says awkwardly. Silence hangs in the air.

As they sit down, Ivy asks, 'So, you're an old friend of Martin and Wendy?'

Bob shifts in his seat. 'Well, we don't know each other that well. I used to work with Martin many moons ago. We haven't been in touch for years. I was a bit surprised to get the invite tonight.' Martin coughs at this. 'It's always lovely to see the two of them, of course.'

Ivy's annoyance grows. The poor man wasn't part of this plan at all. She can see exactly what's happened. Wendy trawling through a list of potential suitors for her. A small pool – eligible bachelors over seventy. However, she decides she can't take it out on Bob and gratefully takes the glass of wine Martin hands her.

The conservatory is stiflingly hot despite the doors being open wide and Wendy calls them to the table inside. She's looking a bit flushed from the heat of the kitchen.

'Well, isn't this nice?' Wendy says. 'I hope you two have been getting on well.' Ivy cringes at her lack of subtlety. 'Anyway, it's shepherd's pie. It's a favourite of ours. And who doesn't love a shepherd's pie?'

'Did you know the difference, Bob, between shepherd's pie and a cottage pie?' Martin asks.

'Isn't a cottage pie made of lamb and shepherd's pie beef?'

'The other way around,' Wendy interjects. 'It originated in Scotland.'

Ivy smiles politely between mouthfuls, wondering when she can leave without it seeming rude. 'Delicious,' she says.

'You like all sorts of food, don't you, Ivy? Some of the things she eats I've never heard of,' she tells Bob. 'What was that mushy grey thing you were eating the other night?'

'Baba ganoush. It's made with aubergine and tahini.'

'Never heard of it,' Wendy says, pulling a face. 'I must say, it didn't look too appetising.'

'I love Middle Eastern food,' Bob says. 'Maggie and I used to travel a lot. We liked trying different foods, experiencing different cultures. We didn't go on the usual touristy routes. More off the beaten track.' His eyes sparkle with the memories.

'Really?' Ivy says, interested. 'So, where did you go?'

'Madagascar. Fantastic wildlife there. We did Central America. The Mayan ruins in El Salvador. Fascinating. We went to the Galapagos Islands one year.'

Ivy is impressed. Wendy and Martin, who generally holiday in Weston-super-Mare, seem less so. 'How interesting! I'd love to do some more travelling,' Ivy says. 'I know it's a cliché but they say travel broadens the mind.'

'I quite agree,' Bob says. 'Most of it we did in school holidays. Maggie was a teacher and then we both retired. We started with a camper van and did most of Europe and then became a bit more adventurous, going further afield. We packed a lot in in those few years before she became ill.' His smile subsides. 'Fortunately.'

'I really want to go to Scandinavia,' Ivy says, 'and New Zealand. And I was reading once about Bhutan. It's between India and China. They measure their GDP by happiness. Can you believe it?'

'Maggie and I loved New Zealand,' Bob says. 'Sublime landscape and stunning fjords. I'd go back in a heartbeat.'

At this, Wendy shoots Martin an *I told you so* glance. *Didn't I tell you they'd get on?* The evening is darkening and Martin switches on a lamp.

'Can you give me a hand to take these into the kitchen, Ivy?' Wendy asks. Bob rises, too. 'No, it's fine. Us girls will manage.' Ivy cringes at being referred to as 'girls'. 'Perhaps you can top up Ivy's wine, Martin?'

Once in the kitchen, Wendy turns to face Ivy. 'Well?'

'Well, what?' Ivy is not going to make this easy for her.

'What do you think of Bob, of course? Isn't he just the loveliest?'

'He seems a very nice man,' Ivy says.

'As soon as Martin and I remembered Bob, we thought he'd be perfect for you. He's a bit eccentric. Has some funny ideas. But his wife has died. Perfect!'

'Really, Wendy?' Exasperated, she sighs. 'I don't want to meet anyone. I can't be plainer. It's only two years since Jim died and, to be truthful, I want some time to myself. I *need* some time to myself.'

'I've made a lemon posset,' Wendy says, ignoring Ivy's comments and artfully arranging a few raspberries around it. 'All I'm saying is that it's not natural for a woman to be on her own.'

Ivy bites her lip and helps Wendy carry in the plates.

Ivy likes the citrussy tang in her mouth. As the conversation falters, she watches a moth fly into the conservatory, its wings fluttering around the lamp.

'Did you hear about the pole dancing classes that have started up in Morlan?' Wendy asks Bob. 'I know Narberth is liberal in attitudes and you'd expect all sorts there, but Morlan has decent folk.' She spears a raspberry with her tiny fork. 'Disgusting, really. And totally inappropriate. Some of us ladies in the village are getting a petition together with Idris Hopkins, our councillor, to get it closed down.' She turns to Ivy. 'You can sign it later.'

Ivy's stomach churns. She feels like flipping some of her lemon posset in Wendy Gower's face.

Summer is the first to arrive, looking a bit flustered from walking up the hill with her two little ones in tow.

Taking Nia's hand, Ivy says, 'Well hello, Nia. I've got a surprise for you.' Ivy's living room and dining room have been knocked into one and she leads her to one corner where a bright pink plastic kitchen is situated, utensils hanging from its frame. 'Perhaps you can bake us a cake.'

'She'll love that,' Summer says. 'Anything different to her own toys. Jordan is asleep. I've only just fed him.'

'I did want Tabitha to have something less gender-biased, less girly, but Matthew insisted that this was what she wanted.'

Summer laughs, 'You can't fight it.'

Gwen turns up next and then Meg, fifteen minutes later with apologies, 'Sorry, everyone. I'm feeling a little delicate.'

'Ooh, do tell us how your date went,' Ivy says.

Meg smiles widely, 'Good. Well, better than good. He's lovely.'

Summer nudges her. 'So, where did you go? Tell us all.'

'Only St Davids – he's moved house there. He's starting as a GP in Haverfordwest tomorrow.'

'Well, we certainly need more of those,' says Ivy.

'Did you go back to his place?' asks Summer, pretending to eat a plastic cake Nia has handed her. 'Yummy!' she says in an exaggerated voice.

'A lady never tells!' Meg grins. 'No, we might have had a little kiss, but I don't want to rush things.' Something crosses her face and Ivy wonders if she's been hurt in the past.

'I would be happy if I never saw another man,' Gwen grimaces. 'Take your time, Meg. They're all rats.' Ivy pats her knee in sympathy.

'Anyway, you're not the only one who had a date last night.' Ivy laughs at their shocked faces and then relates the disaster of the previous night. 'Honestly, the poor man had as little idea he was being set up as I did. He was very nice, don't get me wrong, but I am happy to spend time alone. Why does everyone want me married off so quickly?'

'Misery likes company,' Gwen muses. 'Speaking of misery, Gareth is over tonight to pick up the rest of his stuff. It's the first time we've properly been in a room together since he left. I can't say I'm looking forward to it.'

'It's lovely, darling,' says Summer to Nia. 'Can you make me another one?'

'We'd better get started,' says Ivy, 'I need to get those steps in my head before Thursday. I don't have a pole, unfortunately, but we can practise the first bit before we do the spin.'

'Meg, you've got to help us,' says Summer. 'You're the only one who can do them.'

'I loved dance when I was a teenager,' says Meg. 'I got up to grade seven.'

'What made you give up?' asks Summer.

'I was unwell for a time and then sort of gave up,' she admits. 'So, point your toe forward like this and pretend the pole is in your right hand.' The subject is closed, Ivy notices.

After twenty minutes, Jordan is crying for a feed and Nia is following the women, copying their steps.

'I am actually corrupting my children,' Summer laughs.

'I'm not sure I'm any better than I was at the start,' says Gwen, 'but it's good fun. It's the only time I don't think of any of my problems. It forces me to concentrate.'

'I know what you mean,' says Ivy, bringing in some lemonade. 'I made this yesterday and I've put lots of ice in it.'

'You have a lovely place here,' Gwen says. 'I like what you've done with the house. It's amazing what you can do on a tight budget.' She winces, 'Sorry, I didn't mean that. I can't help myself putting my big foot in it.' She flushes.

'No offence taken,' Ivy smiles.

'It must be such a sense of achievement to think you've done a lot of the work yourself.'

'All Aled wants is a man shed. He leaves all the house design to me,' says Summer, 'which is just as well as he'd want black walls everywhere.'

'That's very on trend at the moment,' Ivy says.

'I wish my gran was more open-minded like you,' Meg confesses.

'I wish the people of Morlan were more open-minded full stop,' says Ivy. 'Wendy says there's a petition going around to stop the classes, driven by our esteemed Councillor Idris Hopkins.'

'That interfering old turd,' says Gwen. 'We had trouble from him when we were building the house. He took delight in opposing us at every stage.'

'Wendy tried to get me to sign the petition, but I cried off with a headache and came home early. I will have to come clean sooner or later. I hate confrontation and have avoided it all my life.'

'Well, there's strength in numbers, Ivy. We're in this together,' says Summer.

Ivy smiles, feeling a warm glow. It's been a lovely afternoon and even Wendy's curtain twitching as the women leave doesn't dampen her spirit.

Chapter Sixteen

Summer

The headline catches Summer's eye as she stoops to collect the paper that's just landed on her welcome mat. The *Morlan Village Voice* is hardly a fountain of juicy gossip – most weeks the front-page story concerns a pesky pothole on the main road, or a stolen marrow from local allotments – but this week things are different.

The title reads 'Sordid Sex Classes in Morlan Village Hall: Villagers Protest' with an image of the hall's facade on the front page. Summer is in disbelief. What nonsense!

She hears Nia stirring over the monitor from upstairs, and prays she has two minutes to read the article before her children wake up from their naps. She drops the other assorted junk mail on the table and sits with paper in hand.

The local community was stirred when posters started going up in March to advertise pole dancing classes. Was this a figment of someone's imagination? Or the plot of a Hollywood movie? We would like to hope so, but the village was rocked when Feather Starr pitched up in Morlan with an array of poles to corrupt local women.

Her eyes skip further down the page.

'It's pornography, is what it is,' Councillor Idris Hopkins told reporters. 'If we don't take action, this could be the start of a slippery slope towards chaos for the village. I've seen it happen before, drug problems, prostitution, you name it. It will infect the minds of our youth.' When asked what Mr Hopkins would like to happen to the classes, he said, "Shut them down, of course! Someone has to put a stop to them. Restore the peace and respectability of our community. End this criminality immediately. Sign our petition." The petition Mr Hopkins is referring to is gaining traction throughout the village, with over five hundred signatures and counting . . .

Summer nearly can't read the rest of the article. It's so ridiculous and over the top, she could gag. How did this pass for reporting? She had thought pole dancing classes were saucy, but calling them pornography and criminality is ludicrous. If anything, it makes Summer even more determined to keep going to the classes, show those old fogies in the WI and the local council just what Morlan women are made of. If only she could get a babysitter for this week.

Has anyone seen the absolute trash in the Morlan Village Voice *this week?* Summer types quickly on the WhatsApp group. They'd made the group when they were rehearsing at Ivy's yesterday. Summer had the distinct impression that Gwen had never used WhatsApp before, but Ivy was certainly a natural. She'd changed the group icon to a cartoon pole dancer and named them the Pole Stars by the time Summer had walked home.

We're famous! Meg types back almost immediately. *Just seen the post office copies. Pornography . . . are they mental?*

Summer sends a laughing emoji as Ivy types, *They clearly haven't been to any classes.*

It's only a matter of time before Gwen's involved too. *Did you see what they said about Feather Starr? Criminal record??*

Summer's eyes scan wildly for what she's missed. Towards the bottom it talks of the instigator of these 'sordid classes' as Feather Starr and mentions her having 'done time' in vague terms.

There has to be a story there, Meg has typed while she's been reading.

It hardly makes her a witch, and there's Idris Hopkins wanting to burn her at the stake!

Ivy's right, the language used is horrendously old-fashioned.

You'd like to think we live in a progressive community . . . Gwen writes.

Nothing progressive about Morlan, Meg replies.

I hope it's not put anyone off going to the classes, Summer types now.

God no!

Absolutely not! the women respond. Summer hopes she doesn't sound desperate, but she's come to realise how much she values the classes, and these women in particular. It was a respite spending time at Ivy's yesterday. It lifted Summer's soul. She isn't ready to give them up yet.

Although that brings her on to her next task of the day,

finding a babysitter for Thursday. Aled went back to work four days ago, and Summer wishes she could say the house has been quiet since, but the usual chaos and destruction have resumed. She feels sometimes that she is the only one who can't control her own children; they were good as gold in Ivy's yesterday, and they always seem on best behaviour when Dad's home. Although it's not like Aled has the golden touch, the shambles of last week's pole dancing class demonstrated that much.

At least he is another pair of hands, and now Summer has no one. She hears the familiar snuffling sounds again over the monitor, the heavy breathing and pause of a few seconds, before the lung-shaking cry that signals nap time is over. Summer trudges upstairs with a heavy feeling in her heart. She was hoping to have a babysitter sorted by now, but it's another burden she'll have to deal with while entertaining the kids.

'Hello, darling,' she says, when she gets in the bedroom. Jordan is napping in the bedside crib, still sharing a room with Summer and Aled. 'Shhh, Jordan. What's this all about?'

The baby falls silent in her arm, and without thinking about it, Summer inhales his smell deeply, relishing these moments. She can't believe that one day he'll be a teenager, all smelly socks and wanking, and he'll be embarrassed to be seen with her, let alone enjoy a cuddle. He's too precious for that. If she could only freeze her perfect little boy like this forever.

Nia has a sixth sense for when Jordan's awake. She has the biggest FOMO of all, not wanting to miss out on the party, and Summer goes to greet her daughter in the nursery. It's now time for the routine of changing, feeding, playing and settling down on the sofa, which Summer does diligently, driven by muscle memory while she brainstorms possible babysitting options.

She daren't call her mother for help, that was a one-time aberration that ironically got her into the pole dancing classes in the first place. Her next-door neighbour looked after Nia when Summer had her scans while pregnant with Jordan, but that was begrudging at best. She remembers the wry look when Summer said that she owed her big-time, the lack of protest. Cold bitch! The chocolates hadn't even thawed her when Summer finally had time to go to the supermarket.

'Rita? It's Summer.' She tentatively calls Aled's mother.

'Summer, how are you? Is everything OK? With the children? And Aled?' Her voice crackles down the phone with concern. Summer likes that she doesn't even pretend to be interested in her.

'Everything's fine. How are you?'

A weary sigh. 'Not good at the moment. I've got another appointment at the hospital next week. Nothing showed up on the MRI last time, but they're thinking of doing another one.'

'It must be frustrating,' Summer sympathises. Rita has one of those chronic pain syndromes, with no medical cause found. She knows Rita gets tired, and struggles with activities around the house, but Summer doesn't quite understand the whole picture. Rita seems to be well enough to attend ballroom dance lessons with her friends every week, but can't do her own shopping or cleaning. Summer doesn't think Aled understands either. He always waves a dismissive hand whenever Summer suggests a visit there.

'More than frustrating, it's infuriating. The consultant said they could start a new medication . . .'

Summer wants to listen but multitasking with Jordan's burping is taking priority. She rubs his little back, watching him dribble down his Babygro. Rita's story goes on for a while, and Summer almost forgets the reason she's called.

'Well, I hope things go better with this MRI,' she says, hoping she's been diplomatic enough to end this stream of medical history. 'I was just wondering . . .' she hears the trepidation in her voice, knowing what Rita's answer will be already, 'whether you'd be able to look after Nia and Jordan Thursday night? I have a . . . an exercise class and I have no other options really. I wouldn't ask otherwise. It would only be for an hour, probably, plus twenty minutes for travel.'

'Oh, Summer.' Rita's permanent state seems to be sighing. 'I'm just not up to it at the moment. You understand that, don't you? I can't look after a baby.'

Summer tells herself to be strong, to hold firm. 'Jordan's usually asleep at that time of evening, Nia too. They wouldn't be any hassle.'

'The doctors have said I need to rest. Aled always tells me what a handful they are. He's so tired when he's home, and I know having the two kids on his own is a strain for him. It's different for a man, working like that . . .'

Summer's eyes roll back into her head. Why did she fucking bother?

'I won't cope with them. You know that. If you want to stop in with them, though, that would be great. Afternoons two 'til four are my best times.'

'I will do soon,' Summer says through gritted teeth. 'I'll see if I've got time later this week.'

'I tell you what would be marvellous, if you could pick up my medication on the way? I struggle to get to the clinic these days,' Rita moans. 'And the pharmacy is so close to Morlan.'

'Isn't that marvellous?' Summer knows she shouldn't, but sarcasm is all she has. 'Like I said, I'll let you know if we've got time. Nice to chat, Rita. Take care.' She hangs up before she can cause any more relationship damage.

She knows she should be more sensitive and sympathetic to Rita's issues, but Summer just wants to cry with self-pity. She can't have one hour to herself. Just one class a week.

Just had the pleasure of speaking to your mother, she begins to type to Aled, then deletes it. Moaning to Aled will just cause a fight, and then she'll be in an even worse state. Aled seems to be able to complain all he wants about his mother, but as soon as Summer says anything he jumps to her defence.

Summer huffs in frustration. Nia looks at her curiously before turning back to the television.

I don't think I'm going to be able to come to classes any more. I love them, but it's just too hard getting someone to look after the kids and we can't afford a childminder. Maybe when Aled's back I can come for a few sessions. It's been nice getting to know you all. I'll come and watch you in the village fête, Summer types on the WhatsApp group to the women. She decides she needs to lighten the tone. She sounds like she's breaking up with them. *I'll be in the front row – you know I love a bit of pornography!*

She sees Gwen and Meg start typing straight away.

WHAT? With a crying emoji from Meg.

That's a shame. Are you sure there's no one else who can help? It's been nice to get to know you too. Gwen's message is ultimately pointless; Summer's explored every avenue she can. But she appreciates the sentiment. Gwen Vimpany really isn't as bad as people make out. Summer senses that Gwen needs these classes as much as she does. At least Gwen can carry on attending.

You can't break up our little group! Meg has typed again. *Are there no babysitters in the village?*

None that will take a baby under six months. Sorry everyone! Summer puts the phone down in a sulk now. There's no use trying to get people to see. No one's in this predicament but Summer.

Her phone pings, and Summer almost feels too dejected to look at it. But she does.

I might have the answer. From Ivy. *Give me two mins.*

Summer doesn't want to get her hopes up. It's kind of Ivy to care, but Summer really has tried everything. Short of bringing the kids to class with her, there's nothing she can do.

When her phone rings a literal two minutes later, Summer is surprised to see Ivy's name on screen.

'Have you ever met Zoe Jones?' Ivy dispenses with the usual greetings.

'No, I don't think so,' Summer says.

'She's my neighbour, Wendy's, granddaughter. Lovely girl. Can't say the same about the grandparents, although that's another story.' That's the closest Ivy gets to moaning about someone, Summer thinks. 'They're decent people.'

'Right?'

'She's just deferred a university place in Cambridge. She's going to study veterinary science, but she's working on Gwion's farm to save some money first. She's going to be here for a year.'

'Okay.' Is this going anywhere?

'Well, she's just agreed to babysit for you. Ten pounds for the hour's class. Fifteen, if you come to the pub afterwards.'

'Wha . . . why would she do that? That's too kind.' Summer feels flabbergasted. Strangers just don't help out like this. How has Ivy managed it?

'Her grandmother owes me for the other night. Plus, Zoe's a sweet girl, and she needs the money. She's happy to do it.'

'Ivy, you are an absolute angel!'

'Nanny Ivy?' Nia overhears. 'Hello, Nanny Ivy!' Summer didn't realise Ivy's had a promotion from Nia, but in her opinion, Ivy deserves saint status.

'How can I thank you?' Summer asks, mentally planning a hamper of treats, maybe even a lottery win if she can orchestrate it for Ivy and her neighbour's granddaughter.

'By bringing your sorry behind to class on Thursday night. See you there!'

Summer can't get over the turn of events in a few minutes, but she's beginning to think stumbling into that pole dancing class was an act of fate. And meeting Ivy definitely was.

Chapter Seventeen

Gwen

Gwen keeps looking out onto the drive, waiting for Gareth to pull up in the Merc. She doesn't know how she feels about seeing him again now that the white-hot rage of a couple of weeks ago has dissipated. She's wearing her navy Jaeger shift dress and has made a special effort with her hair, visiting that ludicrously expensive hairdresser in Haverfordwest.

Not that she wants him to desire her. That ship has sailed. The last thing she wants, though, is for him to think she has fallen apart since he left, imagining he would find her lying prostrate on the sofa surrounded by empty crisp packets and Boris licking her face. No, she is going to show him that she doesn't need him and his philandering arse in her life any more.

She wonders where Gareth's staying at the moment. Lynne lives in Kilgetty. Gwen has visited her cottage a couple of times. It's very Cath Kidston, very twee. Somehow, she can't imagine Gareth there, as he favours chrome and clean lines, rather than floral curtains and muted soft furnishings. He can't enter a room without knocking an ornament over or spilling something on the carpet. Lynne will find that a trial, no doubt.

The purr of Gareth's engine pulling into the drive forces her back to the present. She quickly reapplies her lipstick and opens the door. He struts like a peacock towards her, wearing an open-necked shirt and beige chinos, casual and confident, his comb-over lifting slightly in the mild breeze.

'Gareth,' she nods. There is an awkward moment on the doorstep when he looks as if he doesn't quite know what to do.

'Gwen.' His tone is clipped, sharp. His eyes look behind her into the hallway, 'Is Lydia home?'

'No. She's with Sophie for tonight. I don't think she's ready to see you yet.'

'I hope you haven't poisoned her against me,' he says, and Gwen fights to keep her temper. *Don't rise to it*, she tells herself.

'I told her the truth, Gareth. She is owed that, at least.'

'I see. Shall we sit down? We need to be rational and reasonable about this.'

'I agree. Let's go in the kitchen. Do you want something to drink? Tea? Coffee?'

He pulls up a kitchen stool to the island. 'Coffee will be fine. Thanks.' The air between them is arctic.

'Everything is as you left it, so you can pack up the rest of your clothes and anything else you need.'

'You haven't thrown them into black bags like a heap of rubbish as you did the other night, then. Clothes that cost a bloody fortune.' He shakes his head. 'Madness.'

He's not making this easy. 'I was hurt, Gareth. I had only just found out. What did you expect?' She turns to face him. 'Instant OK?' She knows he likes filter coffee but he daren't complain. She hands him the coffee. 'So, where are you

154

living now? I need to know for the business. Are you staying with Lynne?'

'Not that it's any of your concern but I'm renting a flat in Haverfordwest.' He sips his coffee and winces.

'Not my concern,' Gwen says, taking a seat opposite him. 'Gareth, we've been together since we were nineteen years old. We lived like paupers in that council house in Haverfordwest when you were just a small-time car mechanic eking out a living. We ate spaghetti hoops on toast more times than I can remember.' She shakes her head. 'I was there by your side when we started this business. You would never have done it without me.' She pauses. 'And you know it.'

'Yeh, go on. Tell me again that I would be nothing without you. That I wouldn't be the success that I am. That Vimpany Motors would never have existed without you.' He rolls his eyes.

'You ungrateful bastard! You know that it's true.'

'I had *some* part to play in it too, Gwen. Shit.' Drops of coffee spill down the front of his shirt.

'You were screwing my best friend under my nose. How do you think that makes me feel, you pompous turd? You didn't have the decency to just leave!'

'Best friend?' he snorts in derision. 'She's never really liked you.' The comments cuts Gwen like a knife. 'Lynne actually wants me,' he goes on. 'She doesn't lie like a corpse next to me in bed. Do you know the last time we had sex?' Gwen says nothing, having done the calculations herself not so long ago. 'Do you? I'll tell you when. It was over seven months ago.'

'I can't switch it on like you can, Gareth. Did you ever think to ask me why I didn't want to make love any more?' He

155

sniggers at this, and Gwen feels breathless with indignation. 'Do you think that Lynne would have given you the time of day if you didn't have any money?'

'Not everything comes down to money,' he spits. 'She's not materialistic like you. Forty thousand we paid for this kitchen. With you it's all about impressing people.'

'That's rich coming from you. Every item of clothing you have has a label. You paid sixty thousand for the car! Sixty thousand. It lost money as soon as it left the showroom. You say that yourself about all the suckers who buy cars from you. At least a house rises in value.' She feels the heat prickle her skin.

'This is getting us nowhere. I have come to get the rest of my stuff and I'm getting the hell out of here. I might have known I couldn't have a civil conversation with you.'

'You want me to be civil, do you? Well, I'm off to my solicitor in the morning and we're going to sort out the mess that is our marriage. I am going to make you pay for the way you've treated me. I deserve respect, Gareth.' His face pales at this.

Tears prick Gwen's eyes but she's determined not to show him. He spends the next hour packing up the rest of his clothes. Only when he pulls away from the drive does Gwen allow the tears to spill from her eyes and drip down her chin. She doesn't bother to wipe them away.

Gwen pushes open the door to Boniface and Sons Solicitors in Haverfordwest. Justin Boniface was her solicitor when she was left a small amount of money by her aunt a few years ago. She couldn't use Selby's, the one they use for the business as there would be a conflict of interest. She isn't keen on Justin Boniface.

He's far too pompous for his own good. He's quite an eccentric dresser, often favouring waistcoats and a cravat instead of a suit and tie. He has a floppy fringe reminiscent of Hugh Grant and she has the distinct feeling Justin looks down his nose at her. As if owning a car showroom is a bit chavvy. No doubt he'll not feel too superior to take her money when the divorce is finalised.

'Mr Boniface has a client with him at the moment,' the perky receptionist says, glancing behind her thick glasses. 'He shouldn't be too long. Take a seat and help yourself to a glass of water from the water tank.'

How very generous, Gwen thinks, especially as Justin Boniface's fees are extortionate. She just hopes that he is experienced and ruthless enough to secure her a good deal when she and Gareth part.

She manoeuvres herself into the red tub chair in reception. The magazines on the coffee table, *Country Living*, *House Beautiful*, *Vogue*, seem aspirational, to reflect the kind of clients Justin Boniface wants to attract. She picks up a copy of *Pembrokeshire Life*. It's a few months out of date and she idly flicks through the adverts for holidays, a review of local restaurants and the property section. She wonders how much her house in Morlan is worth now. It has to be over nine hundred thousand, perhaps nearing a million in the current market. Lots of Londoners have been making their homes in Pembrokeshire since the pandemic, with the flexibility of working from home.

She glances at the oversized clock behind reception. Ten past ten. It annoys her that she's kept waiting and she feels nervous about what Justin Boniface will say. He's been in touch with

Gareth's solicitor in the past week and should have got the ball rolling financially.

Gwen reads about a young couple who have renovated their house in Saundersfoot. It's a small fisherman's cottage but they've gone all out with the Hamptons' beach effect in soft furnishings of blues and beiges. The couple look proud as punch of their modest home and she pauses at a picture of them drinking wine in their small back garden, softened with fairy lights and quirky painted tyres filled with lavender and delicate white geraniums. She and Gareth were like that once, embarking on a grand adventure. Building their lives, the business, having the girls, improving their home. Their happiest times were when they had the least. There's a knot of sadness in her stomach and she turns the page quickly.

Her phone beeps in her pocket and Jas's name appears on the screen. Jas rarely messages her. She's so busy now that she's finished travelling and has started a new job in Southampton and with her relationship with Rupert, that needy boyfriend of hers. Still, she seems sympathetic to her with this mess. Gwen spoke to Jas as soon as she could when her father left and she knows Lydia has filled her in, too. It makes her feel better that they are on her side.

Gwen reads the message: 'Good luck today at the solicitors, Mum. Is it OK if I use you as a guarantor for the apartment we're buying? I'll chat about it 2nite xx.'

'Mrs Vimpany, Mr Boniface is ready to see you now.'

Justin Boniface comes around his desk to shake her hand vigorously. 'Mrs Vimpany. I'm sorry to keep you waiting. How lovely to see you again. It's been five years, I believe.' He sinks back in his seat, his velvet jacket opening as he sits down. 'I was just looking at the notes before you came in.'

Gwen looks at the file he has in front of him, notices Justin's gold signet ring as he opens the pages. 'I'm sorry to hear about your divorce. It's always a difficult time,' he says with as much sincerity as he can muster.

Gwen nods in agreement. 'It has been challenging. Most unpleasant.' She could be talking about a leaking pipe, she thinks. 'There's a lot to sort out with the business and the house, of course. We do have a couple of houses we rent out in town. I expect I'm entitled to half.'

He pauses. 'Would you like a cup of tea, Mrs Vimpany?'

'Please call me Gwen. Nothing for me.'

'Well, Mrs Vimpany, uh Gwen. I have been in touch with Mr Vimpany's solicitor, Trevor Gibson, and he's put me in the picture.' He coughs. 'He's shown me the figures, the houses and the business and the investments.'

Spit it out, Gwen thinks. 'I help with the books, Justin. I know full well what the business is worth. The house in Morlan is architect-designed and—'

He coughs again. 'The figures aren't as healthy as I imagined they would be . . .'

'What on earth do you mean?'

'It's a well-established business and one of the biggest car showrooms in Wales . . .' He sips from a glass of water on his desk.

'Yes, the third. What's the problem, Justin? Do be plain with me.'

He looks her in the eye and she sees a flash of sympathy,

159

perhaps pity. 'This is rather awkward,' he begins, 'rather embarrassing. Your husband has made a series of bad investments. Catastrophic investments. And it rather seems that he kept you out of the picture.'

Gwen feels her throat reddening. 'What do you mean *bad*?'

'Bad. Very bad. He sold the rental properties you had in town. A couple of years ago. I'm afraid the business is in trouble. A terrible mess.' He looks down at his hands and fiddles with the signet ring. 'He took out a second mortgage on the house in Morlan. He might need to file for bankruptcy.'

Through the open window, Gwen hears the noisy engine of a bus trundle up the hill.

'What? How has he done this without my knowledge? It's not possible.' She can hear the panic in her own voice.

'Well, your signature is on the relevant documents. Do you remember signing them? Perhaps you have forgotten.'

'Of course I haven't bloody forgotten them! I mean, sometimes I have signed things, petty things, about employees or something, and not checked them . . .' Her voice trails off as she scrabbles through her memories.

'It's quite feasible then that he told you they were for something else and—'

'And I trusted him,' Gwen finishes. 'The bastard!'

Chapter Eighteen

Meg

'Are you sure you're not free to join us today?' Josh asks down the phone. Meg is lying on her bed, in sports bra and knickers, sweaty after a morning yoga session. Josh had interrupted her before she could finish in her final pose, savasana, although she would have used the time lying down to daydream about him anyway.

She's met him once this week since the date in St Davids, and she is learning that Josh is more of a phone call kind of guy than a texter. She doesn't mind that – in fact, Meg quite likes how old-fashioned he is. It's refreshing compared to the Tinder guys who try to play it cool by waiting three hours to reply to a text with a one-word answer. Josh likes her and he isn't afraid to show it. And that makes Meg very happy.

'I can't, I promised I'd work in the post office today,' Meg says. It's half-true, she supposes. She *is* planning to work in the post office with Hannah, but it isn't exactly a promise, and she knows Hannah can cope perfectly well without her today. She has another member of staff coming to cover the café area. Meg will just be a helping hand to carry stock around.

'I'm sure your grandmother would understand if you told her you had a hot date,' Josh says.

'Hot date, is it? You know cockiness is a real turn-off for me. I'm not sure my grandmother would approve,' she teases.

'Fine.' He gives an exaggerated sigh, and Meg laughs. 'I'm just desperate to introduce you to all my friends.'

'I'd love to meet them,' she says genuinely. Josh's friends from medical school are coming down to see his new place, with one of them even driving from Swindon. 'So, is it surfing you have planned with them?'

'The weather's meant to be decent so I'm thinking a day at the beach will be perfect,' Josh says. From what he's told her they all sound quite outdoorsy, with tales of hikes in medical school, to an adventure obstacle course for one of their stag parties last year. 'I think they'll be keen to hire surfboards and wet suits, get in the water. Which beach is best for that around here?'

'Newgale has the best surf, or Freshwater West, which is probably a bit quieter,' Meg says, as if she has any authority on the subject. She used to like surfing as a child; her father took her when she was big enough to use a bodyboard. She remembers the cold slam of the board against her stomach, the feeling of exhilaration when she caught a wave and was sent barrelling forwards.

'A natural,' her father used to call her. Then school and the business of being a teenager got in the way, and then came her illness. Meg wouldn't be seen dead in a wetsuit now, let alone skimpy swimwear, and she wouldn't know what the changing situation would be – what if someone saw the stoma bag?

Besides, the abdominal friction wouldn't be safe against the delicate skin and attachment. So, really, she'd had no choice but to refuse Josh.

'Oh well, maybe we can do something tomorrow. I don't think they're going back until the afternoon so you could come for lunch with us?' Josh asks tentatively.

'Maybe, I'll check in the post office first,' Meg says, worrying their surfing might extend into a two-day session. 'I'm usually knackered after pole dancing too.'

'I can't wait to tell my friends about that,' Josh jokes now. 'They'll be wanting to move to Morlan.'

'And ogle the old women in sportswear? No chance.'

'Well, I'd love to ogle you,' he says. Meg giggles, knowing that she's safe for tonight. No one will be ogling her on a pole any time soon.

'Enjoy today,' she rings off, smiling a Cheshire Cat grin. She's forgotten how good this feeling is. The new relationship feeling. Meg would never call it a relationship to his face, it is far too soon for that, but she has a very good feeling about Josh.

She just needs to tell him about her condition.

Meg hears the Hoover start up from the hallway. 'Nan, I'll do that now!' she shouts. She'd better get to work.

After a warm and sunny spring day, the weather has broken and sheets of rain are pelting Morlan like a disaster movie. Attendance at pole dancing is understandably thin on the ground when Meg arrives. Feather Starr is there, nevertheless, and dressed for a night in Ibiza in some sparkly Strictly-esque number.

163

'We'll give it a few minutes for anyone else to get here, maybe they're stuck in traffic,' Feather says, fiddling with buttons on the old-school CD player she's brought with her.

'I don't know what traffic she's on about,' Meg says to Summer. 'Most of Morlan is staying indoors. Most sensible people, anyway.'

'Not me, I've finally got a regular babysitter so not a chance I was missing this,' Summer says.

Meg unzips her raincoat and throws it on the heap of jackets in the corner.

The door opens, bringing with it the roar of wind. Gwen enters, not a drop of rain on her, but a face like thunder.

'Hiya, Gwen,' Meg calls her over.

'Hi,' she nods, stiff-lipped. Meg looks to Summer and shrugs. Something's up with her.

'Gareth?' Summer mouths.

'Where's Ivy tonight?' Meg asks.

'Is this the week she's visiting her son? I can't remember when she's going.' Summer says. 'She didn't want to miss the class, but her son must have guilt-tripped her.'

'Right, let's start,' Feather yells from the front as though she's commanding a crowd of hundreds. 'As you can see, there's fewer of us tonight, so we can use a pole each instead of the usual group work. Practise our technique. We can demonstrate how it's done to the others next week.'

Summer grimaces, and Gwen mutters to them, 'That sounds hard.' Meg's glad she seems to be loosening up.

'As we've talked about before, movement on the pole is all about momentum and rotation. The more momentum you have, the better, the less pressure on your wrists and other joints to support yourself.' Feather Starr demonstrates walking around the pole, before wrapping one leg around it and allowing the other to trail on the floor. 'This a basic move, known as the flamingo.' She uses two hands to hold her weight on the pole. 'You want your weight to be spread evenly between all contact points.'

The others try it, with varying degrees of success. Meg finds she's out of breath and panting after just a few minutes. She's usually sharing the pole as a group of four, so she gets a breather in between. She can hear laboured breath from Summer and Gwen on poles either side of her.

They continue for a while, swapping legs and directions until they can all just about spin around. Meg feels jerky and uneven, but smiles when Summer shrieks, 'You look amazing, Meg.'

'Now, an easy transition to do from the flamingo is to go into the fireman.' Feather Starr hooks her other leg around the pole so she is now suspended, and lets go of the pole with one arm. 'Let's try it, first as a static position.'

Meg feels she is clinging to her pole like a koala bear, but she can hold herself up. There is a horrible juddering sound from around the room, as several sets of thighs slide down the pole in protest. Gwen can just about stay in place, but Summer looks out of breath and exasperated.

'I think I took a few layers of skin off with that one.' She rubs her inner thighs.

'This is so much harder than usual,' Meg says to them both.

'That's it,' Feather Starr walks around giving encouragement.

'Now let's try it with rotation. You'll hook your right leg around first, then push off with the left, leading you into the spin.'

More flesh complains against the poles as the women try the spin. 'Believe me, the looser you grip the pole, the more movement you get and the easier it will become.'

Meg tries loosening her grip, worried she'll slide off it, but Feather is right. She's secretly thrilled to find she can do these moves well. Definitely not an expert yet, but on her way.

'That's looking brilliant,' Feather Starr encourages her as she walks past her pole. She pauses to get her breath back and watch the others. It's rare that Meg feels sexy, but spinning around with her hair trailing down her back, she actually thinks that maybe it wouldn't be the worst thing in the world if Josh was to see her now.

'Eventually you'll be able to do this,' Feather Starr has mounted her pole again now onstage, and demonstrates moving from the flamingo, into the fireman, and then letting go entirely, allowing her legs to hold her on the pole. She arches her back to an angle that looks entirely unnatural, and splays her arms, totally upside down.

'She's just showing off now,' Gwen moans, but Meg notices she is smiling.

'If I could do that, I'd feel like Superwoman,' Meg says.

'That'll probably be next week for you,' Summer jokes.

They work on a few different grips on the pole, with Feather Starr talking them through the different names, from the elbow and forearm grips to the twisted grip.

'So, let's try the fireman a few more times, but now we're going to cross one leg over the other, which should create enough tension in the legs to allow us to let go of the pole with our arms. Again, let's try it as a static position first. This is a great workout for the core.'

Meg tries it, and this time her thighs burn in protest, her stomach muscles also, holding her body weight up.

'This is why we do the pelvic floor exercises first. You'll see.'

'Bloody hell,' Meg hears Summer swear under her breath. It looks as though Feather Starr also hears her, as she catches Meg's eye and laughs. She's a real teacher's pet now, but Meg's having a great time.

'If you can hold yourself up, you can try it with the rotation now, but don't worry if not. This really takes some work.' Feather Starr nods at Meg to encourage her to have a go.

She feels under pressure, knowing she's keeping an eye on her. Meg tries pushing herself into the fireman, then crossing her legs as she spins round. It takes her a few times to get enough rotation before she can let go of the pole.

Meg just about has it but finds the new position, without her arms holding her in place, means her abdomen is pressed right up to the pole, and she feels an uncomfortable pulling sensation on her bag. It's as if her stoma wound is grating against the pole. She quickly puts her arms back on and jumps down, but she can feel something has dislodged.

Meg glances around to make sure no one is watching her, then puts her hand under her sports top. She can feel the stoma bag needs readjusting; it will start leaking if she doesn't act quickly. And then everyone will notice.

Her thoughts are spinning, and Meg knows she needs to act naturally. She makes a play of fanning herself down with her hand, as though she's hot and needs a break. She jogs to the back of the room, where she has left her jacket and water bottle. With her back turned to the class she can quickly assess the damage. It's hard, with her underlayer holding the bag in place. She can't properly adjust it like she needs to, and she can see fluid coming from the stoma wound. *Oh shit.* Meg's heart is pounding now.

She whips back around to see Feather Starr and Gwen looking at her. She motions that she needs two minutes, and smiles in what she hopes is reassurance that she's OK, but is probably a little exaggerated through her panic.

She pushes open the door to the lobby leading into the hall. She knows she doesn't have long but can pull the band of material holding the bag in place, and properly click the bag back. She grabs a tissue from her jacket pocket to wipe around the opening, then lets out a big exhale. It's fine. No one has seen. No one is any the wiser. She can calm down.

But when she turns round, Gwen is standing in the open doorway. Meg tries not to gasp. How much has she seen? Gwen has a strange look on her face, or is that Meg reading too much into it?

'I've just come to check you're OK,' Gwen says.

'Fine,' Meg smiles, probably not very convincingly. 'I just needed some air.'

Gwen frowns. She's definitely seen something, but Meg can't tell what, and she wants to scream. Gwen looks as if she's about to say something, but seems awkward about it herself. Meg could just die on the spot.

'Are . . . are you sure? I think we're cooling down now.' Gwen still has that strange look on her face.

'I'll be in in a second,' Meg says. She's relieved when Gwen shuts the door behind her. She can imagine Summer's quizzical look, Gwen's shrug, everyone's suspicions. It feels as if she can't lead a normal life, as soon as things start to go well, she has this massive secret threatening to drag her down. A massive label around her neck, that won't go away no matter what she does, no matter how much fun she's having. A reminder that she's ill and needs to hide herself.

Meg is almost tempted not to go back. To leave her jacket and walk home in the rain. Never go to classes again.

But that would raise more questions. So, she makes sure everything is tucked back where it should be, and she forces herself to go in.

'Great work tonight, my lovelies,' Feather Starr is just finishing up, leading the women through a cool-down routine that consists of neck rolls, body twists and leg stretches. Meg joins in, without making eye contact with the others. 'You're all a bit stiff, though. We need to get looser, to embrace our inner goddesses. Shake it up. You're too inhibited.'

Feather Starr has no idea how inhibited Meg is, she thinks.

'There's an easy way to loosen ourselves up, but I don't know if you're ready for that yet,' she looks conspiratorially from woman to woman. There is an uneasy air in the class. 'Leave it with me, but expect the unexpected for the next few weeks,' Feather says. Meg thinks it's almost a threat. All this talk of inhibitions, loosening up, embracing inner goddesses. Meg knows it won't be pleasant.

'Sometimes I wonder why I put myself through this,' Gwen

169

says to Meg and Summer, as they walk to put on their outerwear.

'We're all suckers for punishment,' Summer laughs. 'Anyway, think of the ab muscles.'

'Yes, but I don't like the sound of the unexpected,' Meg says.

'I thought you were up for anything?'

'I know what I am up for. The pub,' Gwen says to vehement nodding from Summer. 'Coming, Meg?'

She wants to hide inside. She wants to go home to safety. She wants to avoid Gwen's awkward looks, Summer's joking, and Rhys's teasing in the pub. But Meg likes these women. And she always enjoys the post-class pub visit.

'God, yes. I need a drink.'

Chapter Nineteen

Ivy

'It's our secret, Tabitha,' Ivy tells her four-year-old granddaughter, as she hands her the cone with chocolate ice cream. Tabitha's eyes brim with glee.

The ice cream man taps his nose conspiratorially, 'What the parents don't know doesn't hurt them, eh?' He laughs loudly at his own joke.

Tabitha's tongue rakes the ice cream, and a brown river drips down her sleeve, staining the cuffs of her dress. Oh lord! A frown crosses Ivy's face. Matthew and Rachel will kill her if they find out. Everything has to be organic and bought from Fothergill's, that ludicrously expensive farm shop, where a second mortgage is needed to buy a few organic sausages and a box of vegetables you could quite easily grow yourself with a little bit of effort.

Ivy and Tabitha have spent the afternoon in the local park and had a picnic. It's Inset day at school and Matthew had asked her to stay over for the weekend and it's Tabitha's birthday party too, with a few friends invited from her class. Ivy had relented in the end, deciding one missed class wouldn't make a difference. Under the watchful eye of Rachel, she'd made up a little lunch box for Tabitha and herself: hummus and carrot wraps with celery sticks, grapes and some almonds. *Rabbit food*, Jim would have called it, and Ivy would have agreed for once.

They sit down on a bench and watch the ducks in the lake, weaving between the sage green lily pads, gossamer thin as they float on the surface.

'Can we feed the ducks, Grandma?' asks Tabitha.

'Of course, darling,' Ivy smooths Tabitha's hair. 'Finish your ice cream and we'll give them the bread we've brought.'

Ivy treasures this time with her granddaughter. She reminds her so much of Matthew when he was this age, with her dark brown curls and large, expressive eyes. Although Matthew was perhaps more serious than Tabitha. Instead of going through that stroppy teenage phase, he seemed to morph into a middle-aged man overnight. He started saving all his pocket money and knew everything about stocks and shares. Still, he sailed through an economics degree at LSE and now has a high-powered job in finance in Bristol. Nonetheless, Ivy would have liked to see him take a gap year, have a few piercings, get paralytic at Glastonbury. Perhaps even get arrested for something. Minor, of course.

Tabitha's hand delves into Ivy's handbag and she scoops up some bread from the paper bag, spilling most of it over the bench.

'Careful, Tabs,' Ivy says. 'Let's try to break up some of these bigger pieces.'

Then Rachel is even more staid than Matthew. A primary

school teacher, the daughter of a headteacher and teacher, she's followed in her family's footsteps. She plays piano and cello to grade eight, speaks French fluently and can rustle up an iced vegan courgette cake that would make Mary Berry weep.

'Can we come to the park every day when you live with us, Grandma?'

'Yes, darling,' Ivy says absentmindedly. 'What? What do you mean when I come to live with you?'

'Mummy and Daddy said you're going to sleep in the shed in the garden.' She looks up at Ivy with eyes full of concern, 'Will there be spiders there?'

Ivy frowns. She knows Matthew is keen for her to move closer, but to live there with them. 'No, Tabs, there won't be spiders. They won't hurt you, anyway.' She begins wiping Tabitha's face, 'Come on, let's get you cleaned up. Mummy will be home soon from her meeting.'

When Ivy and Tabitha arrive at the house, they can see that Rachel is home, her blue Audi Q3 parked outside. The house is in Belgrade Road, a substantial period family home, estate agents would call it. It's beautiful, of course, and elegantly decorated, but being three storeys, it's far too big for the three of them. With four bedrooms, four reception rooms, three bathrooms, it's just as well they have a cleaner. It's a status symbol rather than a home, Ivy thinks, then berates herself for being mean. The views over the Mendips are breathtaking. She would miss the sea, though. Nothing beats that view from her humble little cottage in Morlan that you could fit into one of the reception rooms here.

'Mummy,' Tabitha yells, running down the hallway, 'I've

had chocolate ice cream and crisps.'

Rachel scoops Tabitha into her arms and frowns at Ivy. Will Ivy be relegated to the naughty step? 'It was a nice little treat,' Ivy says, 'and it's such a hot day.'

'You won't be hungry for your dinner,' Rachel smiles, 'you greedy little monster.' She tickles Tabitha and she gurgles with joy. 'I'm baking a cake. Come and help me, Tabs. Tea, Ivy?'

'Can I play in the garden?' Tabitha begs.

'Yes, darling, if you want.'

The kitchen is bathed in light and Tabitha runs out of the back door, dashing to the slide. Rachel goes back to grating carrots.

'What are you making?' Ivy asks, sitting on a stool at the kitchen island.

'Carrot cake. Reduced sugar. I'm making a large one so the children can have it tomorrow when they're over for her tea party. Did you have a nice afternoon?'

Ivy watches Tabitha run around the garden, Jasper, their russet Springer Spaniel chasing after her. 'Lovely. Although Tabs did say something quite curious. She mentioned that I'd be coming to live with you and sleeping in the garden shed. She's worried about spiders.'

Rachel flushes, 'Oh, you know what kids are like. They get the wrong end of the stick sometimes. It was just Matthew and I talking the other night about you living here, and perhaps we'd knock the shed down and build an annexe. We know how you like your freedom.'

'I don't intend to move, Rachel. I have made that clear to Matthew.'

'Yes, I understand that. He just worries about you. You know what Matt is like, a proper mother hen sometimes.'

Ivy sighs. 'I may be seventy-two but I am very active, as you know, and I want to travel a bit. I've got a life in Morlan and have good friends there.'

'Matthew means well, Ivy.' She sighs. 'You have to face up to it, though. You're eight years away from eighty. Few are able to live alone without any care as they become elderly.' Rachel beats the eggs vigorously. 'I thought you might prefer living with us – well, in your own annexe – rather than going into a care home.'

Ivy suddenly feels quite hot. 'Ah, so you've discussed a care home, too. Perhaps Matthew is keener on the price he'll get for the cottage than my welfare. Really, Rachel! That's so insensitive of you both.' She climbs down from the stool and says tightly, 'I think I'll have a lie down. I've got a bit of a headache.'

For a minute or so as Ivy wakes up, she thinks she's in her own bed at home. Looking at her phone, she sees that she has slept for over an hour. She sits on the end of the bed and feels guilty. She snapped at Rachel earlier and she admits reluctantly that they only have her welfare at heart. At least Matthew wants her near him, and it was wrong to suggest that he's after the money for the cottage. He's never mentioned that. She'll apologise to them both.

She has to stop being oversensitive. It's just that she wants to experience life before it's too late. Visit beautiful places, listen to the cadences of different languages, taste exotic foods, see sunsets on different shores. Even going to the classes on

Thursday nights have energised her, given her a new lease of life. As if on cue, her phone pings.

Summer messages her. *You didn't miss much last night. Only a few of us there. Filthy weather kept everyone but us diehards away. Feather was hinting about us needing to lose our inhibitions. She's cooking up something – God knows what! We missed you xxx.*

A broad smile spreads across Ivy's face.

Matthew gets home around six forty-five. He comes in to kiss Tabitha whilst Ivy reads her a story, *Lola the Llama*.

Ivy adopts an exaggerated voice, '"No, Mummy I don't want to eat broccoli-eee," said Lola.'

'Daddy! Daddy! You're home!' Tabitha yells.

'Tabitha, my little curly wurly girly,' Matthew says, and she jumps into his arms. 'Had a good day, Mum?'

'We went to the park, Daddy, and had crisps and ice cream.'

'No, you didn't,' Matthew says. 'You're not allowed them.' He rolls his eyes. 'Anyway, Tabs, it's time for bed. We're off to Bounce Kingdom tomorrow and you're having your tea party. You need to be fast asleep very soon.'

'Yay! Can I go on the big trampoline, Daddy?'

'We'll see if you're tall enough. Right, missus, bedtime.'

Ivy smiles. She likes to see Matthew like this with his daughter. It reminds her he has a fun side. He's a good father.

They eat at seven-thirty and the air is a little frosty at first, despite Ivy's profuse apologies.

Ivy spoons more of the butternut squash and chickpea curry on her plate. 'This is delicious, Rachel. You are clever. Do you follow a recipe?'

'I just use them as a guide and add my own twist.'

'I don't know how on earth you have time,' Ivy smiles. 'So, how was work, Matthew?'

'Stressful. One of our biggest clients is in Singapore. It has a hundred and sixty partners and nine hundred and fifty employees. Aiden has asked me to go out there next month. With any luck, Rach and Tabs can come out there for a couple of weeks if it falls in the summer holidays.'

'That will be nice,' Ivy says. She hasn't a clue what Matthew's real work involves but she knows it's very important and the salary is generous, otherwise they wouldn't be able to afford a house in such an affluent area. Ivy sips her Châteauneuf-du-Pape. 'This is a real treat. So smooth. I'll have to watch if we're up early for Bounc—'

'Oh my God, Mother. What the hell is that?' Matthew splutters. 'Is it a tattoo?'

'Matthew, watch it, this is a white tablecloth,' Rachel scolds, although she stares wide-eyed at Ivy's wrist.

'Do you like it?' Ivy says coolly, amazed they have taken so long to spot it.

'Are you out of your mind? For God's sake. At your age! Seventy-two!'

'I wish you two would stop reminding me of my age. I am quite aware of how many years I've been on this earth.' She gulps her wine. 'Besides, age is just a number. Judi Dench had her first tattoo on her eighty-first birthday.'

'Tell me you're not having another,' Matthew pales. 'What on earth is it? A butterfly?'

'No, it's a bluebird.' Ivy runs her finger over it. 'It symbolises freedom.'

'Has Tabitha seen it?' he asks.

'I don't think so. I'm sure she won't be corrupted by it, though.'

Matthew's lip curls. 'Well, I think it's cheap, distasteful.' Rachel touches his thigh, a warning he's gone too far perhaps.

'It's lucky, then, it's me that has a tattoo and not you.' Ivy pushes her plate away. 'You've never been very open-minded, Matthew. Besides, if you think that's cheap, what will you think when you hear I've joined a pole dancing exercise class?'

'Didn't I tell you there was something wrong, Rach?' He turns to his wife. 'I don't know if you're having some sort of late life crisis or—'

'Or what, Matthew – early onset dementia? Really! It's an exercise class.' Ivy is exasperated. 'I thought you might be happy your mother is finally living her life and having a bit of fun.'

'It's not normal behaviour, Mother. That's all I have to say about it.' And he clams up.

The atmosphere is strained after this, all three of them eating their carrot cake in silence. Rachel attempts conversation several times, 'Tabitha is so excited about tomorrow. She's only been to Bounce Kingdom once before . . .' Her voice trails off.

Ivy pleads a return of her headache and takes herself off to bed. After reading for a while, she turns off the light. It's going to be a long weekend, she thinks, as the room is plunged into darkness.

Chapter Twenty

Summer

'Ted tired,' Nia holds her teddy bear aloft for Summer to inspect. She picks the bear the and examines him.

'He does look tired,' she says. 'Maybe you're tired too?'

Nia thinks about this for a second, before shaking her head, but Summer knows better.

'I think you are. And I'm not surprised.' She takes a wipe from the kitchen cupboard and cleans Nia's sticky hands and feet. A combination of Play-Doh and glitter glue in a botched art project on the living room floor, which involved running around on a big sheet of paper with painted soles and palms. 'Zoe's going to put you to bed tonight.'

She's surprised this doesn't get a bit more of a reaction. Nia had taken to Zoe when she babysat for the first time last week. Summer didn't know whether to be offended or not with how well she'd seemed to cope without her. She should be grateful really.

'Will you miss Mummy?' She knows she shouldn't be fishing for compliments from a two-year-old, but a week of kiddy-conversation has reduced Summer to this.

Nia shrugs, distracted by a bird at the window.

'What about Ted? Will Ted miss Mummy?' This time Nia nods furiously, and Summer takes that as the reassurance she needs.

She hears the doorbell ring as Zoe arrives. Summer rushes to the door as though welcoming a celebrity guest. Zoe may as well be. She handled the kids with such ease, Aled should be ashamed of himself.

In fact, Summer is planning to keep Zoe on as a babysitter for pole dancing classes even when Aled is back next week. He won't be complaining when he sees the bouncy-boobed, blonde-locked Zoe. Maybe Summer should be worried about the potential of a clichéd affair between the dad and the nanny, but she is just too relieved to have some help around the house.

'How are you?'

'You're not dressed for class yet?' Zoe says in dismay. 'Here, let me take this little rascal, and you go and get ready.'

'Thank you,' Summer exhales, passing Jordan on to her.

An absolute saint.

She races upstairs, noticing the ache in her thighs that's still present after last week's class. Feather Starr really gave them a workout on those poles; Summer feels she gained about thirty thigh muscles and lost several layers of skin trying to cling on to the pole like a frog. It came naturally to Meg, but the rest of them struggled.

Summer puts her workout clothes on, hoping she can get away with the burgeoning hole at the waistband of her leggings. She really needs some new stuff. Her bra is small and pinches at her swollen boobs. Maybe when Aled's home, she can convince him to come shopping with her and the kids. She's usually too preoccupied with entertaining Nia and trying to manoeuvre the double buggy around tight clothes aisles to take time for herself. Aled will probably say they can't afford anything new, but he can't argue with this – Summer can now put her fist through the hole in the leggings.

She kisses both of her children goodbye, reminding Zoe that she's left enough breastmilk for Jordan, labelled in bottles in the fridge, then heads out.

These nights are the highlight of Summer's week. She adores both of her utterly scrumptious children, but this night of freedom, with music and movement and adult female company, really makes up for the other six where an occasional glass of wine on the sofa after bedtime is the best she can hope for.

'Welcome, everyone!' Feather Starr is shouting at the front of the class. 'Glad to see we have everyone back this week.'

Summer is pleased to see Ivy, home from Bristol.

'How was the trip?' She squeezes her arm as she joins the group of three women in the hall.

'Eventful, to say the least. I'll tell you later,' Ivy warns the women. 'Catch up in the pub later?'

'Of course,' Gwen and Meg chorus.

'I have the wonderful Zoe in my house until nine, so I am definitely up for it,' Summer smiles.

The women start with a warm-up, then a recap of last week's moves.

'Who can do the fireman?' Feather Starr shouts to the crowd. The women look to Meg, who appears suddenly nervous.

'I can't remember it,' she says now, her arms crossed in front of her body. It's not like Meg to be shy, but Summer supposes she wouldn't remember her own name if she was the one called out in front of the class like this.

'Go on,' the other women encourage, to much head shaking from Meg, all apart from Gwen.

'I'll have a go,' she says, raising her voice. Summer's surprised by this. Gwen isn't usually so keen to demonstrate her moves for the class. And she doesn't remember Gwen especially mastering the fireman. She looks at Meg, who smiles appreciatively at Gwen. It's kind of Gwen to step up for her.

Gwen does a poor demonstration of the fireman, wrapping both legs around the pole.

'Well done,' Feather says with insincerity, before doing the move herself like a circus performer.

'Does that woman have a spine?' Ivy says to Summer in admiration.

'She can't possibly,' Summer agrees.

'I'll give you some time to try it in your groups.' Feather Starr puts music on, and the women regroup around their pole.

'It's your turn, Ivy,' Gwen says. 'Let's show these youngsters how it's done.'

Ivy hooks one leg around the pole, then the other, staying perfectly in place while the muscles in her arm tense around the metal.

'God, Ivy, you make it look easy,' Summer says, in genuine admiration. 'Are you sure you haven't done this in a former life? You weren't even here last week.'

'Or had some secret youth as a pole dancer you haven't told us about, you dark horse?' Gwen joins in. Summer notices Meg is still a little quiet. She encourages the others to try again first.

Summer feels equally as hopeless as the first time she did the move, but she enjoys the time they spend giggling and egging each other on.

Before Meg can have another go, Feather Starr informs them they'll be running through the routine again. Summer lags behind the others as they remember and perform the steps naturally. A few women in the class are behind, with her, and they catch each other's eyes conspiratorially.

'Let's add a few more steps this time,' Feather says, then demonstrates how to end the routine with a spin and a drop-bend at the hips, which segues into the flamingo position on the pole. Meg's back to her goddess-like performance again, showing off the moves with ease.

The hour passes quickly, and Feather gathers the women at the end of the class.

'Some of you might remember when I mentioned I'd be shaking things up over the coming weeks,' she says. Summer had forgotten this, but the dreaded words come back to her now. Something about *loosening up* and *embracing inner goddesses*. Summer doesn't think she has one. She feels so tired now, and her whole body is sore, especially her boobs.

'Well, next Thursday, instead of a class, we're going to go on a little field trip. It won't be far, but it will be a fun exercise for you, and I think you'll appreciate it. Meet me here at nine-thirty.' She says the words with mystery.

'Under cover of darkness,' Summer whispers to Meg, who looks pale with terror now.

'I wonder what it is?' Meg says.

'Hopefully going to the pub again,' Summer tries to reassure her.

'I hope it's not some bonding exercise where we have to fall backwards into each other's arms,' Gwen says as they walk out.

'It'll be something like that. Or build a campfire and tell two truths and one lie,' Ivy supposes.

The women get to the pub, and Summer's pleased to see that Gwen leaves her car behind in the hall car park.

'What's everyone having?' Meg says, before rushing off to order. The others take up their usual seat in the corner.

'Do you think there's something going on there?' Ivy nods her head towards the bar, where Meg is chatting to Rhys, the bartender. They're leaning their heads closer than they need to – the bar isn't that busy – and Rhys says something that makes Meg laugh uproariously.

'She said he likes someone else, but I'm not sure,' Summer says.

'She's got her new guy, anyway. I think Rhys likes her, though. That's obvious,' Gwen says. 'He should see her in class.'

'She could give Feather Starr a run for her money,' Ivy smiles.

Meg rejoins them carrying a bottle of rosé and four wine glasses.

'Ivy, tell us about Bristol,' she prompts as she sits across from them, probably a strategy to stop them probing about Rhys.

'It was lovely to have some time with my Tabby.' Ivy gets her phone out and shows them a picture of her beautiful granddaughter, licking a chocolate ice cream cone, the brown liquid trailing down her arm.

'She's gorgeous,' the women coo.

'I hope Nia keeps her blonde curls like that,' Summer smiles. 'I don't know where she's got them from.'

'Of course, I'm not allowed to call her Tabby,' Ivy shakes her head now. 'It's strictly Tabitha or Tabs for short if they're feeling agreeable, and no ice cream or artificially-sweetened food, according to my daughter-in-law.'

The women laugh and Ivy frowns. 'I shouldn't say this. I'm being bitchy now.'

'Hardly,' Gwen encourages.

'I'm still feeling a bit frosty towards my son. He had the cheek to tell Tabitha I was moving up to live with them.'

'What!' Summer asks, dismayed that Ivy could be pulled from the group.

'He thinks I'm struggling without Jim. Said I must be having some kind of late-life crisis,' Ivy takes a large gulp of the wine that's been handed to her by Meg and thanks her.

'Ugh, men,' Gwen sighs.

'He thinks the tattoo and the pole dancing are evidence of it.'

'I hope you told him where to go,' Meg says in between her sips.

'He's not used to being told, that's the trouble,' Ivy admits. 'Anyway, I missed the class last week and our weekly catch-up. It's such a tonic.'

'I was thinking that earlier,' Summer agrees 'It's just a bit of fun and frivolity, but it's the only night a week I feel myself again. Aled says it's the one night I'm not grumpy with him on the phone.'

'After solo-parenting all day, I'd be surprised if you weren't grumpy,' Gwen says. 'I was so glad when the baby stage was done, although toddlers are even more exhausting.'

'I think I've been worse lately, though.' Summer thinks about the last few weeks, realising it's true. She's happy as anything with Nia, then one thing sets her off and she feels the world is ending, like earlier when Nia spilt some juice on the carpet. Summer had nearly cried, yet the painting fiasco later on was no drama. 'I'm going through mood swings worse than a teenager.'

'Me too,' Meg smiles. 'It's not your time of the month, is it?'

'No,' Summer says, then sips her wine, questioning whether it should be. Jordan is only a few months old, and her periods were all over the place after Nia. The last period was six . . . seven weeks ago; Aled's been home twice since then. Was that normal?

'How did you leave things with Matthew, anyway?' Gwen asks, moving the conversation on, but Summer's too distracted to listen.

Mood swings. No period. The ability to fall asleep at any moment.

The first sign with the last two was the sore boobs, but Summer's boobs are always sore these days when she has a tiny human pulling and draining them every day like she's cattle. Maybe she hasn't noticed it as much, but maybe this bra isn't tight and uncomfortable for no reason.

Maybe she's pregnant.

Chapter Twenty-One

Gwen

The Mariners is packed and another group elbow their way inside. Tourists, by the looks of it. 'Unchained Melody' is playing on the jukebox and Gwen remembers how she used to love this. It was out when she met Gareth. She was only nineteen. She watched *Ghost* at least a dozen times, Gareth more than willing to indulge her in those days. She'd even had her hair cut like Demi Moore but looked more like an eleven-year-old schoolboy than achieving the sex symbol chic she'd hoped. She still hated photos from that time. And without fail, she cried at the end as Patrick Swayze floated to heaven.

Sipping her wine, Gwen says, 'God, it's been a shitty couple of weeks.' She flushes when she realises she's said it out loud. 'I'm sorry, I don't mean to dampen everyone's mood.'

Ivy casts her a sympathetic look, 'Don't apologise, Gwen. You're entitled. You've had a horrible shock with Gareth.'

'It's not just the cheating,' Gwen says, 'he's got himself into a mess financially. Or I should say *us* in a financial mess. We're almost bankrupt. I doubt I'll be able to keep the house.' She gulps her wine.

Ivy touches Gwen's arm, 'I'm so sorry.'

'Fuck!' gasps Meg.

'God, you're well rid of him,' Summer announces. 'I'd barbecue Aled's testicles and feed them to the dog if he treated me the way Gareth has you.'

'Remind me not to cross you,' Meg says.

'What are you going to do?' asks Summer.

'I have no idea. Find a job, a house. No doubt some people in the village will love this.'

Ivy frowns. 'Don't worry about other people, Gwen. I've done too much of that myself. Hold your head up. You've done nothing wrong.'

'Ivy's right,' says Summer.

'You can always stay with me,' Ivy offers.

Gwen smiles gratefully at Ivy. 'I couldn't impose on you like that. It's telling the girls that's the awful bit. They know their father has been having an affair but nothing about the finances. Jasmine is home tomorrow. She's hoping I'll help her with buying a new place in Southampton. They'll be devastated.'

'You'll get through this,' Ivy reassures her. 'I know it's tough now, really tough, but you're stronger than you think.'

Gwen fights hard to keep back the tears, feeling none of the confidence Ivy seems to have in her. She could never have imagined confiding in other women like this. She never really knew how important female friendship was. Her fault, of course. 'I don't think I'd have got through the last couple of weeks without the classes and you three.'

'It's funny, isn't it?' says Summer. 'I feel like we've known each other forever.' She glances quickly at her watch. 'Shit, it's quarter past. I told Zoe I'd be back by nine.' She stands up, draining her glass. 'Anyone else dreading what Feather Starr has in store for next week?'

'Totally!' says Meg.

They drift off when Summer goes and, when Ivy and Meg leave her halfway up the hill, Gwen is left alone with her thoughts. Breathless, she turns to look at the sea. Swathes of ochre streak the sky as the sun sinks into a sea on fire. She's always used the view as currency. The house is worth a fortune because of the sea view. Now, she doesn't want to lose that daily sight of the ever-changing sea, the headland stretching out its protective arm. When they settle their debts, will she be able to afford something, a deposit on a place in Morlan? It's so humiliating but in her heart of hearts, she feels perhaps she deserves this. Like it's karma of sorts, for feeling she's better than everyone else.

When she nears the house, she can see all the lights on. Lydia is probably in her bedroom but the downstairs is lit up like Blackpool Illuminations. Well, that will have to change soon for all of them. They'll never be able to take money for granted again.

After kissing Lydia goodnight, she has a bath by candlelight, watching the winking lights of the village below. Her head is so crowded with thoughts of the future and what she'll do that sleep eludes her until at least dawn, when she lapses into fitful and broken slumber.

Gwen spends the morning cleaning. She's had to let Paula go, making some excuse about her being ill to Lydia, who's shocked

189

at the sight of her mother changing beds and scouring the family bathroom. Not that she offers to help. Bleaching the toilet bowl and scrubbing the shower quell Gwen's embattled mind.

Jasmine is due to arrive at lunchtime and Gwen prepares a salmon and asparagus quiche, homemade for a change. She used to love cooking but has got out of the habit, preferring to buy from Marks and Sparks or having meals out.

As Gwen brushes the pastry with an egg, she wonders how she'll tell Jasmine and Lydia. Jasmine left home when she went to university at eighteen, then went travelling. She's building her career in HR and doesn't earn that much. Her boyfriend Rupert works for the charity Teach First. She's always used her parents as a safety net, living the life of Riley as a student, kitting out her accommodation with stuff from Barker and Stonehouse, not IKEA like normal students. She had a brand-new white Audi A1 for her eighteenth birthday. Then there were the skiing holidays, summer breaks in the Maldives. Yes, they were spoilt rotten.

Boris's tail curls around her calf and he miaows insistently. 'Yes, Boris, even you have been spoilt.'

Lydia has only just got out of bed when Jasmine pulls into the driveway. There's no love lost between them and Lydia flops onto the sofa, showing no enthusiasm for her sister's arrival.

'Jas!' Gwen envelops her eldest daughter in a warm hug. 'You look gorgeous.' She's wearing a long floral green midi dress which suits her statuesque build. 'I love the hair.'

'Do you like it? I had the highlights done last week. That salon is super expensive, but worth every penny. Ooh, that smells nice,' she says, dropping her weekend bag in the hallway and heading to the kitchen.

'I've made a quiche. Lydia, come and say hello to your sister,' Gwen says. 'Was the journey OK? You must be shattered.'

'It wasn't too bad, apart from Newport. It's always a bloody nightmare there. What about you, Mum? How are you feeling about everything?'

'Come on, sit in the kitchen. I'll put the food out and we can have a proper chat over lunch.' Jasmine and Lydia exchange glances. Gwen tries to lighten the atmosphere. 'I've been slaving away at the cooker all morning for you two.'

At the table, Jasmine regales them with tales of her job and her creepy boss and the parties she's been to.

'So, what did you think of the apartment, Mum? Isn't it marvellous? It's on the top floor with views over the city. There's parking underneath, though. It's so modern.' She reaches for her phone, scrolling through the images. 'Did you have a good look when I sent them?'

Gwen nods, taking a sip of water. 'Of course I did, darling. It looks really nice.'

'Honestly, the estate agent says we're getting a bargain.'

Lydia snorts, 'They all say that.'

'What do you know about it?' Jasmine shoots her a look. 'Anyway, Mum, we've put the offer in. It's asking for bids over three hundred thousand. Rupert's parents are able to help us a bit with the deposit, so we were kind of hoping you and Dad might be able to go half. I mean, his parents aren't that well off. His father has retired now, and they've just bought a place in France.'

Gwen feels her stomach flip as she struggles to swallow a piece of quiche.

'Oh, God, here's me wittering on about my life,' Jasmine says, 'and you're going through this awful thing with Dad. I can't believe what he's done to you. Are you really OK, Mum?'

'Now you show an interest,' says Lydia. 'About bloody time. It's been horrible for Mum. You haven't been here, but I've heard her crying in the night.'

Gwen feels guilty, promising to be more discreet in future. 'I'm OK, you two. It's a shock, but I am handling it.'

'And with Lynne, too. It's so horrible, Mum,' Jasmine says. 'If I hadn't been so busy at work, I'd have been here.'

'Look, there's nothing you could have done, Jas. Your father has been a fool.'

'I hate him,' says Lydia. 'I don't want to see him again. He has been ringing but I haven't answered.'

'He's still Dad,' Jasmine says. 'I'm angry at him and I have told him. He still loves us, though.'

It crosses Gwen's mind that Jasmine might change her mind when she knows the full story and that there'll be no money forthcoming for her deposit. 'Let's have coffee,' Gwen says. 'I need to talk to you both about something.'

Gwen arranges some biscuits on a plate and they sit on the patio. It's quite warm outside with a promise of summer in the air.

As Gwen sits down, she braces herself. 'I have been to see my solicitor about the business, the houses we rent out and this place, of course. There's a lot to sort out with a divorce. And to be straight with you, we're in financial trouble. Your father

192

has made some bad investments. I was kept in the dark about them.' Gwen looks at her daughters' faces and sees the horror reflected in them. 'The long and the short is that there is very little money left. Almost nothing when the debts are paid.'

'We can keep this house, though, Mum?' Lydia says.

'Little money?' Jasmine says at the same time.

'No, I'm afraid we can't keep this house. We owe too much. It looks as if the business will fold, and we'll have to sell as much as we can to pay everything. I'll have to look for something small, modest. Hopefully in Morlan. And I'll look for a job. Although at fifty-two, it might be difficult, but I have got my bookkeeping qualifications . . .'

'So, you won't be able to help with the deposit for the apartment?' Jasmine asks.

It strikes Gwen that Jasmine's first thought is her own situation rather than the repercussions for her mother and sister, for all of them. Lydia, often given to histrionics, is unnervingly quiet. Shock, Gwen assumes.

'I can't believe it,' Lydia says at last. 'I hate him.' This time Jasmine doesn't contradict her and Gwen feels the same.

Lydia looks back at the kitchen, 'I love this house. I don't want to move.'

'Neither do I,' Gwen says quietly.

'What if I try to get a job?' Lydia asks. 'The Mariners are always looking for bar people. I could work it around school.'

Gwen kisses her head. She doesn't tell her that a month's wages won't cover the electricity bill for The Haven for a week. It has hardly turned out to be a haven, Gwen thinks. Gareth had wanted to call the place Morlan Manor when they first moved in, but she had put her foot down at the pomposity of such a ridiculous name.

'Did you honestly not have an inkling about what he was doing, Mum?' Jasmine asks.

'Well, the affair was not a surprise, to tell the truth. Well, the first time he did it, yes.' Both girls look aghast. 'The money, though, is different. I was doing the books. I should have known but your father is clever. He hid things.'

'Stupid, you mean,' Jasmine says.

'I don't know how long he's been burying his head in the sand. A long time, I should think. He must have known it was going to catch up with him finally.' They fall silent for a moment. Gwen continues, 'I wonder what Lynne will do when she finds out.'

'Dump him, probably,' Lydia says.

They all laugh. 'That's some consolation, at least,' Gwen says. 'We'll survive. The Three Musketeers.' But there's no conviction in her voice.

Chapter Twenty-Two

Meg

'Are you sure you don't need me today?' Meg asks, already knowing the answer.

'Of course not. Go and enjoy yourself,' Hannah clucks. 'You look gorgeous. Do you need a jacket, though?'

'I've got my denim one.'

'I mean a real jacket, it's not that warm out there today.'

'It's June, Nan,' Meg says, aware she sounds like a teenager.

'I'm only saying. Your parents want me to look after you.'

Meg decides she should leave before Hannah starts suggesting coat options. *Must start looking for flats*, she tells herself. Summer is only one year older than her, but she has a house, a husband, and two kids. Meg is starting to wonder if she'll ever be treated as someone that's finished puberty.

'Be safe today. I'll text you when I'm on my way back,' Hannah shouts.

'Enjoy the play,' Meg calls. Hannah's going to see *A Midsummer Night's Dream* in Llansteffan Castle with some friends in the village on a coach trip.

She checks her appearance in the hallway mirror, pleased

195

that the new dress she ordered online fits. There are absolutely no clothes shops in Morlan, or anywhere nearby that would cater for anyone under the age of sixty. Apart from the odd charity shop find, Meg has to resort to online shopping. It's like playing size roulette at the best of times, but Meg has learnt she has to be extra careful to get something that will fit around the stoma bag and the protective belt she wears. Sizing up works, but then the rest of her looks a shapeless blob. Another post-stoma problem the hospital didn't warn her about.

Luckily, the lilac flowery dress she ordered for the date with Josh is perfect. Floaty but flattering, just what she wanted. And not too dressy with the denim jacket and trainers.

She shuts the door behind her and exhales. It will be Josh's first trip to Morlan, and Meg is inexplicably nervous about showing him her hometown. She wants him to see how special it is, and plans to walk him around the village to show off the best sights – the sea view and maybe even the lagoon. On the other hand, Meg knows everyone in Morlan and everyone has an embarrassing story to tell about her or her nan. She hopes seeing her walking with Josh won't draw too much attention. They'd held hands when she met up with him last week, and although Meg loves the public display of affection, she has a feeling she'll be more self-conscious in Morlan.

As she walks the main road to the village centre, she passes beneath the winding driveway and steel gates to Gwen Vimpany's house. Meg looks at it there, perched above the village with the best view of the sea and the private landscaping. All glass and modern lines. She knows it draws envious eyes from the villagers, and that Gwen and her family probably enjoyed that, but Meg can't help feeling sad for her friend.

It will cause quite a stir when it comes up for sale, and poor Gwen won't be able to hide what a shitty time she's going through. Being cheated on and then losing everything you own. Meg can't even imagine what that must feel like. At least her illness has crept up on her over years, the surgery a gradual adjustment that she can hide. To have such a public downfall must be excruciating. She's glad that Gwen has her, Summer and Ivy. They'll have to think of something they can do to cheer her up.

As Meg is lost in thought, she hears a car door slam up ahead. She's surprised to see Josh get out. He notices her at the same time and a big grin spreads on his face.

'Hello, you,' he says, making Meg's insides tingle.

'Fancy seeing you here.' She goes to hug him, and enjoys how he squeezes her, how his hands linger on her arms as she pulls away.

'You look gorgeous. Am I all right to park here? I don't want to be booked outside someone's house.'

'You're fine. There's no parking wardens in Morlan. The worst you'll get is an angry message on the village Facebook group.'

He falls into step beside her as they drift towards the village centre.

'I love a village Facebook group,' Josh laughs. 'People get so angry about nothing.'

'Someone let off fireworks at 9 p.m. last weekend,' Meg says. 'You would have thought there'd been a murder, the amount of angry messages.'

'I bet the pole dancing classes get some attention on there?' Josh asks. Meg had told him about the petition and the angry article in the newspaper.

'God, yes. There's almost a daily tally of signatures on the petition. Every day going up by one. It's hilarious.' She can laugh about it but she just hopes it doesn't go any further. 'Tons of speculation about what goes on in classes too.'

They happen to pass the village hall. 'In fact, that's the hall where we have the class every week.'

Josh pauses to take it in. 'So that's the wild sex club?' She hits his arm playfully. Josh grabs her hand and puts it in his. Meg hopes her palm isn't too sweaty, but the warmth of his feels delicious against hers. And she decides that she doesn't give a damn if anyone sees her.

'How come you're off on a Friday, then? I thought GPs were weekday people.'

'I don't finish until seven the other four nights of the week. I get Fridays off to make up for the long days,' he explains as they walk.

'How are you finding it?'

'Throughout my training I've always been supervised. It's nice in some ways, now I'm a fully-fledged GP, to have the independence of working on my own. But terrifying in other ways.'

Meg laughs. She likes a guy that's modest, willing to admit when he's out of his depth.

'Of course, I get told by my patients that GPs are lazy and have done nothing throughout the pandemic, but apart from that it's great.'

'That's true, though, isn't it?' She says, joining his sarcasm. She hopes he doesn't speak to Hannah anytime soon, or else he'll get a lecture about the phone queues to make an appointment with the Morlan GP.

'I don't really remember the two years of sitting at home rejecting people in need and watching Netflix, but then I must be mistaken,' Josh smiles. 'What's the plan for today, then?'

Meg encounters her first spectator. Rhys is walking in the opposite direction across the street from them. It's the first time he's known her to have a guy, and any hope she can have of going unnoticed is dashed when his eyes light up. She tries to send him daggers across the street, and he must get the message, not before he puts his hands together in a heart shape at chest level.

'Who's that?' Josh asks, noticing Rhys.

'Just a friend from school,' Meg says, pulling him away quickly. 'We're going to Calon Café for lunch, then a walk around the beach and lagoon.'

'I hope that's the best restaurant in Morlan?'

'Try the only restaurant in Morlan, unless you count fish and chips from the van on the beach on a Friday night, or The Mariners, Morlan's answer to Wetherspoons.'

'I trust you,' Josh whistles.

They order fish finger sandwiches, a bowl of chips to share and two beers.

'I'll probably regret eating this,' Meg says, once their food arrives in the little café.

'Are you a bit of a health freak?' Josh asks, squirting tomato ketchup onto his plate and off the side. 'Oops.'

'Aah,' Meg starts. How much to tell him? 'A little bit. I've had some . . . issues . . . with my digestion in the last few years.' She doesn't know whether to reveal more. She had built herself up to tell him today, reasoning that he seemed sensible enough not to worry about the stoma bag. He is a GP, for goodness' sake. But now the opportunity is here, Meg is very tempted to keep shtum.

'Anything serious?' he asks now, taking a bite of his sandwich. 'Mmm this is delicious.'

'Kind of,' she begins, then stalls by biting into her own sandwich. 'I've had to have surgery.'

'A mate of mine does gastric surgery,' Josh says now. 'He tells me the best stories. You wouldn't believe what they find in people's colons. Twelve LED lightbulbs were my favourite. Part of a string from a Christmas tree.'

Meg smiles thinly, feeling unsure of herself. She doesn't know if this diversion about his friend is meant to make her feel better, but it doesn't. Can he sense her tension? What if he just doesn't want to hear what she's got to say? She definitely doesn't want to tell him now.

'That's . . . strange.'

'Not as weird as what the A&E guys hear of people *falling* on to, arse first.' He smiles now, seemingly unaware of her discomfort.

'I bet,' Meg's voice is faint, and she hides behind her sandwich.

'The angel from the top of a Christmas tree, whilst we're on the festive topic,' Josh laughs. 'The one perk of my job is the crazy stories. Sorry, we probably shouldn't talk about this while we're eating.'

Meg feels simultaneously disheartened that he hasn't listened to her, and relieved that she hasn't had to talk about it. Josh probably isn't in the mood for heavy conversation. Their relationship is still early, they are still sounding each other out. Keeping things light is for the best. Besides, he probably doesn't realise how serious her story is. Best that she hasn't said anything.

'You must have some great patients?' she asks now, wanting to move the topic along. Meg eats and listens half-heartedly. Has she done the right thing in not pushing the subject of her illness? Is she being cowardly? She's probably just overthinking it.

'Well, we may as well go the whole hog and order the brownie for dessert,' Josh says, eyeing up the blackboard of specials above Meg's head.

'Definitely.' She tries to sound more enthusiastic. 'We need our energy for this afternoon.'

'What's this afternoon?' Josh lowers his tone.

'A walk, nothing else,' Meg says, knowing he wants something saucier.

Things grow easy again between them as they finish up in Calon Café, and Josh pays the bill.

'Thank you so much,' Meg says. 'It was definitely my turn, though. I feel I owe you something now.'

'Just spending the day with you is payment enough.' He takes her hand again as they head out into the sunshine. True to her plan, Meg walks Josh down the narrow path to the beach, where a paved track parallels the sand, running the length of it and up the hill to Morlan lagoon.

'This is beautiful,' Josh says, showing the appropriate awe she'd hoped for.

'I'm glad you think so.'

'I can see why you wouldn't want to leave here.'

'I'm not sure about that. I love Morlan but I do want to see more of the world. I'd like to study journalism one day.' Meg hopes he doesn't ask more questions about that, why she hasn't been to university yet, but again it's glossed over.

'Well, it really is beautiful. My parents think I'm nuts for moving so far away and to such a remote place.'

'Are they still in Reading?' Meg asks.

'Yes, they'll never leave the city. I always felt I never quite belonged, though, somehow. Even though my family was there, I longed for the summers we spent on the Welsh coast. It got under my skin. It seemed right when I got into Cardiff Med School. A hint to move further west. And then I met you.'

He stops Meg in her tracks, pulls her closer. A couple walking in the other direction pass by, and they have to step off the path. Josh places his hands on her waist. Meg is all too aware of how close his hands are to the stoma bag, but doesn't move them, not wanting to draw attention to that area.

'You really are beautiful, you know that,' he says. It's been far too long since she's heard those words, and Meg decides to forget the stoma bag. She allows Josh to kiss her, and enjoys the sensation of his lips on hers, his hand tangled in her hair. She moves her body closer, relaxing into him. She really feels like a teenager now, snogging on the beach path in broad daylight, but Meg loves it. The beer with lunch has gone to her head, and the dizzying feeling of Josh's attraction is wonderful.

They pull apart at the sound of footsteps nearby. It's Ivy, much to Meg's dismay.

'Good afternoon,' Ivy greets them both, smiling as if she hasn't just witnessed their teenaged antics.

'Afternoon,' Josh smiles.

'Ivy, this is Josh,' Meg introduces, in lieu of knowing what else to do. 'Ivy is in the pole dancing classes with me.'

'We're all in awe of this one,' Ivy tells Josh. Meg feels herself blush, ridiculous as it is. 'You should see her.'

'I'd love to,' Josh squeezes her waist.

'We were just heading to the lagoon for a walk,' Meg tells Ivy, hoping she takes the hint.

'I'm running errands for my next-door neighbour. Told her I'd pick up some milk from your grandmother. It gives me a good excuse to pop into the antiques shop next door.'

'Let me know if you find anything,' Meg waves her off, then steers Josh purposefully. She can't risk kissing in the open here again, much as it amuses Josh.

'This is what I love about Welsh villages,' he says, following her.

'It's what I hate about Morlan,' Meg laughs. The lagoon is Caribbean blue in the reflection of the sky, and tucked into the cliff in its own private cove. You wouldn't know it was there if you weren't a resident.

'You're lucky it's a school day or else this place would be crammed with teens,' Meg tells him.

'Getting up to no good?'

'That's about the measure of it.'

'That's what I plan to do,' Josh says. He pulls Meg towards

a wooden bench at one end of the lenticular-shaped pool of water. They are sheltered here, but Meg still feels self-conscious.

She lets Josh kiss her, though, and tries to forget herself. He's perfectly gentle, teasing her lips with the tip of his tongue. She feels a flicker of desire and tells herself to relax. Josh puts his hand on the outer edge of Meg's thigh and runs it slowly up her leg. It does feel good. She pushes back against him with her mouth. It feels nice to be so desired, and to fancy him equally. She needs this.

'I could do this forever,' she moans, and Josh takes it as encouragement. He runs his hand further up her leg, over her hip, and to her waist.

Meg's instant alarm bells raise. She doesn't want him to discover what's there. Not like this, not without warning him first. She slips her arm under his, as though she's grabbing for his hip, and manages to move him away, back down to her leg. She hopes it's subtle, but the kiss now feels mechanical. Meg's thoughts whirr too much for her to enjoy it like she did a moment ago.

It seems Josh hasn't noticed the change. She pulls back, for a second, pretends to check to see if they have company. The lagoon is quiet.

'I wish we could go somewhere more private,' he says.

'Me too,' Meg lies. She doesn't want him getting any more handsy. She's treading a murky line here with Josh, wanting to satisfy him, but wanting him to keep clear of the danger areas on her body.

'Come here.' He kisses her again before she can stop him. His hands are back where they shouldn't be. She wishes he wouldn't go for the waist. He doesn't seem to notice anything is up. Without warning, he lifts Meg's legs and scoops them on to his lap. She can feel how stiff he is through his jeans. This position is less comfy, but it's slightly harder for him to grab her waist. His hand naturally reaches around her back now, to safety.

Meg doesn't know how to stop this. She's consenting, but certainly not comfortable. 'Josh,' she tries to say, but he's reached up her back, pulling her close. She settles for, 'Not here.'

'No, you're right,' he says. Thank God he's listening. Meg lifts her legs off his and moves apart on the beach. He exhales, smiles at her sudden bashfulness.

'Maybe we could go back to yours?'

Oh, God. He wants to continue this.

Meg cringes inwardly as she says the words, 'I can't. Sorry, my grandmother is there.' She can't remember if she told him about the play, but the disappointment from him is palpable. She doesn't know how he will react. She worries he's going to be angry, that she's going to lose him.

'I wish we were in St Davids,' he sighs now, but smiles at the same time. 'Don't worry about it.'

'Sorry,' she says again.

'I'll just have to keep waiting for another time,' he shrugs.

'It'll come,' Meg says now, eager to please.

'It better had,' Josh grins. 'Sorry, I don't mean to pressure you.'

She's relieved he's said that. 'You didn't,' she reassures, although she's felt pressured ever since that first kiss. 'I want this too.'

'I'm so glad to hear you say that,' he says now, and kisses Meg lightly. She kisses him back now, eager, but unsure why.

Josh ends the kiss this time, stares out at the still water, their only company a seagull overhead.

'Do you fancy another drink in the pub?' she asks now.

'I'd better not. I'm driving back and I'm up early tomorrow for an extra shift,' Josh gets up and they start to walk back. Meg finds she chatters loudly as they stroll, babbling to fill the silence. She can't tell how Josh feels about her. Wouldn't he stay longer if he really liked her?

'Should we do something next weekend? We've got some weird group bonding thing with the pole dancing class on Thursday night. I don't know what it is yet.' She talks while Josh listens politely.

'I'll have to see about next weekend,' he says as he gets to his car. 'My parents might be visiting.'

'Sounds nice,' Meg smiles. Is he going to ask her to join? Like he did with his friends?

'If not, then that would be nice,' he says. He unlocks the car from his pocket, then turns to Meg. She wobbles from one foot to the other, unsure how to end this strange date.

'Great, maybe see you then,' she says.

Josh kisses her again. A peck on the cheek, French-style. She hooks a hand over his shoulder, then feels awkward, like she is his grandmother. She lets go quickly.

'Do you want a lift home?' he asks as he gets in the car.

'I'll walk, don't worry. Thank you, though.' The car's moving and Josh is gone, almost before she finishes her sentence.

Meg moves to head home but realises she doesn't want to go

there. She doesn't want the silence of the post office flat. She's confused and disappointed, and really needs some company.

Did she misread that whole situation? Or was she right, Josh really couldn't get away fast enough once she'd turned him down? Does he just want her for sex? She can't believe that is true; he doesn't seem like that kind of guy. She's met enough of them on Tinder to know. Josh is sensitive and caring and funny. And normal. He isn't that shallow, surely. He'd apologised for pressuring her at the lagoon. She already feels guilty for pushing him off.

Is that ridiculous? She knows she is a strong, independent woman and shouldn't feel guilty for protecting what she wants. But she likes Josh, and the foundations of their relationship are tentative. She hopes that's not the last she'll see of him. She should have just come clean about the stoma bag.

Meg is relieved the car park to The Mariners is empty. She pushes open the door, hoping she has the place to herself. Apart from Gwion Morgan in the corner, she does.

'What happened to the date?' Rhys asks as he sees Meg. She smiles. He is exactly who she wants to see now. The antidote to the uncomfortable afternoon she's had. Comfort food in a human.

'He had to get back for work,' she explains, wishing she believed it.

'At 5 p.m.? Is he a bouncer? He didn't look big enough for that,' Rhys teases.

'We can't all be built like a mountain.' She raises her eyebrow at his shape.

'Honed from pork scratchings and pale ale,' he says, patting his stomach.

'You should write your own diet book,' she jokes with him, already feeling her tension easing.

'How did you meet him, then?' Rhys asks. Meg suddenly doesn't want to talk about Josh, not to Rhys.

'A long story involving a trip to the hospital.'

'Best place to meet potential love interests,' Rhys says. 'Maybe I should try that?'

'I don't think Natalie Jones hangs out in hospitals.'

'Ouch,' he pats his chest, while taking two gin glasses out and placing them on the bar. 'I assume we're having gin?'

'You know me too well.' While Meg waits for him to pour, she wonders if that is the problem. The guys in Morlan she knows too well, and the others are a mystery.

'Watch it.' She throws a stale peanut, from a bowl on the counter at Rhys' head. 'I'll never make it home.'

'Please, this is a called a healthy measure.'

Meg feels a vibration from her pocket. She quickly checks it, feeling a combination of nerves and excitement when she sees Josh's name.

I'm sorry if I seemed weird today. I had a bit of a difficult time at work yesterday, been a bit off my game. It was great to see you. Parents are coming next weekend so maybe a weekday might be better? I'll think of something really nice – maybe a day out in the big city of Haverfordwest? Xxx

She reads it quickly, her mood soaring. Josh does want to see her again. And a day out no less.

'Lover boy?' Rhys asks.

Meg wishes she could stop grinning. 'Shut up.'

Chapter Twenty-Three

Ivy

Ivy is leaning over to look at the paint. There's a lovely Farrow & Ball colour called 'Sloe Blue' that will look fantastic on one wall in her bedroom and achieve that beach look she's after. She takes a quick snap on her iPhone so she can call into B&Q to find a similar colour at a cheaper price.

The woman behind the counter looks at Ivy over her glasses. 'Are you OK, there? Anything I can do to help?'

'I want to show my daughter this colour,' Ivy says, crossing her fingers. 'I can never make decisions myself.'

Ivy is in Narberth, in a lovely, shabby-chic furniture shop but the prices are eye-watering. Nooks and Crannies, who came into the WI a few weeks ago, is closed for lunch. Ivy's going to start on her bedroom this weekend and she's already bought some stripy blue bed linen. Last week, she rescued some driftwood from the beach, and she's been searching YouTube for how to make a frame for a mirror. She'll see if she can pick up some shells later. They'll make fantastic ornaments for her chest of drawers.

'Ivy? It is Ivy, isn't it?'

She turns around and a familiar face is in front of her, the name eluding her for a moment.

'It's uh, Bob. How are you?'

He's the 'date' Wendy and Martin had arranged for her the other week. Ivy feels a little awkward. He's a very pleasant man but it's embarrassing to think how obvious Martin and Wendy were in trying to set them up.

'Grand. Keeping busy. I'm making a doll's house for my granddaughter and wanted some paint. It's quite a project,' he laughs.

'It's really expensive here,' Ivy warns.

'Oh, Lord, I don't buy it here. This just gives me ideas and I buy paint somewhere cheaper.' Ivy suppresses a smile. 'Do you fancy a coffee now that you're in the rarefied air of Narberth?' he asks.

'I seem to remember Wendy describing Narberth as some sort of Sodom and Gomorrah,' Ivy says. She winks, 'Perhaps that's why I like it so much.' She picks up her shopping bag. 'A coffee would be lovely.'

'Let me get that,' Bob says. 'You'll have to indulge me, I'm an old-fashioned man in some ways. He thrusts out his arm for her to take it. 'I know a lovely little coffee shop around the corner that does fabulous homemade cakes. I highly recommend their coffee and walnut cake.'

Ivy loops her arm in Bob's rather awkwardly, but he's so good-natured that she can't take offence.

Once they're ensconced in the cosy window at Serendipity, they scan the menu.

'Well, I will have to try the coffee and walnut cake seeing as it comes with such a glowing review,' she teases.

'Hmm, as you're twisting my arm, I guess I'll have the same.'

Ivy notices his eyes when he smiles, the fact they're a brilliant blue. 'So, did you know what Wendy and Martin were up to when they invited us round for dinner?' she asks.

'Of course,' Bob laughs. 'Subtlety is not Wendy's superpower. She mentioned our widowed status at least a dozen times, as if it's guaranteed to draw us irresistibly together.'

'I'm so sorry,' Ivy rolls her eyes. 'I honestly had no idea. I thought it was strange she'd invited me over for dinner and she was so insistent.'

'I gathered, but if you don't mind me saying, I wasn't at all disappointed. I rather enjoyed the night and the chance to meet such a lovely woman.'

Ivy blushes. 'I have to say, I did enjoy hearing all about your travels.'

'I haven't been as much since Maggie passed. Twice, actually, and it was a disaster both times.' He stirs two sugars into his coffee. 'The first time I went away was about eighteen months afterwards, to Costa Rica. But it was too soon and I had a thoroughly miserable time.' He looks up. 'Sorry, I don't mean to be depressing.'

'What about the second time?' Ivy asks.

'Well, I went on one of those Rhine cruises. Beautiful. However, I'm not suited to pre-packaged, manufactured fun. It's just not my thing. I prefer exploring places off the usual tourist trail. I also prefer travelling with a companion. It's not the same if you have no one to share it with.'

After a pause, Ivy says, 'My Jim never liked travel. Nothing wrong with that, mind. He just never had itchy feet like me.' She sighs, 'There are so many places I want to see. Petra in Jordan is on my list. I know that's a Mecca for tourists, but it fascinates me.'

'The red rose city,' Bob says. 'Maggie and I went there about ten years ago. It's incredible. I'd definitely go again.'

'You said you worked with Martin,' Ivy says, changing the subject.

'Yes, at BT. Martin's a depot manager. I was in technical training. I enjoyed it and it paid the bills, funded our jaunts. I retired three years ago when I was sixty-five.'

'Oh, I thought you were the same age as me. Sorry, I didn't mean that you look as old as me.'

Bob laughs, 'I didn't come here to be insulted. How old are you?'

Ivy sips her tea and doesn't look him in the eye, embarrassed. 'Seventy-two.' The term 'cougar' flashes in her head, something she's heard on TV and she thinks how ridiculous it is.

'A very youthful seventy-two, if you don't mind me saying. You could certainly give Wendy a run for her money. And she's what, twenty years younger than you?'

'You are awful, Bob,' Ivy laughs.

'I like your tattoo, by the way.' He rolls his sleeve up over his bicep. 'Mine's of a sunset. It reminds me of Lake Wakatipu in New Zealand. Maggie and I spent a few days in a lodge there.'

Ivy smiles. They have such a lot in common, she acknowledges to herself. And he is attractive! Her face reddens.

They are quiet for a moment. 'I don't want you to think I'm still in grief. I'm not. The pain lessens in time, even if you never forget. I have moved on, though.' He sips his coffee. 'It's

212

much more recent for you, of course.'

Ivy nods, appreciating his sensitivity.

'Look, let's chat about something more cheerful,' Bob says.

'It really is a gorgeous cake.' Ivy balances a large piece on her fork and a walnut drops onto her plate. 'Oh dear!' she grins. 'Tell me how many grandchildren you have.'

'Three. My eldest son Jack has two sons, Oscar and Oliver. Adam has one daughter, Millie; she's the one desperate for the doll's house. She's five. The only girl in the family.'

'I bet she's spoilt rotten. A bit like my Tabitha.' Ivy suddenly looks at her watch. 'Gosh, the bus leaves in ten minutes. I'll have to go.' Bob is easy to talk to and an hour has flown by. She gathers her shopping.

'Do you drive, Ivy?'

'Yes, but I haven't got a car. I am thinking of getting one.'

Bob stands up. 'Let me take you back.'

'Honestly, there's no need,' Ivy says. 'The bus takes me right into Morlan. I've got a WI meeting later.'

'Well, if you won't let me take you back, come for lunch with me next week. I'll book somewhere in Fishguard and pick you up.'

'That would be lovely,' Ivy says. They exchange numbers and Ivy just makes the bus before it pulls away. The last hour or so with Bob has made Ivy feel quite heady. Is the lunch next week a date? She wants to see Bob again. Desperately. He's interesting and interested in her. It's so totally unexpected. She smiles as the bus heads out of town, her stomach filled with butterflies.

* * *

213

Later, Ivy walks into the village hall for the WI meeting. A historian is presenting a talk on the background of Pembrokeshire.

'Find out how Pembrokeshire was an important centre of Bronze and Iron Age culture. Evidence of tombs, cairns and hut circles abound in the county of Pembrokeshire. Come along to learn about megalithic remains found in Morlan itself. Local historian and retired university lecturer, Frank Abbott, will reveal all the exciting secrets that Pembrokeshire holds.' Ivy is quite interested – she's always enjoyed history.

In the foyer, a crowd is gathered around making no effort to enter the hall. Ivy can see a lone man sitting behind a table, Frank Abbott presumably, in the empty room. Several women have their backs to her. She can see Wendy, Sally, the treasurer Cynthia and several others she recognises.

Liz Pocock, who organises lots of the speakers, is holding something up. She turns around and Ivy sees it's a banner. 'Backward Step for Feminism!' it reads. On the table, others are spread out. 'Morlan Rejects Filth!' 'The Slippery Slope!' another reads.

Wendy had a black marker pen in hand. She's crossing out the 'S' on a banner reading, 'Ban the Poles!'

'This just makes it sound like we've got something against Polish people,' she says in dismay.

'What do you think, Ivy?' asks Cynthia. 'We're holding a protest against the pole dancing classes. We've invited the press and we'll form a line outside the next class, hopefully stopping as many as we can from entering.'

'But, why?' is all Ivy can trust herself to say.

'It contradicts all that we stand for in *our* WI. In Morlan.' She pauses as if announcing the start of World War III on a podium. 'As women.'

Ivy begins to tremble. 'You mean a woman's right to exercise with a group of other women? What harm is it doing?'

The other women fall silent, sensing a confrontation and not wishing to miss a moment. Even Frank Abbott seems to be looking their way curiously. Cynthia coughs. 'I really thought you'd understand. It's not right. It's unseemly. There are other ways to exercise without the sexual element. Morlan is a decent place with decent folk.'

'Surely there are better ways of spending the WI's time than petty protests like this. I joined the WI because I thought I'd meet like-minded women, women who would inspire me. After all, it is in your mission statement.' Ivy has never spoken so frankly before and she senses a ripple of shock amongst the others. 'To think I've always defended the organisation. Tried to dispel the myth that the WI isn't all about knitting and spinsters stuck in their ways.' She flushes. 'I've always thought of it as an organisation reflecting modern women.' Some of the others shift uncomfortably at this.

'You are taking this the wrong way, Ivy. I thought you, of all people, would be keen to put an end to such wickedness. Anyone would think you had some sort of personal interest in it.' She smiles patronisingly.

'Indeed, I have,' Ivy announces. 'I go to the class every week without fail. And I enjoy them. Now, if you don't mind, there is an interesting talk I have come here to listen to and I don't intend to keep our speaker waiting a moment longer.' She sweeps into the hall.

The others follow with much whispering behind her. Unfortunately, Frank Abbott is not a natural speaker. He sounds as if he's reading from Wikipedia, making no eye contact with his audience and speaking in a low voice. Ivy imagines he must have bored a generation of university undergraduates to death.

'There's little evidence of villas or Roman building materials reported by medieval or later writers. Some remains have been discovered near Dale and these were tentatively identified as Roman by topographer Richard Fenton in his *Historical Tour* of 1810.'

A few of the women stifle a yawn and some take surreptitious glances at their watches or phones. There's a stony silence when Frank asks expectantly, 'Any questions?' The awkwardness of earlier still lingers, which doesn't help matters. There's a collective sigh of relief when Cynthia releases them all and thanks Frank.

'That really was fascinating, Frank, and we feel privileged that you were willing to share your expertise with us this evening. I would like to thank you on behalf of Morlan's WI, an organisation that values expanding cultural knowledge.' She looks pointedly at Ivy.

Much clapping follows and Ivy gets up quickly, leaving before Wendy can say anything or, God forbid, offer her a lift home. As she crosses the car park, she's aware of someone trying to catch up with her.

'Ivy, wait!' She turns around to see it's Sally. 'Well, I'd have paid good money to see that, Ivy. Good on you! I wish I had half the guts you have. That really put Cynthia and that bunch of hypocrites in their place.'

Ivy slows down. 'Honestly, I do feel annoyed. It really is harmless. Have they nothing better to do than gossip and interfere?' Pausing, she says, 'I'm not sure I want to belong to the WI when women like Cynthia and Wendy rule the roost. I don't include you in that, Sally.'

'I know, but it's exactly women like you who are needed. Generous, open-minded, kind. And modern.'

Ivy laughs. 'I'm seventy-two!'

'Age is a just a number,' says Sally. 'A cliché but true. I'd love to meet this Feather Starr. She's certainly stirred things up in the village.'

'She's very charismatic and a talented woman, actually,' Ivy says. 'She's got a knack of making us relax and giving us confidence. Although she still thinks we're all a bit uptight.'

'I'm totally uncoordinated,' Sally says, 'so I'd be hopeless at it. I certainly don't intend to join the protestors, though.'

'I have a feeling it will come to nothing.'

Sally stops at the footpath leading to her cottage. 'I really do admire you, Ivy. You have principles.'

'Thanks, Sally, that means a lot.' Ivy continues up the hill, the breezy night air dispelling the frustration she felt earlier.

We're so lucky to live here, she thinks. Why can't people just appreciate that? She feels her phone buzz in her pocket, knowing it will be Matthew's nightly check-in, but when she checks her phone, it's from Bob.

Lovely to catch up with you today. I'm away next week but do you fancy lunch the following Monday? He ends with a smiley face. Kisses would be too much, of course. Ivy smiles and reaches home, just as Wendy and Martin close their front door.

Chapter Twenty-Four

Summer

Issue with the exhaust I reckon. I've called AA. Three hour wait – bloody typical! X

Aled sent the text three and a half hours ago. She's rung twice since then. He's stood waiting on some country B road, with one bar of signal and a dwindling phone battery.

Any sign of them?

Summer messaged twenty minutes ago but has had no reply.

'Mummy, me Anna,' Nia reprimands, handing her the correct *Frozen* doll.

'Sorry, darling,' she forces a smile. 'Let's go to the shop,' Summer says, trying her best to concentrate. She moves her doll to follow along the top of the coffee table.

Nia's doll suddenly launches an unprovoked attack on Summer's. Summer should probably worry about Nia's propensity for violence and is sure other mothers would intervene at this point, but her heart just isn't in it today. She lets her doll get beaten up, feeling that her soul is the one taking a beating.

The one thing she has been counting on today is Aled getting home. She hasn't told him yet about the positive pregnancy test upstairs, or the backup one she did yesterday. She thought about doing it over the phone but just couldn't. She needs to see him face to face, needs to read the same horror in his eyes as she felt when she found out. It's been three days now, and she can't keep it in any longer.

When Summer saw that digital word 'Pregnant' the night she got back from the pub, the first thing she did was vomit. Loudly and messily, just making it to the toilet. The next thing she did was cry. And since then, all she's felt is numb.

How could they have been this stupid? Nia and Jordan took up so much of their time, sex was the last priority. Last time it had barely even counted, the TV was on throughout – Alex Jones on *The One Show*, talking to long-lost siblings that found each other accidentally on a blind date – and they'd both laughed at the ridiculousness of the story while Aled was still inside her. They were both so tired, Summer had wondered to herself if she wasn't the only one faking an orgasm, Aled's seemed suspiciously quick and overexaggerated.

How the hell was that the real deal? Enough to make baby number three? Summer hasn't been on birth control, relying on breastfeeding and pulling out when needed. Maybe it wasn't a great plan, in hindsight, but she still can't believe it.

What a fucking idiot! And what a fucking disaster!

'Oopsie,' Nia's knocked over her selection of doll clothes, sending plastic shoes and miniature clothing in flammable materials flying across the living room. She looks to Summer, waiting for the telling off that's usually imminent in situations like this.

'Why don't you show Mummy what a big girl you are and

tidy this up, please? While you do that, Mummy'll go and put the oven on for your dinner, Missy.'

Nia nods, eager to please, and Summer softens. She's taking it out on Nia and she shouldn't.

She needs to get away, even for a second, to the kitchen. She's bored of toddler afternoons. Bored of games with imaginary rules. Bored of referring to herself in the third person, 'Mummy needs to do this', and 'Mummy wants you to help with that'.

Summer just wants to scream. She feels a pressure cooker inside, emotions threatening to burst out. Aled was meant to be home now, and she was meant to have some relief. And she knows she should be grateful for her two beautiful and healthy children. She is, really she is. But today is too much. She hears her phone ping.

Still no sign of AA. I'm freezing out here. And bored. Worst day ever. I just want to be at home with my team x

Summer almost scoffs. He wants to try being trapped in the house with a baby and a toddler. He couldn't even manage it for one pole dancing class. She'd love to swap places with him now, be wrapped up on the side of a country lane in the rain and darkness. Just to have three hours with her thoughts whilst she waited for the AA. No Internet and no one vying for her attention. Bliss.

I can't wait for you to come home. Be safe driving x

Summer sees there are unopened WhatsApp messages from her pole dancing group but she can't bring herself to read them today. She can't sympathise with Meg's dating life or hear about Ivy's wholesome upcycling adventures. Funnily enough, she thinks the only one she could stomach to listen to is Gwen. Her

220

life is falling apart more than Summer's right now.

She considers calling her but decides it would be too awkward. Summer only needs to hear one sympathetic voice and the truth might come pouring out of her. She needs to hold it in until Aled's home.

She sets the temperature on the oven, tumbles a few chicken nuggets on the tray for Nia, then changes her mind and adds more for herself too. What's the point of pretending she's an adult with real food, when the rest of her life is taken up with toddler tantrums and dirty nappies? She might as well eat chicken nuggets for dinner with Nia at 5 p.m. Besides, Aled will probably eat en route home, and Summer can only eat from a select palate of beige and brown foods without triggering her morning sickness.

Potato smileys complete the frozen articles on the oven tray. Summer will cook up a few peas and baked beans, just to pretend she's feeding her daughter vegetables.

She changes Jordan's nappy and bathes both children while the food is cooking. She scoops them both out of the bath at the same time, one in each arm. She can handle two children, just about. She has the ideal number of limbs. What do you do with a third baby? How do you even carry it without having a kangaroo pouch sewn into your midriff?

'Daddy feed me,' Nia pouts, when put in her high chair.

'I know, I'm sorry darling,' she says. She wants Daddy to be home too.

'Daddy read story in bed?'

'Maybe,' Summer answers, checking her phone again. There's still nothing from him.

Somehow, she gets through the feeding and breastfeeding, the repeat nappy changing, and burping, and ends with two children snoozing away in their respective rooms. Jordan sounds like a farmyard animal when he sleeps, all squeaks and whinges, but she knows not to disturb him. She loves those noises.

Downstairs, she changes into fresh pyjamas and finishes off a few mouthfuls of potato smileys that have gone cold, then loads the dishwasher. It's this time that she would love a glass of wine. Anything cheap and red to soothe her aching mind and muscles, but she makes do with some of Nia's squash in a wine glass and her feet up on the sofa.

When the front door opens, Summer is asleep. Her mind feels foggy and confused, before she realises that Aled is finally home. The anticipation to tell him the news should have kept her awake, but he enters the living room to see her rubbing her eyes and making the same sounds as Jordan.

'What a bloody nightmare, the car had to be towed! Three hundred quid to take it to the garage and drop me off here.' He spreads his arm. 'But honey, I'm home.'

She stands to hug him, unsteady on her feet.

'Is it wine time already?' Aled asks. Summer laughs, the irony of his question a private joke for now.

'I've missed you,' she says and pulls him towards her.

'I've missed you too. I was desperate to get home.'

She feels suddenly nervous now, jumpy. When does she tell him? And how?

'Shall I get the rest of the bottle?' He asks.

'Go on, then. There's food in the fridge,' she tells him.

'I had a Maccies on the way home,' he says, predictable

as ever. She hears the rustling of chocolate wrappers from the kitchen, nevertheless.

'How are our terrors?' he asks, coming back in, wine bottle in hand.

'Asleep, at last. Nia was disappointed you couldn't read to her,' Summer says, hoping she's masked her own disappointment well enough. She wanted to have this conversation about three hours earlier, not groggy from a sofa nap and with chicken nugget breath.

'Anyway, sit down. I want to talk to you about something.' There's no use in beating around the bush.

'Uh oh. I know I'm in trouble now,' he laughs it off. 'Don't worry, you're not as mad at me as I am at myself. If I hadn't offered to give Mike a lift to Newcastle Emlyn, I'd have been home before the car broke down. I've been swearing at myself for the last six hours.'

'It's not that,' Summer says, although Aled left out that detail earlier when she spoke to him. 'I'm mad at both of us.'

'Both of us?' He looks confused.

'We've been really stupid, Al. Ridiculously stupid,' she sighs. 'I'm pregnant again.'

There. It's out now. She remembers telling Aled about Nia, how he'd jumped for joy and they'd stayed up until two in the morning talking and imagining their future with a little one in it. Aled had been the one to suggest Summer was pregnant with Jordan, noticing her symptoms before she'd put two and two together herself.

She knows this time will be different.

'You're pregnant?' he repeats. 'Are you sure?'

'No period and two positive tests. And raging morning sickness. Yes, I am. Hundred per cent.'

'But how?'

'Last time you were home. With *The One Show*? Turns out pulling out wasn't such an iron-clad plan.'

'What?' Aled shakes his head. He's sitting opposite her on the sofa, one arm slung lazily round the back of it. Only now it's gripping the sofa cushion with tension. 'You can't be.'

'My thoughts exactly,' she says. She waits for what's to come, for him to go through the same maelstrom of emotions she has in the last few days. She knows he won't cry and vomit like her, but she needs to see panic. She knows it's coming.

'You're pregnant,' he repeats, as though confirming it to himself. 'We're having another baby. That's . . . that's fantastic.'

Summer's head snaps up to look at him. 'What?'

'Three kids. That's what I've always imagined. It's amazing, babe.' He claps his hands to his mouth like an *X-Factor* contestant being told he's through to the live shows.

She scours his face, wanting to check he's serious. She wants signs of sarcasm, of dismay, of something. Not this pure joy.

'I can't believe it! We're having another baby!' He pours himself a glass from the bottle. 'I wish we had champagne in.'

She checks again, incredulous. She feels she's in some comedy sketch, a send-up.

'When did you find out?'

'Thursday, after class.'

'And you waited all this time to tell me?' He's practically bouncing up and down like a child. 'What do you think?'

Summer feels wrong-footed now. She doesn't know where

to start. This wasn't supposed to happen. Aled is supposed to be angry, and confused, and as terrified as she is. Not giggling with joy, like Nia being tickled.

'I don't know how we're going to survive,' she says, the words barely audible.

'We'll make it work. Maybe I can take on a few extra days on the rig. It's not ideal, but I'll think of something.'

No. No, no, no. Aled can't be away longer. That's the opposite of what they need.

'What about me?'

'You'll be the best mum of three. I know it! Everything's going to work out.' He rubs a hand on her stomach now. 'Our third little one, growing in there. Our hat-trick.'

It's this moment when Jordan's snuffles become louder on the monitor, a sign he's waking.

'Do you want to?' she says, gesturing to the monitor.

'Can you? I'm still absorbing the news. A new baby,' Aled says. Summer goes to her current baby, ready for the routine of change, cuddle, feed and put down. She needs the space from Aled, needs to replay what just happened.

How can he think this is a good thing? It's a horror movie to Summer, the idea of three kids. How can he possibly feel they'll cope with a third child?

But then he won't need to cope, will he? Life won't change for Aled. He'll still be away for weeks at a time, while all the work will be hers. He can play the doting father-of-three, a part-time dad, a minimal change in role for him. She's of half a mind to tear downstairs and yell this at him.

But he's *absorbing* it downstairs. He's had a long day and

she's just dropped a bombshell. The panic might be about to set in. We all react in different ways to life-changing news. Maybe this is just the initial reaction, the shock of it. Summer's had three days to digest the news. She just has to hope Aled will catch up.

Chapter Twenty-Five

Gwen

After leaving Harding and Barlow, the estate agents, to sign some final documents, Gwen's feelings are all over the place. The sign will go up tomorrow and then everyone in Morlan will know that she and Gareth are moving out. And how long before they know, if they don't already, that he's left her for another woman? Does it really matter? People have their own problems and she doesn't feel so alone with Lydia and Jasmine behind her, and the pole dancing girls, of course.

Pippa Barlow told her that she'll put the house up for nine hundred and seventy-five thousand. 'Although the way the current market is, it's likely to go over one mill,' she said casually, as if she was talking about selling a second-hand wheelbarrow on eBay. When she smiled, she revealed lipstick-stained teeth. 'People are offering over the asking price these days. Expect things to move quickly.' She crossed her legs, her pencil skirt riding up over her heavy thighs.

Gwen had done a quick mental calculation, figuring that after paying their debts, they should have about seventy-five thousand pounds each, thankfully avoiding bankruptcy. Not much to start again at fifty-two. It wouldn't buy her a house, but she'd have a deposit and perhaps selling the car would give her extra cash. Get something more modest. She'll have to get a job, though, if she needs a mortgage. If Gareth were here now, Gwen thinks she would give him a piece of her mind, if not kick him where it hurts.

She scans the houses on offer in the window as she leaves. There's one for ninety thousand in Goodwick, but it was an old shop and is now a tiny two-bedroom bungalow on the main road. The windows will need replacing and the roof is in a bit of a state. Gwen has no money in the pot to do any renovations. There's a small cottage in Abercastle, which isn't far from Morlan. It has views over the quaint harbour and looks like it just needs some cosmetic work. Gwen can handle that. It has a handkerchief-sized garden and the asking price is reasonable.

She goes in to book a viewing, aware the staff will talk about her when she leaves, thinking what a comedown this is. She has had to develop a thick skin in these last few weeks. It's Lydia she feels for, though. Her bedroom at The Haven has its own en suite, even a small dressing area. She loves having her friends over for parties in the hot tub. She hasn't had anyone over for weeks, even Sophie, she of the braying donkey laugh. Perhaps Gwen, Lydia and Boris can re-establish their little haven in Abercastle.

Haverfordwest is packed, and by the time Gwen comes out of the estate agents, it's gone 2 p.m. It will take her half an hour to get home. She can't stay in town too long as Feather Starr has asked them all to meet up at the village hall tonight

228

instead of a class, refusing to tell them what she has planned. Deciding to have lunch before she leaves, Gwen finds her usual haunts too busy. She ends up ordering a jacket potato in Marks and Spencer, scrolling through Zoopla as she waits for it to arrive.

Outside, it's beginning to spit with rain. She doesn't want to be too long. She'll cook something nice for Lydia before she leaves for the village hall this evening.

'Gwen. Uh, Gwen.' Lynne stands before her.

Gwen is so shocked she doesn't know what to say. She has fantasised about seeing Lynne, her husband's mistress, her friend, but it involved Gwen calling Lynne a cruel, selfish, husband-stealing bitch. Another fantasy saw Gwen egging her car or throwing a brick through her window.

'Do you mind if I sit down?'

Gwen nods, swallowing.

'I know that I'm probably the last person you want to see.'

'It was inevitable at some point,' Gwen concedes.

Lynne sits down. She's had her hair freshly highlighted, Gwen notices. Lynne pours tea into her cup and her hand is trembling.

'This isn't easy for me,' she says.

'How awkward for you! Bumping into the wife of the man you have been having an affair with. Oh yes, and that wife happens to be your friend.'

'I suppose I deserve that,' says Lynne. 'Although I don't think we were particularly good friends.'

'That's patently obvious,' Gwen says sarcastically.

'I just wanted to say that we never meant for it to happen.

Gareth's been under a lot of stress. Covid put pressure on the business, and he was working long hours and . . .'

'Yes, you forget I was the mug waiting for him at home! You're not the first, Lynne. I hope you realise that. Gareth has never been able to keep it in his pants.'

'Jacket potato.' The assistant whips away the table number and places the meal in front of Lynne.

Lynne moves the plate towards Gwen, 'You're hurt, I can understand that, but making these sorts of catty comments about him doesn't help.'

Gwen snorts, 'God, if you're so naive as to believe him, good luck to you. I hope you have a nice life cosying up in your twee little cottage with your floral cushions and polka-dotted curtains and your pink bedspread.' Gwen's aware that she's becoming petty.

'He's not living with me,' Lynne says. 'He has his own apartment.'

'Oh, that makes everything better,' Gwen sniffs. 'He did tell me, but I don't believe a word that comes out of his mouth. The marriage is in tatters but he's not living with you! Well, he might soon be. You know that Vimpany Motors is dead in the water. We've got hardly any money left and The Haven is up for sale.' Gwen picks up her knife and fork. 'And now, if you don't mind, I'm going to have my lunch.'

Lynne rises from her chair. 'I'm sorry, Gwen. I truly am. That's all I wanted to say.'

Gwen doesn't look up until she sees Lynne's retreating back. Did she know about the business? It's hard to tell. How dare she sit there and pretend she's sorry. She pushes her plate away, her appetite gone.

Gwen can barely reach her car before tears spill down her cheeks.

Gwen makes Lydia a lasagne, her favourite, and tells her all about bumping into Lynne earlier.

'What a bitch!' Lydia says, making Gwen feel heaps better.

'Well, I don't know what she expected me to say to her.'

'I'd have told her to fuck right off!'

'Lydia!' Gwen scolds, but her heart isn't really in it. 'Anyway, the house is up for sale from tomorrow. I picked up these today in the estate agents.' She hands the leaflets over to Lydia.

'God, this one is hideous,' she says. 'Please say we're not going to buy this one. It's so old-fashioned. This looks OK.'

'The one in Abercastle? Do you want to come and see it with me Sunday?'

Lydia nods unenthusiastically, and Gwen's stomach is in knots. How can that bastard do this, Gwen thinks. What he's done to her is bad enough, but the effect it's having on the girls is so much worse.

'I'm off to Sophie's, Mum,' Lydia says. 'Her dad is bringing me back.'

'If you're drinking, don't have too much. You're only seventeen.'

Lydia rolls her eyes, but kisses Gwen's cheek. 'See you later, Mum.'

* * *

231

There are eight of them when Gwen arrives in the hall. She is ten minutes late, but has messaged on their Pole Stars' WhatsApp group to ask them to wait for her.

'Right, my lovely ladies. Thank you all for coming tonight, especially as this is later than usual.' Feather Starr's bracelets jingle as she speaks. She seems more animated tonight, even a little jittery. 'We're going to do our usual deep-breathing exercises. So, grab a mat and sit with your legs crossed in front of me.'

Outside, the sky is darkening. Gwen notices Feather has not set up the poles tonight. 'Close your eyes,' Feather says, her long purple hair falling over her shoulders. 'Now, I have asked you here as I think you all need a little help in calming your anxious thoughts, and releasing tension and with it, your inhibitions.'

Gwen's right eye peeps open, and she catches Meg's puzzled look. There's a nervous frisson in the hall tonight.

Feather goes on, 'I want you to lie back slowly and notice how it feels when you inhale and exhale normally. Mentally scan your body. You might feel tension that you never noticed. Take a slow, deep breath through your nose.'

Gwen can hear the steady breathing around her. Feather has got one of those deep, breathy voices, a bit like Joanna Lumley but less posh. It has a terrifically calming effect, Gwen thinks, as the troubles of her day and her annoyance at meeting Lynne seem to disappear into the darkness of the hall.

'Notice your belly and upper body expanding,' Feather says. 'Exhale in whatever way is most comfortable for you. Try sighing out your breath and pay attention to the rise and fall of your belly.'

232

Gwen feels quite sleepy.

'I want you all to focus and vocalise as you exhale. Think of a word like safe or calm. Keep inhaling slowly for a count of four seconds. Hold it for seven. Then exhale, saying your special word for eight seconds.'

Gwen struggles to think of a word. 'Cheat' is the first word that springs to her mind, but then she realises she's come out of her mindfulness breathing and plumps for the word peace, hissing the word as she exhales.

Seeming to read her mind, Feather says, 'When you get distracted, gently bring your attention back to your breath and your word. Imagine your inhale washing over you like a gentle wave.'

It is lovely, Gwen thinks. Feather has this knack of calming them all down.

'Imagine your exhale carrying negative and upsetting thoughts and energy away from you,' Feather continues in her Joanna Lumley voice. 'Any anger you have inside. Perhaps it's embarrassment. Anxiety. Feel all those negative thoughts and emotions drifting away with your breath. No emotion has that power over you any more. You are in control.' After a beat, Feather says, 'Right, ladies, you can sit up and open your eyes.'

After a bit of shuffling, everyone does as they are told. Gwen has no idea how much time has passed in this deep-breathing session.

Feather seems to be building up to something. Gwen can sense it. 'I have thought in the last few weeks that while you are progressing with the moves, there is still some hesitancy, some anxiety about letting yourselves go. So, I have come to the

233

conclusion I need to do something, something that will push you out of your comfort zones. Morlan's fête is in a few weeks, and it will not work if you allow your inhibitions to hold you back.'

Shit, what is she planning? Gwen wonders, and the nervousness from earlier returns.

'I can see some of you are a little hesitant. This exercise I am planning is one I have done before and it works. Put aside your reluctance. This will be life changing.' She smiles, 'I know you probably think I am exaggerating, but I have seen the transformative power of this exercise in the past.'

There is an undercurrent of tension now and some murmurings of disquiet. *Spit it out*, Gwen thinks.

'I have some towels with me and all of us are going to the lagoon and we're going for a swim.'

'But we don't have our swimming costumes,' says Carol, the woman who always wears a red leotard.

Feather pauses and smiles, 'Exactly. We're going to swim nude.'

Suddenly, the hall erupts into gasps. Gwen catches some of the protests, *You've got to be kidding me!* And *No Way.* Then *Fuck no!*

Summer pipes up, 'That's where lots of the teenagers hang out.'

'A lot of women swimming naked isn't going to interest teenagers. It'll be dark. Most will go once they see us,' Feather says vaguely.

'Well, I'm not doing it,' says one woman called Elin, who has missed some of the lessons.

'That's OK, my love,' says Feather, undeterred, as Elin rises and walks determinedly out of the hall. 'Right, the rest of you, grab a towel. It's a beautiful moonlit night and we are going to experience the thrilling sensation of cold water on our naked bodies.'

'And have chilblains,' says Carol under her breath.

'This will be like an epiphany, a watershed moment,' Feather grins. With this, she hands out towels in a business-like manner. 'Leave your stuff here. I will lock the hall. Let's do this!'

Gwen giggles to herself. Can she really do this? Ivy has already bounced onto her feet. Summer seems bemused, no doubt looking forward to telling Aled when she gets home. Gwen turns around to look for Meg. She is still sitting on the floor and her face is deathly pale.

Chapter Twenty-Six

Meg

All of Meg's worst nightmares have come at once. This feels like the worst thing that could possibly happen to her. Public humiliation. Forced exposure of her stoma bag. This can't be happening. She can't do this.

'Are you all right, Meg?' Gwen is asking, her hand outstretched as though to help her from the floor.

'Fine,' she says, wanting to hide her utter terror.

Why did she say that? She could feign illness, say she's going home. She can't do an Elin and storm off, but she could make an excuse, couldn't she?

'Actually, I'm feeling a bit peaky . . . I feel a bit sick too.' She sounds as unconvincing as a teenage girl crying period to get out of school PE.

'The fresh air and water will help with that,' Feather Starr overhears, dismissing Meg's troubles in one swift sentence. 'Everyone, come along.'

Meg lets herself get helped to her feet by Gwen. 'Are you sure?' she asks, quietly this time.

Meg nods. 'I'll be fine.' She sounds shaky. Meg is the absolute opposite of fine. She feels a sense of horror settling so deeply, it's restricting her breathing.

She had a bad feeling about this so-called 'exercise' of Feather Starr's. She knew it would be something outside her comfort zone, but she didn't bank on skinny-dipping, which is so far outside Meg's comfort zone it may as well be on the other side of the planet.

She trails behind the others as they file out onto the pavement, making comments about the cold night air.

'It's going to be bracing in that water,' Summer is saying.

'I've read cold water bathing is good for immunity. Something about it reducing stress levels and antioxidants,' Ivy says. 'It was on TikTok the other day.'

'Ivy, you do not use TikTok,' Summer is incredulous. On a good day Meg would join in, calling Ivy a perpetual dark horse, but she feels anything other than jovial. Meg just wants the world to end. She wishes she hadn't come tonight. She wishes she'd followed her instincts, could just go home to her comfy bedroom in the post office and forget the whole thing.

Gwen is quiet too, walking in step with Meg. Meg avoids her eye. Does Gwen know something?

'My daughters would be mortified if they knew I was doing this,' Gwen says. 'That's what makes me think I should do this. Maybe Feather's right.'

She appreciates that she's trying to make small talk, but Meg isn't in the mood tonight. She just wants to retreat into herself and decide what she's going to do, how to get out of this.

The walk to the lagoon in Morlan usually takes ten minutes but they seem to reach it in seconds tonight, as they turn to the narrow path leading from the village to the lagoon. There is an air of nervousness amongst the women, but definite excitement too. Meg imagines none of them will feel comfortable about doing this, but no one will feel like she does.

What is she going to do? She has two options, fight or flight, fuelled by the adrenaline flowing through her veins, causing her breathing to speed up and her heart to pound against her chest wall. The easiest option is definitely to run. To cry some family emergency, or an early start tomorrow, or anything. The others might not believe her, but so what? She's an adult, she doesn't need to answer to anyone but herself. And she does not need to be forced into showing her stoma bag.

The other option is to stay and fight. And practically, if she is to do this, can she get away without anyone seeing the bag? She could strip off but keep her protective banding on. She mentally scans her actions when she was getting dressed earlier, how she'd chosen the black strap tonight. Damnit. That was hardly subtle. People would definitely see. But then it is dark outside.

What the hell is she going to do?

The excited chatter gets louder from the women as they reach the lagoon. It occurs to Meg that this will be the second time she's been humiliated at this lagoon. Josh has been particularly attentive after their disastrous date last time when he brushed her off, but it is still a bad memory. It can't come close to what's going to happen tonight.

Feather Starr is right, it's quiet here tonight. It's late enough to be dark but early enough that no teenagers are out yet.

'Here we are, the scene of the crime,' she addresses the group now, smiling. They stand around her, disbelieving that this is truly happening. Meg just wants to bolt, her legs urging her to run. She doesn't have to do this, doesn't have to be here, she could just go. But for some reason she stays rooted to the spot.

'It's going to be cold in there, ladies, but nothing the human body can't handle. Take deep breaths throughout your entry into the water, and you'll soon adjust. It's colder on land tonight than in the water,' she says. 'Oh, and try to enjoy the feeling of air on your naked skin. It's freeing, a celebration of the human body, a beautiful thing.'

Meg doesn't want to be celebrating anything.

'I want you to capture this feeling to take you through the next classes and the performance. You'll need positivity and confidence for the routine and costumes I have planned.'

There are shrieks at this point, but the women seem largely on board. Meg feels utterly sick. Skinny-dipping. Costumes. It's all moving too fast for her. What was once a safe and enjoyable experience is now a nightmare.

'I'll go in first, show you how it's done.' And with that, Feather Starr unzips her coat and whips her dress off underneath. In seconds she's down to her bra and pants, mismatching numbers that Meg wouldn't want to be seen in public.

'I think if I'd planned this whole thing I'd have gone for better underwear,' Summer sniggers to Gwen behind them.

Feather Starr then turns her back to the assembled line of women, unbuckles her bra and slips her knickers down her legs. Immediately she's running, flesh jiggling as she goes. It's a wonder to see; Feather isn't skinny, but is confident and owns her body, not a shred of insecurity about her. It's dark but Meg

239

can make out the tattoos that adorn her thighs and spread up her buttocks.

She lets out a 'woohooo', as she hits the water, not breaking her stride, and plunging quickly into the still lagoon.

There are nervous giggles from the women as they look around, daring each other as to who will go next.

'Come on in!' Feather shouts in encouragement.

Silence. Maybe Meg isn't the only one hating every second of this. Someone is going to break this awkwardness.

'Go on, then,' Ivy suddenly says. 'It's my year to try new things, I promised myself after Jim.' She's unzipping too, shivering as the air hits her exposed skin. She's in good shape, although her skin isn't as taut as Feather Starr's. Meg can just make out slender musculature, before Ivy is jogging down to the lagoon too.

'You know what they say, if you can't beat 'em . . .' Summer begins stripping off before Ivy is in the water. A few of the other women are joining now, removing layers and shrieking at how cold it is. A few link hands, egging each other on. Summer's post-partum stomach jiggles, but she seems happy, whooping as she starts running.

Meg realises she's smiling, enjoying the others' glee. If only she could join them. They look so carefree, so happy, all different shapes and sizes. But no one has a problem like her. A reason they can't do this. Now is the time. Now would be the time.

But she just can't.

The last few women go, and Meg feels frozen still.

'What's the problem?'

Meg is surprised to see Gwen.

'There is a problem, isn't there?' Gwen's gentle, moving closer to Meg.

'Uhhh . . .' She can't speak. Can't bring herself to say it. Gwen has that same knowing smile, the one she saw the night she readjusted her stoma bag.

'I know something's stopping you from doing this.'

Meg feels tears prick her eyes. She's never told anyone outside the family about her stoma. She's never known how people will react, whether they'll be disgusted or supportive. It's been so hard to hide, though. Meg wishes she didn't have to hide it.

Maybe she can tell someone. Anyone. Gwen.

'I've had surgery,' she says, hearing the wobble in her voice. 'A stoma. I haven't told anyone about it.'

'Oh, darling,' Meg can hear the sympathy in Gwen's voice, and it makes the tears want to tumble out now. She gulps.

'I don't want people to find out.'

'Why not?' Gwen asks gently.

'I'm . . . scared.' It's all Meg can say while she figures out her next move. 'I haven't accepted it myself yet. How can I expect others to?' It's true. She barely looks at it in the mirror, avoids seeing herself naked if she can.

'But you're safe here,' Gwen is saying, moving closer to squeeze Meg's shoulder.

'Come on, ladies!' A few shouts are heard from the water. Gwen waves them off.

'Feather Starr's right. We need to embrace who we are. I've relied on Gareth for years, and have had complete humiliation in front of the village. It's time I become my own woman, accept what's happened, accept myself.'

'It's not the same,' Meg wipes her eyes, although she appreciates Gwen's words.

'Aren't you sick of hiding yourself?' Gwen asks. 'I know I am.'

'Maybe.' Meg *is* sick of hiding it. Of keeping such a massive part of her life secret. In truth, she's not imagined how other people will react to her stoma. She's projected her own disgust on to them. People might accept it. It's just an illness, a life event, like any other. She saw a glimpse of Summer's caesarean scar when she ran to the water, and Ivy's tattoo marking the beginning of her new life alone. Why is her stoma anything different?

Everyone's hidden something, and these brave women have bared all tonight.

Isn't it time Meg did the same?

'I'm . . . nervous, though. I can't do it alone.' She looks at all the women ahead of her, swimming around, laughing. They've formed such a sisterhood in these classes, women from different walks of life, tied together by this community. If she's going to show herself to anyone, it's going to be them.

'I'll do it with you,' Gwen says. 'Come on, no more thinking. It's time, Meg.'

Meg copies Gwen's actions, unzipping her coat. She removes her dress, already feeling naked as the bump of her stoma bag is exposed underneath her leggings. She slowly takes them down, now in her bra and pants, with her protective banding in place.

'Here we go,' Gwen says, removing her own underwear at the same time.

'Here we go,' Meg repeats, more to herself than Gwen. She can do this. She is going to do this. It is going to happen tonight.

She's naked now, apart from the banding. A hush descends over the women, as though they sense this is a monumental moment for Meg. She can't look at them, but she slowly removes the banding. Her stoma bag is revealed.

Her secret is out.

Before Meg knows what's happening, she's following Gwen into the water, feeling the rush of air past her nipples and her abdomen, areas that she has never exposed. The women are watching but Meg realises that's OK. They know now. And she is as entitled to do this as anyone else. In fact, she's enjoying herself.

The women cheer as Gwen and Meg get in the water. Her thoughts are spinning so quickly, she can't even process how cold the water is. She's in.

'Go, Meg!' Summer shouts.

'You look gorgeous, girl,' someone else in the class shouts.

'Our superwoman,' Feather Starr winks at her as she meets her eye. 'Well done, ladies. We've done it!'

Ivy and Summer swim over to Gwen and Meg and embrace them in a hug. A totally naked, totally unexpected moment, that Meg knows has cemented this bond between them.

'What would I do without you?' She's talking to Gwen now, tears still fresh on her face.

'I've done nothing. You've got this strength inside you,' Gwen says. Summer and Ivy agree.

Meg swims a little, relishing the feeling of the water on her skin. She hasn't swum since her surgery, hasn't exposed

243

herself like this. It feels exhilarating.

'Thank you,' Meg says as she gets closer to Feather Starr.

'It's my pleasure,' she says, giving her a knowing smile. They all swim around, before declaring how cold they are.

But Meg doesn't care any more. Meg knows this is the happiest she has felt since her stoma bag first arrived.

'Shall we get out?' Feather shouts to the group, before a bright flash goes off unmistakably from the top of the path. The women whirl around, covering their chests quickly. A dark head disappears from sight. Someone with a camera.

'Who was that?' the group murmur to each other.

'I couldn't see,' Meg says.

'I saw,' Feather declares. 'Idris bloody Hopkins.'

Chapter Twenty-Seven

Ivy

The women loop arms as they walk up the hill towards the village hall, Meg with Gwen and Ivy with Summer, the others trailing behind. Ivy can hear Meg and Gwen speaking in low tones beside them.

Summer's breaths are punctuated by excitable giggles. 'Oh my God, I never thought I'd do that in a million years. Fair play, Ivy, you really went for it.' Summer laughs again. 'If my body looks half as good as yours in my seventies, I'll be well pleased.'

'You young girls worry far too much.'

'I've got stretch marks all over my thighs, bum and belly. God knows what I'll be like if I have another.' Summer is suddenly serious.

'That body of yours has given you two gorgeous babies. Who cares about a few imperfections? You're a lovely young woman, Summer, and Aled is lucky to have you.'

Summer kisses Ivy's cheek. 'Thank you, Ivy. You always make me feel better.'

As they congregate outside the hall doors waiting for Feather to get the key, Gwen whispers to them, 'Don't you think someone tipped off Idris Hopkins?'

'Definitely,' agrees Meg.

'Surely not,' Ivy shakes her head.

'How the hell did he know that we'd be there, swimming naked? We didn't even know we'd be swimming naked,' Meg says.

'That means it's someone here,' says Ivy. The women fall silent. After a pause, she says, 'Perhaps he was trying his luck, saw some of us entering the hall and decided to follow us.'

'What will he do with the photos? I don't like it,' says Meg, and Gwen squeezes her arm.

'We were doing nothing wrong,' says Gwen. 'It's a free country and we can swim naked if we want to. Besides, what *can* he do with the photos?'

Feather is leading them briskly through the hall, taking their towels from them. They gather up their belongings and leave, the mood much more subdued than earlier.

At home, Ivy has a quick shower to get rid of the salt water. The swim tonight was invigorating. She feels alive, her body electrified by the shock of the cold water. She's always wanted to try wild swimming and being naked didn't faze her. She feels comfortable in her own skin, but it took her all these years to accept herself.

Sometimes she feels as if she sleepwalked through her life with Jim. She pours herself a glass of red wine and sits in the armchair in the window. The sea, a deep, velvet black tonight, lies on the horizon, omnipresent and reassuring. This friendship, the Pole Stars, feels transformative. What will they do when the fête is over, though? When the pole dancing classes finish? Which they will, Ivy has no doubt.

Ivy saw Feather Starr on the beach the other day. She rents a caravan on the field on the way out of Morlan, towards Fishguard. She was walking with someone, her hair blowing, a halo of implausible purple. Ivy couldn't make out who she was with. She's certainly a curious character.

Her thoughts are interrupted by her mobile bursting into life on the coffee table. With a sigh, she answers.

'Hi, Matthew. Is everything ok?' He doesn't usually call so late.

'I'm fine,' he says tightly. 'I rang earlier. Have you seen Facebook?'

Ivy's heart sinks. 'You know I rarely look at Facebook.'

'Well, I'll send you a screenshot of the Morlan Community Page. Alex Knight sent it to me. I think you have some explaining to do.' She's forgotten Matthew is still in touch with some of his pals from school.

His message pings through and Ivy sees a photo of the women getting out of the water earlier, the scene lit up by the flash of the camera. You can't see much bare flesh, but from glimpses of their shoulders, the back of Meg and, unmistakably, Ivy, smiling widely as she rises from the water, it's obvious they have no clothes on. The message underneath reads:

'Members of Morlan's Pole-Dancing Class swimming naked in the lagoon tonight. They obviously don't care who sees them. I, for one, want to restore decency to this village of ours. I've reported the incident to the police and intend to get these classes closed down once and for all. Sign the

petition below if you agree. Councillor Idris Hopkins.'

There have been twelve 'likes', which doesn't seem much, Ivy thinks. Several comments beneath agree with Idris Hopkins: 'Disgusting!' 'What is the world coming to?' An equal number, though, are supportive: 'Looks like they're having fun – I'd have gone for a look if I'd known!'

'Oh dear!' Ivy says.

'Is that all you can say, Mother? Are you out of your mind? Pole dancing! Swimming naked in public. At your age! Don't you even think how embarrassing this is for me?'

'You're overreacting. We weren't doing any harm.'

'Anyone could have seen you. Anyone!' Then he pauses. 'What would Dad have said?'

Ivy feels her hackles rise. 'Don't bring your father into this, Matthew. I'm trying to make a new life for myself, can't you see?'

'I understand that you are enjoying your independence, I really do,' Matthew says, more gently now, 'but why do you have to humiliate yourself with this sordid kind of behaviour?'

'There's nothing sordid about it. Honestly, Matthew, can we just close the subject? I am doing some exercises that happen to involve a pole! I went swimming with a group of women and we took off our clothes. It's not a crime. No one would have been the wiser if Idris Hopkins hadn't come along. Anyway, let's speak tomorrow. I have a headache.'

Ivy drains her glass. Matthew seems to encapsulate the small-minded, ungenerous and mean spirit of some of the people of Morlan, much as it shames her to admit that about her own son. The excitement from earlier has well and truly disappeared and Ivy turns off the light, making her way up to bed.

On Monday, at midday, Ivy hears the tooting of a car horn and sees Bob turning into her road. Ivy catches herself in the hall mirror. She has on a floral dress with trainers after agonising earlier about what to wear. She likes to keep up with fashion. She wouldn't be seen dead in the A-line skirts and elasticated trousers some women her age wear.

Would it be a pub lunch, she wonders – there are a few nice ones in Fishguard – or a little café somewhere and perhaps a walk? The red lipstick was a last-minute decision. Siren Red. Is this a date, she wonders? The thought gives her butterflies. As she locks her front door, she spots Wendy looking out.

'You look lovely,' Bob says as Ivy climbs into the car. 'I think we have an audience.' He glances over at Wendy. 'Shall we have a snog to give her something to talk about?'

Ivy laughs. 'You're wicked, you are. I have a feeling it's not just us that will keep the gossipmongers going today.'

'That's intriguing.'

'I'll explain later,' Ivy says, wondering if she should tell him at all. She looks across to him. Catching the scent of his musky aftershave, it's clear he's made an effort too. He's wearing a light blue shirt and jeans. 'So, what do you have planned for us?' she asks.

He looks at her sideways. 'A picnic and a walk. Is that ok? There's a lovely river walk if we start from the Harbour Car Park in the Lower Town.'

Ivy is impressed, 'You made a picnic? That sounds lovely.'

'I'll have you know I am famed for my picnics,' he smiles. 'I've packed some tapas for us. Bread, olives, hummus, frittata, grapes. I've never met a woman who doesn't like tapas.'

'You know women too well. I wish I'd brought something now.'

'I wanted to treat you. I've even brought two small bottles of Prosecco for you. I won't have any because I'm driving, of course.'

Ivy is touched, unused to such attention. He really is such a thoughtful man. Perfect, in many ways. 'It's a lovely day for it,' she says. Flipping the sun shield down, she turns to glimpse at the sea as the car meanders its way over the hill. It's beguiling today, reflecting the midday sun and shimmering like liquid gold. 'I never tire of that view.'

'There's something about the sea. It speaks to the soul.'

'I know what you mean. I do feel so lucky to live here, but I long to see other places.'

'You will, Ivy. I promise.'

Bob is so easy to talk to. Ivy feels herself relaxing, the twenty-five-minute journey whizzing by. There's a strength about Bob. He's masculine but open with his feelings.

The old harbour is bustling with visitors. Houses, little fishermen's cottages, hug the curve of the bay, painted in soft pastel shades of blues, mint and candyfloss pink. Small fishing boats bob in the water, their sails spiking the sky.

'I haven't been here for ages,' says Ivy, as Bob gets the cool bag from the boot.

'Come on, we'll find a quiet spot overlooking the harbour, away from the crowds.' Bob reaches for her hand as they walk from the car. Ivy feels self-conscious. It's an intimacy she doesn't expect. His hand is warm, firm, masculine. Bob looks at her hesitantly, as if to ensure she's fine with it.

It's awkward. What is this? Is she ready for it, whatever *it* is? She doesn't know, but decides to go with the flow. She squeezes Bob's hand and they pick up the pace, walking in an arc around the harbour and then escaping into the coolness of the woodland.

Ivy lays the tartan blanket Bob has brought in a clearing they find. Between the sycamore trees, they catch glimpses of the harbour glittering in the distance.

'You've thought of everything,' Ivy says. 'Thank you.'

'I don't often get the chance of lunch with a lovely woman like you. So, tell me what's this gossip you hinted at earlier?'

She tells him about the pole dancing classes, the skinny-dipping, and even Matthew's reaction. 'It's a fuss about nothing, really,' Ivy insists, watching closely for his reaction.

'You are a dark horse,' Bob laughs.

'I've been called that several times in the last few weeks. I have no idea why,' she says, wide-eyed and grinning.

'Good for you. Although no son likes to think of his mother getting her kit off.'

'I am a trial to him, I suspect.' Bob pours her Prosecco into a plastic cup. 'Now you're letting the side down, Bob. I was hoping to have a proper glass.'

'You seem to be enjoying your freedom.' As he takes out paper plates, he says, 'I'm sorry. I didn't mean that to be insensitive.'

'You're right, though,' Ivy agrees. 'I know it sounds a cliché, but I feel that I'm beginning to find myself. I'm having the most fun I've had in years, if ever.' She pauses, looking out at the harbour. 'I love Pembrokeshire, but I'm longing to go explore the world.'

'Home is wonderful to come back to but if you have a wandering spirit, there's nothing like the joy of discovering new places, seeing new things. Maggie had a real sense of adventure. It's one of the things I miss most about her.'

'You were lucky to have her, I think.'

They eat some bara brith that Bob has brought. 'Bought it in Narberth, I'm afraid. My cooking hasn't improved since I've been on my own.'

Ivy closes her eyes, enjoying the feel of the sun on her face. Bob tells her about the yellow Volkswagen camper van he's done up.

'We called her Nellie. It took me months to make her comfortable. It has everything, a fridge, pull-down bed, mini camping stove. Very bijou. I haven't taken her out for a while. If you come over next week, you can take a look at her.'

'She sounds wonderful,' Ivy says. 'I bet you've had some real adventures.'

'I'm planning my next one. In September when the schools go back. A European tour. I've been sorting out my route. I'm starting in Croatia and then moving to Riga, Latvia. Then Macedonia, and Belgrade. I want to see the Mostar Bridge in Herzegovina and then Prague.'

'Gosh, you are brave. It sounds very exciting.'

'Like I told you, it took me a while to be strong enough but it's seven years now since Maggie passed and I'm more than ready to move on.' He looks at Ivy pointedly.

'Good for you.' Ivy feels something shift between them.

'Come with me,' Bob says suddenly. 'I know you must think I'm crazy but there's something between us. You must feel it.' He seizes her hands in his. 'I wouldn't force you before you're ready, wouldn't expect anything from you. But we're so alike. What do you think, Ivy? Come with me.'

Chapter Twenty-Eight

Summer

Summer walks back from the pole dancing class absolutely exhausted and covered in sweat. The last few pole dancing sessions have really tested their commitment. What seemed a lot of fun at first is now something more serious. After the communal bonding session a few weeks ago , Summer had thought Feather Starr might lay off them for a while, but lately the sessions have been harder than ever.

'We need to get our heads in the game ahead of the fête,' Feather had opened with this evening. 'Show the village what we are made of.'

They are a pole dancing group in the middle of nowhere, not a high school American football team, Summer thought. But they'd spent the class rehearsing the routine, adding new moves and working in formations, so some were on the poles whilst others were doing 'floor work' as Feather called it.

Summer's pleased to feel the cool night air on her face, but she thinks it will take a while for her heart rate to go back to normal.

'That was intense,' Meg says, beside her. They've started the journey home together. There was no appetite amongst the women to go to the pub this week after the exhausting session.

'Do I look like I'm constipated?' Summer asks. She's convinced she's swinging her body weight from side to side in a waddle, but her thighs ache too much to walk normally.

'You're fine,' Meg laughs. 'I can't lift my arms beyond this.' She holds them slightly out to the sides, like a penguin flapping its wings. 'I don't know how the older women do it. Ivy's a powerhouse.'

'You're the same,' Summer says. 'You look so strong on that pole, and barely break a sweat. And you're the only one that can do that upside down move.' It wasn't a coincidence that Feather decided Meg should do that move alone in the fête, with the others all fanning out along the floor to highlight Meg's talent.

'It's funny,' Meg starts, 'I never would have had the confidence to do that before the skinny-dipping.'

'I don't know why,' Summer says, although she understands Meg's feelings about the stoma bag must be complicated. 'You hid it so well.'

'I had a long time to practise,' she shrugs. 'Now I wonder if I've been silly all these years to hide it. What's the big deal if people know I have a stoma bag. I'm sick of holding it in. It's a relief in some ways, now it's out in the open.'

Summer puts an arm around her, proud of Meg and her newfound confidence. 'Have you decided what to do about the costumes yet?' Feather showed them a mock-up of her plans earlier. She wants the women to wear black crop tops or T-shirts, with an assortment of sequinned shorts in different colours. It would definitely show Meg's stoma bag. Summer had seen her look of dismay, although she wasn't the only one that didn't look too happy at the revealing outfits.

'Probably wear a normal black T-shirt. It's different with you women, but I'm not ready to show it off to the whole village yet,' Meg says, shaking her head.

Summer knows she should probably reassure Meg, but her thoughts are on her own predicament. She wants to hide her stomach too. She's only seven weeks pregnant now, but her body's already starting to show it. Muscle memory from the last two seems to have paved the way for her bump to start developing. Aled loves it, of course, kissing the new bump every night and touching it every time she passes. Summer isn't so sure. She's reluctant to break out the maternity wardrobe, not that she ever had the time or need to put her maternity jeans away after Jordan was born, but she's going to need it in the next few weeks.

Everyone will know then.

If they don't already, Summer thinks. When she saw that image of the women at the lagoon, blurry and pixelated though it was, Summer's eyes were drawn straight to her lumpy outline. She was convinced she could see everything under the water, from her caesarean scar to the growing paunch at her midriff.

They turn the corner to the village square, where the post office sits between the bus stop and the antiques' shop.

'Do you fancy coming in for a cuppa?' Meg asks.

'I'd better get home to the terrors,' Summer says, waving her off. She only has one more night at home with Aled, before he's away again. She still hasn't really told him how she feels about the baby. He'll be gone again tomorrow, and she'll be left to worry about things alone.

Summer needs to say something, but she just doesn't know what. She knows they will keep the baby, it's the right decision for them, but she feels deep down that something needs to change. They can't carry on as they are. Summer will have a breakdown. The stop-start on-off family life Aled has is constant for her, and she struggles with just two babies. With three, she's not just outnumbered, but completely overwhelmed.

Summer sighs, turning on to her street. She remembers when they moved in, vowing that they'd save up for something bigger when they could. Aled's parents had paid half of their deposit, and they'd taken out an enormous mortgage. But Summer was pregnant, and they needed the extra bedroom. It's fine now Jordan is small enough to sleep in their room, but Summer doesn't know where he'll go when he's big enough, let alone baby number three.

The house is small, in a line of terraces, with on-road parking spaces that are impossible to find come 5 p.m. She and Aled share the one car, but even then, they're often parking across the street, carrying shopping bags and sleeping children into the house in multiple journeys.

She remembers their plans to move, find something detached, with a driveway, their own parking. Life gets in the way, as always.

'I'm home,' she calls quietly, shutting the front door.

'It's just me,' Aled greets her. 'The kids have been good as gold, so I sent Zoe home early.'

He's getting better then, she thinks. Or is this to prove to her that he can cope with another baby, the cynical side of her wonders.

'Do you want a cuppa?'

'No, I'm parched. I want something cold like . . . ooh, a chocolate milkshake,' Summer says.

'And so it begins,' Aled jokes. 'Remember the first time round, when you sent me to Tesco to buy a box of Nesquik at midnight?' Summer remembers, how Aled missed the opening times, and ended up driving halfway down the Welsh coast to Carmarthen to buy her some, while she lay at home on the sofa, trying to satisfy her pregnancy craving. She laughs along with the story.

'At least it was something normal. Lucy in Mother and Baby said she craved Imperial Leather handwash throughout her pregnancy.'

'There's posh,' Aled says.

Summer collapses against the sofa and shuts her eyes. She remembers that first pregnancy, how she'd been so tired throughout the first trimester, stealing naps whenever she could after getting back from school. Aled used to tiptoe around her, doing the cooking and washing-up so she didn't have to, waking her to drag her up to bed at night.

She didn't have the luxury of sofa naps now; how she used to indulge every whim, with Aled treating her like royalty or precious cargo. That was the best part of pregnancy, let alone the excitement of the creature growing inside you, Summer loved feeling special. Though still magic, it wasn't the same the second and third time, when you had another child prodding your stomach and running rings around you.

'We've still got some in the back of the cupboard,' Aled says, handing her a small glass.

'I'll have to get some more Nesquik next week.'

'And I'll be back to rig food,' Aled flops next to her on the sofa. He gives her a self-pitying look, and it's almost more than Summer can handle. Now is the time. She has to say something.

'Aled, I've been thinking . . .'

'Uh oh,' he says, and Summer rolls her eyes.

'I'm not sure we can carry on like this, with you going away. Not when we have three kids.'

He gives a sigh, as though this is the last conversation he wants. 'Not this again. I know it's hard with me going away, trust me. We can't afford for me to get a different job.' He rubs her thigh. 'You know that.'

'I know but . . .' She starts the familiar answer, then realises what she's doing. 'Surely there's something you could do.'

'We need the money now more than ever, though. If we didn't have this one on the way, then maybe . . .'

'No, you're wrong,' Summer says, more forcefully than intended. 'There must be a way to make it work. Otherwise . . .' She sighs, unsure whether she should say what's next. 'Otherwise, I'm not sure I can carry on like this. It's too much for me. Obviously, I love our children to bits, but I can't take on three all on my own like this.'

'You're not on your own,' Aled says but can't meet her eyes.

'At the moment I may as well be. Aled, you couldn't even take care of them for an hour. I have this day-in day-out, it's like I don't know who I am any more. I don't have a personality, my own interests, anything.'

'You have pole dancing.'

'One hour a week. And thank God for it. If I'm honest, that's been the only thing keeping me sane, the only respite I have.'

Aled looks defeated for a moment. 'I'm trying my best, Sum.'

'I know you are. But I'm saying we need to do something. For our family,' she swallows, getting going now. She feels she needs to say this before she loses the courage. 'When I found out I was pregnant again, I have to be honest, the first thing I felt was terror. I knew I couldn't raise another child, not on my own, like this. Not only is it more chaos, but it's just longer before I can get back to me, get back to what I want to do.'

'What are you saying?'

'I want to go back to work,' Summer says, nodding. 'I need this. Obviously not right now and probably not for a while after the baby's born, but maybe I could do some temporary teaching assistant work. Boost our family income and all that.' She's been thinking about it. Seeing Gwen talk about saving her family life by working again, and Ivy grabbing life by the balls at her age, it's made Summer realise what's missing from hers. She loves her children, but she needs a life outside the house. She needs other people and structure and her own income.

'Well, how are you going to do that? We've got no one to look after the kids,' he says, then suddenly leans across to get Summer's chocolate milkshake and takes a big swig. The action makes her laugh, incongruous in this conversation.

'We can make it work, if you're closer to home. I'd only work one or two days a week. Aled, I really need this,' she says.

'Let's think about it. We've got nine months,' he says.

'Nearly seven months. That's not long,' Summer says.

'If this is something you really want, why have you held your tongue for so long? Why not just tell me?'

'Well,' she shrugs, 'I knew I wanted it, but I didn't know if I had the confidence to go back to work. I was planning to do my teacher training one day. I wouldn't mind getting back on that path, at least having some kind of plan for my life in the future.'

'We have sort of derailed your career plans, haven't we?'

There's another reason, though, Summer thinks. These pole dancing classes have done something to her. Given her the mental space to think through what she really wants, and the confidence to follow through and go for it. Without them, she was just stuck, saying yes to Aled, running after the kids, and not even thinking about herself. Going through the motions of life.

'Are you sure this is what you want?' Aled asks.

'Yes, it is. And not just me. Nia would love having you home more. We both miss you so much when you're away, Jordan too.'

'It does break my heart when I come home and pick him up, and he starts crying,' he says. 'It took a while for Nia to learn who I was and that I would be coming back each time I went away.'

'They need their dad around,' Summer snuggles up against him.

'I suppose I could start asking, see if Jonesie knows of any jobs round here,' Aled says.

'Would you do something similar?' Summer asks, wanting

him to stay on track. This is the closest she's got to demanding what she wants in years with Aled.

'Unless there are plans for an on-land oil rig, then I doubt it,' Aled says, sarcastically. 'I'm sure the lads will know of something.' He pauses, 'You know I'd do anything for you and the kids, don't you?'

'I do,' Summer says. She wasn't sure until tonight, but now she feels more content than ever. 'But who's your favourite?'

'Hmmm, it would have to be this little one as number one, then Nia and Jordan as joint second, and you number three.'

Summer play-punches him but feels in total heaven. And with that, the crying starts on the baby monitor.

Chapter Twenty-Nine

Gwen

Shoes and handbags litter the floor of Gwen's dressing room. She's been sorting out her wardrobes in readiness for the move, even though that won't be for a while yet as she hasn't found anywhere suitable. That cottage in Abercastle has been the most promising so far. She and Lydia had a viewing a couple of days ago and the estate agent, Pippa Barlow, showed them around, using the word 'bijou' so frequently, Gwen was amazed she didn't blush with embarrassment. The view was beguiling, glimpses of blue showing through the kitchen window and the front bedrooms upstairs. Nothing as majestic as the view from The Haven, but a view of the Irish Sea, nonetheless. In a corner of the living room, though, the old-fashioned wallpaper was peeling away with damp.

'This is just a bit of mould,' Pippa had told them dismissively. 'Easily remedied.'

The only bathroom in the cottage was situated downstairs. Not great when they were used to their luxurious en suites.

Lydia became quieter and more reserved as the viewing progressed, despite Gwen's best efforts to put a positive spin on things. 'What a cute little back garden. We could soon give this a Mediterranean makeover. A few pots of blue paint and some flowers' and 'Ooh, a wood burner! Think how cosy it will be in the winter'.

In the car on the way back, Lydia had gazed miserably out of the window. 'It was OK' was all she offered in terms of an opinion on the cottage.

Later, when she went into Lydia's bedroom to say goodnight, Gwen's heart broke when she saw her daughter's tear-stained face.

Gwen had taken her into her arms. 'I'm sorry you're having to go through this, my love,' she'd said.

'I don't hate that cottage, Mum, but it is embarrassing going from this,' Lydia swept her arm in an arc, 'to that poky little place. And Sophie has been such a bitch because I've pulled out of the Zante trip and she's gotta share a room with Amelia and Rachel. It's hardly my fault.'

'I could try and scrape the money together,' Gwen started, but bit her lip, knowing that in reality they had to save every penny they could. 'Sophie is not a true friend to you if she doesn't understand.'

'I know,' Lydia agreed. She sat up in bed. 'Dad came to meet me after school yesterday.'

'Oh,' was all Gwen could say, slightly taken aback that Lydia had not mentioned it before then.

'I went back to his flat in Haverfordwest. It's horrible. It's above the kebab place and smells. He says he doesn't even smell it now, he's so used to it. Lynne wouldn't let him stay, saying they weren't really right for each other.' Gwen couldn't help but feel some satisfaction at this. 'He kept saying he's been a fool and if only he could turn the clock back.'

'And how do you feel about him now?'

Lydia had paused at this and held her gaze for a moment, 'Angry. Annoyed at him. But he's still my father and I still love him. Mixed feelings. I definitely don't think you should have him back,' she had said with vehemence.

Gwen hugged her. 'I'm proud of you, Lyds. We'll get through this.' She experienced mixed feelings like Lydia, but any last vestige of love for Gareth had disappeared. She felt angry, bitter and sad all at once. Why couldn't he have come to her when the business was struggling? Why did he turn to Lynne? Why did he have to put them through all this?

Looking through her old clothes, some with the tags still on, she feels embarrassed at how much she used to spend on clothes. When did she become so superficial? When had she allowed material things to make up for the aching hole in her heart? Her stomach suddenly lurches when she spots the box at the top of the wardrobe, where her wedding dress has been lovingly stored in a nest of gossamer-thin tissue paper. Like some sort of treasure. Gwen snorts at the irony. Lifting the box, she places it on the floor. Now, as she gently lifts the tissue, she catches sight of the flouncy sleeves, a cheap imitation of Princess Diana's dress. Not worth much but she felt like a princess in it. The wedding took place in Haverfordwest's Registry Office, and Gareth wore a grey suit, the one he wore for interviews and the only one he owned at the time. Gwen thinks about their first dance in the rugby club to Seal's 'Kiss from a Rose'. It was the way Gareth looked at her, as if she were the only woman in the world. They had no money then but they radiated happiness. They could spend hours just talking through the night, about their plans for the future, the children they'd have, the business they'd create, the life that would be theirs.

It's hard to imagine how they've gone from those heady days to this. Gwen's realistic – that excitement can't last when you've been married years. But the venom Gareth has for her now, the way he's treated her, the lack of respect. The first time he'd cheated, it felt like a physical pain. Jenny, the receptionist. It took Gwen two years at least to get over it. Then it was Lisa, the antiques' dealer who sold him his desk, a dark brown monstrosity he felt gave him some gravitas. The bloody fool! She recognised the signs of old – the late nights, the care in getting ready in the morning, his phone velcroed to his hand. Now, Lynne.

Sighing, Gwen folds the dress back in the box. Time to move on, she thinks.

She can hear Lydia clattering around the bedroom next door. She's started work at The Mariners three nights a week and Gwen thinks that it's good for her. It's getting her out of the house, and she doesn't ask her for money now.

'I'll walk down with you,' Gwen says, meeting her on the stairs. 'I need some fresh air.'

Outside, a bruised sky threatens rain and Gwen pulls her jacket tighter around her. Lydia chats about the pub.

'There's a live band on Saturday, so it should be busy. An indie rock band. Kudos, they're called. Rhys, the bar manager, was telling me it'll be heaving at the fête. You wouldn't believe how much money people pay for drinks, Mum. One guy spent a hundred and twenty quid last Thursday.'

'I can well believe it. More money than sense,' Gwen says, thinking that Gareth often spent a fortune when he went out, but she had wasted money too. 'I'll pick you up later,' Gwen says, as they veer off in different directions. 'Save you walking home in the dark.'

Gwen heads down the hill, breathing in the salty air. She never walked anywhere before, never felt the desperate urge to achieve ten thousand steps a day as most women did. Why walk when you have a car, especially as returning home meant a hike up the steep hill?

Now, though, she likes the way a walk clears her head. The sky is the colour of blackberries, dark and brooding, and the sea churns below. The beach is desolate for this time of year and the rocks, like serrated steel, form a boundary between the road and seashore. Gwen thinks about heading back but sees a figure on the bench.

'I'm not the only mad one out and about, then, Ivy?'

Ivy, lost in thought, turns to Gwen. 'I love it when the beach is quiet like this. You might be right, though. It's threatening rain.'

Gwen sits down. 'So, what's dragged you out?'

'I love it when it's quieter, when the visitors go. You?'

'I had to get out. I've been trying to do a clear out of the house.'

'Yes, that stirs all sorts of memories,' Ivy says sympathetically. She looks out to sea. 'Morlan's such a tiny place. I want to look at the ocean from a different country. I want to see beyond that horizon.'

'At the moment, I would quite happily spend the rest of my days in Morlan. I don't want to move from here,' Gwen says quietly. 'It's never too late for you to travel, Ivy. There's nothing stopping you.'

Ivy evades the comment. 'You'll find something, Gwen. Besides, there's lots of beautiful places along the Pembrokeshire coast, as beautiful as Morlan.'

'You're right, of course. What about you, Ivy? Are you going to do a bit of travelling?' Gwen asks.

Ivy nods. 'Yes, I think so. St Augustine said the world is a book and if you don't travel, you have only read one page. That about sums me up. I want to see new things, experience new sights, inhale new smells. It's like an ache in my heart. I know it might sound foolish coming from a woman my age.' Gwen shakes her head, then Ivy goes on, 'Do you remember me telling you about Bob? He's asked me to travel around Europe with him in September.'

'Well, that's a surprise. I didn't think you knew him that well.'

'I don't,' says Ivy. 'He's lonely and he has wanderlust. Like me. There's nothing in it, nothing between us. He lost his wife seven years ago and he wants companionship.'

'What do you think, Ivy?'

'It's quite tempting. He's a nice man.' She looks out to sea once more. 'I always thought I'd do it on my own. I longed for freedom when Jim was alive.'

'Would you go for a long time or are you talking just weeks, then?'

'Bob has planned an itinerary for a few weeks. The point is, though, I'd like the freedom to go where I want, for as long as I want.'

'Being alone terrifies me,' Gwen confesses. 'I was unhappy with Gareth. He took me completely for granted, but it's all I've ever known, being part of a couple.'

'You're stronger than you think, Gwen. Don't forget you've brought up your two lovely daughters, you've provided a wonderful home for them. You played your part in a successful business.'

'Huh, fat lot of good I was. I didn't realise that Gareth was siphoning off cash, that he'd been making bad investments. I was supposed to be good at accounts. I did a bookkeeping course years ago. Enjoyed it, too.'

'Gareth cheated on you in more ways than one, but you mustn't blame yourself or doubt your abilities.'

'What can I do, though? I'm out of work, will soon be out of the house. We've already got some people interested in buying it. A couple from London.'

'Have you thought of advertising and setting up on your own? A bookkeeping company maybe,' Ivy prompts.

'I wouldn't know where to start.'

Ivy shakes her head. 'Come on, Gwen. Vimpany Motors was once one of the biggest car showrooms in Pembrokeshire. That wasn't all Gareth. You must know about marketing and social media. Get a business account on Instagram. Find a niche. Women-only businesses. Or people starting again after a crisis. An angle that will attract customers.'

'You could be right. I'll have to have a think,' Gwen says. Both lapse into silence for a beat. 'You know, I joined the pole

269

dancing fitness class having all these preconceived ideas about it being something sexy rather than fitness, but everything about this class has surprised me. It's not just been a distraction, it's more like therapy.' Gwen laughs, 'I'm not getting any better at it, though.'

'I know exactly what you mean. Look at young Meg. She's blossomed. Really come out of her shell. That skinny-dipping has done wonders for her confidence. It was just the boost she needed.'

'Hmm, Feather Starr seems to have worked her magic on all of us. Although she has certainly ruffled a few feathers of her own. Personally, I could do without any more drama in my life.'

A lone figure walks along the shore, throwing a stick out to sea for his black Cocker Spaniel to retrieve. Both women watch him, lost in their own thoughts.

Gwen sighs. 'The fête's not far away. I doubt I'll have all the moves nailed by then.'

'I don't suppose it matters,' says Ivy. 'It's only a bit of fun.'

'I just want to get through it without embarrassing the girls too much. Since Gareth left, though, Jas and Lydia are making more of an effort with me. They're under no illusions about their father any more. And Lydia used to be such a daddy's girl.'

Suddenly, fat droplets of rain fall and both women rise quickly to their feet.

'Gawd, why didn't I bring an umbrella?' Gwen moans.

They are drenched before they can reach the bottom of the hill and Gwen laughs at the state of the two of them, like drowned rats!

'Do you want to come into mine?' Ivy offers. 'You can warm up with some brandy and it might stop soon.'

'It's OK. I'll dry off at home and then take the car to pick up Lydia.' As Gwen continues up the hill, she feels more hopeful about her situation. Ivy has given her a lot to think about.

Chapter Thirty

Meg

Meg is strangely nervous before the date today. She hasn't seen Josh since he came to Morlan and had left in such a hurry. They'd been texting though, and Meg could detect no weirdness in his messages, no hesitation in replying or hint of things fizzling out. He'd pleaded pressure of work and Meg imagines it must be hard for him settling in a new job and new place. They say absence makes the heart grow fonder and Meg's desperate to see Josh again – he contacts her on an almost hourly basis, and it feels nice.

The nervous anticipation in her stomach has been building throughout the morning. She needn't have worried. As soon as she pulls up outside Josh's flat, she sees he's been outside, waiting for her, and she knows it will be a fantastic date. Especially with the eager snog he plants on her as soon as she gets close, not caring about the family passing across the street, walking in a line to navigate the narrow pavement. It is a glorious, sunny day today, and Meg couldn't be happier.

There's another reason she's been nervous about today, though. Meg is going to tell Josh about the stoma bag, once and for all. She's chickened out all along, and if she waits any longer, it will be too late. It's terrifying, but if Josh reacts anything like the pole dancing women, she will be fine.

'Top up?' Josh offers the bottle, sweaty from the ice bucket and vastly overpriced.

'I shouldn't if I'm driving home,' Meg says, already anticipating his flirty comment.

'Well, you could get a taxi,' he surprises her. 'Or you could stay over.'

'I could, could I?' she repeats, satisfied with his interest in her.

'If you want to. No pressure of course,' Josh sits forward all of a sudden. His face looks familiar now, but she still delights in every millimetre of it, from the stubble that fails to mask the dimples either side of his mouth, to his lagoon-blue eyes. 'You look absolutely gorgeous today. I don't think I've told you that enough.'

Meg blinks, slowly, like a cat, enjoying his attention. It's nice to feel so wanted, so fancied. And the feeling is absolutely mutual.

'Ahem,' the waitress standing nearby interrupts. They move apart, reluctantly, like two teenagers in the vicinity of a teacher. 'Have you decided what desserts you want?'

'Chocolate fondant,' Meg says, unable to resist the most chocolatey of desserts if it's on a menu. She should remember to check her teeth afterwards for chocolate sauce.

'Same,' Josh orders, barely looking at the waitress before his eyes are locked back on Meg. She should use this interruption to tell him, but he starts talking before she can.

'So, I made a decision yesterday,' he says, clearing his throat.

'I'm intrigued.'

'I've been looking forward to today so much, especially as we haven't been able to see each other with work being such a pain in the arse. I've missed you. I just couldn't wait to see you, and I was thinking . . .' He looks coy, and Meg reaches out to slip her hand in his across the table. 'I decided to delete my dating apps. Not that I've used them lately, don't get me wrong, but I was thinking that it's pointless when I don't want to meet anyone else.'

'Is that the modern-day equivalent of saying we're exclusive now?' Meg asks, hearing the term on *Love Island* last week, and wondering if it would ever come her way.

'Exclusive,' Josh turns the phrase over. 'Well, I've never heard it, but I'm wondering if that's the modern way of saying boyfriend and girlfriend?'

Meg hopes the ecstasy doesn't show too much on her face, when really she wants to stand up and dance, or spring across the table to straddle Josh and kiss his face off. She tries to be confident, feign nonchalance. 'I could go for that.' She's smiling, though, hoping he feels the same.

'I should ask you properly. Do you want to be my girlfriend?' Josh asks.

Meg pretends to consider it for a few seconds, then laughs. 'Yes, of course.'

'Thank God for that,' Josh sighs. 'I might have already told my parents you are.'

Meg laughs now, even happier. 'I haven't told anyone, but now I can tell the world you're my boyfriend.' She didn't think this day would ever come, that she, Meg Thomas, would have a boyfriend. The Pole Stars will be delighted when she messages them later, she thinks.

There's something nagging at her, though.

'I should probably tell you something first,' Meg says. She waits for Josh's smile to fall, but it doesn't. He just nods.

'I've sort of mentioned to you before that I've been ill and had operations,' she says. Oh God, here goes. 'This is something I've been ashamed of for so long, something I try to hide from people.' Josh is intensely focused on her, but Meg feels she's having an out-of-body experience, watching herself admit the words. 'I'm learning, though, to be more confident of it. I have a stoma bag, see. It's meant to be temporary, until I can have another operation when my bowel settles, but last time they mentioned it might not be possible. For a while, at least. I hated it when I first had it, it held me back so much, but I think I'm coming to terms with it. The pole dancing has helped a lot, strangely enough.'

Meg's aware she's babbling now and hasn't made eye contact with Josh since she started talking. She forces herself to look at him. He's still smiling, although there's a fleck of concern in his eyes. Oh God, she hates that concern.

'I'll be fine, I'm dealing with it, learning to love it . . . or at least, not hate it. I completely understand if this changes things for you, though. Especially after the conversation we've just had. I know, I should have told you sooner, I'm sorry.' Meg pauses for breath. 'If I could go back in time, I would. I just get so nervous telling people. In fact, I haven't told many people up 'til now, and . . .'

Josh's hand encloses hers on the table. 'Are you finished now?'

Meg smiles brightly, to cover her embarrassment. 'Sorry, I talk when I'm nervous. I'll completely understand however you feel, whatever you want to do next.'

'However I feel? I'd have to be pretty shallow for that to change my feelings for you, wouldn't I?' Josh says, seriously.

'I should say it's happened before, but in reality, I've never really told anyone like this,' Meg says truthfully.

'Meg, I'm a doctor, stoma bags are not a new thing for me. True, I've never been with someone who's got one, but that's ok. It changes nothing,' he says.

'Are you sure?'

'Of course,' Josh says, squeezing her. He takes his hand away, but Meg wishes he'd keep it there a bit longer. 'I'm glad you've told me.'

'Me too. It's such a relief,' Meg says. She meets his eyes, paranoid as to what she'll find, and searches his for any sign of a change, or of him pulling away, but nothing. He looks just as happy, and she feels elated.

'Two chocolate fondants.' The waitress places the plates between them. 'I'll get you two spoons.' Meg feels slightly nauseous with the drama of telling Josh, but the chocolatey pudding does look delicious.

'I tried to make this once,' Josh says. 'Complete disaster. You have to get the oven temperature and the timing just right.'

'Oh,' Meg says. 'I've never tried, I'm not much of a baker.'

'I baked a lot with my mother growing up, then stopped in uni . . .' He starts telling her about some cooking disaster in university. Meg is a little surprised the conversation has moved on from her stoma bag so quickly. It's such a major thing for her, she expected it to take up a large portion of the dessert, at least. She thought he'd have questions for her, how long she's had it, what it's like, when she can have the next operation, that sort of thing. She guesses he's more comfortable with it than she expected, maybe because of his job. Or maybe he feels uncomfortable asking. Should she say anything, she wonders, then decides to be confident for a second time today.

'That's funny,' she says, as he finishes his story. 'You know you can ask me anything about the stoma, don't you? I don't mind.'

'I know,' Josh says. She's not sure if she imagines the note of defensiveness, but she's probably being paranoid.

'So, there was another time in uni we decided to make Christmas lunch for everyone in the flat. We planned it for weeks . . .' He moves on again. Meg can't help but feel a little hurt, or is she just being overly sensitive?

She lets Josh tell his stories, laughing in the right places and eating chocolate fondant in between. It's hard to concentrate on the gooey goodness, though, her mind whirring over the events of the last few minutes.

When Josh finishes his, he puts his fork down purposefully.

'I'm sorry, I need to go to the toilet,' he says. Meg smiles, and he squeezes her shoulder as he goes past. He does like her, she tells herself. He's not shallow and he does understand the stoma bag. Life is good.

She sits at the table, resisting the urge to pull her phone out and message the women right away. She's come to think of them as her friends; in fact, they know more about her than her official friends do, and she can't wait to tell them about her date. But she stops herself. If she can't be comfortable in her own company for at least a few minutes, then shame on her.

Meg watches the other diners around her, the first time she's taken her eyes off Josh since she's been here. A family is eating, the parents chatting, teenagers both looking bored. There are another few couples, one of them in their eighties. She wonders if any of her fellow diners have just been through a momentous conversation like her. She wishes she could rush right round and tell people, she has a boyfriend!

Meg looks to the toilet door, as the waitress comes to clear their plates.

'All good with the chocolate fondant?'

'Delicious, thanks.'

'Would you like anything else?'

Meg glances again, not knowing what Josh wants to do. 'I'd better check with him. Nothing for me, though.'

She wonders how long he's been in there, shifts uncomfortably in her seat. She gives in to the urge to check her phone, surprised it's got so late, and scrolls through some messages on the WhatsApp group. Summer has shared pictures of the kids and Gwen has sent a listing for a cottage nearby. She also has a message from Hannah asking if she should save Meg some shepherd's pie for dinner, and whether she'd be willing to work tomorrow. Meg types a reply, then slips her phone away. Josh will be back now.

Or not. What if he's stood her up? Left early, slipped out the toilet window? She checks his seat, but he wasn't wearing a coat and must have carried his phone and wallet with him. It would be easy enough for him to leave.

No, that's ridiculous, Meg thinks. Josh is a normal human being, and she is a paranoid psychopath. She should just chill out.

Maybe he's having explosive diarrhoea. That would at least be better for Meg's ego, but poor Josh. It would put a bit of a downer on their date.

Finally, the door opens, and Josh comes back looking a little pale.

'Are you OK?'

'Yes,' he sits down. 'Actually, no. I've just found out my grandfather isn't very well. He's been in and out of hospital a lot recently, but my mum's said I should come up now. It might be my last chance to see him.'

'Oh my God, Josh, I'm so sorry,' Meg says. And there she was thinking he'd left without her. She can be so superficial sometimes, she thinks, she should never admit that to anyone. 'Are you going to Reading?'

'Yes, I'll have to go now.' Josh shakes his head. 'I can't believe this is happening tonight.'

'Please don't give me it second thought,' Meg says. She motions for the bill from one of the waiters. 'Do you want me to drive you up?'

'No, I don't know how long I'll be there for,' Josh says,

stony-faced. 'I'd better take my car.'

'Let me pay, then,' Meg says as the bill arrives.

'Are you sure?' Josh's protests are weak, but Meg can see he's distracted.

'It's my turn,' Meg says, although Josh hasn't let her pay for anything so far.

Within minutes, they are back out on the street outside Josh's flat. 'You go, I can call a taxi from here,' she tells him.

'I'm sorry, Meg. Thanks for today,' Josh hugs her. Meg feels herself clinging on, sad that the date is ending like this, before admonishing herself. She will have plenty of time with Josh, her boyfriend, in the future. He needs to be with his family now.

'Hope you're OK,' she says as they break apart.

'I'll message you later,' he tells her, and then he is gone. Meg calls a taxi, then waits on the wall a little way down from his flat.

What a whirlwind of a date!

Meg texts Josh later that evening. A simple *Hope everything's OK with your grandfather. I'm thinking of your family xxx*

It's more kisses than she would usually send, but then he is her boyfriend now. By the time she goes to bed, he hasn't replied. Poor Josh, he must be having such a crap night. Meg wishes she had a picture of him on her phone, but they haven't got to that stage yet. She has to make do with a grainy Facebook picture of him that hasn't been updated for about five years. Still, he looks gorgeous, and Meg stares at it for an embarrassingly long time. Her boyfriend.

The next morning there's still no reply, so Meg sends

another one. *Let me know how you are when you have time today. Hope everything's OK xxx*

At lunchtime, there's still no reply. He must be having the worst day ever. Meg can't imagine how she'll feel when the time comes for her own grandmother to get old and be in hospital. She hugs Hannah extra tight at the end of her shift in the post office.

Dinner comes and still nothing, so Meg decides to call him, but no answer. Poor Josh. *Don't worry about calling back if you're busy. Just checking on you xxxxx*

She tries not to obsess over her phone, and to ignore the whiff of desperation her unrequited messages give off, a one-sided conversation in blue on her iPhone. She really should put fewer kisses next time. But then the man is grieving. He doesn't need her constant messages. Meg will limit herself to sending just one tomorrow, if she doesn't hear back from him by then.

The next day comes with nada.

Let me know you're ok and haven't been in a horrific car accident on the way to Reading . . . Meg starts to type but deletes it instantly, instead sending a simple *Let me know you're ok x*

She pops round to Summer's for a cuppa with the other pole dancing women, but instead of enjoying their conversation and banter, she finds herself wanting to check her phone every few minutes, mistaking every sound for an incoming message vibration. She decides not to tell them about the whole boyfriend/girlfriend thing, just in case.

In case of what, Meg isn't sure, but this somehow doesn't seem like a good omen. She isn't sure if she's being obsessive, bunny-boiler style, or realistic. Surely, he would have replied by now?

In bed that night she refrains from sending another message, but decides to internet stalk him instead. She Googles his name, and multiple different combinations, from Cardiff Medical School to St Davids Practice. There's a picture of him on the GP website, along with a short bio, but nothing else to satisfy Meg. She struggles to sleep that night.

Meg finds herself annoyed when she wakes to a blank phone screen the following morning. There must be something up. She's sure that even if he's grieving for his grandfather, he could type a quick reply.

I'm beginning to think you don't want to talk to me . . .

She sends, then quickly follows with a *Sorry if that sounded aggressive. Just let me know how you are. I'm worried x*

She works in the post office again, resolving not to check her phone until she has a break, but it is still blank.

'Oh, I've just found out my car's sorted in the garage. They're dropping it round later,' Hannah says as she passes Meg. 'Do you want me to take you to get yours?'

'That would be fab, thanks Nan,' Meg says. She hasn't had a chance to collect it yet, waiting instead for Hannah to help. If she's going that way, she wonders whether she should call in to Josh's. Find out what's happening for real.

He can't be ghosting her. He's too nice for that. It's fine if he doesn't want to be with her – well, not fine, but his own choice – she just wishes he would tell her straight. Is it the stoma bag, Meg wonders? Surely Josh isn't that shallow. He seemed fine with it on their date. Scarily fine. Maybe too fine. What if it was all an act?

She still hasn't heard from him by the time she's in the car later with Hannah. Hannah drives about ten miles an hour, painfully slowly, and Meg is more impatient than usual. She can't decide whether to knock on his door or leave him be. She's going to decide in the moment.

Mercifully, Hannah can't wait outside Josh's busy road, so Meg waves her on and walks to her car. She notices Josh's lights are on in the flat.

So, he is in. She feels anger flare in her chest. He could at least reply to her if he's not in Reading. The window to his flat leads on to the pavement, and Meg hesitates before strolling past, glancing inwards.

She sees the light of the TV illuminate faces on the sofa. Male faces, all around Josh's age. She can't see him, but she can hear laughter and male voices.

She pauses on the pavement past the window, then turns round, hoping no one's watching her right now. She peers in again. This time she sees that it's football on the television, and there, standing next to the screen, beer in one hand and remote in the other, is Josh. He's talking, saying something that receives whoops from the other guys.

The absolute arsehole.

Meg feels momentarily stuck. She wants to run but can't look away.

Then Josh looks up at the window. Before Meg can move, his eyes meet hers and his expression changes.

Heart pounding, Meg makes a break for the car.

She manages to get in and pull out of the space, thanking the man behind who's let her out. It's only when she gets out of St Davids that Meg's heart breaks.

She cries the whole way back to Morlan.

Chapter Thirty-One

Ivy

Sipping home-made lemonade on the patio at the back and enjoying the morning sunshine, Ivy hears her phone ringing in the kitchen. A butterfly lands on the back of her chair, its wings as delicate as silk. Reluctantly, she gets up to answer.

'Mum, it's me, Matthew,' he says with little preamble, an urgency in his tone.

It's odd Matthew ringing in the day, she thinks, and a Wednesday, too. 'Is everything OK?'

'I'm in Cardiff Gate at the moment. I had to stop to get petrol. Are you in? I was going to call round.' He makes it sound as if he lives just around the corner.

'Yes, I was about to make lunch. I'll hang fire until you get here.' She can't but help wonder what the reason is for this impromptu visit but she refrains from asking. He'll tell her, no doubt, but Ivy feels a knot of anxiety. He never calls around like this. Matthew plans everything, from the socks he's going to wear to his sandwiches for lunch.

'I'll be there in about an hour and a half. Looking forward to seeing you, Mum.'

Most odd. Ivy was going to start sanding down and painting the kitchen cupboards this afternoon. She's seen some beautiful, Mediterranean-style kitchens on Pinterest with navy blue cupboards and bright yellow mosaic tiles. Instead, she makes a spinach and goat cheese frittata with salad and new potatoes. She and Matthew spend little time together, so it's nice to cook for him.

As Matthew's BMW pulls up outside the house, Ivy watches him. He's wearing jeans and a checked shirt, buttoned to his collar. Even when he's dressed casually, there's a stiffness about him. He never really lets go. The familiar twitch of the curtains tells her Wendy has spotted his arrival too.

'Hi, Mum,' he says, as he kisses her perfunctorily on the cheek and hands her a bouquet of flowers. 'Not very exciting, but it's all they really had in the services.' His eyes are bloodshot, she notices.

'What a lovely surprise to see you, Matthew. Peonies. My favourite. I've set up the table in the back. I'll just top up the lemonade. I made some this morning.'

When Ivy walks back through the lounge, Matthew is looking out of the front window. 'It is a beautiful view. I took it completely for granted when I lived here,' he says.

'I thought you were a city boy through and through these days.'

'I am. I love Bristol and there's not much work in these parts. Sometimes I wish we were nearer the countryside for Tabitha's sake. Children need fresh air and open spaces. And the beach.'

'You need to bring her more often, Matthew. It's been ages

since she visited Pembrokeshire.' He nods. 'Come on, let's go and have some lunch. I'm ravenous.'

Matthew butters the French loaf and helps himself to another slice of frittata. 'You always were such a good cook. I don't think Dad ever appreciated it.'

'I don't think he did,' says Ivy. 'He wasn't very adventurous. Liked his roasts and stews.'

'Rachel likes to bake, but she's always so busy with work. When Tabitha's in bed, she settles down to mark or prepare for the next day. There's always something she has to do for school.' Is there an edge to his voice? Ivy can't quite work it out, but Matthew seems to be floating on the edges of the conversation. It's stilted, strained. Perhaps he and Rachel are going through a difficult patch. Matthew has never been very open or effusive with his emotions.

'Why don't you bring Tabitha down here and leave her with me for a week or even just a couple of days? I'd love to spend time with her and I could take her to the rock pools. It would give you and Rachel some time together, just the two of you.'

'Yes, perhaps. I think you and Tabs have a special bond.' Matthew pushes his glasses up his nose, looks directly at Ivy. He seems to be searching her face and he speaks very carefully, as if his words are rehearsed. 'Rachel and I were hoping you'd reconsider our proposal.' He coughs awkwardly. 'I mean, to come and live with us in Bristol. Not with us in the house,' he corrects. 'You'd have your own space. We'd build an annexe in the garden.'

'Matthew, I told you, I like things as they are. I don't want to live in Bristol. I want to see Tabitha, of course, but I can come up more often and you could bring her here more. And—'

'Rachel's pregnant,' Matthew blurts out. 'She's already twenty weeks. We don't know what to do.'

'Oh, that's wond—' The words catch in Ivy's throat. There isn't joy in his face. 'What do you mean, you don't know what to do?'

'We can't afford for Rachel to give up work and we can barely afford the childcare costs. We don't know where to turn, Mum.' He stares at the ground, reluctant to meet her eyes.

'I thought you were doing so well, Matthew.'

'The house is a huge drain on our finances. It's far too big, really, and the mortgage is astronomical. We had to take a second mortgage to do the renovations. If you came to live with us, well, it would solve a lot of problems. You would be able to take and pick Tabs up from school, look after the new little one. Not every day, of course.' He pauses. 'And perhaps you could sell this place. It will help free up a bit of cash, help fund the annexe.' He flushes with embarrassment. 'I know it's a lot to ask, but we don't know where to turn. There are redundancies at the company and my job is likely to be secure, but they're talking about cutting back larger salaries. A gesture to the others . . .' Matthew trails off.

The bread feels stuck in Ivy's throat. Freedom has been at touching distance, just within her grasp. She chokes back the tears that threaten.

His hand reaches for hers. 'I haven't been a good son. I know that. I've been a pompous arse. Selfish.' Ivy smiles but doesn't contradict him. 'I never wanted to be like Dad, but

288

I've been more like him than I care to admit.'

It's as if her destiny is always to care for others, her own desires sidelined. God, what is she going to do? She's desperate to travel a bit, take some time for herself. But how can she refuse? Matthew's eyes are full of anguish, and she feels her heart lurch. 'I will think about it, Matthew, I promise. Give me time.'

After he makes his confession, he seems to relax. 'Tabs is doing ever so well in school. Her vocabulary is really advanced for her age. She makes us laugh every day.'

'Children are a joy and it is wonderful Rachel is expecting again,' Ivy pats his hand. 'Do you want to stay tonight, Matthew? You're more than welcome.'

'I've got work in the morning so I can't really. I'll take a walk on the beach this afternoon, perhaps, and go around four-ish. Do you want to join me?'

The sea is mesmerising as they make their way down the hill. It glitters in the early afternoon sunshine and the beach is busy with dog walkers and sunbathers. On the horizon, sail boats cut lazily across the water.

'I do miss this,' Matthew says. 'The salty air. I hardly seem to take a breath sometimes.'

'With work?' Ivy asks.

He nods. 'I was always ambitious and wanted to get to the top. It was all about money and success.'

'You were always driven, very determined. Even as a teenager.'

'Sometimes I wonder if the sacrifice is worth it. More often than not, Tabs is in bed when I get home and I've lost count of the times I've had to work weekends sorting one crisis or another.' He gazes at the sea again. 'I don't think life is meant to be like this.'

'You can change things, Matthew. You're young. You have a lot of years left in work.'

'Don't remind me!' he says with feeling. 'Anyway, I'm not sure forty-two is classed as young. In Rachel's last antenatal clinic, someone told her she's a geriatric mum. At thirty-seven! Madness.'

'If work is too much, perhaps you need to find something else. I'm not even sure I know exactly what you do. I know it's in finance.' Ivy grins sheepishly.

'Don't worry. Not many people do. I work in hedge funds. Basically, we invest other people's money and examine global macroeconomic trends. You know, imbalances between countries in things like economic growth, interest rates and other things.'

'I'm sorry I asked,' Ivy says, smiling. 'What would you do if you had your time again?' They reach the bottom of the hill and cross the road to the beach.

'Ivy. Hey, Ivy!'

Ivy turns around to see Summer struggling with the pushchair and Nia in her arms.

Ivy reaches for Nia. 'What are you doing, little monkey?'

'She's saying she's too tired to walk and I can't carry her all the way up the hill.'

'I'll help,' Ivy volunteers straight away. 'This is my son, Matthew, by the way. Summer is in my exercise class.'

'Oh,' Matthew says, looking unsure what to do and Ivy thinks how socially inept he is. He looks like he doesn't know whether to shake hands with her or not.

'Yes, I'm from the infamous pole dancing class,' Summer laughs. 'We're bringing wickedness and evil into Morlan!'

Ivy wonders if Matthew feels embarrassed at his reaction to the pole dancing.

'Idris Hopkins is trying to get the performance banned from the fête. He is such an old fart,' Summer goes on. 'All he seems to do is generate more publicity for us and it doesn't seem to bother Feather in the slightest.'

'Funny that!' says Ivy thoughtfully. 'Nia is two,' she says to Matthew.

'Ivy is always talking about her granddaughter and she's wonderful with Nia. She's got a gift, I think,' Summer says.

Matthew rubs his chin, 'I agree. I've been trying to persuade her to come and live with us in Bristol and she can put her child-whispering skills to good use.'

Summer glances at Ivy, remembering what Ivy said about her last visit to Bristol and her reluctance to change the status quo.

'Well, I wish my mum, and Aled's for that matter, were half as good as Ivy. The kids barely see them.' Nia's pulling on Summer's hand. 'She's spotted the ice cream van. We'll be fine walking up the hill when Nia's got a 99 in her. You two go and enjoy your walk on the beach. The rain's coming in tomorrow.'

'She seems nice,' Matthew says, as Summer crosses to the ice cream van.

'I've met some wonderful friends at this class. It's been a tonic. What we'll do when it finishes . . .' Ivy stops herself, knowing Matthew is single-minded now in his determination to get her to move. She tries a different tack. 'Can you imagine your father's face if I'd joined the class when he was alive?'

'He never let you do anything, did he?'

'I didn't think you noticed. I feel guilty talking about this now, but he liked things his way and I wasn't strong enough to resist him. The trouble is your life can pass you by pleasing others.' They tiptoe their way across the stony entrance to the beach.

'He was a powerful character,' Matthew agrees. 'I never felt I was good enough for Dad, you know. Never manly enough. I wasn't into sport, and I felt I failed him in some way as I didn't share his passion for cricket. Then when I got into LSE, I thought he'd be over the moon.'

'He was,' Ivy says quietly.

'Well, he never showed it. We were very different, I think.' They head to the lagoon. The tide is fully in and the water is a deep indigo. 'This is where the teenagers used to hang out, I remember.'

'They still do,' Ivy says. 'We were interrupted earlier. What did you say you would have done given the chance?'

'Become a teacher,' Matthew says ruefully. 'Rachel thinks I'm mad because of the hours she works, but she loves it, really. Always talking about the kids in her class.'

'You should think about it, if that's what you want. Make it happen.'

Matthew shrugs. Something has shifted between them. It's the first time Matthew has opened up about his father.

'You and Dad weren't the same. You always made me feel loved, Mum.'

Ivy loops her arm in Matthew's. 'Come on, we'll head back. You'll hit all the traffic if you don't leave soon.'

Chapter Thirty-Two

Summer

Jordan is curled up asleep on Summer's chest, amazingly, while she bounces around with Nia.

'Mummy, I want "Wheels on the Bus," Nia demands, not for the first time.

'I can't, Ni. I can't hang up now,' Summer checks how long she's been on hold in the queue to speak to the GP receptionist. Thirty-six minutes. She can't quit now.

The twinkly piano music stalls for a moment while the robotic voice tells her she is number two in the queue. At the same time Aled's name pops up on screen calling her. She'll call him back later. The music begins again.

'Woohoo, let's shake it about.' She tries to sound upbeat for Nia. Inventing a dance to the GP queue music. There is no end to the creativity motherhood brings, out of necessity of course. Last time she'd called, when Nia had chicken pox, Summer had managed to make an entire fish pie while in the phone queue.

'Hello, Morlan Surgery,' the grumpy voice eventually answers. Summer pounces on the phone faster than she's moved in her life.

She FaceTimes Aled back as soon as she's off the phone. 'Sorry about that, just waiting to speak to the GP.' She rolls her eyes exaggeratedly so he can see.

'What for?' Aled asks. She can see he's wearing his uniform but is in the tiny bedroom he shares on the oil rig, about to start his afternoon shift. Despite the lack of baby clutter, it looks minute, and has a distinct university halls' vibe to it.

'I told you yesterday, Nia's rash is back,' Summer tries not to snap. She's convinced he doesn't listen to her, like when he recommended a film to watch that she'd been begging him to see for months.

'Yes. How is my little pudding?' he smiles, and Summer flips the camera round so he can see Nia, still dancing around the living room.

'She seems fine, but it's worse than last time. I don't think that cream helped,' Summer muses. 'I could only get an appointment in two weeks. They offered next Friday, but we've got an extra rehearsal for the fête.'

'Shame I can't take her,' Aled says.

'Yes, it is,' Summer agrees. That would be one of the thousand things he could help with when he changed jobs. It is a fantasy dreamier than sex, Summer thinks.

'I'm dreading starting my shift now. I'm knackered,' Aled moans.

'Only . . . eight days to go 'til you're home to these two,' Summer moves the phone so Aled can see Jordan's face all cwtched into her. He's taking annual leave to spend time at home and to see the fête. 'Any news on jobs, then?' She tries to sound casual, but she's getting more and more impatient as every day passes.

'It turns out that job Jonesie mentioned a while ago was in Vimpany Motors, so I guess that's a no-go now,' Aled says, amused. 'I'm sure something will come up.'

'We need to be looking, though,' Summer says. A passive approach would get them nowhere. It's been over a week since their conversation, and he hasn't acted on it at all, from what Summer can tell. Even though he agreed to search for something closer to home, Summer worries it's an empty promise.

'Don't worry,' Aled says. 'Look, I'd better go. I'll ring Paul in St Davids when I get time, see if he knows of anything going.'

Summer resists the urge to ask why this morning didn't qualify as time he could have called. She's frustrated, and Jordan must be picking up on it as she can tell he's stirring.

'That would be great,' she smiles. 'This one will want to chew on my boob any minute. Have a good shift.'

'Love you.'

Aled's job can't come soon enough. Summer hates to be the nagging wife, but she needs to be this time. Standing up to Aled once wasn't enough, she needs to make sure he knows. She's not in a rush to go back to work – the idea is terrifying and exciting in equal measure – but it would be nice to know there's something in her future. Something other than breastfeeding and silly dances and GP visits. A taste of the independence that pole dancing has given her.

A WhatsApp from Meg chimes on the group. *I'm saving you a nice table xxx*

'Shit,' Summer says under her breath. Then noticing Nia's

puzzled look, Summer covers with 'Ship, ship. Come on, we need to move. Ship on out of here. Nia, get your pink jacket.'

'Ship, ship,' Nia copies as she toddles off. Summer follows to zip Jordan into his pramsuit.

It's hardly needed as they emerge from the house to a mild day. With Jordan in the sling on her front, Nia in the pushchair and a bag balancing on the back, Summer feels like the Michelin man.

She gets to the post office and spots Gwen and Ivy at a table in the little café area. 'I'm sorry I'm late.' She manoeuvres the pushchair around the other tables and parks up beside theirs.

'Let me help you.' Ivy's straight in to greet Nia and swoops her into a hug. Her granddaughter must be so lucky to have her, Summer thinks. She's not sure her son is so grateful, though, after meeting him on the beach yesterday. He seemed a bit of an uptight snob to Summer.

Even Gwen surprises her by offering to hold Jordan while Summer gets settled in.

'Don't worry, I need to breastfeed him soon. I didn't get a chance in the house,' Summer says. Gwen ushers her into her vacated seat, which is more discreet and hidden from the eyes of the other customers.

The post office café is no-frills to say the least, with sticky tablecloths and mismatching cutlery, but they've met here today instead of at Ivy's house as Meg couldn't get out of work. Summer starts feeding her son while Ivy and Gwen are still fussing over Nia and the doll she's brought with her.

'Hiya,' Meg greets Summer as she carries a tray over to the table. 'I've got you a latte, I hope that's OK. And for this superstar, I've made a summer sunshine cocktail,' she offers Nia a plastic glass with orange liquid, and a tiny umbrella balanced on top. 'Apple juice and sparkling water,' she whispers to Summer, who smiles gratefully.

Meg sits at the final empty seat and sighs. 'Have you guys seen this?' She reaches back to take a newspaper from the stand next to her. The *Morlan Village Voice* is slapped on the table in front of them.

'"Boycott of village fête has 1000 supporters on Facebook: We don't want to see pole dancers!" Gwen reads aloud with incredulity. 'Not this rubbish again.'

'When will Idris give it a rest?' Ivy glances at the women nervously. 'One thousand supporters seem a lot. That's got to be half the village and their extended families.'

'We'll be performing to an empty hall by the sound of it,' Summer says once Jordan has latched on.

'How tragic is that?' Meg mutters.

'Well, people say they won't come but they probably will out of curiosity. It's just a Facebook page,' Gwen reasons.

'I don't know,' Ivy says. 'The WI will probably be all over this.'

'It says further down that Idris is knocking on doors, and the school has sent out letters advising parents of the "potentially explicit" entertainment at the fête,' Meg paraphrases.

'What do they think we're doing, getting our bits out at the fête?' Summer says. 'Then again, I suppose we did at the lagoon.'

The women sigh collectively. 'Maybe it is a lost cause,' Gwen says.

'I didn't like the sound of the performance from the start,' Meg agrees. She takes a sip of her drink. There is a dejected air over the table. 'Did you say your son was down yesterday, Ivy?'

'Yes,' she smiles tightly. 'A flying visit, but it was nice to see him. How was your date last week?'

'Oh . . .' Meg pauses. 'It was OK. Not much to report.' She goes back to drinking, then seems to think better of it. 'Actually, it was bloody awful. If I was allowed to swear today, then the air would be blue.'

'Why?' Summer asks.

'He asked me to be his girlfriend.'

The group looks confused. 'That's . . . nice?' Summer asks, tentatively.

'Not really. I decided to tell him about the stoma bag and he made an excuse that his grandfather was dying to get out of there. Wait for it! Then he ghosted me. Completely stopped replying to my text messages. Didn't answer the phone. I saw him having a whale of a time with mates the other day. His grandfather's fine. Men, eh?' Meg tries to laugh it off but Summer can tell she's really hurt.

'Bastard!' Summer mouths. She hands Nia her phone, knowing she will always gratefully accept phone time. 'This situation calls for swearing,' Summer says. 'Are you sure he's not just busy?'

'Of course, he's not just busy. He thought of the stoma bag and thought, no, I can't deal with that. And he's a doctor, no less!' This time tears do spike Meg's eyes. 'Sorry, I don't want to waste any more time over that arsehole. I just feel like my whole life is stuck sometimes. I'm never going to get a real life.'

'Seriously, what is the problem with men these days?' Gwen says. 'I thought it was just Gareth that was the arsehole, but it's encouraging to know it's not only me that picks the worst ones. Sorry, Meg, that was insensitive.'

'Maybe it wasn't because of the stoma bag,' Summer says. 'That hardly makes it better, though. What a total wanker! You're right, Gwen, men are pathetic.'

'Wanker!' Nia repeats, and Summer is aghast.

'Why is it always the swear words that get stuck in her head?' Summer says, and the others laugh.

'Have you seen Gareth recently?' Meg asks Gwen, seemingly keen to move the conversation on from herself. She dabs at her eyes with a napkin.

'No, but I just get so annoyed when I think of the total upheaval he's caused the girls. Not only do they have to come to terms with the fact that their father's a cheating arsehole, but they have to leave their childhood home. He's broken their hearts, and we haven't had an apology or anything.' She huffs, and Summer senses that huff is covering up a lot more than just frustration. 'I feel so angry.'

'How's the house search going?'

'There's nothing in Morlan, obviously. So, I'm looking further afield, St Davids, Haverfordwest. The further I go, though, the less chance of work if I do have to start bookkeeping again. At least people know me around here, word of mouth. We looked at a crumbling little cottage the other day. *Lots of potential*, the estate agent kept saying. There's only potential if you have the time, money and ability to do it. I've got nothing.' She runs a hand through her hair.

'You're stronger than you think, though,' Meg says.

'You carried Gareth along, and he knows it,' Ivy agrees.

'Yes, if anyone can start again it's you,' Summer nods.

'I don't have a choice,' Gwen says. 'I just wish I could find something nice for my girls.'

'Well, I might have a house going for you,' Ivy says. It's a flippant comment, but unusual for Ivy.

'You're not selling, are you?' Summer thinks of what she heard Matthew say yesterday. Ivy can't leave Morlan to live with her son. She's part of the fabric of this village, and she's too independent to rely on her son and daughter-in-law's wages.

'No, I'm not. At least I don't think so. My son wants me to move in with him,' she explains to Gwen and Meg. 'To help with childcare now he has another one on the way. They need help financially too. It would make sense for me to move to this annexe they want to build, but I don't quite feel ready for that. It sounds selfish and, don't get me wrong, I love spending time with Tabitha. It just feels like I'm signing up to being shackled down again.' Summer catches Meg's eye. It's rare for Ivy to speak so candidly about her private life. 'Matthew and Rachel haven't thought about how this will impact my life. They need the help, though. It's very hard for me to refuse.'

'I don't know what to say,' Gwen sighs.

'There's nothing you can say. It's a decision I need to make on my own.'

'How far along is your daughter-in-law?' Summer asks.

'Twenty weeks.'

'A good bit further than me, then,' Summer slips out, then gasps. She hasn't told the women yet. She doesn't know why, maybe something about avoiding their congratulations. Summer hasn't felt like being congratulated over what's been the most stressful news of her life.

'Well, I would say that's fantastic, but how are you feeling?' Ivy asks, perceptive as always.

'Three under three. That's going to be tough,' Meg says.

'Exactly. You know how much of a struggle these two terrors have been. Angelic, though he looks,' Summer smiles at Jordan's sleepy, milk-drunk face. 'I've asked Aled to move back. It's not what he wants but I need the support.'

'Too right,' Gwen says.

'He's taking his time with it,' Summer confides. 'I get so frustrated when he's away. It's like he can just shrug off his role, step into his work shoes and the problems just go away. I'm not sure he wants to come back to twenty-four-seven mayhem. I'm urging him but I think he's just placating me.'

'He doesn't really have a choice,' Ivy says, gently.

'I know.' It's Summer's turn to sigh. Silence falls on the women as they drink their warm drinks.

'Does anyone want a Welsh cake?' Meg offers the plate. Ivy and Summer accept, with Summer breaking hers in half to give to Nia.

'We're a right sorry bunch today, aren't we?' Meg says. 'It's not like me to wallow.'

'I think you've got good reason to, though. We all do,' Summer says. 'Although we shouldn't let men do this to us, walk over us like this.'

'It's hard not to when it's our lives they're playing with, our happiness,' Gwen says dejectedly.

Summer strokes Nia's hair to reassure her, whilst deep in thought. They are on a downer, and they're not usually like this. She's used to seeing these women so strong, so vibrant, in the pole dancing classes. That's what started it for them, and the classes have worked wonders. Without them Summer would be sitting inside today, not talking to her three lovely new friends. She's gained so much from the classes.

'You know what the answer is, don't you?' she says.

The women perk up. 'Please tell us,' Ivy laughs.

'We need to channel Feather Starr,' Summer begins. 'No, seriously. What would Feather Starr do? She wouldn't let her husband work away like I'm doing. The next time I speak to Aled I need to demand answers, demand help.'

'Know your worth,' Meg trots out one of Feather's favourite sayings, smiling.

'When I started the classes I thought that was just mumbo jumbo rubbish,' Gwen agrees. 'But the woman does have a sort of wisdom. A strength to her. She certainly wouldn't mope over Gareth and the house.'

'She'd see that she could stand on her own two feet,' Meg says. 'Like I need to do. Josh was a knob. Why am I crying over someone like that?'

'Exactly.' Summer's pleased. She thought this would be a harder sell to the women. 'I've learnt so much from pole dancing, that doesn't involve cocking my leg like a Border Collie, but strength, independence and so much fun.'

'You're right,' Ivy nods.

'Do you think that philosophy could help you too, Ivy? With your son?' Meg asks.

'We'll see,' Ivy says, thoughtfully. 'There's a few things I need to think about first.'

'We can all do it, solve our problems. And we can solve this one too,' Summer points at the newspaper. 'There has to be an answer to the boycott. Something we can think of, together. We can do anything.' She's getting going now. 'There must be an answer. We haven't come this far to just let the performance fail like a damp squib. We have a point to prove to this stuffy village.'

Meg and Ivy are nodding.

'What do you think, Gwen?'

Gwen pauses, then smiles. 'I think I might just have an idea.'

Chapter Thirty-Three

Gwen

Gwen pulls up outside the cottage. With its position on a busy road, she has to park the car halfway on the pavement. There's only space for one car alongside the house. An archway of white roses, pink gerberas and lemon Alstroemeria welcomes visitors up the garden path. Not that Gwen is that familiar with the names of flowers. Clive, their gardener, handled all that. Gwen can imagine the house in *Ideal Home* with its wisteria-covered porch and the leaded windows. Inhaling the scent of honeysuckle, she hesitates before ringing the doorbell. Suddenly unsure if this is a good idea, her stomach flutters with nerves.

As she reaches up to ring the bell, there's a moment of confusion as the door swings open and Lynne stands there, a bag over her shoulder, obviously intending to go out. Lynne's hair is a bright blonde and she wears a scarlet lipstick. She's always kept herself trim and Gwen can see why Gareth was tempted.

'Gwen?' she says, puzzled.

'I can see you're going out, but can I come in for a moment?'

Lynne's face flushes. She looks at her watch, then says

305

reluctantly, 'Yes, it can wait. I'll put the kettle on.'

'Thanks,' Gwen says. At least this time, it's Gwen who has the upper hand, she thinks, as she follows Lynne into the kitchen. The kitchen is drenched in sunlight and everything is spick and span, all polished surfaces and floral oven gloves and matching tea towels tucked into the handle of the Aga.

'Coffee?'

'No, it's OK. I don't want to keep you too long.' It makes Gwen sad to think that she once considered Lynne a friend. It wasn't like the friendship she has with the girls at the pole dancing class. Ivy, Meg and Summer have her back. They fill her with a feeling of warmth, safety. True friendship. Lynne kept her at arm's length. She'd only ever been to Lynne's twice for coffee.

Lynne flicks the switch of the kettle. 'I'm having one. So, tell me, to what do I owe this pleasure?'

'I'm sorry to catch you like this. I have a favour to ask you.'

'Now I'm intrigued. I can't imagine what *I* can do for *you*.' She sits down as the kettle bubbles behind her.

'Is your brother still working for BBC Wales?' Gwen asks and Lynne nods. 'Will you ask him to do a piece on us for the news? The pole dancing class, I mean. We're performing at Morlan's Fête.'

'It's hardly newsworthy, Gwen. Some sad middle-aged women twirling around a pole in a backwater in south-west Wales.'

'Ouch!' Gwen smiles. 'We're all ages, as it happens. I thought perhaps the item could be one of those light-hearted bits they do at the end of the news. You know, *And now for something completely different . . .*'

306

'I could try,' she concedes, 'but why would I do that for you?'

Gwen looks her right in the face, 'Because you owe me, Lynne. For what you and Gareth have done to my girls' lives. I'm old and ugly enough to cope, but Lydia has the embarrassment of moving to some tiny house, wrenched from everything she knows. And Jasmine, even though she's older and lives away, she's devastated by all this. They loved their father to bits, the useless lump of lard that he is.'

'Gareth was the one that messed up financially. And I hardly twisted his arm to have an affair with me.' She sighs. 'Okay, I'll try,' she says, nodding. 'I can't promise he'll take it up.' She gets up and pours two instant coffees. 'I don't have filter, I'm afraid.' She pushes the coffee towards Gwen. 'How will a BBC news item help you?'

'Well, they're trying to boycott our performance at the fête. If it's on the news, Idris Hopkins will hardly want to pull the show. It's worth a shot.'

Lynne looks puzzled. 'This class of yours, why does it mean so much?'

Gwen sighs, 'Because for the first time in my life I've got real friends. I hope that doesn't sound too cheesy. They like me. Not because I'm rich and I've got a fancy house. Not because I'm married to a successful businessman. They like me for me. And I like them. We have a laugh.' She sips her coffee. 'Last week in the pub, one of them, Summer, was telling us about putting her son down after feeding him and she answered the postman with her breast out. I laughed so hard, wine came out of my nose. Daft.' She smiles at the memory. 'It's my own fault. I never really tried with women. Thought they were all catty, jealous bitches. Thank God I've realised that's not the case.'

Lynne says nothing. She twists the bracelet on her wrist, avoiding Gwen's eyes.

'Why did you go with Gareth, Lynne? Did you really want him?'

Lynne looks up and gives a wry smile. 'That useless lump of lard? You wouldn't understand.'

'Try me,' urges Gwen.

'It was because I could, I suppose. I never had much in life. I'm fifty next year and I've never been married, never had kids. I've nursed both my parents. My father had cancer and my mother died of Parkinson's two years ago.'

Gwen nods, remembering.

'This is their house. It's not much to show for a lifetime. I should have gone away, but I'm an only child.' She shrugs. 'Life deals you the cards. You don't get to choose them. And then you, you had everything. The house, the successful husband, two beautiful girls. The perfect life. I wanted some of it.'

'And Gareth made himself available, I should imagine.'

Lynne nods. 'I do regret it. I never loved him. You have to believe that I never meant for it to go this far.'

'I believe you,' Gwen says quietly.

'He wanted to move in here. He was panicking about the business. It would never have worked. I didn't want him and he never really wanted me.'

'It's sad, really,' Gwen says. 'Lives ruined, for what?'

'This would have happened at some time, Gwen. You're the

brains behind the business, though. Everyone knows that. He's nothing without you.'

'Thanks. I think you're right, if that doesn't sound too arrogant.'

'So, what will you do now?'

'I'm going to set up a bookkeeping business of my own. I know a bit about marketing and when you have a teenager, they're all over social media. Lydia is making up all sorts of TikTok videos. This has brought us closer.' She smiles, 'And the girls at the class have all sorts of contacts. But it's not going to be easy.' Gwen sips her coffee. 'And what about you?'

'I'm starting in Withybush Hospital next week. An admin post. I'm quite excited about it. It'll be more interesting than cars.'

'I'm glad, Lynne. Neither of us deserved Gareth in our lives. He's far too selfish. He'll certainly survive. He's like a bloody cockroach.' Gwen rises. 'I'd better go.'

As Lynne sees Gwen to the door, she says, 'I will ask Tristan if he'll do a story.'

'Thanks,' Gwen says, as she leaves.

'You are an absolute genius,' Ivy beams. 'Do you think it will work?'

'Who knows,' says Gwen, 'but Idris will be so spooked by the BBC cameras coming, that he'll dare not pull the plug on us. Even if they don't turn up, it might work.' Gwen leans against the kitchen counter, 'Are you really going to sell up, Ivy?'

'I'm in a real quandary. I don't think I have any other option. Matthew and Rachel are struggling at the moment and with

309

another baby on the way . . . well, they'll never afford childcare.'

'But it's not what you really want to do?'

'I did hope to travel a bit. I can go a few years down the line, perhaps, when this younger one starts school. If I'm not too old, of course.'

'You'll never get old, Ivy. You've got more energy than anyone else I know.'

Ivy smiles, 'So, what do you think of the house?'

'I absolutely love it. This kitchen is like brand new. I wouldn't have known if you hadn't told me.'

Ivy flushes with pride. 'I painted it last week. I watched a few YouTube videos and voilà!'

'Voilà, indeed! I'm not sure I could do it. I always used to pay someone. It must feel like a real achievement when you do it yourself.'

'Well, yes, it does.' She looks serious, suddenly. 'So, you'd be interested in the house?'

'Gawd, yes,' says Gwen with feeling. 'You could get a very good price for this. It's immaculate. Very modern. I know Lydia will love it and she'll definitely bagsy that front bedroom. Honestly, if you'd seen some of the houses we've viewed!'

'That's all I need to know. You shall have it, Gwen, if you want it. I won't put it on the market.'

'That's great. A weight off my mind. I feel a bit guilty, though, because I know that you don't want to leave, that you're being forced to.'

'Don't worry about me. I won't do anything I don't want to. Let's go and sit out the back.'

'It's so peaceful in the garden, Ivy,' Gwen says as they sit down. 'What about that man you had lunch with? Bob? Aren't you tempted to go travelling with him?'

'Very much so. We're on the same wavelength. I sometimes feel I'm being pulled all ways.' Ivy closes her eyes, 'I'm not going to rush into anything right now. Anyway, what about you? How's the business venture?'

'It hasn't really got off the ground yet. I've taken your idea, though, and in the advert it mentions recovering from a crisis, targeting people who have just started up.' She sighs, 'I'm not sure I can do this. If it was just me, I wouldn't worry, but Lyds depends on me. What if I don't get any interest, no bookings? If I have no money coming in, I don't know how we'll survive.'

'I have every confidence that you'll manage, Gwen. You have been part of a very successful business. And . . .'

'Yes, and one that has almost gone bust.'

'Everyone around here knows you were the one behind the success and Gareth was hanging onto your coat tails.'

'I hope you're right. You're the second person to say that to me today. I've got nothing else up my sleeve, so I'll have to make it work.' She smiles. 'Things are progressing with the sale of The Haven too. A couple originally from Pembrokeshire has made an offer. They live in London at the moment and want to come back.'

'With London prices, it will seem a steal around here.'

Gwen nods. 'Do you mind if I bring Lydia over tomorrow? I know she will love this place.'

As Gwen walks up the hill to The Haven, she feels optimistic for the first time in weeks. The possibility of Ivy's house

311

being for sale fills her with hope. She hears the familiar chug of Gwion Morgan's tractor behind her as it makes its way up the hill, his ruddy cheeks visible through the window. He toots as he passes. Gwen thinks how she would have felt breathless walking up hill only a short time ago; now, her regular jaunts to The Mariners have increased her exercise levels.

She pauses on the driveway. That silly car will have to go, she decides, looking at her previously beloved Audi. She's going to get something more practical – a four-door, for a start.

'I'm in here!' Lydia calls out from the kitchen when Gwen gets in. 'I'm making us dinner.'

'Ooh, what are we having?' Gwen says, surprised.

'Tuna pasta bake. From *BBC Good Food*. It's about time I learnt to cook.'

'I'm impressed. I thought everything you cooked came with a ping.'

'Very funny! Anyway, it'll be ready soon.'

'Well, I think you'll love Ivy's house. Nothing needs to be done to it and it's really modern. The front bedroom has fantastic views. Not as good as this, of course. And when Jas visits, there's a spare room for her.'

'It sounds promising. Better than the one in Abercastle, then?'

'Definitely. I thought you liked that one.'

Lydia wrinkles her nose, 'I only said that because I thought we had no choice, and I didn't want to hurt your feelings.'

Gwen wraps her arms around Lydia's waist, as she searches for the cutlery. 'I love you, darling.'

'Mum, get off. I want to lay the table. Just sit down and I'll bring it to you.'

Gwen looks out at the sun sinking into the sea, a perfect globe of crimson. You only appreciate things when you are threatened with losing them. She decides she'll never tire of that view, a sunset in Morlan.

Chapter Thirty-Four

Meg

There is a buzz in the air tonight as the women gather in the hall. The last pole dancing class before next week's performance. It feels like the end of an era, and the level of chatter in the room belies the nerves and excitement of the women.

Meg pushes open the door, spotting her female team of Gwen, Ivy and Summer. She's glad to see them as she has news for the women, a decision she's made, but that can wait until the pub later.

It's funny, she thinks, how they were put together in a group by chance, but have become firm friends. She's started to think of them as her closest friends, despite their differences in age and background. She wouldn't have recovered from Josh without them.

And she is recovered from Josh. Seeing him with his friends was a kick in the guts, which was ironically what Meg wanted to do to him afterwards. He deserved more than that, with Hannah saying she wanted to rip his bollocks off when she told her, the first time she'd ever heard her grandmother swear. It was hard to come to terms with the fact that someone so seemingly nice and caring, a doctor no less, could treat her so callously. Meg still has the occasional moment of incredulity and intense anger towards him, but it is getting less often.

He obviously wasn't right for her. Meg can see that now. Will she ever find the right man? Goodness knows, she thinks. The ever-decreasing pool of available men are either self-obsessed, or insensitive, or immature, or any combination of the above. Meg just needs to focus on herself for the moment, herself and these women around her.

'Evening,' she says, rushing over to see them. Summer gives her a quick squeeze.

'Look at you in the tight top,' she notices, 'looking amazing.'

Meg blushes. She hoped no one would notice. She's worn this top before, but has decided to let her stoma bag go free tonight, no protective banding. That was mainly to hide it before, and there's no point doing so now. It just gets in the way, Meg has decided. She appraised herself in the mirror earlier – you can definitely tell there is something going on under her top, but Meg actually thinks it looks better this way. She's spent so long hiding. And after Josh, it feels like the worst has happened. People know about her stoma bag. They've talked. She's been dumped. It sucks, but life has to move on. What's the big deal?

'Thank you,' she forces herself to say.

'I can't believe this has come around so quickly,' Ivy says now.

'I had a nightmare about the routine last night,' Gwen says. 'That I was performing onstage to crowds and the cameras, and when I looked down my clothes had fallen off.'

Summer laughs. 'The classic naked-in-public dream. At least

you didn't do it for real, flashing the postman.'

The others join in. 'People have already seen us in our birthday suits courtesy of Idris Hopkins,' Meg says. 'Any news on the cameras, by the way?'

'Apparently Tristan seems interested. I had a message from Lynne today,' Gwen explains. 'Still not confirmed, though.'

'Well, word seems to be out there,' Ivy says. 'I've heard the group has disappeared from Facebook.'

'Already? You know what they say, word travels fast in Morlan.'

'I'm surprised Idris has given in so easily,' Ivy says.

'I can't help thinking he might have something else up his sleeve,' Summer says, rolling her eyes.

Meg feels a buzzing in her pocket. She checks the screen, about to decline the call, when she sees Josh's name. What could he possibly have to say to her?

'Good evening, my lovely ladies!' Feather Starr, energetic as always, bounds onto stage. Whatever Josh has to say can wait. 'Welcome to all of you. We're down to our last couple of rehearsals before the fête next week. Tonight, I want to see fire. I want to see flames onstage as you're dancing. I want to see spice and drama and passion. Let's give it some . . .' and then she takes a deep breath before letting out a roaring sound akin to something on a David Attenborough documentary.

The women look at each other bemused. Meg remembers Feather's original poster, something about needing feisty, fierce women, with no inhibitions, and how that had seemed a world away from her. She wouldn't say she's feisty now, but there's something about being able to hold her body weight up on a pole while contorting upside down, that makes her feel pretty powerful.

'No more namby-pamby, doing the steps politely onstage. I want to see real attack, real vigour in your performance. Can you do that for me?'

There is embarrassed nodding around the room.

'I said, can you do that for me?'

Meg resists the urge to roll her eyes at the panto-style beginning. A few women say yes, before Feather has them all shouting, all laughing at their collective 'YEEESSSS!'

'But first we warm up,' Feather leads them through the now familiar routine of stretches and breath-work, the obligatory pelvic floor exercises.

'This has done wonders for me,' Summer says, while Feather sets up the sound system. 'No more peeing myself every time I cough.'

The familiar sound of 'Lady Marmalade' comes on. A cliché perhaps considering the link to the *Moulin Rouge* film, and Meg wonders how it will go down in the fête next week. To think, they'll be up onstage, strutting their stuff for the whole village and now TV cameras.

'Come on, then, starting positions please,' Feather instructs. Meg leans against a pole back-to-back with Ivy, one arm wrapped around the metal. They run through the routine, from the synchronised dance at the start to the demonstration on the poles, and Meg's final upside-down flourish. She feels pretty happy with it, and notices Feather smiling as they finish. It's funny how much she wants Feather's approval.

'Not bad, not bad. A few bits to refine, but you women are going to look hot next week!'

Meg's hair feels damp and sticky by the end of the class, after running through the whole song several times.

'If I never hear that song again, it'll be too soon,' Gwen grunts at the end. 'My daughters are going to have a fit.'

There are a few clunks outside the door to the hall and a few of the women turn their heads.

'Just some staff setting up for the fête next week,' Feather says to them. 'We're actually going to do the routine one more time, but I'd like to see it dressed. Ladies, your outfits have arrived!'

Meg hadn't noticed the cardboard boxes sitting at the side of the stage. She feels a familiar sense of dread. The costumes.

She knows Feather wants them to wear sparkly shorts, and the Strictly-style sequinned numbers that she's pulling out of the boxes now are just that, and a black top. She told them she has a variety of black T-shirts and crop tops. The women 'ooh' and 'aah' as they see she has had them printed with a pole dancing logo and 'Feather's Angels' written on the back.

'She hasn't held back,' Meg whispers to the group, although inside her stomach is churning. To crop top, or not to crop top? That question has been on her mind for a while now.

At the start of this journey, a crop top would have been out of the question, with even a T-shirt seeming too risky. But doesn't her newfound confidence and acceptance mean that she should go for it? Stop hiding and put it all out there?

Meg isn't sure whether she's ready for this last step. And she doesn't have long to make a decision as the women are asked to form a queue at the boxes to collect their outfits.

Will she regret it if she doesn't make this final leap? Or should she stick with a T-shirt, probably feeling more comfortable and confident for the dance? Everyone's eyes will be on her at the end of the routine. Can she handle the pressure?

'Flamingo pink for our hot mamma,' Meg hears Feather say as she hands Summer her outfit.

'Forest green for our pixie,' Ivy's handed a green pair of sparkly shorts. Gwen's given purple.

'I'll look like Diana Ross in these,' Gwen jokes as she passes Meg.

'And the star of the show,' Feather says as Meg is last in the queue. 'Gold shorts for you, and what else?' Meg feels her cheeks redden. 'I wasn't sure if you wanted a crop top or T-shirt?'

'No,' Meg shakes her head. 'I'm not sure either. Probably a T-shirt.' Her voice sounds small and uneven.

'Why don't you take the two?' Feather suggests knowingly. 'You can practise at home in both and see how you feel.'

'Okay,' Meg doesn't want to delay the decision any longer, but looking at herself in costume in the mirror at home will help.

She takes the clothes from Feather Starr, grateful she hasn't made a fuss in front of everyone.

'Right, ladies, you can get changed in here. Use the screens dotted around,' Feather instructs. A few screens are left out from the monthly blood donation sessions and school plays, and some of the women huddle behind them. Meg waits her turn, before hastily stripping into her shorts, which fit perfectly, and what she thinks is the T-shirt. Once her arms are through the holes she steps out, rolling the material down her body. It stops just below her belly button, leaving the stoma bag exposed.

'Oh,' she mutters, and spins to get changed. She wants privacy before wearing this for the first time. As she slips behind the screen, she notices the door to the hallway is open and the clunking means more supplies are being dropped off. Before Meg can move, she makes eye contact with Rhys, who happens to be outside staring at her. She didn't realise he would be helping with the supplies, but of course he would, as most of the booze for the fête is coming from The Mariners.

She moves the screen to shelter her, but there's no way he didn't see her. No way, Meg thinks as she quickly changes into a T-shirt.

Oh well, if Rhys didn't know about the bag before, then he definitely does now.

The women look a rainbow of colours in their outfits as they perform the routine again. Whether it's the sparkles or the louder music, they definitely seem to have more pep as they do it.

'Fantastic!' Feather Starr cries at the end. 'That's the level of energy we need. You look a picture up there. That's it for tonight, ladies, you're ready!'

'Woohoo!' a few male shouts and wolf whistles come from the back of the hall where some of the staff, including Rhys, have stopped to peer in. Meg's eyes meet his again.

'Push off!' Feather shouts.

'Just a sneak preview!' someone calls, at the same time as another man gives a seedy, 'Looking good!'

Meg has noticed that only one woman in the class has opted

for a crop top. Carol, the one that wears the leotard most weeks. She doesn't have the best body, but she looks confident in her crop top, and excited.

'You look amazing, Meg,' Summer says. 'Are we off to the pub tonight? Zoe's told me she's happy to stay later with the kids.'

'Yes,' Meg says. 'I need a drink.'

'My sentiments exactly,' Gwen says. This time she drives them to the pub, all of them too exhausted and sweaty to bother walking. In the car park, Meg remembers Josh's call. She sees he's tried again and left a voicemail.

'One second,' she says to Summer, hanging back. Meg takes a deep breath and presses dial on the voicemail.

'You have one new message,' the robotic voice tells her. Click. 'Meg . . . Hi.'

Her pulse quickens and she feels slightly nauseous just hearing his voice. The anger and upset he's caused her. 'I'm sorry for calling. I wanted to explain. You've been on my mind and I feel so guilty for not replying. I feel awful about it.' Meg turns cold. He feels *guilty*. He doesn't have a right to assuage his guilt like this, as if one phone call can take it away. It's not fair.

'I should have just told you the truth, Meg, I'm sorry. It's just . . . I'm not ready for a relationship right now.' Meg gasps and hangs up before she can hear any more. What utter bullshit! She knows it's not true. He's just not man enough to admit what the real problem is.

Meg knows instantly what she needs to do. She needs to get rid of him.

Why should he get the last word? Meg can take control with

one touch of a screen. She deletes his voicemail. She deletes his number. She deletes his WhatsApp. She deletes him from all social media. And she blocks him for good measure. Wiping all evidence she ever knew him from her phone.

Meg exhales. Josh is out of her life for good. She makes a vow to herself to never date a toxic man again. She knows she's too good for that.

Meg is moving on.

She pushes the pub door open, leaving the digital world behind. The Mariners is quiet tonight, with only a few locals knocking around amongst the women from the pole dancing class.

'I'll order us a bottle,' Meg says.

'We've saved the usual table,' Ivy tells her, as they tuck themselves into the cosy corner table.

As Meg queues at the bar, she notices Rhys serving, glancing at her. Oh no, will this be awkward? He's seen pretty much all there is to see now. She doesn't want things to be uncomfortable between them.

Carol orders a bottle, and even Feather Starr has come to the pub tonight.

'Meg,' Rhys says, when she gets to the counter. 'The usual tonight?' He coughs, and looks a little nervous, if she isn't imagining things.

She decides to nip things in the bud and confront what happened. 'Yes please. Although I don't think there's anything usual about tonight.'

'I don't know what you mean,' Rhys says, but his teasing smile is back.

'You certainly had an eyeful,' Meg says. 'I should apologise. No one needs to see us in our skimpy costumes.'

'I wasn't looking at anyone else,' Rhys places a bottle of rosé on the counter but stops. It's Meg's turn to feel embarrassed now. She has to pull herself together.

'I'm sure that scarred you for life, then.' She's joking, but Rhys doesn't smile.

'Why? You looked fucking hot, Meg.'

She waits for him to smile, say it's all a joke, but he doesn't. And there's something arresting about his words, his eyes, that Meg's never noticed before. No one's said anything like that to her before, so sincerely. She's never been called hot.

'Ha ha,' she tries to laugh it off. 'Not as hot as Natalie Jones, I bet.'

'Natalie Jones? I fancied her for about a month in sixth form. She's not who I like now. And that crop top,' Rhys shakes his head slowly.

'Oh,' Meg can't quite bring herself to speak. 'I thought you liked her.' Her heart's beating loudly, her eyes looking into his, just like they did in the hall.

'And I thought you were taken?' Rhys asks.

Meg smiles. 'I'm not. I'm not taken at all.'

'That's good to know.'

'Is it?'

'It is.'

Does Rhys like her? Has he always liked her? She's never thought of him in this way, convinced he was into someone else. She feels like Anne Elliot in *Persuasion*. Which would make Rhys her Captain Wentworth. Is Rhys her Captain Wentworth?

'Excuse me,' a man says behind her. As though the spell is broken, Rhys moves to open her bottle.

'On the house.' He passes her the wine glasses. The whole exchange is over in a few seconds, but Meg feels her world has been rocked. Everything she thought she knew about life in Morlan has changed. 'What can I get you?' He moves to serve the impatient customer behind.

Meg carries the bottle and glasses to their table, her legs shaking.

'Thanks, Meg,' Gwen says.

'Don't say you had it free again,' Summer teases.

'Why not? That's the reason we send Meg for the drinks when Rhys is in!' Ivy jokes.

Meg smiles, remembering their teasing when they've been in The Mariners before. She's brushed it off, thinking that it's impossible someone like Rhys would be into her. Maybe it's not impossible. Maybe it's true and she just hasn't believed it before.

'We were just discussing how strange it feels that we've finished the classes,' Summer says. 'And talking about what's next for us. Obviously for me, it's number three on the way. And Gwen's going to conquer the world with her new venture. What's for you, Meg?'

She hopes she isn't blushing thinking about Rhys. She doesn't know what's next for her love life, but she does have news for the women.

'I've applied to university. I'm going to Cardiff at the end of the summer to study journalism.'

Chapter Thirty-Five

Ivy

'She's in good nick,' says Bob, flopping down onto the seat in the back of the camper van. 'Fantastic for 1974. A classic Type 2. There doesn't seem much headroom, but the roof pops up.' He stands up to show her the lever. 'It'll be totally adequate for one. You'll just have to take the bare minimum.'

Ivy nods, pulling down the door of the oven. 'I know. I can do that.' The worktops are sparkling and there's a small stainless-steel sink. Everything she could hope for. 'I'm amazed so much can be packed into such a small space. It's marvellous.' Her stomach flutters with excitement.

'How many miles are on the clock?' he asks.

'Eighty-two thousand.'

'That's to be expected for her age. There's not a bit of rust on the old girl. You'll have to be careful, though, Ivy. She needs gentle handling.'

Ivy sits down next to Bob, looking across at him gratefully. When she saw the advert for the mint-green and white Volkswagen camper van, she immediately fell in love. 'Thanks for coming with me. I can't be trusted in choosing. Think with my heart rather than my head.'

'She *is* gorgeous. I bet you've already thought of a name for her.'

Ivy grins, 'Daisy. Isn't she perfect?'

'Don't go straight in with the asking price. You need to haggle. Get it down a bit.'

'Oh, I hate doing that.'

'Get used to it, Ivy. When you're on the road and looking for somewhere to park for the night, you must try and knock down the rate for campsites, especially if it's out of season. The ball's in your court, remember.'

'You're a mine of information.'

'You'll soon get used to everything. There's nothing quite like an open road and the excitement of visiting new places. You're the one in control. You get to decide where and when to stop.' His eyes sparkle. 'The world seems full of endless possibilities. There's nothing like it.'

'You're the one who has spurred me on. Your enthusiasm's infectious, like no one else I know. Not in Morlan, anyway.'

'You'll love it,' he says for the umpteenth time. Suddenly, his brow is furrowed in concern. 'You must make sure the van is secure, though. Lock it up at night. You never know, especially as you're on your own.' He's thoughtful, 'You're very brave, Ivy.'

'Brave or mad?' she asks.

'Brave,' he says firmly. 'I would prefer it if you were with someone. Not necessarily me, as much as I'd like that. Just that it would be safer.'

'I know. I have to do this on my own, though. It's hard to

explain. It's almost like I've got to prove something to myself. And it means I get to see places I've only dreamt about. I want to gaze at a sunset in Bologna, breathe in the sights of Bilbao, roam the streets of Bordeaux . . .' She laughs self-consciously.

'You're preaching to the converted, don't forget. You've thought about this for a long time, obviously.'

She nods. 'I have. I am hoping you'll help me plan my route.'

'You try stopping me,' he grins. 'Come on, you promised me a pub lunch for helping you. Do you think this is the one, then?'

'Yes,' she says, rising to her feet. 'Let's test my bargaining power. You can give me marks out of ten.'

It's almost four when Bob drops Ivy outside her cottage. He kisses her on the cheek.

'I've had a lovely afternoon,' she says. 'You're welcome to come in for a coffee.'

'My granddaughter is over later so I'd better go. I'll see you before you leave, of course. I wouldn't miss Morlan's fête for the world. You are a woman full of surprises, Ivy Bevan.'

Once in the house, Ivy switches the kettle on. Her phone pings in her pocket. It's a message from Bob. *I'll be in Riga at the end of October. If you change your mind and want some company, meet me at the Freedom Monument. Just name a time and I'll be there. Keep in touch. Bob xxx*

Ivy smiles. She just might.

Ivy turns the volume down on the television. Her hands are shaking as she taps on Matthew's name. The phone rings out and Ivy feels relieved, but as she makes herself some cheese on

327

toast, Matthew's name flashes on her screen.

'Hi, Mum. Sorry, I missed your call earlier. We've just come back from a summer concert at Tabs' school. It's a shame you couldn't be there.'

Ivy swallows. She's forgotten all about that. 'I couldn't get out of something. I'm sure she was great.' She feels guilty for being so self-absorbed that she'd forgotten her only granddaughter's concert. Bob would never do that.

'Oh, she was. Even Miss Marks said she's talented. A voice like an angel. Anyway, is everything all right?'

Ivy has been dreading this call, but it's unfair to keep Matthew hanging on. She gulps her wine. 'Matthew, I've been thinking about your proposal when you came over the other day.'

There's silence on the other side, an intake of breath.

'I've had the house valued. In fact, I have someone interested in it. I've decided I am going to sell up and I'll give you a portion of it. To help you and Rachel out.'

'So, are you coming to live with us?' There's hesitation in his voice, uncertainty.

'I've decided to go travelling. This afternoon, I bought a camper van.'

'You've done what?'

'Bought a camper van. I'm going travelling. Six months, a year, maybe. I don't know yet. I'm leaving in a couple of weeks.'

'You're not going to live with us, then?'

'Matthew, you must let me do this. With your father's insurance and a healthy profit from the house, you and Rachel will be fine. You'll be able to pay a good proportion of your

328

mortgage off and you should be able to afford childcare. You can start building the annexe. And if,' she corrects herself, '*when* I'm ready, I'll come to Bristol.'

'You seem to have it all worked out. I'll worry about you,' he says, recognising the note of determination in her voice and deciding he can't fight against it.

'I know you will, but you know this is something I have to do. I have a lot of years left in me, and I don't want to waste them.'

'What about the new baby? Don't you want to see him or her?'

'You know I do, Matthew, and I shall travel back when Rachel gives birth. I'm starting in Europe first. Dipping my toe in, so to speak. It'll be easy to come back to see you all, even if it means catching a flight.'

'What about your furniture?'

'I've booked storage. I won't need all of it and some items I've already put on eBay. I'm just keeping the things I need when I eventually move to Bristol.'

Matthew sighs, 'You really have thought of everything. I know I can't argue with you when you're in one of these moods.'

'There's nothing to argue about. I think it's a brilliant compromise. You and Rachel get to survive the financial trouble you've got into and I'm not blaming you for that at all. And I get to indulge my wandering feet.'

'You're right, of course. Do you know, I had no idea when Dad was alive that you wanted to travel, no idea you liked furniture upcycling. Or pole dancing, for that matter.'

'I didn't know either,' says Ivy. 'Now I'm free to do what I want. I hope you don't think that's disrespectful to him.'

'No, I don't. I'm glad you're finding yourself, Mum, and doing what you want to do.'

'Don't make my mistakes,' she says with vehemence. 'I think you should pursue teaching, Matthew. You need to fight for what you want. These pole dancing classes have awakened something in me, given me a courage I never thought I had. I feel I can do anything.'

'Will I get to see you before you go?'

'Well, the fête is on Saturday. You and Rachel could come down with Tabitha. The girls and I are putting on a performance. It's just dancing, exercise, nothing indecent. I'll understand if you think it's inappropriate.'

'I'll see what Rachel says.'

'The BBC cameras might be there. Just so you know.'

'What?' Matthew quickly recovers himself and sighs. 'Thank you, Mum. I do appreciate this.'

'I know. I love you, Matthew.'

'Love you, too.'

It's a long time since Matthew told her he loves her. Ivy feels a burden has lifted as she flicks the light switch off before going to bed.

Ivy pulls into Gwen's driveway in her mint-green and white camper van. Gwen races out, followed by Summer and Meg.

'Well, look at you! When did you pick it up?' asks Gwen.

Ivy switches off the engine and hops out, 'About an hour ago from someone in St Davids. It takes some getting used to. I feel like I'm driving an Owens' haulage lorry or something.'

They all laugh and Meg says, 'I love it. It's very you, Ivy.'

'A bit rickety and seen better days?' Ivy grins.

Meg shakes her head, 'It's beautiful. Quirky. Vintage. A perfect metaphor for you.'

Ivy opens the side door, 'You have such a way with words sometimes, Meg. Do step inside, ladies.' She sweeps her arm towards the camper van.

'Oh my God,' says Summer, 'it has everything. You'd better hide this from Nia or she'll be wanting to sleep in it tonight.'

'The seats pull down like so,' says Ivy, tugging at a handle beneath with some difficulty. 'It eventually lies flat for a bed.'

'I can't believe you're doing this. This is definitely classic Ivy. I wish I had your guts sometimes.' Gwen says, helping Ivy pull the seats out.

'What are you talking about? You're setting up your own business.'

Gwen smiles. 'I know and I'm terrified. Anyway, I've got coffee on and we waited for you, Ivy. I swear I've forgotten all the steps. I'm so grateful to have another practice before Saturday.'

As they enter the house, Summer peeps in the travel cot by the dining table. 'He's still fast asleep, love him. It's so kind of you to find the cot, Gwen.'

'It was just gathering dust in the attic. I don't need it. You might as well make use of it.'

'I've got less than an hour before I need to pick Nia up,' Summer says, looking anxiously at her watch.

'We'll put the music on quietly,' Gwen says, pouring Ivy's coffee.

'Don't worry about Jordan. He'll sleep through it.'

331

'Well, let's just have ten minutes to gird our loins.' Gwen hands Ivy her coffee.

Summer turns to Meg, 'I have to say, you and Rhys seem to be getting on like a house on fire.'

'Don't start that,' Meg says, blushing. 'After my last disaster, my arsehole radar needs fine-tuning!'

'I don't think you need worry about Rhys,' Ivy says. 'He's not like that Josh. What you see is what you get.'

'So, who's going to do the talking to the TV crew?' Meg asks, changing the subject deftly.

'I don't mind,' Gwen says. 'I'm not even sure they'll be there. I'm more worried I'll forget what my feet are supposed to be doing. Come on, let's get this practice done, so I can at least say I've tried everything. You know, I always fancied myself as a Strictly dancer, but even a small routine like this has got me in a tizz. And that's after months of lessons.'

Summer snorts, 'Sorry, Gwen, I can just picture that. Even you admit you've got two left feet.' She turns to the kitchen, 'Alexa, play "Voulez-Vous Coucher Avec Moi".'

Meg nudges her, 'I've never heard that said in a more Welshy accent before.'

'Aled seems to like it,' Summer grins. 'What's worrying is that Nia was singing this in nursery the other day and I've had to prise the feather boa from her. She runs around the house with it.'

'Girls, let's concentrate please,' Gwen says in a mock-teacher voice. 'Seriously, I'm never going to get all these steps right.'

'Nobody'll be looking at us with Meg around. I'm sure you were a pole dancer in another life, Meg. A dancer or stripper in the Moulin Rouge in Paris,' Summer laughs.

'Alexa, play "Lady Marmalade",' repeats Gwen.

As the music starts up again, Meg steps forward expertly, swinging her hips and twirling around an imaginary pole as the other three gaze down at their feet, and step forward in their best attempt at a rhythm.

'Oh, bloody hell. They're at it again!' Lydia stands in the kitchen, her hands on her hips. 'I'll be glad when this fête is finished. Follow me,' she tells Sophie, who gazes with her mouth open at the four women.

Suddenly, Jordan begins whimpering in the cot, before bursting into a hundred-decibel scream.

'Shit, I'm leaking,' says Summer. 'Oh no, I've got to get Nia, too.'

'I'll take you in Daisy,' says Ivy. 'Feed him now and we'll make tracks.'

'But we haven't really had a practice,' moans Gwen.

'It'll have to do!' Summer says firmly, above the yelling.

Chapter Thirty-Six

Summer

Summer manoeuvres the double buggy around a parked car and onto the pavement. It's usually quieter in Morlan at this time of evening, but the village is busy preparing for tomorrow's fête. Bunting is being strung across the village square by men on ladders, looped between the post office and the corner shop across the road in a myriad of coloured triangles. The entrance to the village hall has been festooned with balloons, and the field to the back of the hall is awash with white tents and speakers.

Preparations for the fête are not usually this extensive, and Summer has the distinct impression it has something to do with the BBC van parked outside the Morlan Guest House. There certainly aren't any signs of a boycott now. Summer even spots Idris Hopkins carrying a box of goodness-knows-what along the little path to the field.

Nia's talking has tailed off, and Summer notices one arm dangling outside the pushchair. Hopefully, this slumber won't disrupt her sleep later. It's just nice to get out of the house, and Nia is exhausted after all that riding round in Ivy's camper van.

The phone rings in her pocket. Aled.

'I'm all packed and ready to come home,' he announces proudly. 'I can't wait to see my little team tomorrow.'

'We can't wait to see you,' Summer keeps her voice quiet as they turn down the road leading to their house and she spots another mother out for an evening walk around the block.

'I should be back by ten,' Aled says.

'Perfect. We've been told to be there by eleven to rehearse before the performance at one. I wonder if the cameras will want to interview us first; Gwen mentioned they might. It's so exciting.'

'My wife, the pole dancing star,' Aled teases.

'Shut up, it's Meg that will be the breakout star tomorrow. Anyway, we should be finished by 2 p.m., so I was thinking we could just wander around the fête then. Nia's desperate to get her face painted. Let's hope she doesn't get a rash like last year.'

'Oh no,' she hears disappointment in Aled's voice. 'I won't be able to come round with you. You'll have to take the kids off my hands as soon as you're done.'

'Why?' Summer tries to keep the frustration out of her voice. It's Aled's first day home. 'I was hoping we could at least have the day together. Nia and Jordan are excited to see their daddy.' She doesn't say that she's looking forward to the break too, the division of labour as much as the family time.

'I'm sorry but I couldn't get out of it,' Aled says. Summer breathes in the cooler evening air, hoping to quell her disappointment. 'I don't think it would look too good if I cancelled a job interview.'

'No,' Summer agrees. It takes her a minute to register what he's said. 'A job interview? And you're telling me this now!'

'It's all a bit last minute, for an engineering firm in Cardigan. When they heard I was looking, they said they wanted to see me straight away, even though it's a Saturday!'

'What?' Summer is incredulous. 'That's amazing. It sounds promising.'

'It does.'

'Do you want to do it, though?'

'Well, it's a step on the ladder. And it brings me closer to my family. I don't want to get our hopes up, but it's kind of perfect.'

Why hadn't they heard about this before?

As though Aled can read her mind he says, 'They don't usually take anyone outside their apprenticeship scheme, but they've taken on some massive project and need urgent help.'

'Hopefully, you could start soon then,' Summer says.

'Fingers crossed. I'm coming home, babe.'

'We'll just get some crowd shots, and then we'll come inside and interview a few of you, once you're in costume, if that works,' the BBC cameraman instructs, trailing complicated-looking equipment behind him.

'No problem,' Feather positively beams. The village of Morlan is certainly putting on a show, Summer thinks. It looks an idyllic picture, with hundreds of people old and young gathering in the field in the sunshine, sipping cold drinks from the bar, which Rhys is manning, and milling around the stalls and displays set up.

The women have gathered in the hall, ready for their costume change and a dress rehearsal.

'Right, women, let's give this village something to talk

about!' Feather barks. 'Costumes, make-up, go, go go!'

Half the group are shipped to a make-up artist, whose purpose seems to be applying as much glitter as possible to the cheeks of the women, with the other half getting changed behind the screens again.

Summer feels like a bit of a tit in her flamingo pink sparkly hot pants. She doesn't think she's worn anything like these since she was a child, and now she's three months pregnant. In for a penny, in for a pound she thinks, plus Nia will adore them. She hasn't shown Nia yet, wanting to surprise her daughter. She steps out from the screen in full dress.

'We look like the pride flag,' Gwen says, laughing in her matching purple shorts.

'Where's Meg?' Summer asks, noticing their group is one woman down.

'Here,' Meg says, and she steps out in her gold shorts and little black crop top.

'Woohoo!' Summer shouts as Ivy says, 'You went for the crop top!'

'Good on you,' Gwen says.

'In for a penny,' Meg shrugs, gaining a smile from Summer. That should be their motto. 'I didn't think the T-shirt covered much more, especially while I'm upside down on that pole, and, anyway, why should I hide myself?'

'Exactly!' Ivy affirms.

'We're so proud of you,' Summer says, and she pulls Meg in for a hug. The other women join. 'You're such a good role model for Nia.'

'For all girls when they see you on BBC news,' Ivy says.

'Stop it, you're going to make me cry,' Meg grins. 'And I haven't been glittered yet.'

'You look amazing,' Gwen says. 'The men's tongues will be wagging. Rhys is a lucky man.'

Meg clams up, suddenly shy, but Summer winks at Gwen. They all know that Rhys is like a puppy dog when he stares at Meg. It will only be a matter of time before they're a couple, Summer thinks. Josh probably did Meg a favour, revealing his real colours. She's much better with Rhys, someone who really appreciates her.

The women change and get ready. Summer allows her face to be glittered up, knowing Nia will be jealous and will want a similar pattern when she sees her. Her skin feels weighted down by the amount of make-up applied, and she thinks she looks like an Irish dancer when she looks in the mirror.

They really look the part, though.

Some of the women talk to the camera crew while they prepare. Feather Starr moves them to the tiny backstage area of the hall while it fills up ready for the performance. Summer would love to go out and check on Aled and the kids, but they are under strict orders to stay in the hall. The poles have been set up, and the voices of the crowd are floating through the thick curtains.

'Oh my God, have you seen how many people are here?' Meg says, peeking out through a gap in the material. 'Is it too late to change our minds?'

'Just think, that's a fraction of the people that will see us when we're being shown on BBC news.'

'Summer, that's not helping,' Meg jabs her arm.

'You'll be fine,' Ivy says, moving to peek through herself. 'Look at Idris Hopkins in the front row. You'd never guess he was opposed to this just a few days ago.'

He does indeed look every inch the supporter in the front seat, holding his clipboard schedule and glancing round for the cameras.

'I can see my girls,' Gwen says after her turn. 'Jasmine's home for the weekend.'

'They really look like you.' Summer peers through. She spots Aled somewhere near the back, holding a sleeping Jordan. Nia is running around in front of him with another girl her age. Aled looks every bit the doting father, and her heart swells with love for him. To think they could make regular outings like this as a family is so exciting. Summer scans her eyes through the crowd again. The whole village seems to be crammed into the hall, she thinks, as she notices Hannah Thomas chatting to Rhys. 'Ivy, you didn't tell me your son was coming to watch you.'

'He's not, is he?' She scrambles to check herself.

'That's lovely, he's come to support you,' Gwen says.

Ivy looks almost white when she pulls away from the curtain. 'Well, that's a turn up for the books. He didn't tell me!'

Maybe he's finally come around to what his mother wants to do, Summer thinks.

'He's brought Rachel and Tabs too. Did you see her playing with Nia?'

Summer puts an arm around Ivy, pleased her family are supporting her.

'Right, ladies. It's 1 p.m. Are we ready to show that village what we're made of?' Feather says. Summer's stomach flips.

'Here goes,' she turns to the women. 'Good luck, everyone.'

They line up at the side of the stage, ready to go on. The lights dim, and the chatter of the crowd dies down. Summer suddenly feels more nervous than she ever has in her life. Six months ago, did she ever think she would be up here, dancing with a group of women and performing to the whole village as well as her family? It's a thrill to think about how this class has changed her life since then.

The women move into position, and it feels a painfully long time before the music comes on. Then Christina Aguilera's sultry voice booms out, the lights brighten and the routine begins.

'That was fantastic!' Aled says, rushing over to give Summer a kiss. 'You looked damn sexy up there.'

'Sexy!' Nia repeats and Summer rolls her eyes.

She picks Nia up to give her a cuddle. 'What did you think of mummy up on stage?'

'I like the pink the most!' She puts her arms in the air and wiggles her hips.

'Oof,' Summer puts her down. 'I'm not going to be able to carry her much longer,' Summer rubs her stomach.

'I thought I could spot a little bump up there,' Aled says. 'You looked gorgeous.' Summer decides to take the compliment instead of worrying about her shape.

'I'll walk you out to the field and then I'll have to head off,' Aled says, as they stroll out of the hall with the rest of the crowds.

The routine was a success, mostly. Summer definitely

tripped up on one movement, using the opposite arm to the rest of the women, and she saw Gwen do the same more than once. Carol used the wrong pole at one point, forcing Summer to move to the next one. But Meg obviously looked incredible, a natural, twirling around and around in a dizzying show of fitness. And from looking at their smiles when the music stopped, Summer is willing to guess the others enjoyed it as much as she did.

She bids farewell to Aled, while allowing Nia to drag her towards the bouncy castle and slide set up in the field. It's a scorcher of a day, and the scene looks worthy of the *Vicar of Dibley*. She watches as Nia plays on the slide, her boundless energy carrying her up and down with the other children. The hairstyle Summer did for her has come loose, and she has something sticky down her top, but the happy shrieks tell Summer she's having a good time. Summer cuddles with Jordan and keeps an eye on her daughter.

'I thought you might fancy an ice cream.' Ivy brings a tray of ice lollies and tubs of chocolate ice cream over to the slide.

'Thank you, Ivy,' Summer says. She calls Nia over and hands her an ice lolly, imagining the trails of red liquid she will find on Nia's clothes later. Matthew has joined her with Tabitha. The two girls begin playing again.

'Are you staying for long, Matthew?'

'Unfortunately not. Rachel has an inspection in school starting Monday, so we're heading back tonight.'

'They're coming to see my camper van first, though,' Ivy says, beaming. 'Bob's meeting us there.'

'Tabitha will be obsessed with it if she's anything like Nia,' Summer tells him.

'You should bring Nia and Jordan,' Ivy offers. 'We're going to have a drink in my garden. I need to drink the cupboards dry in the next few weeks. You'd be doing me a favour.'

'Oh, don't remind me you're going again. We will miss you,' Summer says.

'Gwen, do you fancy a drink back at mine? Ask Jasmine and Lydia too,' Ivy says as Gwen joins them.

'I'd love to. We need to celebrate.'

'You look happy,' Summer notices.

'I've just got my first client,' she grins widely. 'Hannah Thomas of all people, gave my name to someone looking for bookkeeping work.'

'Congratulations,' Summer says. 'I wonder if that was Meg's doing.'

'Where is Meg?'

'I just saw her,' Ivy says, taking a lick of her ice cream. 'Chatting to lover boy.' The women laugh. Summer spies Meg chatting to Rhys across the field. They're both leaning against a tree, with Meg still in costume. It's clear to see Rhys's attraction; in fact, Summer doesn't think it's physically possible for two people to stand closer together. 'I'll tear her away from him soon to see if they want to join us. Hannah Thomas too.'

Summer looks round, remembering all those times when she was alone with Nia and Jordan. She doesn't feel alone any more with her gang. They are like family, with all of their families merging into one this afternoon.

'Do you think we should invite Feather Starr?' Gwen asks.

'Good thinking,' Ivy says.

'I was joking!'

Summer can't imagine socialising with Feather Starr outside of class. But now the classes have finished, she supposes it would be nice to get to know the woman behind it all.

'Where is she?' Summer asks, looking round. At the same time, the women spot her purple hair in the crowd.

'It seems she's occupied,' Ivy says.

'Is that . . . ' Gwen trails off. Feather is in deep conversation with Idris Hopkins.

Epilogue

Frances sits on the steps of the caravan, inhaling the fresh, salty air. It's five in the morning but she has never been a good sleeper. The headland is wrapped in an ethereal mist, which she finds quite enchanting and mystical. She's always been very spiritual, intuitive. She can read people well, judge their characters in their eyes. She's always trusted herself, her gut instincts. Since she was a child, she's seen signs around her, things most people ignore. It's a sense, a feeling and that scares people; most like to deal with facts. Frances reads signs in the air, auras. When she was a child, she knew she couldn't trust that neighbour. It was his grey eyes; they were soulless. And so it proved. She still remembers the gossip and whispers when he disappeared one day.

It's not cold despite the early hour. Frances has a silk scarf over her shoulders, purple with signs of the zodiac in silver embroidered onto it. The wind chimes tinkle in the light breeze. She sips her peppermint tea, enjoying its almost medicinal hit in the back of her throat.

Behind her, everything in the caravan is packed up. It's time

344

to move on. She doesn't feel sad. Rather the contrary. Travel excites her. Meeting new people, discovering new places. The crystals tell her where to go. She doesn't think she can ever stay too long in one place. She guesses it's the traveller's blood in her veins. Her father was an Irish traveller. He gave her his wandering spirit and his thick, curly hair. She'd never met him but she loved the idea of the romance of her parents, a love that transcends people's censure, so powerful, it can't be stopped. This part of Pembrokeshire makes her feel close to her father sometimes. It's touching distance to Waterford and Wexford, his stomping ground. She doesn't know if he's still alive, but he comes to her in her dreams. She has that one photograph of him, and even though it's black and white, she can see his olive skin, his hair as black as midnight and his petrol-blue eyes.

Morlan is not new to her, of course. She was brought up not far from here and she knew one day she would come back, even if for just a short visit. She wanted to see Idris again, the randy old goat. He hasn't changed a bit. More grey hairs, sprouting from his nose and ears, as well as his head. But then she, too, has suffered the ravages of time. Her hips are wider and her belly jiggles when she dances. Poof! What does it matter? It never bothers Frances. Women are far too hung up on their bodies. It all still works and Frances enjoys sex, giving and receiving pleasure. The sweat, the visceral grunting, the bliss at the end. It's messy, chaotic, real. Men don't give a hoot if her thighs have cellulite or her breasts aren't as pert as they used to be and neither does she.

The reunion with Idris has been everything she had hoped for. When she heard he and his wife had divorced, she couldn't resist coming to visit the old devil. He doesn't need a map to find his way around a woman's body. He knows exactly how she likes to be touched and it has been electric. They had spent a few afternoons here in the caravan and they'd had loud, noisy sex. It's a wonder the caravan hadn't shifted from its breeze block piers. She grins at the memory.

'I'd forgotten just how hot you are, Frances Smith. Or should I call you Feather Starr,' Idris had whispered into her neck.

Her ample breasts lolloped onto her arm as she turned to face him. 'Do that to me again and you can call me what the hell you like.'

They had heard birds pecking on the roof of the caravan, the cacophonous cry of seagulls overhead.

'How's the petition going?' she had asked him then.

'Slow, but I'm doing my best. I'll get a thousand names by the end of the week. I was going to catch them coming out of chapel on Sunday.'

'Good idea. The more you stir things up, the more publicity I get.'

'They're like trophies for you, aren't they?' he'd grinned, his mouth suckling her breast.

She moaned in delight. 'All publicity is good publicity.' She laughed, as he bit on her nipple.

Frances gets up to toast a slice of teacake, smiling. She'll miss Idris. She'll pack up and hit the road soon.

Honestly, why people make such a fuss about sex, she'll never understand. Some women don't know how to let go. Frances takes her plate and sits once more on the steps outside. The mist seems to be lifting; it's going to be a lovely day.

She's run her classes in many places, but this group of women was especially satisfying to work with. She loves empowering women, allowing them to harness their own strength. Pole dancing is a perfect vehicle for this. That hoity-toity one Gwen, for starters. Frances could see she thought she was better than everyone at first. Barely spoke to the other women. Frances had seen her husband on TV adverts and in the *Pembrokeshire Herald*. Fancied himself as a hot-shot businessman. All talk and no trousers. It must have been humiliating for her but she's better for the experience, Frances decides.

Then Ivy. A sparky character. Game for anything, despite her age. She's got some courage that one and she's off travelling. A kindred spirit. Too often women can be held back by men.

The two younger ones, Summer, in the fog of motherhood. She can't dance to save her life but the classes have been good for her. Reminded her she's a woman, as well as a mother. And the final one in that foursome, Megan, granddaughter of that acerbic Hannah Thomas. She's been like a butterfly emerging from a chrysalis. Frances thought something was up when she first came to the class. So self-conscious for one so young. Couldn't see the power she had. She's fantastically supple, a natural dancer. Frances wasn't sure she'd strip off naked that time at the lagoon, but it did her the world of good. The world's her oyster. Those four have become firm friends and they needed each other. The classes have been therapy for them.

Frances has been considering where to go next. Maybe that little village in mid-Wales. The crystals seemed to suggest it last night. She trusts them. She used to visit there when she was a teenager and she remembers vividly the young farmer she had a fling with one hot summer. Fine memories, indeed. Frances wonders if he's still there.

Yes, it's time to move on from Morlan. Her work here is done!

Acknowledgements

Thank you first and foremost to the wonderful Bill Goodall, our agent, who had faith in us and *Poles Apart*. You have no idea how joyous it was to receive your first email telling us how much you loved the book. Your edits and keen eye for detail made the book immeasurably better. We can't say it enough, thank you for your hard work and support. Apparently, only one in a thousand novels submitted actually get published, so we'll be eternally grateful to the lovely Lesley Crooks, and the team at Allison & Busby, who have made our dreams come true!

Writing is tough and a network of supportive people is vital. So, a big thank you to family and friends, who have buoyed us up and spurred us on. Frazer, you have been a fabulous support, listening to our endless chatter about the book, and keeping baby Harry busy when deadlines were looming and chapters needed writing or editing. And Harry himself, son and grandson, and the convenient times you slept to facilitate the writing process and even times when you interrupted it! You are our inspiration (and an extremely cute distraction)! Nadine Riley, you are, as always, our wonderful cheerleader, being as chuffed as we are with our successes and a shoulder to cry on during crises of confidence. And thanks to you, dear reader, for buying our book. We're keeping everything crossed that you enjoy it.

ANNA BURNS is a psychiatrist and JACQUI BURNS is a lecturer. Mother and daughter write their novels while living over two hundred miles apart, emailing chapters back and forth, focussing on strong but relatable women at the centre of families and communities. *Love at Café Lompar* was shortlisted for the RNA Debut Novel Award and with *Poles Apart* and *Escape to Pumpkin Cottage*, they have been writing stories set in their native Wales.

@annaandjacqui
annaandjacquiburns.com